THE
THIRD
GENERATION

"... for I the Lord thy God am a jealous God,
visiting the iniquity of the fathers upon
the children unto the third and fourth
generation of them that hate me."

—EXODUS 20:5

CHESTER HIMES

THE
THIRD
GENERATION

THE CHATHAM BOOKSELLER
CHATHAM, NEW JERSEY

ACKNOWLEDGMENTS

Four lines of *Memory Lane,* on page 192, Copyright 1924 by Harms, Inc. Reprinted by permission.

Two lines of *Collegiate,* on page 192, Copyright 1925 by Shapiro, Bernstein & Co., Inc. Copyright renewed. Assigned to Shapiro, Bernstein & Co., Inc.

Two lines of *Chloë,* on page 192, lyrics by Gus Kahn, music by Neil Moret, Copyright 1927 Villa Moret, Inc. Rights controlled by Robbins Music Corporation. Used by Special Permission.

Four lines of *Where'd You Get Those Eyes,* on page 209, Copyright 1926 by Leo Feist Inc. Words and music by Walter Donaldson. Used by Special Permission of Copyright Proprietor.

Two lines from *Me and My Shadow,* on page 210, Copyright 1927 by Bourne, Inc. Used by Permission of the Copyright owners.

Two lines from *Gimme a Little Kiss,* on page 216, Copyright 1926 by ABC Music Corp. Used by Permission of the Copyright owners.

Two lines of *Three O'clock in the Morning,* on page 220, words by Dorothy Terriss, music by Julian Robledo. Copyright 1921/22 West's Ltd., London, England. Copyright Renewal 1949/50 West's Ltd., London, England. Leo Feist Inc. Sole and Exclusive Agents for United States and Canada. Used by Special Permission.

Three lines of *When Day Is Done,* on page 255, Copyright 1926 by Harms, Inc. Reprinted by Permission.

Two lines of *Among My Souvenirs,* on page 288, Copyright 1927 by DeSylva, Brown & Henderson, Inc. Reprinted by Permission.

FOR *Jean*

1

Spring was in the air. The bright morning sunshine had dried the dew and warmed the ground, and crocuses,
bordering the front brick walk, bloomed in yellow flame. Rosebushes along the front picket fence were heavy with buds, and
the tiny lacquered leaves of the spreading elderberry tree trembled as if in ecstasy. Everything seemed dazzlingly clean and
dressed for an occasion. Beyond the vivid green of the sprout-
ing grass the small frame house glistened with fresh white paint.

The faces of two small children pressed wistfully against the
front windowpanes gave eyes to the house. It was a pleasant
house, and one could imagine it having eyes, and smiling, too, on
such a morning. Professor Taylor rented it from the college
president.

Upstairs were three comfortable bedrooms, and downstairs
the living room, library, dining room and kitchen, all furnished
tastefully as befitted a teacher's home. But the library, more
than any of the others, revealed both the endowments and pre-
tensions of Professor and Mrs. Taylor. It contained four large,
mahogany-stained bookcases filled with mail-order de luxe editions, leather-backed, gilt-lettered volumes. known as "sets." A
set of Thackeray sat atop a set of Dickens, and a set of Long-

fellow nudged a set of Poe; a set of *Roman Classics* vied with a set of *Greek Classics,* and a set of the Encyclopedia contested the place of honor with a set of the *Book of Knowledge.* They were understandably very proud of their library. With the single exception of the president's, it was the only one in the community, and his was not nearly as "complete."

Occasionally Professor Taylor would recline there in his easy chair and nod over a volume, the brightly burning gas mantle hissing him awake from time to time. Or he would have his cronies in for a glass of elderberry wine and pace back and forth, recounting some story. But the children really enjoyed it. Thomas, at eleven, loved to read, while the tots, five-year-old William Lee Jr. and Charles Manning, sixteen months younger, were enthralled by the pictures. For her part, Mrs. Taylor preferred to read in the living room because of the grand piano. Music had always been her sanctuary and the nearness of the piano gave her a sense of security. Besides, owning a grand piano had always seemed to her indicative of good breeding.

The dining room was rarely used except for Sunday dinners or when they had company. Most of the time they ate in the kitchen at a table covered with printed oilcloth. It was a large bright kitchen looking onto the back garden, equipped with a huge wood-burning range. Twice weekly a woman came in and did the washing and heavy cleaning, but Mrs. Taylor did her own cooking.

At the precise moment the children were staring so longingly at the front yard, she paused in the act of wiping the dishpan to listen. It was not like them to be quiet. Hastily, she hung the pan on its nail beside the table and went forward to investigate. They pounced on her instantly, tugging at her skirt in their excitement.

"Mama, can we go out and play? Can we go out and play?"

"*May* you," she corrected, "not *can* you. And you must call me *Mother*—how many times must I tell you?"

"*Mother* . . . May we, *Mother?* May we go out and play?"

"Let Mother see first," she said, crossing to the window as they clung to her. It would be a blessing if they could, she thought—they were like caged tiger cubs.

For an instant her gaze went toward the entrance to the college, directly across the street, flanked by fieldstone pillars. It was an old college with a fine tradition and had been founded by a regiment of Negro soldiers who had fought in the Civil War. The campus was enclosed by a high thick hedge but there was a knoll beyond and she saw several shirt-sleeved students hurrying along the paths. Then she glanced appraisingly at the blue, cloudless sky. It promised to be a beautiful day, the first warm day of spring.

"Yes, children, you may go out for an hour before lunch," she consented, but called them back as they dashed off. "You must wear your woolen playsuits. There's still a chill in the air and Mother doesn't want you to catch colds."

A few minutes later, watching them run down the steps, she breathed a sigh of relief. All winter long she had had them under her feet. She had never completely recovered her health since the birth of Charles, and there had been times during the dull winter days as they ripped and romped through the house, screaming at the tops of their voices, when she had felt on the verge of nervous prostration.

It was an inviting yard, free of the hazards—stone menageries, sundials, birdbaths, fishponds and rock gardens—that cluttered the more pretentious yards along the street, and she had no fear of the children hurting themselves. But as they dashed wildly about, they seemed so reckless, so filled with explosive energy, she could not repress a mild fear. Should any harm befall them now, when she had nothing else to live for, she would die, she thought.

The children loved the yard. To them the house was a great stone castle and the yard an immense kingdom. Sometimes they imagined the house a fort. Then the yard became the great plains where the redskins roamed. They were always the Indians—"wild Indians," their mother called them. They'd charge the house, shrieking wildly, and beat against the front stoop with sticks in an effort to break down the stockade gates and scalp the pale-

9

faces. It struck their mother as a little strange that they should always want to be the Indians. It seemed to her that at times their own white blood should predominate and they should want to be the palefaces. She disliked this game most of all. She was afraid it might encourage them to hate white people. She wanted them to grow up to love and respect fine white people as she did. And besides, it was such a bloodthirsty game and made her nervous. She hoped that during this summer they'd learn to play another game, or at least play with the toys their father had made for them. She reminded herself to have Mr. Taylor bring their wagon from the shed.

For a moment they paused before the gate, looking about to see if she was watching them.

"Don't you dare swing on that gate," she called. "You know I've expressly forbidden you to open it."

They lingered for a moment longer, testing her determination. Seeing them in that perspective, she noticed with a sense of shock how they had grown since the summer before. William had already grown above the latch but Charles was crowding him fast. They're shooting up like weeds, she thought. William would soon be of school age. Her gaze lingered on him for a moment, and she contemplated his resemblance to his father. His complexion was a flat, muddy brown, and he'd inherited his father's features —and also his father's kinky hair. She felt a mild surge of resentment. She hated to think that even one of her sons would resemble his father, although she knew many people considered Professor Taylor personable, recalling wryly that she herself had once thought him quite dashing.

Actually, away from his home, Professor Taylor was seldom looked upon with such photographic detachment. Only his wife saw him as a short, black man with a wiry, simian body, the bowed legs and pigeon-toed stance of great Negro athletes. But to her, the stigma of his blackness was relieved somewhat by his well-formed head, large, hooked nose and flaring nostrils, which she liked to think of as being Arabic. He was an active man with a facile expression, and others usually saw him on the move, laughing, talking, screwing up his face in a listening attitude, or doing something with his hands which held their attention. In a community where the majority of people were black, his color appeared commonplace, and he wore good clothes which gave him an air of distinction.

Most persons thought him lovable. He had the guile and intuition of the born comedian and could be extremely entertaining, yet he was never quite a clown. Along with an innate servility, which he had almost completely submerged beneath an aggressive demeanor, he had a strong and bitter pride. But unlike many proud men, who carry their pride in silence, he was boastful, and was never so pleased as when recounting with gestures some incident in which he had emerged heroically. He loved to rear back on his heels, his toes pointing inward, unconsciously scratching his head, and boast of what he'd told the college president, the local political boss, a white store clerk, or some similar person in a role of traditional superiority. Deep in his heart he wanted to be a rebel. Had he ever become a hero in the eyes of his wife he might have been a leader. He had the physical courage. Often he thrashed grown students half again his size. But his wife and the circumstances of his life had put out much of his fire. For the most part he was disarmingly ingratiating, not only toward his superiors but toward most persons.

Mrs. Taylor detested this latter characteristic most of all. Anything which, to her way of thinking, savored of being submissive sickened her. Of late she had noticed in William an expression of vague constraint as if he were holding himself back, which seemed to reflect his father's submissive attitude. It troubled her.

On the other hand, Charles was gleeful and spontaneous with a mischievous twinkle in his eyes; he caused her more anxiety though he gave her more delight. Also, his skin was of a lighter complexion. She thought of it as "olive-colored," similar to the complexions of southern Europeans. In reality it was the rosy, sepia hue common to mulatto children. He had a round, smiling face with a small, straight nose and a pretty, well-shaped mouth. The corners of his lips were constantly turned up in a smile and dimples appeared in both cheeks when he laughed. He had straight black hair which hung to his neck in a bob and showed signs of much care.

It was one of Mrs. Taylor's deepest regrets that none of her sons had inherited her own soft, straight hair, which, to the same degree as her straight nose and fair complexion, was indicative of her white blood. She had been reared in the tradition that Negroes with straight hair and light complexions were superior to dark-complexioned Negroes with kinky hair. This conviction was supported by the fact that light-complexioned skin and straight hair did give Negroes a certain prestige within their race.

Of her three sons, Charles was her last hope in this respect. She longed for him to resemble her own father, after whom he had been named. From his birth she had taken great pains with his hair, nursing it along as if his life depended on it being straight. Every night she massaged his scalp with warm olive oil and gave his hair a hundred strokes with an imported brush; and several times each day she gently pinched the bridge of his nose to keep it from flattening out. At times Professor Taylor complained, "What are you trying to do, make a girl out of him?" But she ignored him and continued to do all within her power to cultivate her son's white features.

Although she tried to love her sons equally, deep within her she loved Charles best.

As she stood behind the front screen door, watching the children play, she recalled what a seven-day sensation she had caused by engaging a white doctor at their births. It had incurred the animosity of all the Negro physicians and had provoked great consternation among the faculty. Her face hardened with a vague bitterness and she derived a fleeting sense of pleasure from the memory of her husband's tremendous trepidation at the time. He was afraid of his own shadow, she thought.

The children were crouching down behind the rosebushes, peering through the picket fence. A dog trotted by on the cinder path outside.

"Bang! Bang!" screamed the children.

The dog jumped as if he had been stung and fled down the gulley. The children ran in wild pursuit as far as the yard permitted. She wondered absently what the dog represented.

Her gaze lingered on Charles. She'd wanted a girl when he was born, she recalled, thinking, he looked enough like a girl to have been one. It reminded her of what the doctor had laughingly remarked at his birth, "He is almost a girl, at that."

Unconsciously she sniffed for the scent of flowers, a habit left over from her girlhood when she had tried to tell what flowers were blooming when she passed a garden at night. She had loved flowers and had addressed them as if they were human, scolding those that grew poorly and praising those that did well. There was a wonderful, earthy scent in the air, she noticed. It reminded her of the Easter Rambles held in her home town when she was a little girl. For a moment she reveled in the memory of the good times she had had during her girlhood. "Such good times," she murmured, the words escaping from her lips. She smiled strangely; then the present invaded her consciousness again and the smile saddened and slowly vanished.

Sighing, she smoothed her hair. She wore it parted on the left and brushed loosely across her forehead, gathered in a chignon behind. In repose her features had a slightly drawn and bitter cast and her skin had the slightly pallid hue of one who has been ill for a long time. There were dark circles about her deepset, gray-green eyes, and the lids drooped, giving her a look of weariness.

She was a tiny woman, but she carried herself with such implacable determination that her size was seldom noticed. She had always dressed attractively, even at home. The dark woolen dress she now wore had been ordered from Chicago but she had made the gingham apron. Her hands, clasped loosely across her waist, were slightly rough, and the knuckles were reddened and swollen from washing dishes. Her engagement ring with a solitary pearl and the plain gold wedding band which Professor Taylor had made in his shop from virgin metal gleamed brightly in the sunlight.

Absently, she watched the people pass along the street. A

farmer drove by, his dilapidated wagon, pulled by a brace of mules, piled high with cordwood. She looked down across the front yards and picket fences of her neighbors. It was a pleasant street, flanked by scattered elms, and the weeds had not yet had time to grow high in the gutters. Later, all the trees and flowers would be in bloom, she thought, and when the hedge about the college bloomed it was a lovely sight. Farther down the street was the state prison, bordered by an exquisitely beautiful flower garden tended by the prisoners, and sometimes the forbidding Black Maria passed before their door.

Mrs. Barnes drove by in her new carriage, the perfectly matched team of dappled gray mares kicking up dust from the graveled roadway. It was a pretty sight. Mrs. Taylor had heard they had a new carriage, but this was the first time she saw it. Dr. Barnes must be doing very well indeed, she reflected. In addition to being head of the college hospital he had a very good private practice. They lived in a large colonial-style house in the next block.

Mrs. Taylor was not on intimate terms with the Barneses—Dr. Barnes had never forgiven her for engaging a white doctor at the birth of her sons—and she prided herself on never having "set foot" in their house. But she had heard of their expensive furnishings and she had seen their blooded horses and luxurious carriages passing along the street. And she was no different from the other women of the community who envied them. But, unlike the others, she did not consider them her superior. Despite all their possessions and their great prestige, she felt herself to be their superior. And this was due entirely to the fact that Dr. Barnes was a dark-complexioned man and his wife only a "high yellow" with kinky hair. Mrs. Barnes could have no more than three-fourths white blood at best, and that was highly improbable, Mrs. Taylor had decided. She herself was only one thirty-second part Negro. And in her veins flowed some of the most aristocratic white blood in all the South. Mrs. Taylor thought of racial strains in terms of blood, and of this blood as flowing in her veins.

Mrs. Taylor had not always been so preoccupied with racial strains. Nor had her sense of being a superior person evoked such bitter disparagement. At first it had been protective, a shield for her wounded pride and outraged sensitivity. Quite often it had been constructive, enabling her to set her sights higher than most Negroes would have dared. It extended the limitations of her ambitions. And it also defended her from despondency and defeat. Whenever she felt the urge to give up, she reminded herself of her parents' magnificent accomplishment, of how they had come out of slavery and made a home for themselves, and after great hardship had prospered and educated all seven of their children. She had inherited their determination and stamina and their credo—to want something better, to become educated, to be somebody worthwhile. And in remembering what they had done, she always remembered how they looked.

Her father had been a tall, spare man with light brown hair and a long silky beard. His complexion was as fair as any white person's. Her mother, though slightly darker, had the coarse black hair and high cheekbones of an Indian. Both would have been accepted as white in a northern state. But it had never occurred to them to leave the South.

They had three small children when they were freed. Their one asset with which to face a new, strange life had been their ability to read and write. Both had been "body slaves" and after the Civil War their master had tried to persuade them to remain on the plantation.

"You have never known want, and if you remain with me, you never will," he had promised them.

Dr. Jessie Manning was descended from the English peerage, and had once served in the United States Senate. According to his own lights he had tried to be a kind and just master. Both Charles and Lin loved him. But they had refused to stay. Even though the very thought of freedom had terrified them, they had wanted to be free. Deep inside them had been some compelling urge to flee from the shadow of slavery, to rear their children in the sunlight, to provide them with something better, with education and opportunity. They had heard these ideas propounded by their master; they had listened to the reverence in his voice; they had believed.

For two years they lived in a floorless, one-room cabin with a lean-to on an acre of land they had cleared. Charles had learned brick masonry and did odd jobs in the neighborhood while Lin took in washing and worked as a wet nurse.

But the proximity of the old plantation had stifled their sense of freedom. They moved to a railroad town in Georgia and took the family name of Manning. For a decade Charles worked as a brick mason. Another son and three daughters were born to them there. Mrs. Taylor's Christian name was Lillian, and she was second from the youngest.

Although she was then a little girl, not more than five, Lillian could remember the crisis that had arisen when her father went broke. He had been ill for a long time and one day he had said to Lin, "Hon, we got to sell the house."

They had moved to Atlanta and he had worked for a time as a Pullman porter before finally having to quit. For three years he had been ill with tuberculosis, and for a year he had been confined to his bed. It had fallen Lillian's lot to nurse him. All of the older children had worked desperately to make ends meet. Lillian never forgot the great piles of laundry her mother washed each day. But they had never given up.

When her father recovered, the family returned to the town in South Carolina where the parents had grown up as slaves. Once again they had cleared a plot of land and built another house. The parents were more determined than ever to bring their children up in the church, give them an education and a better start in life. They joined the Presbyterian Church; Charles became a Deacon and the Superintendent of the Sunday School, and Lin became active in missionary work. For years the church had been the center of their social life.

It had been a slow, hard struggle all the way. Despite his ill health, Charles had worked long hours as a brick mason and day laborer, while Lin did washing. But they had sent their children to college, the girls to the church seminary and the boys to a college in Atlanta.

All of the girls had been considered very talented; they played the piano and had "white folks' manners." All had fair complexions and reddish hair. The three eldest had taught at the seminary upon graduation. Tom, the eldest son, had become a successful building contractor. Both Charlie, his younger brother, and his father had worked for him.

During that time the family had gained in prestige and had become prominent throughout the town and state. Two of the girls had married doctors. Lillian's oldest sister had married a minister who had later become a bishop. Both brothers had married schoolteachers.

Lillian had taken piano lessons from the age of six and had been considered the genius of the family. She had been given to daydreaming and was moody and temperamental. When her older brothers and sisters had grown up and began earning their living the family showed signs of prosperity. After the age of ten she had been raised in very pleasant circumstances. It had been during her early teens she had first conceived the romantic notions of her heredity.

She had seen only one of her grandparents, "Grandma Mary," her father's mother, who had lived on the old plantation until her death. Her parents never spoke of the others. She had been a curious girl. Once she had asked her mother, "Where does Grandpa live, ma?"

"Your grandpa was killed in the war," Lin had replied.

"Both of them?"

Lin had stopped ironing and had sat in the rocker by the hearth. "Come here, chile, and I will tell you all 'bout your grandpas. Your Grandpa Manning, your pa's pa, was killed at Chickamauga when he threw himself in front of Ol' Mars to save his life. He caught the bullet that was 'tended for Ol' Mars' heart and fell dead at his feet. And my pa was shot trying to get through Gen'l Sherman's lines to carry orders to the cap'n of the Georgia troops. They never did find his body."

Lillian had known that this was fiction to satisfy her curiosity and had become more curious than ever. After that she had eavesdropped on her parents' conversations. One of her favorite positions was in the dark by the open kitchen window when her parents thought her in bed. Here she had learned that her father was the son of Dr. Jessie Manning, and that her mother was the daughter of an Irish overseer and an Indian slave.

She had added to the story, enlarging and changing the parts she didn't like. The resulting story was that her father was the son of Dr. Manning and a beautiful octoroon, the most beautiful woman in all the state, whose own father had been an English nobleman. Her mother was the daughter of a son of a United States President and an octoroon who was the daughter of a Confederate Army general.

At first it had been a childish game of fantasy. After having received several whippings for recounting it to her wide-eyed schoolmates she had kept it to herself, and in time had outgrown it. As a young woman she had felt a real sense of superiority which, in her home environment, had needed no support.

It was only after the disillusionment of her marriage and the first bitter conflicts about color with her husband and the dark-complexioned faculty wives that she revived it. She never gave the story absolute credence, but it became conceivable. She certainly had a great percentage of white blood, she told herself. And it was quite reasonable it should be the blood of the type of persons who had been friends of the aristocratic Dr. Manning.

She created the fiction of being only one thirty-second part Negro deliberately. It symbolized her contempt and disdain for all the Negroes she felt had tried to hurt her. It was her final rejection of all the people who would not recognize her innate superiority. Because regardless of how much they hated her, or tried to hurt and belittle her, none of them could possibly be her superior, and but a very, very few her equal, because she possessed the very maximum of white blood a Negro can possess and remain a Negro.

At the beginning it was a simple mechanism to bolster her morale. But after all the inroads of hurt, discouragement and despondency, it slowly attained the strength of fact. For a time it became the only fact she possessed. She thought of it as a legacy, and she wanted to pass this legacy on to her children. She wanted to impress on them that in their veins flowed the blood of aristocrats.

18

For a moment her attention was drawn back to the children. They were pulling at the rosebushes. But she checked the impulse to scold them. She should be thankful, she told herself, that they had not begun that awful shrieking and hammering and slaughtering of palefaces.

When she looked up the street again, Mrs. Barnes' carriage had passed from sight. She felt strangely relieved. There were various other professional and business people who lived on the street, but none disturbed her as did the Barneses. Although most of them earned more money than the professors, the professors had the greater prestige.

Negroes put a great value on education, she meditated. They thought of it as both the source and result of all good things. And she, too, believed in its efficacy. That had been the reason she had married Professor Taylor.

She recalled how dazzled she'd first been by the dashing young professor from the state college who had courted her. How impressed she'd been by his education. All the fuss and bother; all the fine talk of his dreams and ambition. She'd been thrilled by the thought of the wonderful things they could accomplish together. They would complement each other like no other two people who had ever lived.

She had come home to live that spring, following her father's death. For the previous two years she had been teaching music at the seminary. She had loved her father dearly, and for a time had been disconsolate, a lonely lady immersed in sorrow. It had given her a rare beauty, vivid but withdrawn, as if she were lost in reverie.

Most of the young men thereabouts had felt uncomfortable in her presence. At that time her eyes were hazel in color, with an attractive tilt at the outer edges; but they had been level and challenging. She had seldom worn the brilliant colors that had been fashionable at the time. Her preference had been for light grays and blues; and her favorite dresses had been silk jerseys with lace collars and white, frilly dickies. She had loved fine lace with a rare passion. Her only jewelry had been a string of pearls her brother Tom had given her on her eighteenth birthday. At times she was painfully intense. Music had seemed to be her only passion.

The young men had thought her cold and unapproachable. Her restraint had dampened their ardor. No one but her mother had known how sensitive and deeply emotional she was inside. Outwardly, she had seemed so conscious of her worth, her beauty and intelligence, that she had repelled most people. She could give little of herself, and only to one she considered an inferior, only in the manner of one bestowing a grace. But she would have been horrified had she known this about herself.

Professor Taylor had come first to call on her younger sister. But he soon became infatuated with the strange, distant, beautiful girl. He had resolved to win her.

At that time he had been head of the mechanical department of the Georgia State College. He had attended Boston Technological Institute. Most women in the town had considered him a good catch, even though he was dark.

But it had not been his position that had first attracted Lillian. It had been his homage. He had given the appearance of worshipping at her shrine, even on occasions when she had acted ridiculously.

Their parlor had been heated by a wood-burning stove that had tiny panes of isinglass in the door. One evening Professor Taylor had called unexpectedly. She and her mother had been sitting in the kitchen. Her mother had answered the door, and when Lin had called that it was Professor Taylor, Lillian had snatched up the kitchen lamp and, running to the parlor, put it in the stove. She had wanted him to think she had been sitting in the parlor all the time. But after a time she had realized it was extremely chilly for so bright a fire to be burning. She had made some excuse about the damper being broken and the heat going up the chimney. But Professor Taylor had smilingly insisted that it was quite warm in the room. He had known the lamp was in the stove. It was an old trick; he had done it many times himself.

Then there had been all the entertaining when they had become engaged. Several times that winter she had visited him at the college. She had been lavishly entertained by the faculty. And he had spent his Christmas vacation with her family.

They had been married the following June.

The "Violet Teas," she recalled, as her memories went completely sour. The "Yellow Buffet," the garden parties, the wedding reception; all the many people, both white and colored, who had turned out to bid them *bon voyage* on their honeymoon. They had engaged a drawing room all the way to Philadelphia. People in the town said they had never seen anything like it.

It now seemed more like a prelude to a nightmare. She couldn't imagine herself as that idealistic young school teacher who had had such high-flown dreams.

She felt the leak of bitter tears. Blindly she turned away from the sunshine and went back to her chores. After twelve years the memory of her wedding night was as vivid as if it had happened yesterday.

2

IT WAS LATE AT NIGHT WHEN THE TRAIN PULLED into the old stone station. A short black man wearing a black derby hat, dark suit and black, box-toed shoes alighted from a Pullman car. The conductor looked away. The short black man stood at the bottom of the steps and extended his hand to a woman. She wore a linen duster over a pale-blue silk jersey dress, and a large pink hat with feathers. Her face was white and strained; her deep-set eyes fixed in an unseeing stare.

The short black man touched her arm. She looked at him. A smile flickered in her stiff white face, flickered out. The short black man helped her down the steps. The conductor's mouth pursed in a grim, straight line; his face reddened slowly.

A Pullman porter followed, carrying two heavy valises and a woman's straw traveling case. The short black man tipped him

21

and hailed a station porter. Then he took the woman's arm and, preening with self-importance, followed the porter through the huge, dimly lit South Station to a dark side street.

"We'll just go straight to the hotel, honey, unless you want to stop for a bowl of hot milk or a glass of wine," he said.

"No," she said.

He looked at her, undecided, as if to interpret her meaning. She seemed passive, acquiescent. He smiled indulgently and patted her arm.

The porter hailed a horse cab and put the luggage aboard, and the short black man, tipping him generously, helped the woman to enter and climbed in beside her. His actions were slightly erratic. He seemed laboring under great emotion, tautened with excitement.

The old cab went clattering through the drab cobbled streets, past row after row of gray stone houses interlocked and identical as peas, in the dim light like prison walls enclosing the tunnel down which she went to her doom. She couldn't help the distortions of her imagination. She was frightened, lonely, homesick. The man beside her, whom she had married that morning, now seemed a stranger. And this seemed a monstrously wrong thing they were doing.

He sensed her need for reassurance and patted her hand comfortingly. But tremors of his excitement passed down through his touch into her skin and she shuddered.

He'd gone to great pains to arrange everything so there would be no embarrassment or anxiety, and her attitude puzzled and angered him.

"It's a big city," he said. "More people here than in all the state of North Carolina."

She looked out at the depressing sameness of the gloomy streets. "Yes," she replied.

They lapsed into silence . . .

. . . as if she were that kind of woman, she was thinking . . .

. . . she'll be all right, he reassured himself doubtfully . . .

The clop-clop of the horses hoofs hammered on the silence. The neighborhood changed. Smell of city slums pressed into the cab. Strident Negroid laughter shattered on the night. The horse cab pulled up before an old dilapidated stone-faced building which carried the faded legend, HOTEL, atop a dingy door. The short black man alighted and helped the woman down. He paid the driver and struggled with the luggage. She opened the door for him and followed across the dusty foyer to the scarred and littered desk. A few moth-eaten chairs sat here and there in the dim light of turned-down lamps and in one a fat black man sat slumped, asleep and snoring slightly. The smell of damp decay hung in the air.

The short black man put down his luggage and smiled at the woman reassuringly. "It's the best colored hotel in town. I thought it'd be better than to try to . . . " his voice petered out, leaving the thought unspoken.

She didn't answer.

The night clerk came from somewhere out of the shadows, hitching up his suspenders.

"I reserved the bridal suite," the short black man said.

"Yas suh," the night clerk said, and teeth came alive in his face as he slanted a glance at the strained white face of the waiting woman. "Yas *suh!*"

The short black man signed the register and the night clerk picked up the luggage and preceded them up the narrow, bending stairs, his footsteps muffled on the threadbare carpet. The night clerk opened a door at the front of the narrow corridor, entered the darkness and lit a lamp, lit the grate, carried the luggage within, and stood to one side, his big white teeth winking at them like an electric sign. The woman looked at him with a shudder of distaste.

Impulsively the short black man lifted the woman across the threshold. Her body was stiff and unyielding. Gingerly he stood her erect, then turned and tipped the servant.

"Thankee-suh, thankee-suh. Ah knows y'all gonna have uh good time," the night clerk said as if it was a dirty joke.

The short black man quickly closed the door. He turned and went across to the woman, who hadn't moved, and tried to put his arm around her. She pulled away and went over and sat on the moth-eaten sofa. The same smell of decay encountered below was in the room, but here it was dry, mingled with the vague scent of countless assignations. Again the woman shuddered as her thoughts were assailed by a sickening recollection. Once, as a little girl, when cutting through a vulgar street in nigger-town, Atlanta, she had heard an obscene reference to her vagina. She had not known then what it had meant, only that it was vulgar and dirty and had filled her with a horrible shame. She had never told anyone, but the feeling of shame had lingered in her thoughts like a drop of pus, poisoning her conception of sex. As she had approached womanhood, she had resolved to make her marriage immaculate. And now it seemed dirtied at the very start by this cloying scent.

The fire sputtered cheerfully in the grate. Beyond was the door into the bedroom. The short black man went and lit the bedroom lamp, then came back and turned down the living-room lamp and went over and sat beside her.

"You go to bed, honey," he said gently. "You must be tired."

She turned and for the first time gave him a grateful smile. "I'm not tired." She groped for words. She spread her hands slightly, inclusively. "It's so squalid."

"It's the best they have," he said defensively.

She arose and started toward the bedroom, then impulsively bent down and kissed him on the lips and, laughing girlishly, went into the bedroom and closed the door. Slowly she undressed before the mirror, glancing furtively, a little ashamedly at her nude figure, letting the realization that she was married come to her.

She was a tiny woman with soft milk-white skin and tiny breasts as round and hard as oranges. Her face was slightly longish and her expression a little austere. Laughing at herself, she slipped into her nightgown and, putting out the light, crawled quickly into bed. She lay looking into the dark, her thoughts pounding, listening to the movements of her husband as he un-dressed in the other room. The latch clicked, the door slowly opened. She tensed beneath the covers, watching him enter the room.

His short muscular body, seemingly blacker than the night, was silhouetted against the faint luminescence of the doorway. *He's naked!* she thought, horrified as by some startling obscenity. And then as he came toward her, his naked body assumed a sinister aspect, its very blackness the embodiment of evil. She felt a cold shock of terror.

"William," she whimpered.

"I'm right here, honey," he said reassuringly.

She felt his hand pulling back the cover. She could scarcely breathe.

He lay down beside her with infinite gentleness. For a time he lay still. Then his hand moved and he touched her breasts. Her body became instantly taut. She could not analyze her fear of him, but she dreaded the feel of his touch. She was still caught in a state of shock. She feared him as something inhuman.

He turned over and kissed her on the throat. She lay rigid in terror. His hand went down over the smooth satin nightgown and rested on her stomach. Then, abruptly, he reached down and drew the gown up about her waist and his hand searched frantically. His breathing shortened and thickened.

"Don't!" she gasped. "Don't! Not now! Not here! Not in this hovel!" Her arms had stretched out, gripping the sheets in the classic posture of crucifixion.

He scrambled over her. His hot breath licked at her face.

"Don't!" she cried again. "Don't!" And then she screamed in terror, "Light the lamp so I can see you!"

But he had gone out of himself and was panting uncontrollably, unaware, unhearing, his head filled with the roaring fire of his lust. He mounted her like a stud. The penetration chilled her body like death. For an instant the vision of her father's kindly white face with its long silky beard flickered through her consciousness. Then her mind closed against reality as it filled with a sense of outrage; her organs tightened as she stiffened to the pain and degradation.

He struggled brutally and savagely and blindly and then desperately to overcome her, conquer her, win her. She fought to hold herself back. He could not control himself; his muscles jerked with frenzy, the vague pallor of her face floating through the red haze of his vision. When she felt her virginity go bleedingly to this vile and bestial man she hated him.

He threw back the covers, leaped from the bed and lit the lamp, unaware of his reason for doing so. Standing naked, the shadow of his black, knotty body with the muscular bowed legs, darker than the night, he trembled with frustration and dissatisfaction, not knowing what was wrong with him.

She lay rigid in the posture of crucifixion, her stiff white face as still as if in death, looking at him through pools of horror. The sight of his black body was incalculably repulsive. Finally she closed her eyes. She felt as if she had been raped, victimized, debased by an animal. "You beast," she said.

He was shocked out of his daze. He groped for reason, sucking at his lower lip, trying to frame in simple thought the basis for her attitude.

"But, honey, we're married now," he said in a soft, placating voice.

"You rapist," she said through clenched teeth. "You don't know what marriage is."

Had it not been for the prospect of facing the night alone in a strange and terrifying city, she would have left him then. But she realized she had no place to go. Her family wouldn't have welcomed her home, she knew. There would have been a scandal. No one would have understood. In view of all the hardships and travail her parents had experienced during their marriage, they would have been appalled by her attitude. So she steeled herself to stay with him.

Vaguely aware that he was losing her, he tried to win her back. Afterwards, he was infinitely gentle. But she never became reconciled. Each time, she received him with horror and revulsion. Although a child was conceived, she never got over that first night. She was never able to separate the blackness of his skin from the brutality of his act; the two were irrevocably bound together in all her thoughts of him.

After they returned to the college in Georgia where he taught, he discovered she hated him. She was cold and distant and shuddered at his touch. He thought it was due to her condition; many women hated their husbands during pregnancy. To lighten the burden of housekeeping for her he brought his sister to live with them and do the housework. Beatrice was a thin, black girl with short, kinky hair. It was her first time away from home. And she stood in such awe of her forbidding, white-faced sister-in-law she was painfully self-conscious and stupid. Mrs. Taylor was ill and unhappy and very impatient with the girl. She thought her mean and sullen, and took out her spleen toward her husband on her.

One day Beatrice burst into tears and begged Professor Taylor to send her home. He turned on his wife and shouted, "Confound you, quit picking on my sister!"

"Then get her out of my house," she retorted. "I can't help it if she feels inferior because she's black."

"Inferior? Because she's black?"

"Yes, that's why she's so sullen and slovenly. It's no crime to be black." For the first time she had revealed her attitude toward color.

He was shocked. Then suddenly it all came clear, the source of her unhappiness, the reason she hated him. "Confound it, who do you think you are, a white woman!" he raved, turning ashy with fury. "You're a colored woman, too, just like my sister. The only difference is my sister and I aren't bastards." It was an epithet black people hurled at light-complexioned Negroes, challenging their legitimacy.

Her face blanched. "You'll live to see the day you regret that vile calumny," she vowed.

"Yes, and you'll live to see the day you'll wish you were black as me," he replied cuttingly.

She pursed her lips and turned away. He knew that he had scored a hit and felt a sense of triumph. But he little knew how deeply he had wounded her, nor how relentlessly she'd seek vengeance. Added to the shock and horror of her wedding night, it completed the destruction of their marriage.

For years she punished him in every conceivable manner. She left his bed and for four years forbade him to touch her. She wasted his salary on expensive luxuries and ran him into debt to embarrass him. All her love and tenderness were spent on her child. She treated her husband with unwavering contempt and made enemies of all his associates. She whipped him with her color at every turn, and whipped all those about him. There came the time when she was not welcome in a single house. Yet her scorn and fury continued unabated. Eventually he was asked to leave the college.

When they came to this college in Missouri, he was beaten. Only then did she feel avenged. After Thomas became of school age she relented and accepted him again as the father of her children. She had resigned herself to marital unhappiness, but now she longed for a family. It was the beginning of her bitter struggle for security, for possessions and prestige and a home, and for opportunities for her children.

By then Professor Taylor had lost all hope and confidence. He refused to share in her plans and seemed only interested in earning his salary. When William was born she became desperate. She tried to fire him with ambition again. But he seemed dead inside. For a time she was sorry for him. She knew she had destroyed him. And she wanted to remake him with her love and devotion. She forgave him for all that he had done to her. When he seemed most despondent and forlorn she responded to him most passionately. Charles came as the result of this tender interlude. She often thought that was the reason she loved him best. All the while she carried him she felt devoted to his father. She thought she was mending him with her love.

When it finally became evident that he was unchanged, her love reverted to hate. She became more disillusioned than ever. She was chagrined as much as infuriated. She hated him for leading her on. All waste, she thought. All her efforts to fire his ambition and spur him on—nothing but waste. Nothing had changed.

Even now, after twelve years, she was still as revolted by him as she had been on their wedding night, she reflected as she went bitterly about her chores. Twelve years of nothing but waste. He had the same type of job he'd had when they were married, with scarcely any more salary. They didn't even own the house in which they lived. Her own parents had owned their home in less than twelve years of freedom, she thought bitterly. But her husband had given up. It filled her with rage and frustration. Even with all his other faults, including his apishness and carnality, she could respect him if he had kept fighting to advance. She could make allowances if he were a success. But he couldn't even succeed at teaching, for which he had been trained.

None was better educated. He was a fine blacksmith and wheelwright. His students had built some of the best carriages and wagons seen in that city. He could make the most elaborate andirons and coal tongs and gates and lampposts imaginable. He had made jewelry and lamps and dishes from gold and silver. He was an artist at the forge and anvil. There was practically nothing he couldn't forge from metal. Many prominent white people from all over the city commissioned him for jobs. He had made the wrought-iron gate for the governor's mansion, and a pair of ornamental silver bridles for the district attorney. All of the school's metal work was done in his shop. He made cedar chests and brass lockers and all manner of things for the faculty members; he shod their horses and repaired their harnesses. Nor could she accuse him of neglecting his own home in this manner. Their house contained numerous fine pieces that he'd made—marble-topped tables with intricately wrought iron legs, hat racks, stools, fenders, footscrapers, chests, cabinets.

And the children loved him too. He made most of their Christmas toys—little wagons, the exact replicas of large expensive ones, with hickory axles and iron-bound hubs, spoked wheels with iron tires, solid oak beds with removable sides, and seats with real springs. They were the joy and wonder of the neighborhood. And he had made sleds with fine iron runners, rocking horses, and miniature garden tools for them.

No one could deny he had the ability. That was what enraged her most. He could if he tried. But when opportunity knocked he seemed to shrink within himself. Often she wondered if his being black had anything to do with it; if in some way he was racially incapable of doing great things. During moments of despondency she regretted having married a black man. She should have known better. Had she married a man her own color at least she would not have to worry about her children being black.

She had long since concluded that he was not going to get anywhere. And regretting it was just a waste of time, she told herself. But she was tied to him by her children. And she would never let him hold back her children.

For a moment she wondered where it was all going to end. Now she was not so certain of anything. But as she worked, a strange set came over her face and her actions became forceful. It was as if she stood with clenched fists, drawing on her heritage, and said over and over again, "I will! I will! I will!"

3

THE CHILDREN BEGAN PLAYING INDIAN. THEY skulked behind the fence, awaiting the arrival of the stagecoach. Soon they would attack the stockade. Poking about the yard in search of tomahawks, they ran across a can of paint and a brush left there by their father when painting the window sills.

It was war paint, they decided, and just what they needed to become big bold braves. Dipping the brush, they sloshed great splotches of paint over each other's face and head. Then, screaming wildly, they ran in circles about the yard.

Hearing them, their mother came running in alarm. Turning the corner, she came unexpectedly upon two apparitions dripping fresh green paint from head to foot and screaming as if in pain. Her first thought was they had blinded themselves. She was frightened out of her wits and for a moment had to steady herself against the house to keep from fainting. "Have mercy, God," she gasped. And then she noticed Charles' matted hair, plastered to his skull. "It's ruined," she moaned, "oh, it's ruined," her anguish as poignant as though he were dead.

Rousing herself, she staggered forward and began wiping their faces with her skirt. It merely smeared the paint. Some got into their eyes. They began to cry.

"My eyes," Charles screamed. "I can't see, Mama, I can't see." She caught sight of his eyes covered with a greenish film. Suddenly she screamed, "Lord, oh God!"

The children were more terrified by her outburst than by their own pain. They clutched her about the legs as if hanging on for dear life and screamed at the tops of their voices.

Mrs. Allen, wife of the English professor, and her cleaning girl, came running from the house next door. They found the mother and her two sons clinging to one another in blind terror, like figures from a Greek tragedy.

"What is it, Lillian? What is it, dear?" Mrs. Allen cried in a shocked voice.

"The children!" Mrs. Taylor sobbed. "The children!"

Mrs. Allen looked at the children who were screaming in pain and terror. "Why, they've got into some paint," she said.

The cleaning girl stood to one side, her eyes popping whitely in her startled black face. "Dey's green as watamelons," she observed.

"Oh, they've gotten it all into their eyes and ears," Mrs. Taylor sobbed helplessly. "Please send for Mr. Taylor."

"Run and get the professor, Lucy," Mrs. Allen directed. Then, gently, she clasped Mrs. Taylor about the waist and got her separated from the children. "Now, dear, get hold of yourself. Let's get the children inside."

Finally Mrs. Taylor came to her senses. "Oh yes, oh yes, we must." She took Charles by the hand and Mrs. Allen followed with William.

Mrs. Allen saw that the children were not seriously hurt, and gave a sigh of relief. But they'd looked so funny, the three of them clinging to each other like Medea bidding her children farewell, she thought, stifling the impulse to laugh. "Now don't you worry, dear, it'll be all right," she said soothingly, as if talking to a child.

"Oh, their eyes and their ears," Mrs. Taylor wailed as she half-led, half-dragged Charles around the house toward the kitchen. "Oh, his hair," she added involuntarily, thinking aloud. "It must be ruined."

In the kitchen they undressed the children and Mrs. Taylor brought bath towels. Carefully they wiped the paint from their faces and necks, but it kept dripping from their saturated hair. "Oh, dear," Mrs. Taylor sobbed. "Oh, dear."

Mrs. Allen wiped methodically. The children bawled.

Lucy ran all the way across the campus to Professor Taylor's shop. Professor Taylor wore blue denim coveralls over his trousers and vest. When Lucy appeared he was burning a hot iron tire onto a wagon wheel. His students were ringed about him. He held the blacksmith's hammer aloft to pound the tire. Lucy dashed into their midst and cried hysterically, "Fess Taylor, Fess Taylor, yo' chillun's done painted theyselves." He understood her to say *fainted*.

Without a word he turned and started to run, still holding the blacksmith's hammer aloft. His wits weren't working. His mind held just the one picture—*accident!* His love for his children was such an integral part of his existence he never thought about it. He never thought of his heart beating. He loved his children in the way his heart beat.

Students and several members of the faculty saw him running across the campus, the hammer held aloft. They thought he'd taken leave of his senses.

"There go Fess Taylor, chasing a ghost," a student remarked.

He arrived in his kitchen out of breath. His gaze stabbed at his wife, flashed toward the children. They sat side by side on an old bench before the stove. Their heads glistened with dark green paint; their skin had a greenish cast. They looked at him out of wide, frightened eyes, whimpering slightly. Slowly he lowered the hammer to his side and looked enquiringly toward his wife.

"What is it, honey? What's happened to them?" His voice was breathless with anxiety.

"You left the paint open in the yard and they've painted themselves," she said hysterically.

"Painted?"

She pointed accusingly. "Look at their hair."

He looked again toward the children. They stared back solemnly. Except for their red eyes they didn't seem injured. Relief flooded over him in a wave of weakness. It was all he could do to keep from laughing. Carefully he averted his face under a pretense of disposing of his hammer.

But she had noticed his expression. "You needn't laugh," she cried. "They've gotten it all in their ears and eyes."

"Now, honey, there's nothing to get so upset about," he said placatingly. "They're all right." He had a deep rich baritone voice and when he attempted to placate his wife it acquired a syrupy tone. "Just put little drops in their eyes—"

"I did," she said harshly. "And I've put sweet oil in their ears."

"They're all right," he soothed. He went over and patted the boys on their heads. His hand got wet with paint and he wiped it on one of the soiled towels.

The children stopped whimpering.

"We were playing Indian," William informed him.

"We were braves," Charles added.

Their father laughed. "See, honey, they're all right. Their eyes are bright as pennies. There's nothing to get upset about. They're all right."

Her mouth tightened angrily. Now that he had gotten over his own panic he was condescending toward hers, she thought. She knew that he could panic as easily as herself and his calmness infuriated her. She felt resentful toward the children also, as if they had let her down by responding to their father's reassurance.

Turning to his neighbor, he grinned broadly. "How d'you do, Mrs. Allen."

She nodded. "Professor Taylor."

"I s'pose you were frightened for a minute."

"Oh, your wife had everything under control," she said impassively.

Professor Taylor removed his cap and tossed it on the table. "They're just boys," he said. He had a habit, when assuming an attitude of indulgence toward his wife, of cocking his head to one side, mussing his short cropped hair, and squinting his eyes off to one side while his wide mouth fashioned a grin. It always infuriated Mrs. Taylor. "They're just Daddy's boys."

Mrs. Taylor turned away in anger and disgust. Professor Taylor looked at Mrs. Allen for support. "Boys will be boys. They're just busters."

Mrs. Allen remained neutral. She knew, as did all the faculty wives, of Professor Taylor's tendency to seek feminine approval of his behavior, and how this enraged and upset his wife. He loved a feminine audience.

"Now, Lillian, honey, you get them dressed and I'll take them over and have Doc Barnes look at their eyes and ears and then I'll have Jethroe clean their hair and by suppertime you won't know they've been in the paint."

"We'll never get the paint out of their hair," she said grimly.

"It's colored hair," he replied slyly. "A little paint won't hurt colored hair."

She knew that secretly he was glad it had happened. She could barely restrain herself. Without replying she left the room. Mrs. Allen excused herself and went home. Professor Taylor began to undo his coveralls. He doubted if the paint would hurt the boys' hair. But even so, what difference would it make after all, he thought.

Unlike his wife, who before her marriage had known but few black people, and none intimately, Professor Taylor had grown up with black people exclusively. His father, Caleb Taylor, had been apprenticed to the blacksmith on the plantation where he'd grown up as a slave. He had been bought by his master at an early age and had no memory of his own parents. He was twenty-seven years old and the father of four, when the Civil War ended. After the war he had remained on the plantation and worked for the owner.

Caleb was a short, powerful man with coal-black skin and incredibly kinky hair. Professor Taylor had inherited his father's physique, but they were nothing alike in temperament. When it served a point, Professor Taylor often feigned anger he didn't feel. But his father had possessed a truly ungovernable temper.

34

Soon after Caleb was freed he had a row with his former overseer and felled him with a singletree. He left him for dead and fled the country. His wife got word in time to flee with her children. He never had word of them again.

A year later, in another section of Georgia, he married again. His second wife was also an ex-slave, but they were married in a church by a traveling evangelist. She was as black as Caleb, but frail. They had five children, three boys and two girls. Professor Taylor was the third born. He was fourteen years old when his mother died of consumption and his older sister, Lou, took her place. The oldest son, Henry, left home and became lost to the family. But the three youngest children became a tightly-knit group under Lou's tender care.

Although Caleb was a good blacksmith, he could barely feed his family. After his trouble with the overseer, he worked only for ex-slaves, and there were but few of them who could afford the services of a blacksmith.

Professor Taylor was the only child to get a college education. All of the others had to sacrifice. He attended a small church college in Georgia and worked at menial jobs to pay for his room and board. It was not until after he began teaching that he could afford to study in Boston. But he didn't let his poverty or color hold him back. Although he hardly ever had a decent suit of clothes, he wore those he had with an air, and his ingratiating manner endeared him with everyone. He was never lost, never without friends. He could always get a girl.

In part his popularity came from his being a magnificent actor. None knew this so well as his wife, who had learned it to her regret. He could dissemble and pose with such validity that his innermost thoughts and emotions were seldom revealed. Mrs. Taylor despised this characteristic almost as much as she did his color. She thought of it as a slave inheritance. Whenever she saw him scratch his head and assume his attitude of subservience, she was reminded of the fictional character, Uncle Tom. Ofttimes she was struck with the queer notion that he, also, might have been a slave.

Only his wife could make him feel inferior. In the presence

of most people he felt a wonderful assurance. But she was so conscious of her white blood she kept him constantly on the defensive. He could never be natural with her. He was either indulgent or resentful. She seemed destined to bring out the worst in him.

Now, added to her contempt for himself, was her attitude toward their children. She wanted to rear them in the belief that they were, in large part, white; that their best traits came from this white inheritance. He wanted to prepare them for the reality of being black. Between them the battle of color raged continuously. But he still wanted her; he still loved her; and deep down he was proud of being married to her.

When he had finished removing his coveralls, he turned to the older child. "Now, Will, you're getting to be a big boy. You mustn't do naughty things to upset your mother."

"He did it," William said, pointing toward his younger brother.

"Didn't, didn't, didn't!" Charles denied.

"It makes no difference," his father replied. "You're the oldest. You have to keep your little brother out of mischief. You must learn to take care of your little brother."

William looked at him solemnly without replying. He didn't love his father with the same intensity as he loved his mother, but he was excited and awed by him. At that time Charles loved his father passionately. He loved to go to strange places with him and hold his hand and be made much of by people. And he loved to hear his father's loud rich voice and his indulgent laugh. His mother he took for granted.

Mrs. Taylor returned with the children's clothes and dressed them. She had a hard, bitter set to her face. She wouldn't look at her husband.

"Now don't fret, honey," he said. "I'll have them spanking clean. I'll get Jethroe to clip their hair—"

"Don't you dare!" she cried threateningly. "Don't you dare have Charles's hair cut." Mrs. Taylor was one of those persons who believed that cutting a child's hair at a tender age would ruin its texture. "Don't you dare! You just have the paint cleaned out and I'll see to it myself."

"Now don't worry, honey, I'll have it cleaned with turpentine," he promised.

But once outside he forgot his promise. He became so carried away with telling all the curious neighbors what had happened, unthinkingly he let the barbers clip the boys' hair and shave their skulls.

At the college hospital their eyes and ears were cleaned and their skins washed with alcohol. The children were excited and happy. It was better than a game. Never before had they been the center of so much fuss and bother. Several members of the staff had gathered about. Professor Taylor told the story again. It was the beginning of a family legend. The students laughed and teased the little tots. The children forgot that they'd been naughty.

In the meantime, as Mrs. Taylor went about cleaning up the mess they had made in the kitchen, she wondered if she'd be able to save Charles's hair. When mulatto children's hair turned kinky, the transformation was termed "going back." To Mrs. Taylor it was more than that. She thought of Charles's hair as being *lost*. First, she'd wash it with tar soap, and then she'd apply hot castor oil. She'd have to brush the life back into it. The thought made her suddenly weary. So much care she'd taken—and now to have this happen.

Thomas came in at two-thirty, swinging his books by a leather strap. He kissed his mother fondly. "Can I have a sandwich?" he asked.

He was at an age when children shoot up like beanstalks. "Thomas has a tapeworm," his mother often teased. "We must feed him enough for himself and his tapeworm too." At eleven he was taller than his mother, but rather thin. His face was narrow and his eyes set a little close together. He had his father's large hooked nose and his mother's thin mouth. Although he was the fairest of the children, his features were strongly Negroid.

She sliced some bread and liverwurst. "The children have gotten themselves all messed up with the paint your father left out in the yard," she informed him.

37

He stood eating the sandwich rapidly. "How, Mother?" he asked with his mouth full of food.

She'd warned him repeatedly against talking while chewing, but now she overlooked it. "Your father is so thoughtless. He *will* leave things about for the children to get into. Sometime he's going to leave his shotgun out and the children are going to kill themselves."

All of the children loved her voice. It was a small and shallow voice but very pleasant. Often she played the piano and sang for them. But they were hurt and embarrassed by the strident tone it took whenever she spoke of their father.

Tom wanted to know more about what had happened to his little brothers. But he wouldn't ask. The intonation of her voice made him feel too ill at ease. He couldn't understand her feelings for his father. It seemed so strange and wrong to him. He thought his father was the greatest man in all the world. He was awed and fascinated by the things his father did.

He'd stop by the shop on his way home from school to watch his father at the forge, see him grip the white glowing metal with the long iron tongs and slam it on the anvil, and then quickly, before it cooled, pound and shape with short deft strokes of his blacksmith's hammer. Sparks flew harmlessly against his father's leather apron. His black face would shine with sweat. The students stood about, frozen to attention.

Tom watched his father work with open-mouthed wonder. He scarcely breathed as the white metal magically took shape and cooled to cherry red. His father would stick the metal back into the forge. A student would turn the handle of the bellows. His father would wipe the sweat from his eyes and see him standing there. He'd smile at him and Tom's heart would turn over with pride. Again the glowing metal would be slapped upon the anvil and pounded into shape. Then his father would plunge the glowing shape into a pail of water to temper it. The water would hiss and bubble. And Tom would breathe again. Finally a student would plunge his hand into the pail and withdraw a plowshare. Tom believed his father could make anything.

He knew his mother didn't like his father. She called him

"Mister Taylor." But it was more than that. It was the way she spoke of him, always accusing him of doing something wrong, and the harsh tone of her voice. It hurt him to see his mother's mouth get so hard and tight. She was so pretty and she had such a nice light way of laughing. It made him tingle inside when she was happy.

He ran up to his room to change his clothes. His mother made him wear a Norfolk suit and long black stockings to school. But after school he could wear his corduroys and let them dangle down his legs.

It was four o'clock when Professor Taylor returned with the children. At sight of their bald, square heads Mrs. Taylor went white. She hadn't believed that Professor Taylor would go against her expressed wish. Then the blood rushed to her face. For a moment she was speechless with fury.

The change was more pronounced in Charles. He looked like a wax doll before the wig has been attached. But he was not his mother's beautiful long-haired boy.

"I'll never forgive you, Mr. Taylor," she said. "You just did it to spite me."

"Now, honey, it's going to grow back," Professor Taylor said in his sugary, placating voice. "The world hasn't come to an end. Our little boys have just had their hair cut, that's all."

She turned her face away and bit back the recrimination that came to her lips. What was the use, she thought. Her mouth closed in a grim, straight line.

When Charles's hair began to grow, Mrs. Taylor brushed it endlessly. But the texture had changed to the soft fuzz of beginning kinkiness. She firmly believed that it had been the shaving of his skull that had changed its texture. It hurt her deeply to know he wouldn't have straight hair. She felt he'd been deprived of his birthright. Until her death she considered it one of the tragedies of his life.

One evening as she was reading to the children before putting them to bed, Charles said suddenly, "I got wool hair now, Mama, just like the black sheep."

Professor Taylor laughed. But tears came to Mrs. Taylor's eyes.

"Yes, darling," she choked, trying to smile. "Just like the little black sheep."

They were sitting about the living room fireplace, the children sprawled upon the hearth rug, and she and Professor Taylor in the easy chairs. Professor Taylor leaned down and rubbed Charles's fuzzy head. Mrs. Taylor gave him a look of venom. Charles laughed delightedly.

"Rub mine too, Daddy," William cried, inching toward his father.

Mrs. Taylor stood up. "It's time for bed, children," she said harshly.

When she returned from putting the children to bed she gave her husband a look of infinite contempt. He squirmed guiltily.

"I suppose you're satisfied," she accused.

"Yes, I'm glad it's turning nappy, if that's what you mean," he blustered defiantly. "The boy has to be what he is."

"And what is that, pray?"

"Just a Negro, that's all; just a Negro. Did you think he'd be white?"

"Must he have kinky hair to be a Negro?"

"I want my children to look like me," he muttered.

"So they can grow up handicapped and despised?"

"Despised!" His face took on a lowering look. "What do you mean, despised? I suppose you think I'm handicapped and despised?"

"Aren't you?" The question startled him. "Can't you see," she went on, "I want the children to have it better, not just be common pickaninnies."

"Pickaninnies!" Her thoughtless remark cut him to the quick. "That's better than being white men's leavings."

She whitened with fury. It was the second time he'd slurred her parents but this time was all the more hurting because they were dead, and she revered their memory. Striking back, she said witheringly, "You're nothing but a shanty nigger and never will be anything else. And you would love nothing better than to have my children turn out to be as low and common as yourself."

He jumped to his feet, shouting with rage and frustration,

"And you're a yellow bitch who thinks she's better than God Himself!"

Upstairs the children lay quiet and listened, scarcely breathing, They trembled with fear and hurt.

Mrs. Taylor looked up at her husband scornfully. "Better than you at least. You don't even want it better for your own children. What kind of father are you?"

"Confound it, woman, I've taken your nagging and bickering for twelve years, and I'm through!"

"Then get out! I'm sick of the sight of you. Go! Get out! Go to your Mrs. Douglas. That's where you've been going with whatever money you can beg and scrape together!"

"That's a lie!" he shouted. "That's a foul, vicious lie!"

The blood came up hot in her face. "Don't you call me a liar!" she cried, standing to confront him. "You black devil! You're the most depraved, despicable liar that was ever born."

They were leaning forward toward each other with their faces jutting and their hands clenched. Their eyes were hot with hatred and their voices screamed and lashed back and forth. The listening children shuddered and prayed for them to stop.

"Woman, take that back!" he demanded threateningly. "If you don't take back that dirty lie I'll—"

"You yellow cur. If you touch me I'll have you arrested. You make this house filthy with your presence."

"Then get out of it!" he roared. "It's my house. I pay the bills. Shut up or get out!"

"I will get out," she declared, drawing herself up. "If it hadn't been for the children I'd have been gone long ago. Don't think I stayed because of you. I hate you! I hate all of you dirty, deceiving, conniving Taylors! You and your cabin brood. Yes, I hate you, you black despicable nigger!" Her eyes brimmed with tears of rage and impotence.

Overcome with fury he slapped her. She drew back, her face hardening and her mouth becoming thin and set. Without saying another word she clutched her shawl tightly about her shoulders and left the house. She walked swiftly to the nearest police station and swore out a warrant for his arrest, charging him with criminal assault. The two officers who accompanied her to serve the warrant tried to act as peacemakers. It seemed a shame to have to arrest one of the teachers of the colored college as if he was a common nigger wife-beater from down in the bottoms. But she was adamant. He was taken under arrest. The children peered around the upstairs bannisters, whimpering and trembling in terror, as he was taken away. She sent them back to bed and took up a lonely vigil in the living room, nursing her outraged feelings.

Professor Taylor was released on his own recognizance. But he refused to spend another night under the same roof with his wife and packed his valise and left. She didn't know where he went, and she told herself she didn't care.

Fearful of the story creating a scandal, reflecting on the college, the magistrate postponed the hearing. But the story leaked out and created a scandal after all.

Mrs. Taylor went about with a tight mouth and a strained frightening look in her eyes. The children were afraid of her. Tom was too ashamed to go to school. She let him stay home that day, but the next she packed him off.

Meanwhile she sent telegrams to her sisters and brothers in the South, asking them for money so she could leave her husband. But they were loath to interfere in a family quarrel. They didn't want to be accused of encouraging her to leave her husband. Nor did they want the responsibility of her and the children. Had she shown up with the children they would have taken her in; but they wouldn't send her the money to leave. She had no money of her own. She felt trapped and abandoned. But her determination to make her husband suffer hardened all the more because of it.

Soon the scandal grew to such proportions the college president had to take a hand. He persuaded Mrs. Taylor to withdraw her charge, and advised Professor Taylor to return home. They worked out a truce. For the sake of the children she would live with him, but never again as his wife. He moved into the room with Tom. She spoke to him only when necessary. The atmosphere was charged with strife and dissension and the children lived in constant fear. She worried about them and tried to act natural when they were about. But she hated her husband with such deadly fury, more for the allusion to her parents than for his striking her, that she was always on edge. How dare he cast slurs on her parents, she thought. He wasn't good enough to mention their names.

Again they became ostracised. There was no choice left Professor Taylor but to resign and seek another post. When the school term ended they prepared to leave. He hadn't told her when they were going and she wouldn't give him the satisfaction of asking. Rarely did she even look at him.

He left a week in advance to prepare their house. She engaged a crew of warehousemen and supervised the packing, all the while unaware of their destination. Not until she received his letter, containing the tickets and instructions for freighting the furniture, did she learn his position was in Mississippi. Had she possessed the means to support her children she would have refused to go. But she had no choice. Closing her mouth in a grim tight line, she prepared to leave. He had won this time, but her time would come. She would put up with him until she could get away. She wouldn't let him have the children. Where the children went, she would go.

4

IT WAS DUSK OF A LONG SPRING DAY WHEN THEY finally arrived at the railroad station where Professor Taylor was to meet them. The train pulled to a stop beside a dilapidated wooden platform. Mrs. Taylor and the children peered through the windows.

Across a level patch of yellow mud stood a false-fronted general store. In lieu of a porch there were two wooden benches on which sat several long-haired white men, clad in faded and patched blue denim overalls, leaning back against the wall. They sat slumped in an indolent mobility, their faces rock red in the strange yellow light, still eyes staring balefully at the resting train, like figures of a long forgotten race carved by a demented sculptor in bas-relief. Two rickety wagons with teams of bony mules, both mules and wagons caught, it seemed, in attitudes of utter lethargy, were hitched to the slanting posts. A single hack with a team of fat gray mules, incongruous with the surrounding scene, was tied to the station platform.

There was no sign of her husband. Her heart sank. At that moment she felt as close to defeat as she ever had. Slowly she began collecting their luggage.

The brakeman came into the Jim-Crow coach to hurry them. And suddenly Professor Taylor was there, smiling at the brakeman to soothe his feelings, and trying to quiet Mrs. Taylor's alarms.

"Now, honey, now, honey, just let me handle things."

The baby boys rushed up and hugged him about the legs.

"My boys, my boys," he said, patting them fondly on their heads and lifting each in turn to kiss him. "My little boys."

They had been frightened but now they were reassured.

The brakeman recognized him as one of the teachers from the Negro college by the fact he wore a suit with a collar and tie. "Thass all right, fess," he said indulgently.

Professor Taylor shook hands with Tom, patting him on the shoulder. And then he turned after an instant of hesitation and kissed his wife. At that moment Mrs. Taylor wanted him to kiss her. She had been without sleep for two days and was exhausted and dispirited. If only for the moment, she had to put her trust in him; she couldn't carry on without help any longer.

In a short time he had them off the train. Tom helped with the luggage. The brakeman waved. The train began to move. They piled the luggage in the hack. Across the street the row of lookers moved, leaned forward, but only the ears of the drooping mules flickered with brief life.

The hack contained three hard wooden seats, one behind the other, covered by a crude wooden top. Professor Taylor sat in the front seat, flanked by the two baby boys, while Mrs. Taylor and Tom sat behind. He picked up the reins and flipped them lightly across the dull gray backs of the mules. The team turned in the dirt square and headed away from town.

Beside the road were fields of corn already at full height, like rows of dark green sentinels in the soft dusk. No one spoke. They could hear the gentle rustle of the cornstalks in the faint breeze. Beyond a grove of white pines a purple-orange cloud hung in the darkening sky. It had rained recently and the hoofs of the mules made suction sounds in the muddy road. The iron-tired wheels swished faintly in the mud.

An atmosphere of serenity enveloped them. Mrs. Taylor dozed, too tired to take notice. Tom stared about him with bewilderment. He felt a vague sense of foreboding. William was soothed by the peaceful scene. But Charles was enthralled. The strange quiet beauty of the long green fields drew him into a state of enchantment. He loved each new sight passionately, the smell of the mud and the mules, the pine spires in the purple sky, the softly sighing corn. It was as tangible and friendly and as wonderful to him as his mother's breast.

The road turned and crossed a stream, the iron tires rattling the loose boards. Then slowly, at first imperceptibly, the road began to sink. The countryside rose higher; corn gave away to green rows of cotton; the banks closed in and the road became narrower. Soon the bank was as high as their heads, and then it was over the top of the hack, cutting off the light. They moved like a boat down a shallow river of darkness beneath a narrow roof of fading twilight. As the road deepened, roots of huge trees sprang naked from the banks like horrible reptilian monsters. Now high overhead the narrow strip of purple sky turned slowly black, and it became black-dark in the deep sunken road.

The mules moved down the tunnel of darkness with surefooted confidence as if they had eyes for the night. They knew the road home. Professor Taylor tied the reins to the dashboard and gave them their head. It was so dark he couldn't see his hand before his eyes. The black sky was starless. As they moved along the old sunken road the dense odor of earth and stagnation and rotting underbrush and age reached out from the banks and smothered them. It was a lush, clogging odor compounded of rotten vegetation, horse manure, poisonous nightshades and unchanged years. Soldiers of the Confederacy had walked this road on such a night following the fall of Vicksburg, heading for the nearby canebrakes.

The little children huddled fearfully against their father. Even Mrs. Taylor was frightened by the unrelieved darkness. Nearby an owl hooted. She gave a start. She felt as if they were coming to the end of the earth. In the distance a hound howled, the long lonesome sound hanging endlessly in the thick night. The road was like a canyon deep in the bowels of the earth, away from all life.

Finally the little children went to sleep. Tom nodded beside his mother. Professor Taylor talked desultorily, but Mrs. Taylor did not reply. She held herself rigid against the surrounding phantoms. After what seemed an eternity the road came again to the surface of the countryside and the landscape stretched out in a faint visibility. But it yielded only vague silhouettes.

They arrived at the college in the dark. The children were sleeping. They stopped before a white picket fence. Beyond, in the shadows, stood the dim outline of a two-storied house. Professor Taylor lifted down the tots. They awakened and whimpered in the strange darkness. Tom jumped to the ground and helped his mother to alight. They went in a group up the uneven walk and entered the strange house.

A fire burned low in the front living room. Their own furniture had not arrived and the room looked huge with its few pieces of homemade furniture. Mrs. Taylor went into the kitchen to warm some food for the children. But the old wood-burning stove was cold. Professor Taylor offered to build a fire, but she declined.

He went after the luggage. And then he had to return the hack and team to the college stables and walk the mile home in the dark. In the meantime she gave the children cold milk and took them up to bed. There were four bedrooms upstairs, barrenly furnished with old iron beds, straw mattresses and crude pine stands, each holding a pitcher of water and a wash basin. It was a cheerless reception. She felt that Professor Taylor should have had someone there to look after things. Without waiting for him she selected a room and went to bed, trying to stave off thoughts of tomorrow. She knew it would take all of her resources to cope with this frightening wilderness.

Professor Taylor returned to the darkened house to find all of them in bed. He was disappointed. He had hoped for a moment to talk with his wife and reach some kind of reconciliation. For a long time he stood in the darkness of the living room before the dying fire. It was oppressively hot. He'd built it to add cheerfulness to the barren house, not because it was needed in the hot Mississippi night. But it had been the wrong thing. He should have built a kitchen fire. Finally he went upstairs and entered the empty room. His wife could have her own room if that was the way she wanted it. At least he had his sons.

In her own room down the hall she heard him moving about. She was frightened and lonely. Had he come to her then she would have welcomed him. She needed him then. Her spirit was at its lowest ebb. She needed a husband to give her strength.

But the bright sunshine of a new day streaming through the curtainless windows across her bed made quite a difference. Even at that early hour she felt its heat penetrating her skin like rays of energy. New life came into her weary bones; her spirits lifted. She heard the children yelling downstairs, and screeching excitedly in an orgy of discovery. She arose and washed in the basin. Then she dressed and went down to the primitive kitchen to prepare their breakfast. A fire was burning hotly and the grits were already cooking. A shy, young, very black girl was setting the table. At Mrs. Taylor's entry she looked up and smiled. She had the long beautiful face with the full mouth, sloe eyes and classical symmetry of the pure African.

"Good mawnin', Miz Taylor. Fess Taylor got me tuh come in an' hep. Ah woulda been heah las' night but Ah din know when y'all wuz comin'." Her voice was soft and melodic, humming-like, almost as if she was singing the words. Her large, strong hands with the long, spatulate fingers moved slightly in a gesture of reassurance, as if she knew what the older woman was experiencing and wished to comfort her. "You jes tell me w'ut you want done. Mah name is Lizzie," she added.

"Good morning, Lizzie," Mrs. Taylor greeted in her light, precise voice, but it was warm with pleasure and she smiled gratefully. "I'm so happy you came." She turned toward the stove. "What are you preparing?"

"Fess Taylor thought you mout lak some grits an' bacon. He got some new cane 'lasses he thought the boys mout lak."

Mrs. Taylor looked at the huge, thick slabs of side meat just beginning to sizzle in the skillet. "Do we have any cereal and milk? The children have cereal with their breakfast. And it would be nice if we had some fruit."

"Yessum, Ah forgot," Lizzie said, getting down a large box of corn flakes and a pitcher of milk. "Fess Taylor bought these 'specially for them." And then she fetched a bowl of fresh strawberries from the storeroom on the back porch. "Ah picked these 'specially for you," she said shyly.

Tears brimmed in Mrs. Taylor's eyes. She put her arms about the girl and hugged her spontaneously.

Although the windows and door were opened, the heat from the wood-burning stove was stifling. Mrs. Taylor stood for a moment in the window. Flies buzzed outside the screen, drawn by the smell of frying.

The backyard was a barren square of baked clay with here and there a thistle weed and tufts of Johnson grass. Beyond was a wire-enclosed chicken coop beside a row of wooden sheds. She recognized the outhouse by the half-moons in the doors. On the other side was a fieldstone circle of the top of a well with a bucket and pulley attached. She wondered if they got their water there. Several fat, lazy Plymouth Rock hens were busy burrowing dust holes in the hard, baked dirt.

Behind the yard was a field sloping down to a point some distance away where a tall tree stood. Later she was to learn it was a pecan tree from which pecks of the fat greasy nuts were gathered in the fall. A man was plowing in the field and her two younger children ran along behind him, barefooted in the turned furrow.

She withdrew from the window and stepped out onto the screened back porch. On the other side she found a pump and cistern and breathed relief. While Lizzie was finishing breakfast she inspected the rest of the house. Across the front were two large, identical rooms, separated by the center hallway which led back to the kitchen, each containing a fireplace. The flues had openings in the above bedrooms for winter stoves.

A porch extended across the front of the house. Except for the entrance it was completely enclosed by morning-glory and honeysuckle vines in full bloom. Rambling rosebushes ran along the eaves and wandered up and down the ceiling posts. Bees were at the flowers, making a droning sound, and several humming birds darted in and out. At one end of the porch was a low, wide swing. It was cool out there and very pleasant in the morning. She went over and sat in the swing and rocked gently back and forth.

The front lawn had been cut and the fence recently painted but already the sun was browning out the grass. Stunted rosebushes grew as wild as weeds. At the corner of the porch was a fig tree with branches up over the roof. Beside the brick walk was an umbrella tree.

The house sat on high brick pillars because of the uneven ground, but the vines screened the opening underneath. Tom and his father came from beneath the house. Mrs. Taylor was startled by their sudden appearance.

"Call the boys," she directed Tom. "Breakfast is ready."

He ran off toward the field.

Professor Taylor came up on the porch and sat down beside her in the swing. "Well, honey?" he asked tentatively.

She looked beyond the picket fence at the baked clay road down which a wagon drawn by two ancient mules came slowly into sight. "It's a comedown," she said.

"You haven't seen it all yet, honey."

"I've seen enough."

There were freshly plowed fields on both sides, separating them from their nearest neighbors. "The boys'll have room to grow up in, honey. In a few years we can build a new house."

She arose to go to breakfast. "It's your choice," she said unforgivingly. "I'll make the best of it."

But as she walked back through the empty house she knew she had her work cut out. He followed humbly, a little uncertainly. The children were already eating their cereal with relish, hurrying to be finished and away again. Their eyes were bright with excitement. She looked at their bare dusty feet and sighed.

5

THE COLLEGE HAD ORIGINALLY BEEN BUILT FOR white students. But some years past, through a political deal, it had been turned over to Negroes. Traces of its former charm still remained.

The original buildings had formed a horseshoe about a spacious campus of shade trees dotting a level lawn. They were built of brick and adorned by the tremendous, two-storied verandas supported by tall marble pillars which had become the architectural landmark of the old South.

At the curve of the horseshoe, overlooking the campus, stood College Hall with its thirty-three marble steps, then in bad decay, ascending to its pillared veranda. A beautifully designed wrought-iron railing, which had been imported from Italy, enclosed the staircase, and some of the original stained-glass windows still remained in the assembly hall, where now the church services were held.

To one side was the president's residence, a large white colonial structure with landscaped lawn and flower garden. The architect who designed this house never dreamed that a Negro would once inherit it.

Beyond was a huge wooden building containing the girls' dormitory and domestic science school, its latticed outhouse extending like a tail behind. Further on were two of the old brick buildings and then several residences for the faculty members. At the edge of the college grounds the dirt road diverged from the horseshoe, climbed a short steep hill, and meandered for fifteen miles through cotton fields and cane brakes to Port Gibson on the Mississippi River.

Across the campus from College Hall was the flat one-storied frame mess hall; and behind it the powerhouse, waterworks, icehouse and laundry

To the other side of College Hall were four of the original old brick buildings, verandas and all, housing classrooms and the men's dormitories. Then came a two-storied frame structure with blistered paint which served jointly as the hospital and science building. And beyond were the doctor's residence and several small frame shacks serving incidental needs.

This was the academic department. The classroom buildings were heated by wood-burning stoves placed in the hallways. There was no heat in the dormitories. Out behind each building were the outhouses, one for women and one for men.

The road on which Professor Taylor lived sprouted from the horseshoe bend and curved down a steep hill behind the science building. Here were the frame houses of most of the faculty members; the Pattersons at top, the Sherwoods next, then Professor Taylor, the Hills on the other side and the Williamses farther down. There, the low clay road, muddy all winter and dusty all summer, took a bend and a half-mile on was the general store, privately owned.

At the top of the hill, leaving the campus grounds, was the road to the railroad station, nine miles distant. Along this road, a mile out, were the barns and sheds housing the livestock and farm equipment, the cannery and silos, and the mechanical building, which comprised the agricultural and mechanical departments. Beyond, as far as the eye could see, extended the thirty-six hundred acres of farm land owned and cultivated by the college.

The mechanical building was the only modern structure at the college. It was a one-storied brick building with tall windows and modern lighting and contained several power saws and lathes driven by belts and pulleys from overhead shafts. Here the wagons were built, the horses shod, the tools and equipment made and repaired for all the rest of the college. This was Professor Taylor's department.

All of the students boarded. They matriculated upon finishing the country grade schools. There were no intermediate schools. The college provided the equivalent of a high school education. Most of the men studied agriculture, the women domestic science. They were grown, eighteen and older, when they arrived. And only a very few could afford to remain four years.

The summer school was attended by country teachers. It opened shortly after Mrs. Taylor and the children arrived. Professor Taylor was away at the shop all day. Mrs. Taylor, with the help of Lizzie and several men students whom her husband sent over, got her house in order. Professor Taylor outfitted the fireplaces and made cabinets, tables and chairs. Their furniture arrived and was brought from the station in the school wagons. When all their familiar possessions had been put in place the house took on a homey atmosphere. When their piano was first unpacked, Mrs. Taylor sat playing it for hours, unmindful of all else, as if visiting with an old dear friend. It made her feel civilized again.

Her chief concern was with the children's food. She was appalled by the diet of the natives. For breakfast Lizzie would eat fried side meat, boiled rice and sorghum molasses, scorning the milk and cereal, eggs and toast which she served the Taylors.

Fresh meat was the great problem. They had no way of keeping it. When the stock was butchered the faculty members got the choicest cuts. But it was mostly pork and Mrs. Taylor distrusted it. She didn't eat the fresh pork herself, and only rarely fed it to the children. She ordered most of her meat in cans from Memphis and Chicago.

Ice was out of the question. A bit was made by the school, but it was scarcely enough for the mess hall. They had a rare treat when Professor Taylor brought home a cake of ice for lemonade or making ice cream. First it would be crushed in a crocus sack; and then carefully packed into the freezer, a layer of ice, then a layer of salt. Afterwards would come the children's job, turning the handle. They'd turn and turn and turn, it getting harder and harder as the ice cream froze. Their strong little arms would ache. But they got to lick the dasher. Freezing ice cream was related to Sunday dinner, fried chicken, fresh linen and visitors.

There were vegetables in abundance. All of the faculty had land to cultivate. Professor Taylor had nine acres around his house. The field behind the sheds was planted in corn. But there was a large truck garden beside the house which he had inherited from the former resident. Already it was yielding English peas and butter beans, squash and greens and Kentucky wonder string beans. Tomatoes, carrots, radishes, spinach and scallions grew like weeds. Professor Taylor added okra, eggplant, cantaloupes and several vegetables unheard of in those parts, such as kohlrabi and artichokes.

The children filled with energy like bursting seeds. Professor Taylor laughingly said the sap had just come up in them. They longed to be out of doors, digging in the ground, running through the fields. She dressed them in denim overalls and wide straw hats such as the natives wore. She couldn't make them wear their shoes. They'd take them off the moment they got out of sight. They found birds' nests and garter snakes and tiny terrapins and toad-frogs, all of which they brought indoors. Their father took them to the barns to see the sows and pigs and cows and calves and mares and colts. They saw the little stud jacks and were amazed to learn that a mule had an ass for a father. There was no end to the excitement.

The first thing each morning they'd explore the garden to see what had grown overnight. They ate anything. Then they'd examine the wigglers in the rain barrels at the corners of the house. From there they'd wander to the field, always inching toward the road which was forbidden. Once Mrs. Taylor found them almost to the general store, all by themselves, walking down the middle of the road, the hot dust squishing delightfully through their toes. They loved the feel of the hot powdery dust on their feet and the taste of the mud in the road after a heavy rain.

She was at wit's end trying to restrain them. The country-side was interlaced with deep ravines and bayous, the ground crawled with poisonous snakes, the woods abounded with de-licious-looking berries and fruits that made the stomach ache. She was worried sick whenever they got out of her sight. But she couldn't watch them every moment. And the moment she turned her gaze they were gone. Professor Taylor assured her no harm could come to them. And in the next breath he'd tell of how some full-grown student had been seriously in-jured.

But the children didn't know enough to be frightened of any-thing. They ate worms and caterpillars on each other's dares. Once Tom showed them how to stuff a bullfrog with bird shot. The frog would lap up the shot with his long darting tongue as if it were fish eggs, until it grew so heavy it couldn't move. The children were anxious until Tom dangled the frog by its hind legs and shook the shot from its mouth.

They ate green persimmons from the tree in Professor Patter-son's yard and made ugly faces when the tart brackish juice drew their mouths. One day they saw a snake fighting a lamper eel in the shallow drain beside the road. The snake and eel were tightly entwined, thrashing in the muddy water. The children got sticks and poked at them.

In front of the general store was a wild cherry tree which they soon learned to climb. One of the summer students told them that the wild cherries would make them drunk. They'd eat the cherries and pretend they were falling from the tree. Soon their mother would come running the long dusty mile, her hair undone and hanging loosely down her shoulders, her eyes harried and distraught, looking like some dusty apparition. She'd switch them all the way home. The neighbors would see them running ahead of her, William screaming as if she were killing him and Charles gritting his teeth and biting back his tears. It fretted his mother that Charles never cried.

But most fascinating of all was going with their father to the general store. If they promised not to tell their mother, he'd give them a nickel to spend. Off they'd race, peeping first into the pickle barrel, and then into the barrel containing salted mackerel floating in dirty brine. They'd filch a cracker from the cracker barrel as they saw the grownups do. And at last they'd stand before the tiny candy counter, eying the delicious sweets. William loved licorice sticks and Charles rock candy. They'd stand entranced by the strange formations of the rock candy in the large glass jar.

Or they'd tag along behind their father and watch him wring the chickens' necks for Sunday dinner and put the watermelon down into the well for cooling. Once he took them with him to the mill. They rode through the country in one of the small school wagons. Professor Taylor gave the miller a bushel of corn for a bushel of meal. He explained to them that a bushel of corn made more than a bushel of meal and that the miller kept the excess for his profit. But they were too interested in the water wheels to listen.

When the sugar cane ripened their pockets were always stuffed with dirty joints which they pretended were chewing tobacco. They'd take a bite and spit out the juice as they'd seen their father do. Tom brought home some bamboo canes and their father made them whistles and pea shooters. Tom was too busy with his own activities to give them much notice. He was either off fishing with the fellows or catching frogs and bringing home the skinned white legs for his mother to cook. As much as she detested them, she'd cook them for him.

One day Charles was bitten by a copperhead while playing in the back field. He cried, "I'm snake-bit," and started running for the house. William sped after him. Their father was at the shop. Mrs. Taylor had gone to the store. They didn't know what to do. They ran through the house bawling for Lizzie. But she was out. The inch-long gash on Charles's leg was open like painted purple lips. They ran out on the porch, screaming.

Luckily, an old Negro vagrant, known about the campus as Billy Goat, was passing in the street. He was barefooted and clad in ragged overalls, with long white kinky hair bushed atop his head and a nappy white beard stained brown with tobacco juice.

"I'm snake-bit," Charles cried, and ran out in the street and clutched him by the leg.

Old Billy Goat looked down at the gash. "Tain't nuddin, boy. Y'all jes cum on now an' ole Billy Goat'll fix it."

He took Charles back to the porch and widened the gash with his rusty knife. Then he put his old tobacco-stained lips to the opening and sucked out the poison. He spat and bit a chew from his dirty plug and when his saliva was rich with the juice he spat into the wound and covered it with dirt.

"Gwine back tuh play, boy," he said. "W'en y'all gits snake-bit agin jes holler fuh ole Billy Goat." Cackling at his humor, he slapped Charles on the rump and wandered off.

The boys sat for a time and looked at the dirty wound. Then they got hoes from the tool shed and went looking for the snake to kill it. But the snake was gone. They didn't tell their mother until suppertime.

Charles stuck out his leg as they were eating. "See that, Mama," he said.

She looked at the dirty, runny sore and jumped from the table.

"That's where I was snake-bit."

"Oh, my God!" she wailed, almost fainting. "Run for the doctor," she ordered Tom.

"Wait a minute," his father said. He turned to Charles. "When were you snake-bit, son?"

"This afternoon." Charles was enjoying the commotion.

"Ole Billy Goat sucked out the poison," William said. "He cut Charles with his knife and then he sucked the blood."

Mrs. Taylor slumped into her seat, too weak to move.

"When did all this happen?" their father wanted to know.

"When Mama was to the store," William said.

"We'd better get the doctor anyway," Mrs. Taylor finally said.

"Now, honey, just wash it out with peroxide and tie it up." He laughed indulgently. "If it was going to kill him he'd already be dead."

But that was the end of their adventures. After that the only time they were permitted to leave the yard was Sunday morning. Professor Taylor always took the children to Sunday school, and afterwards Mrs. Taylor joined them for the church services. They took their baths Saturday afternoon. The children took theirs first. They'd place a tub of water out in the sun and a half hour later it would be hot enough to bathe in. The children bathed on the back porch. But Professor Taylor and his wife bathed in the kitchen.

On Sunday they had an early breakfast so Lizzie could go home and dress for church, and it gave Mrs. Taylor time to dress the children. At the first ringing of the bell the father and sons set forth. Twenty steps up the road their freshly shined shoes were covered with dust, and sweat was running in rivulets down their freshly scrubbed faces. Sunday school was held in the classrooms beneath the assembly hall. Professor Taylor taught a class of older students and the children sat with them. There was no class for tots their age, and Tom didn't want them tagging along with him.

After Sunday school, Professor Taylor took the younger children home and returned to church with his wife. Most of the students were deeply religious. Young men and women ofttimes shouted as enthusiastically as did their elders, jumping from their seats and flapping wildly, as if to fly posthaste to heaven, when the spirit moved them. Frequently the spirit commanded them to beat the devil from their neighbor. There would ensue such bloody fights that the faculty members were hard put to protect the sinners from immediate doom. Mrs. Taylor was afraid her children might be called to their glory before time, so she never took them to church.

Tom went with an older group on Sundays. And he was out visiting most of the weekdays. The other campus children were in awe of him because he'd lived up north in Missouri. He lorded it over them in his strange northern clothes. But he was well liked and was always being invited to dinner by their parents. The popular game for his age group was hide-and-go-seek. It was an ideal game for the surroundings. The various trees and culverts and ravines and buildings made wonderful hiding places. In the early summer evening all but the very youngest children could be heard running and screaming and shouting as they played.

Their mother never let the little children out to play. Sometimes they would swing on the gate and listen wistfully. But it was pleasant on the porch in the cool of evening with the breeze stirring in the vines. Professor Taylor would be home for the day and dinner would be finished. He and Mrs. Taylor would sit quietly in the rocking chairs while the younger children swung recklessly on the porch swing. Other professors and their wives, out for an evening walk, would stop at the picket fence or come in and sit on the steps and chat.

The sun would set at the end of the long summer day, painting the sky with fantastic, brilliant colors; and then the fiery reds and yellows would deepen to a purple-orange. Twilight would come and the crickets would begin to chirp. Slowly the mosquitoes would come out, buzzing about their ears, and keep them slapping at their arms and legs. Charles would leave the swing and go sit on the bottom step and listen to the changing of the earth. He would feel so happy and joyous and excited that his heart would pound against his ribs. And yet it always made him sad. While he watched, the outlines of the buildings and the fence and road would change and grow vague in the deepening dusk. He would sit entranced as a phantom fairyland took shape and the elves and dragons and fairies came out. Twilight affected him with a passion so poignant he'd sit crying inside with ecstasy. Then the fireflies would come out and the spell would be broken. He and William would dash about the yard, shouting gleefully, and catch the lightning bugs. They'd rub their faces with the yellow, phosphorescent tails and pale yellow spots of light would shine where they had rubbed. Mrs. Taylor would watch them absent-mindedly, marveling at their growth. They'd stop for a moment to listen to the shouting of the older children playing tag. After a while they'd slip off by the gate and stand there silently, hoping their mother would forget that they were out. They dreaded the moment she would say,

"It's time to go to bed, children."

6

THE OPENING OF THE FALL TERM WAS AN EXCITING
time. The male students met the first wagonload of women out
at the entrance to the college, unhitched the team, and themselves hauled the wagon the remainder of the distance to the
dormitory. There was always a circus of joshing and buffoon-
ery and many of the faculty members took their families out
to witness the event. It was something of a tradition and took
place rain or shine.

It was a beautiful day and Professor Taylor stood in the
crowd of men, holding the hands of his younger children, watching the wagon come down the dusty road. As soon as they
came in sight the women stood and waved. A roar went up
from the welcoming men. But none went beyond the old wooden
arch that marked the entrance, for it was at this point that the
ceremony took place.

When the wagon finally came into the college grounds, pandemonium broke loose. The men climbed aboard and kissed
the women at random. Most of the women wore gingham
dresses and had their carefully straightened hair tied in bright
bandannas to protect it from the dust. Their black and yellow
faces gleamed with sweat and their dark eyes sparkled as they
put up their faces to be kissed. The big rough country men
milled about the wagon, hanging on the sideboards and jumping to the hubs to get a kiss and see what girl was new. Professor Taylor's children pulled at his arms, trying to get closer
to see what was going on. The men and women laughed crazily,
carrying on conversations that had begun the spring before, as
if the summer hadn't happened. The children didn't understand it. But the excitement was contagious. They danced up
and down.

"Johnny jump! Johnny jump! Johnny jump!" Charles screamed,
adding to the din.

"Hush!" William cautioned. "Hush up! You don't know what you're talking 'bout."

Their father chuckled. Finally the students had the teams unhitched and a long, strong rope attached to the wagon tongue. Then they started running down the road, kicking up so much dust the wagon was enveloped.

In the excitement a woman fell and before the laughing, straining crew could be halted she was run over by the wagon. Charles was standing near enough to see her ribs flatten beneath the heavy iron-tired wheels, and the blood start surging from her mouth and nose. She wore a gray buttoned sweater over a calico dress and her body seemed thin and undernourished. He saw her face with stark clarity. She was a light-complexioned, homely girl with a longish pimply face and her hair was tied carefully in a blue bandanna. He saw her hands grope desperately for the spokes of the first wheel, and then fall limply, jerking spasmodically in the dust as the hurt came overwhelmingly into her bulging eyes. It seemed to come from her in such intensity as to be communicable. He felt her hurt down in his own throat and chest, and he felt as if his ribs were being crushed by the heavy wheels also. The sharp brackish sensation of ruptured blood vessels filled his head as if blood was spurting from his own mouth and nose. His mind could not contain it, and could not throw it off. He couldn't cry or scream or breathe. He felt himself going down-down-down with the dying woman into the cool dark valley of death. He fell gasping to the ground, trembling in the dust. His father fought desperately to keep him from being trampled by the panic-stricken mob. The screams and the wails of the women came into his ears as if he heard them from the grave, and strangely his mind identified the sound of William crying hysterically, but nothing penetrated the incomprehending trance that held him paralyzed. Now, in the cool, dark deep, away from the shock and horror, it was no longer terrifying.

His father carried him home in his arms. His mother saw them coming down the road, her husband straining with the burden, William tagging along in the dust. Her hand flew to her hair. The acid bite of fear coursed through her flesh. She rushed forward and opened the gate, holding to it for support, and the prayer kept sounding in her mind, "*Please, God . . . please, God . . . please, dear God . . .* " When she saw her husband's face, haggard from exhaustion, she cried out in anguish, "He's dead, oh my little baby, he's dead, I know he's dead."

"He's just fainted; he's just had a shock," her husband gasped. But her baby's eyes were open and she knew that he was dead. "My baby, my baby," she cried. "What have they done to you?"

They got him up to bed. His eyes held no intelligence, but he was breathing. She fell to her knees beside the bed and prayed.

"He'll be all right, honey," his father kept saying, helplessly. "He'll be all right."

Down below the front door slammed. "Hey, where is everybody?" Tom called. He came clattering up the stairs, frenzied with excitement. "A girl got run over—" he panted, then stopped. "What's the matter with Chuckie?" he asked bewilderedly.

"Run get Dr. Wiley," his father ordered.

"Lord, dear God, if You'll just give me the strength I'll take them out of this wilderness," Mrs. Taylor sobbed.

"The boy's not hurt, honey," her husband soothed. "The boy's not hurt. He's just shocked; he just saw a girl get run over."

"He saw her die?" she questioned.

"We don't know whether she's dead or not."

She turned her gaze on him. "His soul is hurt," she said condemningly.

The doctor came in out of breath and treated Charles for shock. He was preoccupied and didn't take the matter seriously.

"That girl," he said, shaking his head. "She died instantly, poor thing."

Professor Taylor and the older boys followed him to the door. Mrs. Taylor stayed with Charles, sitting on the bed and smoothing his forehead with her hand. Slowly he came out of his trance.

"I was dead, Mama," he said, looking at her with strange solemnity. "I was dead."

She fell across him and smothered him with kisses. "My baby, my little baby."

He clung to her, terrified again. "She was bleeding from the mouth and nose and her eyes . . . *Mama!*" he cried, feeling himself going down-down-down, away from the terror and hurt.

"Charles!" she cried, trying to hold him back. "My baby!" And then she screamed, "He's fainted again!"

Professor Taylor came running up the stairs. "Let him alone, honey. Don't frighten him anymore."

"We must do something," she sobbed. "You must send to Natchez and get a doctor."

He tried to draw her from the room. "Now he'll be all right. Just let him alone. Dr. Wiley's one of the best doctors in the state."

"Then why doesn't he do something?"

Tom and William rushed into the room and their father caught them and turned them around. "Now let's get out and let your brother sleep."

In a few minutes he was conscious again.

"Does it hurt you?" his mother asked.

"It was just dark," he murmured. "It was just like a funny dream. I wasn't scared at all."

The next day he was up and about. She tried to get him to talk about the accident.

"Won't you tell Mother, son?"

She wanted him to get it out of himself. But when he tried to remember, all the shock and horror returned and he felt himself going away, down-down-down . . .

"I can't!" he cried. "I can't, Mama, I can't!"

She was terribly afraid it was going to affect his mind. For the first time during her marriage she pleaded with her husband. "Mr. Taylor, take us away from here. Take us away."

He was embarrassed. "I can't, honey. You know I can't. I can't just quit my job and leave. We just got here. How would we live?"

"God will take care of us."

"Now, honey, I believe in God as much as you do—"

"Then send us away," she begged. "This wild, savage country will kill the children. They're not used to it. They'll be dead before another year."

"Now, honey, you're just exaggerating. You're letting your imagination run away with you. The boys will like it here. You're just upset. Later on you'll agree—"

"Then I'm going to send Tom away," she vowed. "I'm not going to see him perish in this jungle. I'm going to save one of my children."

"Well, he can go to Cleveland and live with Lou," he relented.

Some years before, his older sister had married a county school principal in Georgia and they had moved to Cleveland. For the past ten years Mr. Hart had worked in the post office. They owned their home and had four children, one of whom, Casper Junior, was Tom's age.

Mrs. Taylor hated the idea of her son living with his father's relatives. It sickened her to think of him living in the home of such black people. But it was too late to enter him in any of the boarding schools. And all of her own relatives still lived in the South. She wanted him out of the South entirely. It was a difficult choice. But finally she consented that he go.

"Now be a good boy, Thomas, and don't let them steal your affections. Mother is depending on you," she said to him in private.

"I won't, Mother."

"You must be polite and courteous, but let no one influence you on things you know are wrong. Your father's people are black like your father and think differently from us. You must make up your own mind. And never listen to anything bad they say about your mother."

Thomas felt ill at ease. It was strange and hurting to hear his mother talk in this manner. But he promised to do everything she said.

After he left she began teaching her younger children at home. Their father brought home two school desks and they turned the front room that had served as a library into a school. He'd contended that Charles was too young for school; but their

63

mother had insisted they begin together, and he'd given in. She hadn't got over her fear of Charles losing his mind. Although she had never again pressed him to speak about the accident, she knew he still retained the shock and horror deep inside himself. He was becoming moody and introspective. She had to put his mind to work.

They had a regular schedule of recitation periods and study hours. For six hours every day, five days each week, they attended school. At first, during the warm, beautiful days of Indian summer, they hated it. They were restless and irritable and had fits of temper and William cried a great deal. They drove their mother to desperation.

But when the cold dreary rains of fall came they began to like it in the big pleasant room with a fire burning in the fireplace. They learned rapidly and it became fun. They loved the feeling of so many books surrounding them in the dark shiny bookcases. During their study hour they would take them down and browse through the pictures. Slowly, the room grew into a world apart, half of which was school, but the other half their own imagination. They experienced a feeling of security and happiness there that they had never felt before. And their mother was reassured.

In other respects the family passed a miserable winter. All summer Mrs. Taylor had fought the dust that came into the house and settled on the furnishings as if they lived in the middle of the road. Now it was the drafts of winter. The old house was never warm. Great volumes of wood were consumed by the huge fireplaces, but most of the heat roared up the flues. In the evenings fires were lit in the stoves upstairs. But all the different fires only served to increase the drafts.

All winter the children had colds. Mrs. Taylor worried constantly. There had been tuberculosis in her family, and she thought the children had inherited weak lungs. She became quite thin and her shoulders became more stooped. She wore an old gray woolen shawl continuously, and kept it clutched about her throat. Professor Taylor developed a deep permanent frown between his eyes. They continued to sleep apart and both suffered a great deal from sexual frustration. They were irritable and short-tempered and flared-up at each other on the slightest provocation. He suffered constantly from piles and she was revolted by his habit of digging at himself. On the other hand he was repulsed by her nightly use of cold cream and always avoided her after she had prepared for bed.

With the falling of the leaves and the dying of the flowers beneath the drawn-out, rotting rain, the surrounding countryside settled into a state of unrelieved dreariness. It was a drear, lifeless rain, beneath which everything took on a soggy, water-soaked appearance, dull and drab. The world itself seemed exhausted, the sun was tired and weak, the sky cried melancholy tears. Mrs. Taylor became unutterably depressed. There were occasions when she felt she couldn't bear it another minute. Then she'd sit at the piano, playing for hours, forgetful of the children's studies, until she found solace of a sort. Only the children escaped the sad and lonely days, living in their half-imagined world.

But Professor Taylor had his work to occupy him. He put on his rubber slicker, knee boots and fireman's hat and went out into the rain. They didn't have a horse and buggy and he walked the mile to work. Sometimes he hired a student to chop the kindling and kitchen firewood. The fireplace logs were ordered by the cord and stacked beside the house. Sometimes Lizzie did the chopping. But more often he did the work himself, standing in the rain and mud, splitting the slippery logs. He'd stand before the hearth and dry himself, steaming on one side and then on the other.

After the rainy season it turned cold. He liked rising early on a frosty morning and going hunting, or taking the children to gather hickory nuts and pumpkins for Halloween. His cronies would ride up in a wagon with the hounds following behind, and he'd get his double-barreled shotgun and fill the pockets of his hunting jacket with twelve-gauge shells and they'd go to the deep woods and shoot whatever they could find. He often told the story of how Professor Norwood shot a hound dog way up in a tree. Or else they'd set out early in the evening with their lanterns and hunt opossum at night. Sometimes he brought home a 'possum or a pocketful of squirrels and Lizzie would cook them for the boys and him. The boys loved the taste of game, but their mother wouldn't touch it.

A war was being fought in Europe that winter and its far-flung repercussions were felt even in that little Negro college in Mississippi. Cotton prices had gone up and the students were more affluent. The college had been granted a larger appropriation. Now the governor took an active interest in its administration. It became commonplace to see his short, pudgy figure about the campus, addressing the students in the chapel, or sitting at the faculty table in the mess hall, waiting for the others to finish eating so he could have his dinner. The governor felt that this was more democratic than having the entire student body and faculty wait for him to finish, since obviously they could not eat together.

He poked his nose into all the departments. "Mah boy, Burt," as he referred to the president, always accompanied him. He made a point of seeing what the faculty members read. He searched their desks, examined their books and papers. But he did it openly and good-naturedly. "Ah jes' wanna see what you Negra fessors are up to down heah with state money."

Most of the faculty members and student body held the governor in high regard. The college had prospered under his administration; the new machine shop was one of his innovations. And from time to time used equipment, machines and books and desks, had been sent from the white university at his direction. The governor was an avowed friend of the colored people and at every opportunity expressed his desire to see them become "good farmers an' good blacksmiths an' good Negras."

Professor Taylor always held a deep, secret fondness for those white southerners in authority. He knew instinctively how to get along with them, just how far to go and when to be ingratiating. As a consequence, he seemed far more audacious than the other professors. His interviews with the governor always gave President Burton a nervous stomach. And yet the governor liked him best of all the faculty members.

There was an unwritten rule prohibiting faculty members from reading Negro newspapers and periodicals that were published in the North. In New York, militant Negroes and white sympathizers had organized a National Association to fight against discrimination. They published a magazine whose editor was a fiery, angry writer, revered among the Negroes as a great messiah, and feared and hated by the whites throughout the South. The penalty for reading this magazine was immediate dismissal and expulsion from the college.

Once, on one of his raids, the governor found a copy of the magazine in Professor Taylor's desk.

"Willie," he said, "you know the penalty for readin' this heah inflammatory trash."

"Governor," Professor Taylor replied in his sly, obsequious pose, "you know I don't believe that trash. I just want to see what those crazy Negroes up North are up to."

"Willie, you let those Negras up there alone," the governor admonished. "They don' mean you no good. An' don' let me ketch you readin' this heah trash no mo'. Heah, give it to me. Ah'll destroy it."

But a short time later Professor Taylor returned to his office and found the governor with his feet propped up on his desk, reading the magazine.

"Governor," he said slyly, "I thought you just told me that trash wasn't fit to read."

"It ain' fuh you, Willie," the governor said. "But it kain' hurt me. Ah'm jes seein' what those Negras are sayin' 'bout me."

On the other hand, the governor raised no objection to the teaching of Negro history. Obscure textbooks and treatises dealing with all phases of American slavery, its inception, slave uprisings, the political aspects, the rise of the abolitionist movement, were taught in special classes and diligently studied. The students learned the role the Freedmen had played during reconstruction; they knew the names of all who'd held public office. The college had obtained copies of the minutes of the various assemblies of the defeated Confederate states to which Freedmen had been elected. The students were informed that immediately following the end of the Civil War, more than half the legislators in the Mississippi Assembly had been Freedmen. They read the biographies of all the famous Negro rebels, leaders, educators. They knew the names of all the great American Negro actors, singers, scientists, writers, teachers; the name of the Negro who invented the railroad coupling; the name of the Negro who died at Bunker Hill. They learned, from these obscure texts, that Negro blood flowed in the veins of the Russian poet Pushkin, the French novelist Dumas, the English poet Browning, the German composer Beethoven. Every student of Negro literature had read the famous words of the Negro general, Hannibal, to which they gave various current meanings: "Beyond the Alps lies Rome." They were taught to be proud of their racial heritage.

Lincoln's Birthday and Emancipation Day were the two most important holidays.

Despite their seemingly easygoing acceptance of conditions, protest was lodged deep in the hearts of all. Debates were as popular as baseball games. The students drew upon their natural acting talent, employing their rich, stirring voices. Never was there so dramatic a moment in any debate as when some young black man with moving intensity pitched forth the mighty challenge that won for the colonies their independence: "An' in the words of Patrick Henry, Ah say: 'Give me liberty or give me death!'"

Professor Taylor liked it there. In spite of the indignities there was a certain inalienable dignity in the work itself, in bringing enlightenment to these eager young black people. It wasn't as if they could come there with the easy assurance of an upper Bostonian enrolling in Harvard. For what they learned, they and their mothers and fathers and sisters and brothers paid in privation, in calico in January, corn-pone diets and pellagra deaths. Professor Taylor was one of them, a little, short, black, pigeon-toed, bowlegged, nappy-headed man; he'd come from the same background with the same traditions; he was just more fortunate. He knew this, knew that he was more fortunate also in the selection of the mother of his sons. He wanted his wife to be happy, and his sons to grow up carrying the heritage of their race for better or worse. Only his wife was unhappy and hated it. And his sons hadn't yet learned that they were Negroes.

But he liked it in spite of this. And he liked that first Christmas they spent there. He worked hard to make it come off and as early as October ordered his Christmas presents. When the week of Christmas came, he and the boys scoured the woods until they found a cedar tree. They gathered arms full of holly with its bright red berries for window wreaths and cut mistletoe to hang from the kitchen ceiling and over the living room hearth. They spent their evenings popping corn to trim the tree. The wonderful scent of hot buttered corn filled the house and the children stuffed themselves. Their mother had ordered tinsel and artificial snow from Chicago. They fastened the colored candlesticks to its branches and clamped the huge gold star atop. And they gathered moss from the old oak trees to make a bed about its trunk.

Christmas Eve the children undressed before the fireplace and hung their stockings on the mantel.

"I'm gonna stay wake and see Santa come down the chimney," Charles said, dancing up and down with glee.

"The san'man 'll throw san' in your eyes," William warned him.

Their mother read them a little story she'd composed for the occasion:

Word went to heaven of the red chaos which raged upon the earth, and God's heart so swelled with compassion that heaven overflowed and purity spilled out in lazily drifting snowflakes to cloak the mad fury with a merciful mantle of white. The snow-tipped evergreens came to watch, and were fascinated by the sight, and stood entranced. And the little lights came from the rainbows and the stars and the sunsets and the autumns and perched upon their branches. And the little voices peeped from lips, and suddenly, inspired by the happy sight, began singing carols. Hearing them, fire looked out of the fireplace and danced and crackled with joy. And all the evil people, bound by hate in the darkness of confusion, saw the dancing fire and heard the singing voices and were cheered by the sight of the beautiful tree, and goodness and mercy strengthened their souls and they broke their bonds and escaped into the light and ran to greet their neighbors, shouting aloud: Come see the miracle; come see the miracle! Christ has come to us again in the form of a living tree! And that is how Christmas trees happened.

The children listened to her light, lovely voice with eyes as big as saucers; and afterwards carried their potties upstairs and went to bed, breathless with excitement.

Professor Taylor felt such pride in his lovely, talented wife, he could scarcely contain it. These were the moments that he lived for.

Early the next morning he got up and built a roaring fire and he was waiting when the boys came down to see what Santa had brought them. Presents from their aunts and uncles, an erector set, gloves, scarves, a fire truck, popguns, a set of lovely picture books from their mother, were banked about the tree. But he'd bought them real bicycles. And for his wife he'd gotten a phonograph and a box of recordings. Tom had sent her a silver comb and brush set, inscribed, "For My Lovely Mother."

The children were delirious with happiness; and she was flushed with pleasure. This, too, was another of Professor Taylor's moments. All day long the children reveled in their toys, pedaling their bikes over the hard, uneven yard until their little legs ached. And yet that night they begged to go with their parents to see the big Christmas tree on the campus that was lit with electric lights.

William clung tightly to his father's hand as they walked up the pitch-dark hill. He was a natural child, in that he was afraid of the dark and strangeness, and expanded only in the familiar. But Charles was drawn to the unfamiliar darkness, and created fantasies he found more real than what the light revealed. Walking

70

through the pitch-black dark to discover in the distance the lighted Christmas tree beneath which the student choir sang carols was to him a venture into fascination. His mother had divined this side of his nature and thought it was due to the horrible accident he'd seen. She tried in every way she knew to win his confidence. But he shielded his fantasies with all his will and she never really got close to him.

All of them derived pleasure from the phonograph. Among the recordings were arias by Caruso and ballads by McCormack; and Fritz Kreisler playing the "Flight of the Bumblebee," which sent the children into ecstasies of glee. But the one they loved best was John Philip Sousa's band playing "The Anvil Chorus." They would shout and yell and hammer on their imagined anvils as they'd seen their father do. Mrs. Taylor never tired of John McCormack's bell-clear tenor voice singing "Martha." Late at night the children would awaken and hear the golden voice coming from below.

One afternoon while she was playing the Kreisler recording of "When A Gypsy Makes A Violin Cry," an old colored beggar came running from the street. He said he thought he'd heard a woman crying. Mrs. Taylor laughed.

"I was playing a recording of a violin concerto on the phonograph," she explained.

He didn't understand. She invited him in and played the recording for him. He was struck dumb with wonder by the magic box. "An' summon's jes' fiddlin'. Ah swow, it sounded lak uh woman cryin'."

Mrs. Taylor was strangely pleased.

Professor Taylor liked hog-killing time too. He brought home a lot of meat. Everyone pitched in and helped to make the hoghead cheese and the dark delicious sausage meat that crumbled like cornbread when it was cooked. They rendered the fat into lard, and the children made themselves sick eating the hot, delicious cracklings. Lizzie made crackling bread and Mrs. Taylor made scrapple.

Professor Taylor had been boasting all that month of how his father cured their meat.

"Cure us some meat, Daddy, cure us some ham," the children begged.

Mrs. Taylor sniffed.

"You just wait," he said. "When we start cooking that good old hickory-cured ham it'll make your mouth water."

All day long he was mixing the brine in a rain barrel, adding salt and saltpeter and eggs and spices and vinegar until it was thick enough to float an egg. The children watched in awe. The following day he selected several fat juicy hams and several sides of bacon and soaked the white fresh meat in the dirty looking brine until it had turned a dark sickly gray. Afterwards he hung the meat from a low beam in a shed and kept a slow fire of green hickory burning underneath. It required a month before they were cured to his satisfaction. He brought them in and plumped them on the kitchen table. There was a dark, smoky cast to the meat.

"Look at these, honey," he called proudly to his wife.

The children came running from their classroom, their mother following, and they stood about and admired the meat to his satisfaction.

"Just hang 'em in the storehouse and they'll keep all year," he said.

But that afternoon, when Lizzie sliced some ham for dinner, it was filled with small white worms.

Professor Taylor was chagrined. "It must have been the eggs," he said. "I couldn't remember whether Pa put eggs in his brine or not."

The children were sick with disappointment. But at the next killing their father brought them some chitterlings to make up for it. Mrs. Taylor took one look at the tin bucket of chitterlings and carried them far out into the field and buried them.

"How'd Lizzie cook the chiddlings, honey?" Professor Taylor greeted her when he came in from work that evening.

"She didn't cook them," his wife replied. Her mouth pursed in a grim, straight line. "I've stood enough. I'm not going to allow you to bring up the children like savages, teaching them to eat all kinds of filth."

"There's nothing more filthy than a chicken," he countered.

"But we don't eat the chicken's craw."

"We eat the giblets."

"Well, I'm not going to let them eat the dirty intestines of a hog."

"I'll just cook them myself," he said, "and you can take the children and go away until I've finished eating them."

"I'll not have them cooked in my house, stinking up everything," she said.

"And who's going to stop me?" he demanded.

"I am, because I've buried them," she informed him.

He thrust his face forward. "You buried my chiddlings!"

She turned and walked away from him.

But the very next day he brought home another lard tin full and cleaned and cooked them himself. She took the children visiting. All that night he was up with acute indigestion, and she derived a perverted pleasure from his suffering.

"Your stomach's going to kill you yet," his wife said acidly the next day.

"It'll be my stomach and not my bile," he retorted bitterly.

All of them welcomed winter's sudden ending. Professor Taylor looked forward to the summer's burning heat that charred him to a cinder. And Mrs. Taylor longed to be rid of the drafty fires and winter sniffles. But none were prepared for the deluge that ushered in the spring.

It was a lush, semitropical country, bordering on the delta land. Mud dominated the Mississippi spring. Creeks and ravines swelled beneath torrential downpours and bridges were washed out and the Mississippi River rose across the delta, flooding farms and cities and killing men and livestock. The roads became inaccessible except for wagons drawn by teams of oxen. Everything for miles around became bogged down in a relentless mire. Old men who lived in houses along the river bank could count off fifty years by the high-water marks on their living room walls, like grains in a board of wood. Year after year it was the same. The natives stayed on as if chained inexorably to their fate, endured the same property damage, the loss of life, the drowned livestock, planted corn and cotton in the rich silt left by the marauding flood, and bore their children who in turn grew up in the same ignorance and died with the same stubbornness, condemning their offspring to the same fate. It was then that Mrs. Taylor became completely convinced that the people of Mississippi, in addition to everything else, were stone-raving crazy. More than ever she felt the urge to escape.

Their own roof leaked first into one bedroom and, when that was fixed, into another. The yard stayed muddy and the children tracked the mud across the floors and rugs. There was no escape from the mud. The moment they stepped outdoors their feet went down into the mire. It was an ordeal tramping across the muddy yard to the outhouse. Nothing depressed Mrs. Taylor quite as much. Professor Taylor built a board walk, but it soon sank into the mire. The mire drew all things down.

Then the water became polluted, and before they discovered it all of them took sick. They had to haul drinking water from their neighbors. The rain water caught so much filth only occasionally could they drink it.

The students were used to the climate. They sloughed through the mud, tracking gobs of it into the classrooms and dormitories with no concern. Out in the barns and corrals they tramped barefooted through the wet manure to save their shoes and laughed at the fastidiousness of their professors.

"Ain' nuttin' but muleshit, fess. Won' hurt yuh."

Then after the rains the sun grew hot. In the rich steaming soil, seeds germinated like magic. Corn grew three inches overnight. You could sit in the early sun and watch the grass come up.

"Mo' rain mo' rest," a student joked.

"W'ut dat you say, boy?" another cued.

"Mo' rain mo' grass grow, massa," the joke concluded.

The trees budded and leaved. And as the sunshine heated, the shade grew cool. Fruit trees over the rolling two-hundred-acre orchard blossomed in rotation, apple and plum and peach and cherry, covering the landscape as far as the eye could see with a profusion of pink and white. Brier patches, where all winter long the rabbits had escaped the hunters' hounds, miraculously became dark green jungles of blackberry bushes, thick with copperheads and rattlesnakes. All day long the young black men, eager, earnest seekers of that vaunted education, could be seen plowing the tireless mules, turning long yellow furrows in the ceaseless race against the swiftly growing weeds.

Honeysuckle and rambling roses, buttercups and black-eyed Susans, purple irises and swamp lilies grew like wild, and marigolds raised their yellow heads. Dogwood trees in bloom and the marble-white magnolia blossoms added their pristine touches to this fantastic panorama. All of nature ran wild.

Yet Mrs. Taylor, in her own implacable way, sought to change all this and bring order to this chaos. She ordered packages of flower seeds and planted them in neat rows in her flower garden, and was startled when their sudden lush growth seemed to envelop her. She was exasperated.

7

TOM CAME HOME THAT SUMMER. THE FAMILY met him at the dreary station. When the train came hurtling in, William broke from his father's grasp and ran screaming. His father caught him halfway across the road and held him in his arms until his trembling stopped. Charles had been as frightened as his brother. But he'd stood rigid in defiance. Both children gave their mother pause, but Charles's reaction worried her the more. She couldn't understand what was in the child; what was hurting him, what was he holding himself against?

Then sight of Tom claimed her attention as he stepped from the Jim-Crow coach. He'd grown as tall as his father and was dressed in city clothes. He looked strange and foreign and aloof in that bleak, dilapidated, sun-baked hamlet. The white men lounging about the station platform stared at him. Then they saw his mother and their eyes drew up short as if they'd been struck blind; their faces got that blank, malignant look that presages violence in a childish mind. But one of them recognized Professor Taylor and called, "Hiya, Willie," and the tension eased. Professor Taylor lifted a hand in salute.

Mrs. Taylor hadn't noticed. She was never a demonstrative person, but now tears flooded her eyes as she embraced her son.

"Thomas, Thomas, my, how you have grown," she sang. Her voice was so filled with pride and affection it embarrassed him.

"Hello, mother," he said with self-conscious affectation.

He shook hands with his father. "How are you, Dad."

His father greeted him as man to man. "I'm fine, son, and you look well."

The tots were hugging him about the waist. He patted their heads as his father always did. "And how're my little brothers?"

"We're not so little," William said.

"We've grown a lot," Charles added.

Their big brother laughed. But they were disappointed. He seemed a stranger with his condescending manner.

"We got bikes for Christmas," William informed him.

"Come, children, let's go home. Your brother must be tired," their mother said.

As before, she sat with Tom on the back seat while the tots sat up front with their father. But this time she chatted gaily all the way. The boys could scarcely get a word in edgewise as they tried to tell him what they'd been doing too. Their father was content to let the others talk. Only when they came to the entrance arch did William make them listen.

"A lady got run over right here," he said. Then he looked at Charles queerly.

"You've forgotten I was there," Tom replied.

"Chuck was lookin' right at her," William persisted. "Blood was comin' all out of her mouth—"

"Hush!" his mother cried. "Hush this minute or I'll slap you."

"Now, honey," their father began placatingly, but she wouldn't let him speak.

"We won't discuss it now."

The little children subsided into silence. Charles looked off into the distance.

Tom was eaten up with curiosity. "What's it all about?"

"Charles doesn't like to hear about it."

Soon they came to the top of the hill, and Tom waved merrily to Edith Patterson working in her flower garden. She dropped her hoe and ran into the house to tell her parents that Tom was back.

But he was very grown-up in his relations with the young folk his own age. He refused to play such childish games as tag, and only on occasion would he condescend to play baseball or go fishing with the boys. Each family tried to outdo the other entertaining him. He enjoyed the picnics and the parties, although he tried to act indifferent. On the eve of Independence Day he had his mother give a garden party such as his Aunt Lou had given for her daughter, and it became the talk of the college.

He was very devoted to his mother that summer. It was like a part in a play that he had learned in school. She was ecstatic with happiness and grew strangely youthful. She lavished affection and attention on him, and wore her prettiest things for him. She wore her hair up to please him and carried dainty parasols. Sometimes they were as gay as lovers.

All that winter she'd worried for fear the Harts would alienate his affection. And now she'd won him back. Whatever the outcome of their precarious existence, she felt she could depend on Tom to remain true to her. She had no doubt that he would make something worthwhile out of himself; he was so sure and positive in his manner. She wanted him to become a doctor but he hadn't decided as yet. But she was certain he would choose a calling of distinction. As for herself, it seemed that she was caught. She seemed to have lost her initiative; she found it quite impossible to take an adamant stand and leave her husband as she'd once planned. She doubted if she'd ever have the strength to leave him now. She'd have to sacrifice for the sake of her children. But she felt confident that someday Tom would grow up and, like a knight in shining armor, rescue his mother from her fate.

He returned to Cleveland that fall. Before he left she talked to him again in private.

"You must never forget, my son, that your grandfather was a United States Senator and you are a direct descendant of a famous United States President and of a great Confederate General—and don't you let anyone ever tell you differently."

Again he was embarrassed by her strange intensity and confusing claims. But he promised to be true to her.

8

Mrs. TAYLOR TAUGHT THE CHILDREN FOR FIVE years. They learned easily and without effort. William was the slower, but he was conscientious and far less trouble because he was obedient. Charles was bright but mercurial. Both boys had sprung up like weeds and now there seemed little difference in their ages. Their color had darkened beneath the hot Mississippi sun and the humid climate had kinked their hair unmanageably. During the summers they wore their heads sheared clean in the fashion of the students. Many of the natives shaved their skulls but they were mostly grownups.

The students of unmixed African ancestry had elongated, egg-shaped skulls, and the square, flat-backed heads of the Taylor children drew their derision.

"Whereat you tadpoles get yo' heads?" one asked.

"They pa made 'em in his blacksmith shop," another teased.

The children were furious. "I'm gonna tell my papa," William cried with rage.

Charles ran up and spat at them. "Bastards!" he screamed. "Bastards! Bastards!"

"Doan you call me no basta'd, li'l ol' boy."

Charles kicked him on the shin. The student tussled with him, half-jokingly, holding him at arm's length. "De hammer slipped an' yo' pa done knocked yo' head so flat you got pancake brains."

"Confound bastard!" Charles screamed. "Confound bastard!"

The student threw him down and ran off laughing.

William told his father. Professor Taylor laughed and said it didn't matter; the fellows were just jealous of their heads.

He was an open and natural child, and when hurt went crying to his parents. He told them everything that happened and sought their approval and affection. Charles was stubborn and secretive. When their mother sought the truth she went to William.

Both had a wild, animal love of the outdoors. They roamed the fields like hunting hounds. There was always something new to be found. They never tired of the wonder of the countryside. Often they disobeyed their parents and went into the deep woods where there was danger of being injured by the wild hogs, "loco" steers and poisonous snakes. No one would know where they were. Their parents took to whipping them quite frequently then, trying to restrain this wildness in their nature. Their father used his razor strap, but Mrs. Taylor made them cut fresh green switches from the trees. William screamed bloody murder when he was whipped. The neighbors, hearing him, thought Mrs. Taylor was unreasonably cruel to her children. But Charles never cried. He gritted his teeth in silence. This made his mother whip him all the harder. Her mouth closed in a grim straight line and her deep-set eyes blazed as she lit into him. And his little mouth tightened and his eyes hardened as he faced her in silence. The grim, white-faced woman and the defiant brown boy looked a great deal alike at such times, and the intensity of their emotion for each other was overpowering. Charles loved his mother heartbreakingly, and yet he hated her. And her love for him was agonizing. She ofttimes beat him unmercifully seeking to control his will. But he stood up to her and never gave in. They tore at each other's heartstrings, hurting each other terribly. Between them raged this love and hatred which never cooled.

Mrs. Taylor rarely kissed her youngest son. All of his intense emotion poured out through his kiss and she was shocked by her own passionate response. She didn't want to favor one child above the others. He was a beautiful child with perfect rose-tan features and deep dimples when he smiled. His dark brown eyes were deep-set like her own, but large and very clear. They were fringed by long black shiny lashes that curled upward. Each time his mother looked at him she could see in his shockingly beautiful face the girl she had wanted when he was born. But he was the most uncontrollably violent of all her children.

Sometimes she let Charles brush her long silky hair. He loved the feel of it on his hands and face. He brushed with long hard strokes until it crackled and sparked.

"It's sparking, mother!" he cried. "It's sparking. I'm gonna turn out the light so I can see it spark."

Laughingly she indulged him. Afterwards he picked up bits of paper with the magnetized comb.

"Lookit, mother. Lookit."

He loved to watch the quick soft motion of her arms when she plaited her hair: they were firm and white as if carved from ivory. Sometimes she let him file her nails. He fashioned gently rounded points of which he was inordinately proud.

"Aren't they pretty, mother? Didn' I do a good job?"

"You did them very nicely, darling."

As a girl Mrs. Taylor had been proud of her tiny feet. But she'd worn shoes too small for her and had developed bunions. She was quite ashamed of them, and sometimes they pained her terribly. Then Charles sat before her on the floor and, taking each foot in turn, massaged them with a strange tenderness. He was infinitely patient with her and slowly, gently rubbed in the ointment until the pain disappeared.

"Does it feel better now, Mother?"

Her love became so intense she was afraid to look at him. "Yes, darling, the pain's all gone. Now you run along and play with William."

William was never jealous of his little brother. But ofttimes he felt neglected and would go and put his head in his mother's lap and she would stroke it gently.

Their parents fought a great deal during that time. Hearing their screaming voices, followed by the sounds of scuffling, Charles would crawl to the head of the stairs and crouch, trembling in rage and fear. He didn't hate his father. But when his parents quarreled he wanted to cut off his father's head with the chopping axe. He felt violently protective toward his mother.

Both children had a complete disregard for physical injury. They were always hurting themselves. Although their father had cautioned them countless times, they'd stand barefoot on the blocks they were splitting. Once William almost chopped off his foot. A half-hour later Charles was back doing the same thing. The difference was his defiance. He challenged danger. He rolled down rocky cliffs as if his body was made of wagon wheels. If he got a few cuts on the face and skinned his hands and knees it didn't matter. Their knees and elbows were always a mass of iodine-colored scabs. Their mother was constantly worried for fear one of them would lose an eye or limb. Charles was balancing a sharpened hoe on his shoulder and it fell and cut his Achilles tendon. A delicate operation was required to join it together. But even then he refused to stay indoors. His mother ordered crutches from Memphis and he went hopping about. They loved the crutches and played with them long after he was well.

Their father built them a rope swing on the branch of an oak tree in the back pasture. Singly, each of them could loop the loop, but they had to try it double. They fell too short from the top of the turn and struck their heads against the limb.

"You'll have to take down that swing, Mr. Taylor," their mother said at supper. "The children are going to kill themselves."

"Now what've they done this time, honey?"

"They're not satisfied with just swinging; they want to be acrobats."

"They're just boys," he began. "Just Daddy's—"

"They're going to be dead, and it'll be you that killed them," she said harshly. "If you don't take that swing down the first thing in the morning I'm going to send for Clefus and have him chop down that tree."

"Now, honey, I'll move it where it'll be safer."

But he forgot about it. The next afternoon Charles fell trying to somersault on a backwards swing and struck his head on an old iron hitching block concealed in the grass. He was knocked unconscious. Lizzie and a passing student carried him to the hospital, with his mother trailing in the dust behind. X rays revealed he had suffered a brain concussion. Mrs. Taylor attacked her husband like a tigress when he arrived at the hospital. She scratched his face and screamed at him while the students tried to hold her.

"You want to murder them!" she cried. "You want to kill them, then you'll have me all alone so you can kill me too."

"Confound it, woman, control yourself!" he shouted back at her. "He's my son just as much as he is yours!"

Charles lay in a nearby room near death. William stood in the corner, cowed and humiliated. Dr. Wiley and his students were painfully embarrassed.

"Now Professor, now Mrs. Taylor, you're both just upset—"

"You murderer!" Mrs. Taylor screamed. "You want to kill all of us!"

"Now hold her arm," Dr. Wiley instructed his assistants. "Now everything's going to be all right, Mrs. Taylor." And he gave her an injection. "Now if you'll just lie down a while."

She fought them like a wild woman.

"Now Lillian, honey, now honey—"

"Take her to a room," the doctor ordered.

The black students were loath to struggle with this wild-eyed, white-faced woman.

"Here, give me a hand, Professor."

Finally they got her to bed.

The next day they brought Charles home. But his mother was determined to take them away.

"If it hadn't been that it've been something else," their father argued. "The boys have to have some outlet. You keep them cooped up like laying hens. You won't let them go to school like other children. You think they're too good to play with the country boys their age. They never go anywhere unless they slip off. They have to have something to do."

"They don't have to kill themselves," she contended unrelentingly, her mouth grim and determined.

"We'll just have to watch them closer."

"Watch them!" she cried. "That's all I've done. God knows, I've tried. But they're becoming savage. I'm not going to stand for it. I'm taking them back to civilization."

"I've got something to say about that," he challenged. "They're my boys too."

"They won't be yours for long," she said. "I'm going to divorce you, Mr. Taylor."

"You might divorce me, honey," he replied with maddening calm. "But you're not going to take these boys one step out of my house."

"That we shall see," she said, her eyes glinting dangerously.

Age and worry and discontent and too much crying had affected her eyelids so that they looked like dead brown skin laced with tiny veins; and when she was angry they dropped half-closed giving her a particularly malevolent look.

But her husband wasn't cowed. "We shall see," he said.

She packed a bag and went to Vicksburg to consult a white attorney. She was told she had no grounds for a divorce.

"You should be ashamed of yourself, Madam," the attorney said. "You have a fine husband, an intelligent man, a good provider, and according to you he's been faithful. But you want to divorce him so you can leave Mississippi. Madam, I think you are color-struck, and in this instance your husband has all my sympathy."

She never told anyone the outcome of her interview, but afterwards she said no more of getting a divorce.

Charles was glad. He loved it there; he loved the sights and smells and seasons. He loved the hot dry summers and the rainy falls. He never saw a wagon wheel churning in the hub-deep mud without feeling all inside him the aching hurt of death. Winter was like that, like the ecstasy of pain. His mother whipping him out of her love for him and his love for her aching inside of him with the pain, their love unable to come through the hard bleakness of their hate—was like death. Winter was like death. He loved to play dead, falling in a pretended faint and lying immobile on the ground, feeling the embrace of the earth, its closeness and its chill. Several times he frightened his mother out of her wits. She knew he had never gotten over seeing the woman crushed beneath the wagon wheels, and she was always terribly afraid for him.

Spring affected him physically. He could feel it rising within himself like a great turbulence and when it boiled out, strangely, he was a flower, a deep red flower, or a green whispering tree. He could change himself into a bird, or he could become a yellow-winged butterfly. It was almost all a dream; he could turn everything into a dream.

He turned the hill up to the Pattersons into the Alps and he was Hannibal; behind him stretched his elephant train. Once he was Horatio at the clattering wooden bridge across the bayou beyond the barn. He stood before the wagon teams, frightened but undaunted, until the drivers got down and moved him bodily. Then he threw rocks at them. His father strapped him.

But that didn't stop him from straying off all day long following a group of students who were searching for strayed sheep. Only he was searching for the Golden Fleece. No one knew where he was.

"We went across the cornfield by the pine grove," William told his parents at suppertime. "But I didn't go into the woods. It was dark in there."

"When was that?" his mother asked.

"This morning."

"My God!" she cried, rushing from the table.

"Wait a minute, honey," Professor Taylor called, and to his son, "Where were you all day?"

"I was waiting."

"Where?"

"By the woods."

Mrs. Taylor had gone out into the road, walking rapidly up the hill. She met Charles coming down the hill. Professor Taylor had just come out the gate. Charles broke into a run. Wordlessly, his mother seized a broken stick and struck at him. He dodged and ran on home ahead of her and his father let him come inside the house.

"Where'd you go, son?"

"Just walkin'."

"But where, son?"

"Just walkin' in the woods."

"You had your mother worried, son. We were all worried. Now tell me where you went."

"I was just walkin'," he replied stubbornly.

"Just walking. But what were you doing? What were you looking for?"

"Nothin'. I wasn't lookin' for nothin'. I just felt like walkin'."

His father couldn't make him out. Then his mother entered with a freshly cut switch, her face grim and determined. He braced himself for the whipping with relief. Now he wouldn't have to tell them anything.

She saw that he was waiting for it. She dropped the switch and fell to her knees before him and took him in her arms. Suddenly she burst into tears. Charles was shocked. He wished he could make his mother happy. He wished he could confide in her and make her laugh her tingling little laugh. She was so beautiful when she was happy. It was her grim, unconquerable look he couldn't bear. She fought so desperately.

On summer days when it rained the children played in the attic. They were entranced by the drumming of the rain on the shingled roof. It was a faraway sound, transporting them to magic lands, and then even William could play Charles's games of dreaming a new existence. There were mud daubers' nests to crack and see the larvae. Sometimes a bat flew blindly about, coming within a hairsbreadth of their faces. They rushed recklessly about, trying to catch it. From below it sounded as if they were fighting dragons. Their mother came flying, panting breathlessly from the steep stairs.

"What is it? What's happened?" Her voice was shrill from strain.

Innocently they looked at her. "We were just trying to catch a little ol' bat," William said.

She sat on the top step, torn between laughter and tears. She knew her children were lonely and constrained. Their lack of companions their own age was a constant source of worry. She longed for them to experience a happy childhood, such as she had had. But what was she to do? At times such as this she ached for them. What would happen to them, she didn't know. It was all their father's fault, she thought. If he only knew what he was doing to his children, bringing them up in that awful environment.

As they grew older they took their books to the attic to read. Any dream was possible beneath the strangely stirring drumming of the rain.

In the wintertime they curled up before the downstairs fire, their parents sitting in the easy chairs. Mrs. Taylor had her bag of darning and Professor Taylor held an open book. Soon he dozed, his bifocals slipping down his nose, and his head fell forward, open-mouthed. The fire blazed and crackled in the fireplace. William showed his mother the picture of Agni. Charles was lost to it. He was reading Poe's "The Raven" with complete absorption. The slow, melancholy beat of the repetitious words spun a sharp hurt through his mind. He felt himself tightening slowly until he couldn't bear it. Suddenly he cried, "Damn! Damn!" His own voice released him from the sinister spell. He looked straight up toward his mother, and cringed from the profound shock that came into her face. She didn't speak. His father stirred sleepily. "Whassat? Whassat?"

"Charles cursed," William said. "Charles said *damn*."

Professor Taylor came awake but he was still groggy and witless. "That right, son? You curse your brother?"

"I wasn't cursing anybody," Charles replied.

Mrs. Taylor saw that her husband was confused. She turned to Charles and said sadly, "Go to the kitchen and wash out your mouth with soap."

86

He went without a word. William followed to see that he obeyed. Charles rubbed the strong lye soap on the dishcloth and thoroughly scrubbed inside his mouth. He didn't know why he had cursed. It was the terror in Poe that fascinated him.

One cold January evening, while sitting in the outhouse leafing through the pages of the Sears Roebuck catalogue by lantern light, he came across sketches of birds. He was sucking a straight pin. Both of the children had picked up their father's habit of picking his teeth with pins. Their mother had tried to break them of it, but they did it secretly.

Suddenly Charles was reminded of the *Albatross*. The whole sinister world of Poe seemed to envelop him. The dark night closed in, phantoms and murderers crept stealthily through the weeds. He swallowed in terror, and the pin disappeared. He didn't feel it in his throat, but he couldn't find it anywhere. If he had swallowed the pin it would puncture his intestines. He sat frightening himself into a trance with thoughts of bleeding inside and dying slowly. No one would know what was wrong with him. He wouldn't tell them. He would say he couldn't eat. He'd become pale and weak. He'd nurture his pain in silence. Finally would come the day when he could no longer stand up. He'd lie in bed, dying. His mother would grieve over him. She'd cry. Then he'd tell her how much he'd always loved her. She'd hold him in her beautiful white arms and kiss him. Then he'd tell her about all his wonderful dreams. He'd say, "You know, Mama, the time I was away all day and wouldn't tell where I was. I was Jason, Mama, I was looking for the golden fleece. I planted the dragon teeth, too, Mama. And the fields were full of soldiers." Then she'd say, "Oh, my darling, you tell me and I will go away with you." And he'd shake his head sadly and say, "It's too late now, Mama." And he'd rest his head on her soft breasts while she held him close in her white ivory arms and he'd die. He was so moved by the fantasy he found himself crying. It shocked him back to reality. Now he was certain he'd swallowed the pin. He was terrified. He ran back to the house, holding his pants by his hands. But at sight of his parents and William sitting so serenely about the fire, he lost his nerve.

"Mama," he faltered. She knew instantly that something was wrong. "I th-think I've swallowed a pin," he stammered.

His parents bolted upright. Professor Taylor ran for his coat and hat. His mother put her arm about him and raised his chin. He could feel the violent trembling of her body.

"Is it in your throat?" she asked, trying to control the rising of hysteria.

William looked at his brother in awe.

"I don't know," Charles said. "I can't feel it."

"Don't you feel it at all?"

"No, I can't feel it anywhere."

"Then how do you know you swallowed it?"

"I-I had it in my mouth and swallowed and it disappeared."

He saw her mouth tighten and her face become grim, torn between worry and anger.

Professor Taylor rushed in, carrying Charles's coat and cap. "I'll take him to the hospital, honey. Now don't you worry."

"I think he's just imagining it," she said.

He looked at his son. Charles had begun to tremble. But he was more frightened by the scene he'd caused than by having swallowed the pin.

"Well, the doctor'll know," his father said. "Come, get into your coat, son."

The hospital had recently installed a fluoroscope. The doctor examined him thoroughly, but could find no sign of a foreign body. Charles was relieved to know that he wasn't going to die. But now his mother wouldn't cry and hold him in her arms. She'd think he'd just made it up to get her sympathy and attention. Perhaps she'd whip him. But there'd be no passion in her anger. He dreaded going home.

She didn't even scold him. On his return she looked at him with contempt and ignored him. It hurt far worse than had she whipped him.

The last time Mrs. Taylor whipped her children was for spying on the women's toilet behind the women's dormitory. It stood on the high bank of the bayou and in the summer was almost hidden by the trees and underbrush surrounding it. The children played a game of standing on the other bank and seeing who could urinate the farthest. It was fun to watch the clear arched streams of urine falling into the tiny stream below. A couple of students came up and took part in the game. But they were no match for the children.

"W'en Ah were yo' age Ah could piss that fur too," one of them said disgustedly.

Charles and William looked at one another and giggled. They were proud of their strength.

The men went down and lay in the weeds and looked up at the toilet. The children followed to see what they were looking for. All they could see were the bottoms of several women relieving themselves.

"They're not doing nothing but going to the toilet," Charles said.

"What you think!" the student exclaimed. "They be eatin' dinner or somp'n?" He and the other student laughed.

Charles didn't know what he'd expected to see—something exciting, like a fight or a game.

William felt uneasy. "Let's go."

"Yare, git de hell 'way frum heah 'fore you draw 'tention."

They got up and started off. Professor Saunders, who patrolled the spot, saw them and came charging. The students jumped like flushed quail and tore off down the bayou. Professor Saunders ran after them. The children followed, tearing through the weeds and underbrush and stumbling along in high glee. This was more like it; this was fun. The students got away. Professor Saunders sat and caught his breath.

"They outran us," Charles said, dancing with excitement.

"They ran like rabbits," William echoed.

"Do you know those students?" Professor Saunders asked the boys.

"No, sir."

"One had a scar on his cheek."

"He had a copper penny 'tached to his belt buckle."

"What were you boys doing there?"

Charles was silent.

"Just looking," William said.

"Looking at what?"

The boys were ashamed. "Just looking around," William replied.

Professor Saunders stood and took them by the arms. "All right, come along with me."

Another professor would have taken them to their father. But he disliked Mrs. Taylor, and he took this opportunity to embarrass her. He marched the boys down the road and up to the Taylors' front door.

"Good day, Professor Saunders," Mrs. Taylor greeted him, wondering what the children had got into now.

"Good morning, Mrs. Taylor," he replied, smiling. He was a tall, thin, dark man with a cone-shaped head and large, yellow teeth. There was always a little matter in the corners of his eyes. "I'm sorry to have to report I caught your sons peeking behind the women's toilet." He licked his lips as if he relished it. "And there were women students using it at the time."

Mrs. Taylor flushed crimson. She felt dirtied and humiliated. "I commend you on doing your duty so meticulously," she said in a tight, controlled voice, "even to the point of ascertaining what the boys were looking for."

Her condescension wiped the oily smirk from his long, horse-shaped face. "I don' know what they was lookin' for," he said roughly, lapsing into his native talk, "but I know what they was lookin' at. An' if you don' whip 'em I'll whip 'em myself."

She gathered the boys to her sides. "If you lay a hand on one of my children I'll horsewhip you," she said, adding scathingly, "You have the effrontery to call yourself a teacher."

Infuriated, he reached for Charles. Mrs. Taylor struck him in the face. He turned ashy with rage and instinctively struck back, the blow glancing off her shoulder. Her face blanched. Without another word she turned back into the house, disdainful of him pursuing her, and went in search of her husband's shotgun.

Maddened by her escape, he turned on the boys, cuffing William on the head. Charles clutched him about the legs and tripped him down the steps, while William fled crying underneath the house.

"You li'l bastard!" Professor Saunders cried as he scrambled to his feet.

Charles kicked him on the shin and fled after William. Professor Saunders followed them, scuttling on all fours underneath the beams. The boys had crawled to the back of the house where there was only a foot of clearance. Looking about for a stick to strike at them, Professor Saunders saw the skirt of Mrs. Taylor's dress as she rounded the corner of the house, carrying the double-barreled shotgun. He crawled rapidly to the far side, losing his hat in the process, and began running across the truck garden, his suit dirtied and disheveled.

"He's getting away on the other side," Charles yelled excitedly.

Deliberately, Mrs. Taylor encircled the house. In his haste, Professor Saunders had stumbled, but he was up, running again, when she came into view. Although he was out of range, Mrs. Taylor, unfamiliar with firearms, raised the gun and fired. The gun kicked her sharply and she uttered a cry of pain. The children dashed from beneath the house to aid her.

Professor Saunders had been running in the direction of the Pattersons' field. But the sound of the shot panicked him and, wheeling suddenly, he jumped the picket fence, snagging his coat. As he tore off down the road in a cloud of dust, she raised the gun and fired again, the bird shot kicking up spurts of dust far behind him. He was well out of danger, but at the sound of the second shot he leaped high in the air, as if he'd been hit, and howled in fear.

"Shoot him again, Mama!" Charles screamed.

Students were converging from all directions, attracted by the commotion. Ignoring them, Mrs. Taylor marched the children into the house, moving with the slow, taut preciseness of an automaton, and placed the gun in the parasol rack. The white heat of her fury had cooled. She felt no more compunction than had she shot at a chicken thief. But she still felt a sense of shame and humiliation and was unbearably vexed with her children.

"What in the world were you doing?" she asked.

"Just looking," William said.

She turned toward Charles. But he was silent.

"What possessed you to go to that dirty, filthy place?"

"We were playing."

"Playing what?"

"Just playing." William sounded ashamed.

She glanced at Charles, her mouth tightening.

"We saw some students looking," William said apprehensively.

She wheeled on Charles. "And what were you doing?"

"I was just looking, too," he said stubbornly.

His reply infuriated her. She ran into the yard and cut long switches from the umbrella tree. A crowd of curious students were clustered about the gate, watching the furious woman with fear and apprehension. They didn't know what she was up to, but several had seen her shooting at Professor Saunders, and someone had already gone for Professor Taylor. But none dared interfere. They stood in awe of the grim, white-faced woman married to Fess Taylor.

She paid them no attention. Returning to the house, she lit into both boys at once, whipping them indiscriminately, releasing her fear and worry and frustration into each hard blow. William screamed so loud the students thought she was killing him, and milled about the gate, muttering indecisively. Finally he ran outside and escaped her. She turned her rage on Charles because he wouldn't run. He jumped and danced in pain. There was a fury and jealousy and strange frustration in her punishment of him. It resembled some horrible, silent ritual. At moments in her passion she felt that she would kill him. She received a vicarious pleasure, hating herself.

Suddenly she was shocked. She dropped the switch and ran up to her room and lay across the bed, sobbing. A strange, shocking doubt gnawed at her thoughts.

After a time, when his pain had subsided so he could walk,

Charles limped upstairs. He went over and stood beside the bed.

"I won't do it anymore, Mother," he said. "I didn't want to worry you, Mother."

She sat up and gathered him into her arms, holding him close. "The things you do hurt Mother so."

"I don't want to hurt you, Mama. I don't want to hurt you." He rarely called her *Mama,* and only when intensely moved.

"But you do, darling, and Mother loves you so."

Downstairs Professor Taylor rushed in, followed by Professor Saunders and President Burton.

"Lillian!" he shouted. "Lillian!"

Sighing resignedly, she arose and went downstairs. Professor Saunders gave her a baleful look, but she didn't acknowledge his presence.

"Now you've gone too far," Professor Taylor began. "I know that you don't like it here and I've tried to be patient—"

"Now, wait a minute, Prof," President Burton cut in, sweating with discomfort. "We can settle this amicably. Professor Saunders was wrong and he's willing to apologize. Now if Mrs. Taylor will apologize—nobody was hurt—we'll let the whole thing drop. Your wife is excitable—we all understand that. And Professor Saunders had no business trying to whip her children —that's for y'all to do—that's between you and your wife. Now if your wife will just apologize—"

Professor Saunders leered vindictively.

"Apologize to *that,*" Mrs. Taylor said. "I'll never! Never!" Turning on her heel, she left the room and went upstairs.

The three men looked at one another.

"I'll get her to apologize," Professor Taylor promised.

"For the time being, we'll just leave it as it is, Prof," President Burton decided. "We don't want any trouble 'tween you and your wife."

But Professor Taylor felt outraged and humiliated. Had she been willing to apologize, he would have been able to turn his fury on Professor Saunders for striking her. But now he was put on the defensive and couldn't assert himself as he felt a husband should. When the others had gone, he rushed upstairs and charged into her room belligerently.

"Confound it, woman, this is the last time you make a monkey out of me—" he began threateningly.

She looked at him with scorn and contempt. "If you dare lay a hand on me, Mr. Taylor, I'll shoot you too," she said.

For a moment he stared at her, trembling with rage and frustration. Then he turned and stalked down the stairs and out of the house and walked out his rage down the dusty roads.

The next day Mrs. Taylor ordered violins for the children. She hoped the music would calm their wildness. The music teacher from the college came three times a week. They approached their music as they did their classroom studies; they practiced conscientiously and learned rapidly. But it didn't get them. It didn't touch them down inside.

With the piano it was different. They enjoyed their mother singing in her shallow, weightless soprano voice, cleared of the harsh undertone that had come into her speech. They kept her at it, and when she tired they begged her to continue playing. Chopin's "Fantaisie Impromptu" was Charles's favorite. Both of them loved Beethoven's "Moonlight Sonata." Charles could ride the liquid, golden arpeggios, doubling back again and again on the mood, as if on a winged steed.

The violin lessons didn't make either of them any less wild. Their mother was constantly after them. "God doesn't like ugly," she said. They hated the expression. It made them uneasy to have God in it. Why couldn't it be just between them?

During that time, following the shooting, their father and mother weren't speaking again. That worried them too. They wondered if their parents loved each other.

They didn't know that the shooting had created a big scandal. Although no action had been taken, everyone knew that a serious thing had happened. The students and faculty alike were stung with curiosity. The faculty wives had it that Professor Saunders was secretly in love with Mrs. Taylor and had become enraged because she had spurned his advances. Few of them, however, took her side. Most wondered what really had happened. There were all sorts of rumors making the rounds. For a time it gave them a subject for gossip. But Mrs. Taylor refused to discuss it with anyone. And they held that against her too.

9

IT WAS ABOUT THIS TIME THE CHILDREN BECAME concerned with racial differences. They had always been aware of the absence of white people at the college. And they'd studied all about the races of mankind. "Brown, black, yellow and white," they rattled off in class. They had learned that Negroes were descended from slaves. They knew their father was a Negro. They'd heard their mother call him a "shanty nigger," but she'd been angry at the time. But they had never thought of the rest of them as Negroes. Tom was yellow, William was brown, Charles was tan, and their mother was white. Only she wasn't white like other white people, because she lived with Negroes.

All their lives, except for the brief train trip south, they'd lived within the confines of two Negro colleges, where white people were seldom seen. Their parents never discussed the subject of race within their hearing. They knew that something happened when white and black folks met. But they'd never thought about it until that year.

The first time they saw this strange thing happen was in their father's shop. A white man, who was having his mules shod, asked, "How you niggahs gittin' 'long down heah, Willie?" The man had sounded friendly. But no one replied.

Their father went about as if he hadn't heard. The students stood rigidly, gripped in a sullen silence. The children didn't understand what was happening. The students often called each other "niggah." They didn't realize the man was talking to their father; they thought he addressed a student by the name of "Willie." But they knew, by everybody's attitude, that something bad had happened.

Then their mother got into trouble in Natchez. She'd gone there for dental service. As usual when alone, she patronized a place reserved for whites. The dentist treated her never doubting that she was white. When he asked her address she gave the railroad station.

"That's down near the nigger training school, isn't it?" he asked conversationally.

"It's the post-office address for the college," she replied.

He thought her choice of words curious, but was not concerned. Leaving his office, she met the brown-skinned wife of Professor Hill.

"Why, Lillian," Mrs. Hill exclaimed. "Why didn't you tell me you were coming to town today? I didn't see you on the train."

"Oh, I just came to have my teeth attended to," Mrs. Taylor replied.

The dentist witnessed the scene from his office window. He rushed into the street and clutched Mrs. Taylor by the arm. "Are you colored?" he asked abruptly.

"You release me this instant," Mrs. Taylor fumed indignantly. "I'm just as white as you are."

Mrs. Hill was terrified. She tried to escape, but the dentist took hold of her also. "You called her 'Lillian,'" he charged. "I heard you. Is she colored?"

"Why—er—ah—she's married to Professor Taylor at the college," Mrs. Hill stammered with fright.

A crowd of white people were collecting. Mrs. Taylor turned and began walking away determinedly. The dentist ran after her and seized her arm again. She struck at him. "How dare you touch me!" she cried, her voice rising in anger.

A policeman came up. The dentist charged her with breaking the law which prohibited Negroes from patronizing white places. She demanded an attorney. The officer took her to the police station and locked her in a cell.

"I'm just as white as you are," she maintained.

The policeman became concerned and called in the chief. It was known throughout the state that the Negro college was one of the governor's special interests. So out of courtesy to the governor, the chief called President Burton at the college. The President sent posthaste for Professor Taylor. He flagged the next through-freight. By that time word of the incident had reached the governor. When Professor Taylor arrived at the police station the chief directed him to telephone the governor.

"You get that yallah woman of yo's outa Natchez an' keep her home," the governor ordered him. "You know better'n tuh let her run 'round tryna pass herself off."

But Mrs. Taylor would not accept defeat. "I'm going to sue you," she threatened the chief of police as her husband dragged her from the building. "I'm going to take this case to the Supreme Court if it's my last act on earth."

That night, lying awake in bed, the children heard their parents discussing it downstairs.

"But you didn't have to pass, honey. There're good colored dentists there. There's Doctor Williamson and Doctor Simpson."

"They're nothing but hacks," they heard her reply in the harsh, discordant tone her voice assumed when something went against her. "I'm not going to have any colored dentist breaking my jaw."

"But you're in the South, honey. When in Rome you have to do what the Romans do. If the governor didn't like and respect me, I'd have lost my job."

"That would have been the best thing that ever happened, Mr. Taylor, I'll tell you that." They could imagine her mouth going grim and her eyes glinting.

"Well, if that's the way you feel about it, you just do as you please and see where it gets you," they heard him say. "These white people aren't as easy as I am. You can't dog them around. You're going to find out that you're colored."

The children knew it was something to do with her being colored. The white people might do something to her because she was colored. They didn't know what, but they trembled in fear for her.

"Will," Charles whispered.

"What?"

"Mama's colored."

"Papa's colored too. All of us are colored, silly."

"I know."

They lay silently, scarcely breathing.

"What's the matter, Chuck?" William asked.

"Something's wrong," Charles murmured fearfully.

"I know."

"What, Will?"

"I don't know," William whimpered.

The next day after recitation period William asked his mother, "Why is it bad to be colored, Mama?"

The question startled her. "Why, William, what on earth are you talking about? Where did you hear that?"

"I—I don't remember," he replied evasively.

Then Charles said, "One day we were coming down the road and we saw a fellow and he said we were going to get it 'cause we were colored," making it up on the spur of the moment.

Their mother looked from one to the other. "Was he a white man?" she asked cautiously.

"No, he was a nigger," Charles replied.

Mrs. Taylor was shocked. She'd never heard the children use that word before. "Don't you dare use that word," she said. "Where did you learn such a word?"

"That's what they call 'em. They call everybody that—sometimes."

"We heard a white man over in Papa's shop say 'niggers,' and he was talking about everybody," William added.

"We heard you call Papa a 'shanty nigger' once," Charles said.

Their mother was sick at heart. "I didn't mean it, children. Your mother was probably upset when she said it. You mustn't hold it against Mother. It's a very naughty word and you mustn't ever use it."

But they weren't satisfied. "Are we bad because we're colored?" William persisted.

"No, children, no!" she cried in anguish. "You mustn't think of yourself as colored. Your mother is as white as anyone. You both have white blood—fine white blood—in your veins. And never forget it!"

But afterwards she realized that she hadn't answered them. She could tell by the questioning looks she caught sometimes in their eyes. She'd hoped it would never come to the point where she had to explain the difference between them and white people. It came from their living in Mississippi, she concluded. And in the end she blamed it all on Professor Taylor for bringing them there.

But once the question had come alive, now it seemed to emanate from everywhere. It was as if the violence had lain in wait for this development. Professor Taylor had words with a white farmer in his shop. The students had an altercation with the white stationmaster. President Burton appealed to the governor to keep the white people off the campus. Reference to white men seeped insidiously into the Taylors' conversation. And then, finally, the children were involved.

For some time Professor Taylor had been taking a correspondence course in automobile mechanics in view of adding it to the college curriculum. He bought a secondhand touring car and taught several of his students to drive it. Ofttimes Mrs. Taylor had one of the men drive her and the children out into the country or down to Port Gibson.

Automobiles were still an oddity on those backwoods roads. Entire families would congregate along the road and stare. The livestock would run and the horses and mules buck and snort at the strange, terrifying sound. Dogs would chase the car, snapping viciously. Whenever they met a wagon or buggy on the road, the driver would stop and shut off the motor until the mule-drawn vehicle passed.

On this day a white farmer had stopped his wagon underneath a hickory tree and sat dozing in the shade. The earnest young black man driving the Taylors stopped the car and went forward and told the farmer he'd like to pass.

"Ef'n y'all will just hol' yo' mules, sah, Ah'll drive by easy as Ah ken make her go."

The farmer was a lank, long-haired, weather-reddened typical Mississippi redneck, dressed in a striped shirt and faded denim overalls. He looked at the solemn Negro student out of sun-faded, pale blue, baleful eyes, and spat a stream of tobacco juice into the hot heavy dust.

The student waited for a moment and then returned to the car. He was worried. "Miz Taylor, w'en Ah ask that man to hol' his team he didn' say nuthin' 'tall."

"Drive on," Mrs. Taylor directed.

"Ah don' know, Miz Taylor," he began hesitantly. "Fess Taylor tol' me not to make no trouble with these rednecks. An' that white man look lak—"

"Drive on," Mrs. Taylor ordered peremptorily.

Suddenly the whites of the young man's eyes seemed enlarged. He cranked the car and, steering far over to the opposite side of the road, tried to pass the wagon. But the mules bucked in terror and bolted off the road. The farmer reached down and got a rifle from the wagon bed. The driver stopped and shut off the motor. The farmer charged forward and stuck the muzzle of the gun into the young man's face.

"Git down, niggah, 'n git mah team back on the road or Ah'll blow out yo' brains," he raved.

The coal-black driver turned gray with fear. William began to whimper. Charles was rigid with rage and terror. But Mrs. Taylor's eyes glinted and her mouth set in a cold, deadly fury. When the driver got down and went to calm the mules, she took a small revolver from her purse and aimed it at the white man's back. Charles hated the uncouth, bestial man and hoped his mother would shoot him.

But William begged hysterically, "Don't, Mama, please don't, Mama, don't shoot him, Mama, he'll kill all of us."

100

His mother lowered the pistol and held it in her lap. When the young man had righted the team and backed the wagon onto the road, he came back and cranked the car. The farmer held the rifle aimed at his back. Mrs. Taylor looked straight into the white man's face, but he didn't look at her. The driver was barely able to steer the car. A mile down the road he stopped the car beneath a tree and wiped his face and neck. He was wringing wet with sweat.

The incident marked the children in a curious way. They felt humiliated. For a time they hated the white man. They dreaded recalling the incident. It took the pleasure out of riding in the automobile. But soon it was time to gather chinquapins and hickory nuts. There were golden ripe persimmons on Professor Patterson's tree. And bushels of big greasy pecans to be gathered from their own back field, the rich yellow meat so fat that oil oozed through the thin brown shells. They'd slip down the front porch roof and climb down the fig tree and run in the cool night dust, and no one was ever the wiser. It was more fun sneaking out at night than riding in an automobile, anyway. And eating the big purple figs when they were ripe, holding them by the stems and sucking the sweet delicious insides right out from the peelings . . .

Running into a mean old redneck with a rabbit rifle. Charles wished his mother had shot him.

10

In the backwoods of Mississippi the major events had a way of passing scarcely noticed. The United States had entered the first World War. At the college, enrollment of male students had slackened. More crops were planted to feed our allies. And the women worked in the fields. Services were said in the chapel for the enlisted men. Prayers were offered for our President, our generals and our allies. Big black headlines in the out-of-town papers screamed the alarming report: Paris was endangered. But the Yanks were coming. "To make the world safe for democracy," President Burton intoned the classic line.

But, for all that there was scarcely any change.

In the Taylor household nothing was affected by the war. Mrs. Taylor had grown increasingly dissatisfied with the passing years. She nagged at her husband. Tom had been home only once in the past three years. He couldn't bear his mother's nagging. He spent his summers in Cleveland, working. Mrs. Taylor knew that she'd lost him. She held it against her husband. One more thing for which he must account. He charged her with driving him away. They quarreled bitterly.

Now she centered all her attention on her younger children. Inadvertently, they were drawn into the strife. Now when the the parents fought at night the children crept downstairs and stood beside her. Her discontent and anguish went inside of them; they shared her moods; when she suffered, they suffered with her. Their father was bitter and alone.

During the last summer of the war, he took them to visit the family of one of his students in the delta country. He thought it might help to break their mother's influence over them.

The Wallaces lived in a section of the country known as Little Africa. The trading post was Alligator. Most of the residents were Negroes who owned their farms. The Wallaces had seventy-nine acres. They lived in a dilapidated, weather-beaten shack. But parked in the backyard, rotting in the hub-deep mud, was a brand-new expensive automobile.

Sudden riches had been dumped into the laps of these poor farmers. Their rich bottom land was planted heavily in cotton that had soared to a dollar per pound. In fertile spots the corn grew eight feet tall; vines of field peas and string beans climbed the tall cornstalks. There was plenty to eat of the food they loved—"Hoppin' John" with hot crackling bread and a pitcher of cool, freshly made buttermilk. And there was plenty of money to be spent wantonly on things they'd always wanted but couldn't use—expensive phonographs without needles

—electric sewing machines in houses that had never had electricity—pianos which no one had ever learned to play—fine automobiles that no one had ever learned to drive.

On Saturday the Wallace boy dug the automobile out of the mud, and the next morning Professor Taylor drove them all to church. There were two Wallace girls beside the boy, the parents and one grandmother, and the four Taylors, but they all got in somehow. The church was a small frame structure, once painted white, with a tilted, wind-broken spire, half-hidden in a grove of pines. They arrived early so the children could attend Sunday school. Professor Taylor was made honorary superintendent and led the prayers.

The congregation came, some walking the dusty roads, some in wagons and by muleback. The expensive cars owned by others had been left behind for want of drivers. The women sat on the grass and wiped their dusty feet and put on their stockings and shoes. Soon the church was crammed to overflowing. A long black preacher in a frocktail coat mounted the pulpit. He began his favorite text—"Dry Bones." His rich, carrying voice was of an indescribable range. He took them with a shuddering whisper down into the deep dark valley of doom, then lifted them with a soaring crescendo to the bright gay streets of heaven, paved in gold.

"Is y'all got yo' wings?"

"We's all got our wings?" the congregation chanted the responses, which were as inflexible as Catholic liturgies.

"Ah say, is y'all got yo' wings?"

"We say, we's all got our wings?" Lulled into a deep, passionate mourning happiness.

"DRY BONES IN THE VALLEY!" he thundered suddenly, the bull roar of his voice shocking them insensibly.

A woman rose, lifting her arms, and screamed in utter terror. Her companions sought to restrain her. But she struggled violently, panting between screams.

"De sinnahs'll burn in brimstone. An' de reek of burnin' meat'll rise to warn dose who dilly wid dere neighbor's wives in de cotton fields . . .

"YOU HEAR ME?"

"We hear you, reb-um!"

"Ah say, does you hear me?"

"Oh, we hear . . . we hear . . . "

He threw back his head and let forth his mighty roar:

"DRY BONES IN THE VALLEY!"

All over the church men and women screamed as if panic had been let loose in their midst. They shouted and moaned and cried and fought. Mrs. Taylor caught her children by the hands and ran.

Women were standing on the pews, eyes glazed, tearing the riotous colored clothes from their strong dark bodies, shouting to their God.

"Ah is pure. Look on me, God. Ah is pure."

Raising strong black arms to heaven, full black breasts lifting, buxom black bodies tautening, their shocking black buttocks bare as at birth.

"Mah soul is white as snow!"

Men were turning somersaults in the aisle, dancing the buck and jig, bobbing to the strains of an unheard banjo playing somewhere deep inside their opened souls.

Mrs. Taylor got the children out. Her hat was gone, her dress torn. "Whew!" she exclaimed, then laughed with relief.

The children were in a state of uncontrollable excitement. They wanted to go back and dance and yell with the others. But she made them sit quietly in the car. It was pleasant in the shade. About them, in the grove, the placid mules were tied to the scarred trees. The little church sat on wooden piers. From inside came the shouting and the screaming and the dancing and the moaning. Over and above was the stentorian roar:

"DRY BONES IN THE VALLEY!"

They sat and watched the little church rock on the wooden piers. They'd never been so excited.

The following week was spent in Mound Bayou, visiting Professor Moseley, principal of the high school. Mound Bayou was the only city in the country inhabited exclusively by Negroes. All of the public officers as well as the businessmen and the proprietor of the cotton gin were Negroes. Only the express agent was white, and he lived in another city. There seemed an unwritten understanding to let the Negroes have this city, of which the governor was as proud as if he had founded it.

"Miss'ippi is the only state in the Union where Negras have their own city," he was wont to boast.

Professor Moseley owned a large brick house. The children were awed by so much splendor. Mrs. Taylor reminded them of the pleasant little house in Missouri where they were born. But they could not recall it.

One afternoon they were coming from the post office. "Is where we were born as large as this city, Mama?" William asked, scuffing his shoes on the strange pavement.

"Oh, much, much larger," his mother replied, a little startled by the question.

"Dunce!" his brother sneered.

"What do you know about it," William said. "You weren't even walking when we were there."

"I was too walking," Charles said angrily. "And I remember it better'n you do."

They were walking on each side of their mother. "Children, it isn't nice to shout."

"He's a liar," William said. "He's always telling some kind of lie."

Charles reached around his mother and hit William.

"Children!" she cried. "You behave this instant."

"Liar!" William shouted.

"Liar back!" Charles yelled, striking William in the face.

"Children!" their mother screamed.

William grappled with his brother. Before she could stop them they were fighting savagely in the dusty street. Several men ran out of a grocery store and pried them apart.

Seeing them fighting on this strange village street, their mother was profoundly shocked. It struck her suddenly that

this was the first time they'd stayed outside the campus overnight in five years. Away from the home perspective, amid these
strangers and strange scenes, she saw how they'd grown.

"These boys is wild, lady," said one of the men who was
holding them apart.

They were big, strapping boys of nine and ten, with their
sheared skulls looking as savage as Indian bucks. The animal
in them was shockingly apparent; fearful was the violence she
had suddenly seen. Their father had to come and take them
home.

Mrs. Taylor was panicky. What had she done to her children? "God in Heaven, if You'll just give me strength I'll get
them out of this savage country," she prayed. On their return
to the college she was overcome with haste. She wrote a score
of letters, applying for a post in some boarding school. It
was already the middle of August. Finally she received an
offer from a tiny church school in South Carolina. She accepted
it.

Tom was entering a Negro university in Atlanta that fall.
He came home for a week before school opened. But his mother
was too filled with her own plans to give him much attention.
The children had grown very vague toward their older brother.
They could hardly realize the kinship. He was a tall, gangling
youth, head and shoulders over either of his parents. Mrs.
Taylor said he'd taken after her father, who was over six feet.
But his manner was very strange. His speech was different,
and his complexion was sallow and pimpled. The darkly
bronzed children were both proud and ashamed of him, but
with no real blood affection. His short stay left scarcely an
impression.

The week following, Mrs. Taylor and the children left.
The boys were grown enough to feel the humiliation and indignity of the Jim-Crow car, one half of the coach containing
the white smoker. It became breathlessly hot in the packed
quarters beneath the blazing sun. Windows were opened. But
black smoke belched inside every time the train turned, first
on one side and then on the other. Mrs. Taylor's new silk dress

was ruined. The children squirmed with discomfort as their mother wiped the cinders from their reddened eyes.

No water or toilet was provided for these passengers. Most of them carried their own refreshments—water, lemonade, buttermilk, corn whisky—in jugs and bottles and buckets. When the train stopped for water, the passengers went into the woods and relieved themselves.

On boarding the train they'd looked so fresh and happy, dressed in their clean cotton dresses, starched overalls and candy-striped silk shirts with peg-topped Palm Beach trousers. Their faces had been washed, their hair combed. Their eyes had sparkled as they waved good-bye to friends and relatives. They'd carried their lunches in neat boxes and baskets, and had brushed off the seats where they sat.

Now, after riding in the hot, cramped car, they were greasy and dirty—mean-looking, sweaty black people with red, evil eyes. Paper and bones and scraps littered the floor. Some were half-drunk. They'd become noisy. The car looked like a pigpen. The passengers resembled dirty black pigs. A man emptied his drinking bottle and urinated in it. Mrs. Taylor was disgusted, sick with frustration.

The train crawled slowly through the baked, barren lands of Mississippi. Scrub cotton stood burnt in the parched fields. Lean, lackadaisical rednecks leaned on their plows, while their mules stood with bowed heads, watching the train go by. The croppers' shacks, with their black rotten walls and curled shingles, stood row on row, blistered and neglected, as poor and downtrodden as the people who leaned in the doorways. The shacks leaned, the people leaned, even the mules leaned; nothing stood straight.

It was evening when they came into Meridian on the Alabama border. Night brought relief. The darkness hid the misery. A brakeman came and lit two gas lights. The train crawled through the darkness, lights flickering through the gusts of smoke coming through the open windows. Snores and stink and smoke, fatigue and pain and discomfort filled the Jim-Crow car.

The children had to urinate. Their mother let them urinate out the window.

"I hope it blows back into those white people's faces," Charles said.

"Charles!" his mother reprimanded.

"Hit ain' blowin' back in they faces but hit sho is blowin' back in mine," a Negroid voice came from behind.

Mrs. Taylor rose in alarm. "Oh, I'm so sorry," she said, fluttering helplessly.

"Set down, lady," the voice said. "Hit ain' de firs' time."

A few minutes later when they were going around a bend the children wanted to have another try, but she made them hold it.

"It's bad enough to be a heathen from necessity," she told them.

They were so excited they couldn't sleep. It was their first night ride since they'd come south. Their eyes strained into the night. The train turned, a string of lights hung across the darkness.

"Oh, look!" Charles cried. "Look, Will. Just like the jack-o-lanterns when Tom had his garden party."

William tugged at his mother's sleeve. "Look, Mother! Look what Chuck found."

The lights flickered and spread, became irregular; a tiny village grew into the night. The train roared through without stopping.

Charles thought of the people living there in that little village. It felt weird and strange to be passing through their lives in the night without stopping. Phantom children played silently in the empty streets. The telegraph poles leaped by. Once a man stuck his head out of a train window and got it knocked off by a telegraph pole. He could see the headless man running along beside the train, dodging in and out the telegraph poles. Thus he amused himself.

Suddenly tracks leaped out from beneath the speeding train. And then more tracks. Dark hulking buildings loomed in the shadows. Dim lights hung at street corners. Gloomy streets tunneled in the distance. And then fire sprang shockingly into the dark night. Round brick structures, like igloos, belched flame from open mouths. Beside them red-hot flames licked up from a row of burning pots, throwing shadowed giants who battled silently in the sky. Souls burned in the vats of brimstone, while naked men and women, doomed into hell, ran screaming soundlessly through the burning pits.

The children held their breath in terror.

"What is it, Mama? What is it?" William asked.

"It's the blast furnaces, children. They're making steel."

They'd come into the steel foundries of Bessemer.

"It looks like Dante's *Inferno*," Charles whispered.

"So it does," their mother said.

Birmingham was next. The passengers stirred. The train pulled into the station. Sitting with their heads hung far out the window the boys watched the strange people rushing past. The Jim-Crow car half emptied. Their mother took them into the colored waiting room and stood while they went to the toilet.

Her skin was blackened and gritty; her hair hung loose. Exhaustion lined her face, pulling down her eyelids like half-closed shutters. She cleaned up as best she could while the boys waited for her. They bought sandwiches to carry. The Jim-Crow car had filled again. Finally the children slept.

The next day they arrived in Atlanta, where they were to change to another train. Gathering their parcels and luggage, they went to look for Tom. Mrs. Taylor had written him when they would be passing through. But he'd not come. She was worried and would have gone out to the university, but was afraid they didn't have time. Their train was due in an hour. She fretted and fussed, walking to the door to look out. It was Sunday and the streets had that deserted Sunday look. He should've come, she thought.

At the street entrance to the white side was a fruit and confectionary stand. Rosy peaches and red pomegranates and shiny yellow bananas were colorfully displayed, the warm fruit scenting the air. Mrs. Taylor and the children were drawn admiringly. They stood on the sidewalk and looked through the doorway at the delicious fruit. Their mouths watered.

"How much are your bananas?" Mrs. Taylor asked, approaching a little closer.

The vendor stared curiously from her to the children. "I can't sell 'em to you," he replied.

Mrs. Taylor bristled. "And why not, I'd like to know?"

"You're on the wrong side, lady." He was a dark, curly-haired man. She thought he was Italian. He looked around and then leaned forward and whispered, "Don't think I don't want to sell 'em to you, lady. But they'd fine me and take away my license."

She sighed. "Oh! Well, I declare."

They trudged disappointedly back to their side of the waiting room. Their train was hours late. Tom didn't come. They'd had plenty of time to have gone out to the university. Now they were tired and frustrated. Even the children were getting fretful; their excitement had worn off. It was late afternoon before their train arrived. They carried their parcels aboard and found a seat.

Mrs. Taylor closed her eyes. The rocking motion of the coach put her to sleep. The children looked disconsolately out the window. It was dark before the brakeman came to collect their tickets.

"You're on the wrong train," he said. White people called most Negro women "aunty." They seldom called Mrs. Taylor anything.

"This is the train to Cheraw," she said sleepily.

"Nope, we go straight through to Charleston."

"But the trainman called this train for Cheraw," she contended.

"Nope, you're dreaming."

"But I heard him call Cheraw distinctly."

Her attitude and manner of speaking irritated the brakeman. "Or else you're lying," he said nastily.

"Don't you dare say I'm lying," she flared.

He flushed angrily. "I'll stop this train and have you put off right here in these woods," he threatened.

"And I'll sue the railroad," she replied. "You just dare."

He stalked from the car. Shortly he returned with the conductor. "You'll have to get off at the next town," the conductor said.

"Then you'll have to give me a return ticket," she demanded.

"I'll give you nothing!" he shouted.

Her mouth tightened grimly and her eyes glinted. "Then I won't get off."

The children sat silent and frightened. The train sped through the night, going to an unknown place. It was like going off the end of the world. They huddled close to their mother, wordlessly. The train slowed and stopped at a darkened station.

"Now get your things together and get off," the conductor ordered.

Mrs. Taylor refused to budge. He stood for a moment, undecided, then went away. The minutes passed and no one came. No one in the coach spoke. The train waited. They all sat in the fearsome night waiting in the silence. The minutes seemed interminable. Finally the conductor returned with a deputy sheriff.

"Now git yo' things together an' come on, les go," the deputy ordered her.

"I'll not move until I have a return ticket," she replied defiantly.

"Then Ah'll have to arrest you."

"Well then, if I'm under arrest, I suppose I shall have to go to jail," she said with great dignity. She arose and gathered her parcels. The children carried the luggage, clinging closely. They descended to the dark platform. The train puffed and went down the tracks. The deputy sheriff stood beside them until its red tail light had disappeared in the darkness.

"Now you jes' set right heah an' you'll git a train back in the mawnin'," he told her.

"I'm going to sue the railroad," she said determinedly.

"Thass 'tween you an' the railroad. If you jes' doan make me no trouble Ah ain' gonna do no more 'bout it."

She turned away and he ambled off in the darkness. They found seats on the dark platform. Shadows prowled the sinister night. Somewhere near was a sleeping village, but it, too, was entombed in darkness. They sat huddled close together, warming their fear. The indignity and the outrage slowly gave way to horror. Now the whole train ride, all the misery and discomfort, was climaxed in remembered nightmare. In the pitch-black dark that comes before day Charles's mind cut loose; reality encroached the dream, death danced as a skeleton leading skeletons to the grave. He sat close to his mother, absorbing the horror of the real and the dream, and couldn't tell them apart.

Down the tracks, across the bright green fields of tobacco, the Carolina sun rose in sheer, majestic beauty. Following their miserable night its wonder gripped and held them.

And then the train came and took them back. They were at the school in Cheraw two weeks. Mrs. Taylor was bitter in her denunciation of the railroad. She wanted to enter a suit, but the Negro attorney in that community advised her against it. She had to content herself with a scathing letter to the president of the line. That fizzling out of her determinations was the major tragedy of Mrs. Taylor's life.

Most of the time it rained. The weathered wooden buildings stood disconsolate in the rain. Boys and girls scurried through the mud, their black shiny faces remote. In the evening a ghostlike quality settled on the scene. The bullfrogs set up their unceasing chorus. Owls hooted startlingly. Mrs. Taylor was vexed and harassed. The children were frightened and lonely. Their own discontent seemed to drench the place. Then the letter from Crayne Institute in Augusta caught up with her. She packed up the children and left.

11

CRAYNE INSTITUTE WAS IN THE HEART OF THE
colored section. It faced a thoroughfare that ran up a hill, passing through a white business district, and came to a stop at a
fort. Originally it had occupied a city square, enclosed by a
high plank fence. But a number of the old buildings on the
surrounding streets had been added from time to time.

Mrs. Taylor and her children arrived in the night and were
driven to the school in an old horse cab. The boys were
turned over to a matron who took them to a room on the third
floor of an old brick building across the street.

"Chuck, come and look," William called his brother to the
window.

Charles went and stood beside him. The building stood on
a height and below lay the city lights. They stared tensely,
quivering like wild colts at civilization's first barrier.

"It looks like Rome," Charles said.

"I wish Mama was here," his older brother confessed.

"Mama said we might not stay with her."

Suddenly William began to cry. Charles went over and sat
on the bed beside him.

"Don't cry, Will."

A frightened desolate loneliness came over them both. There
was no sound from the old gloomy house. They felt abandoned
and lost. Charles bit his lips to keep from crying also. Finally
they put on their pajamas and knelt side by side and prayed:

> *Now I lay me down to sleep*
> *I pray the Lord my soul to keep*
> *If I should die before I wake*
> *I pray the Lord my soul to take.*

Charles lay listening to his brother's lonely sobbing. He
felt torn up by the roots. All was so strange and sad and dif-

ferent. He wished his mother could be happy, then everything would be all right again.

The next morning a boy about their age came for them. "Mi Rainy san ma tu fotch yo fa tu cume brakefost."

They didn't understand a word he said. He was a strange skinny child, bony as a skeleton, with slanting red eyes and a huge egg-shaped head that was completely bald. He looked grotesque in old handed-down clothes.

They stared at each other helplessly. "Brakefost," the boy said. "Brakefost." He was of a curious racial mixture of African, Indian and Spanish, whom the people in that section called "geechies," and spoke a patois of these native tongues combined with English. For generations his people had lived in the swamplands of Florida and Georgia and many had been free long before the Civil War.

He saw that these new ones didn't understand him. "Pomp," he said, pointing to himself, and then beckoning, "Cum."

They followed him out the building and across the street through a side gate in the high plank fence, and were struck by the confusion of buildings. Boys and girls of all ages streamed across the yard. Several turned to stare at them and many of the girls giggled. The children shrank with shame and trepidation, quivering with a strange kind of fear. They were afraid of other children.

The dining room matron seated them at a long board table with others of their age. They searched frantically for their mother, and then kept their eyes glued to their plates.

"Whar you pigmeat come frum?" a bully across from them asked.

Charles looked up, so tense he could scarcely speak. "Mississippi."

The boy snorted. "'Sippi niggers."

In a flash one of the serving women slapped him. "You shet yo' mouth, boy. Usin' dat dirty word."

The boy subsided sullenly. A snicker ran around the table.

"Ah'll git you for that," he threatened Charles when the serving women left.

Charles felt the blood burning in his face.

Their mother came for them at the end of breakfast. They'd never been so glad to see her.

"Children," she laughed delightedly, returning their embraces. "You'd think that I'd been gone for ages."

"We were scared," William confessed.

"Well, it won't be long," she consoled. "Mother will try to get you with her. Now we must go and see Miss Rainy."

The children were shocked by the sight of the big, black, ox-like woman who greeted them in a deep, gruff voice, "So this is Will an' Charles." She had the flat features of the Zulu tribes with short-cropped graying hair, and her gums were a dark, purplish blue. They stared at her.

She patted their heads. "You boys'll have to toe the line even if your ma does teach here. Ah don' make no favorites of nobody's children an' Ah didn' make no favorites of my own when they was here."

"Don't think I've spared the rod," Mrs. Taylor said. "My boys can't say I've spoiled them."

"Speak up, speak up, the cat got your tongue?" the head-woman bade.

"Say 'how do you do' to Miss Rainy," their mother urged.

"How do you do, Miss Rainy," they chorused.

Miss Rainy grinned, her thick dark lips parting over gold-crowned teeth. "Now you boys run along with your ma." Then to their mother, "When you get settled, sister, Ah'll take you over the ground."

Crayne was named after the Senator who had donated the site. Once it had housed the slave quarters of his grandfather's plantation. He'd thought it singularly befitting that it should become a seat of learning for the progeny of those creatures.

But Cindy Rainy was the institution. She'd never gotten beyond the sixth grade of a backwoods school. As a child she'd served in white homes, and after marriage had mothered white children to earn money to feed her own. But it was her greatest ambition to give other Negro children the education she'd missed. Her iron will had raised the Institute from a shanty schoolhouse to an institution of prominence. She'd built it herself; she'd begged every dime.

She'd been hard on herself and she was hard on her students. In her office were two wooden paddles, one of light seasoned cedar with which she beat the girls, and one of heavy, thick oak she used on the boys.

As with many dark Negro women who've struggled to prominence, she had a preference for light-complexioned persons, both as friends and subordinates. Though most of her students were young black folk, a predominance of her teachers were fair. And of these, all but the athletic director, science teachers and chaplain were women.

Mrs. Taylor's position was that of music instructor. Two of her nieces, Martha and Mary Manning, her brother Tom's children, were also on the staff. The relationship was quite marked; both were very fair girls with brown wavy hair. And there were also a number of teachers acquainted with some branch or other of the Manning family. She was delighted to be among her own. Her nieces thought her most elegant and refined and were quite devoted.

She was given a couple of rooms on the ground floor of the faculty house across the street, so she could keep her children with her. The boys had a back room with low windows opening onto a narrow alley. They had but to step outside and they were free.

She saw very little of them that winter. It was as if a dam had broken loose within her. She talked and talked, catching up on the family news. She told and retold the events of her marriage. She became quite garrulous, even a nuisance at times. But she couldn't restrain herself. The words and phrases poured out in an endless stream.

Even the children were astonished. She talked a great deal to them, bringing up bits and sketches of her childhood. That was the winter she told them that their great-great-grandfather, Grandma Charlotte's sire, was General Beauregard.

She would come into the children's room at bedtime and, without preamble, say, "Your cousin, Martha, is just like her grandfather. She likes her coffee scalding hot," smiling reminiscently. "My mother could never get his coffee hot enough. No matter how hot she'd have it, he'd say, 'Lin, this coffee is stone cold.' And she'd have to put it back in the pot and heat it. She got tired of him saying his coffee was cold and one day she put the cup in the oven and got it red hot. Then she filled it with boiling coffee and set it at his place. When he sat down and picked up his cup his mouth was all set to say it was stone cold. But when he put it to his lips we could hear the skin sizzle. My mother was afraid she'd given him an awful burn. It must have hurt him terribly. But your grandfather didn't bat an eye. He just looked across at my mother and said, 'Lin, for once in your life you got my coffee hot.'" The memory made her laugh with pleasure.

The children didn't understand her. She seemed strange. They felt that she was slipping away from them. A vague insecurity threatened them. They became closer to each other.

Their teachers couldn't separate them. They sat on the same bench. Should one falter in his recitation the other took it up. Their mother had taught them well. They were both brilliant in their classes. But they didn't make friends. When one got into a fight the other would rush to aid him. Charles did most of his brother's fighting. But William would help by grabbing his opponent's legs while Charles pummeled him. After several of these skirmishes the bullies left them alone.

Their studies were so easy they soon were bored and took to playing hooky. They'd slip behind the wooden buildings, skirt the playing field, and climb over the fence behind the scoreboard in the corner. There was a grocery store across the street where many of the day students bought their lunch. The proprietor wasn't permitted to sell to the students between hours, but he did to those he trusted. They'd buy a loaf of bread, cut a wedge from the top and fill it with molasses or condensed milk or sardines, and after the juice had soaked in plug it up again. They carried their "sog 'em" to the neighborhood known as the "Blackberry Patch," and there in the shade of their favorite chinaberry tree on the bank of a creek they feasted.

117

Although they were fed plenty in the mess hall—black-eyed peas and rice one day, boiled pork and baked sweet potatoes the next, oatmeal and skimmed milk, hominy grits and hot fat for breakfast—they were always hungry. Their mother supplemented their diet with dry cereals and fruit. Both loved the baked fish that was served on Fridays. The big steaming pan of porgies with onion gravy was set in the center of the table. The other children liked fried fish best, so this one day they had all they wanted.

During supper, the school horse, an old gray mare named Maud, was fed a half-dozen ears of dried field corn in her trough beside the kitchen door. It was great sport with the older boys to try to steal an ear when they came from supper. But Maud was on to their game and snapped at them like a vicious dog, her big teeth clacking dangerously. Charles loved dried corn and once he tried to steal an ear and run. But Maud was too quick for him, and bit him across the cheek and nose. For days he wore a bandage and a tiny scar remained. But he learned how to snitch an ear from the other side when her attention was distracted.

One night the children were awakened by the sound of fire engines. They dressed and slipped out through the window.

Toward the Patch was an orange glow in the sky. All about them were running people. A fire engine turned the corner, drawn by four white horses, smoke belching from its stack. All else forgotten, his brother and mother, the night, Charles went flying in its wake.

"Wait, Chuck," Will called.

But Charles didn't hear him. The urge to run heedlessly, unrestrainedly, like the mad surge of the beautiful white horses, blew out his other thoughts. Soon he was separated from his brother. He ran with a long, smooth, digging motion, down the dim streets, jostling people, through the muddy gutters on into the Patch. Black and yellow people were panicky in the streets. He followed the engine through the milling crowd, came up at the edge of the fire. Police had thrown up a loose, futile cordon. Beyond the shotgun shacks and flimsy hovels burned an immense bonfire. Black people loomed suddenly from the haze of smoke, lugging a straw mattress, a bundle of clothing, a paper sack of cold corn bread. Beds and furniture and clothing and boxes were scattered like debris down the streets of chaos. Over and above the crackling of the fire and the hissing of the water came the wailing and the moaning and the shouting of the people.

Charles was cut loose from reality. The stark raw panic in the black faces transmitted itself to him. He started to run like a crazed horse into the midst of the flames, but was caught up in front of a dark, lonely shack by a woman standing in the door. She was a young mulatto girl, dark hair hanging to her shoulder; a vague shape in a loose nightgown. There was in her posture a strange bitter forlornness more terrible than a Gorgon's head. He was too young to know that she was a whore watching the fire from morbid curiosity. He saw only the infinite loneliness of a strange lost woman in the one left house. He was ineffably drawn to her; he felt an affinity deeper than kin. He went toward her timidly, filled with the great flaming desire to serve her with his life.

"Can I help you, lady?"

She looked at him startled, then cursed. "Git der hell away frum heah an' mind yo' own bizness."

He felt a sharp, brackish shock, turned and fled. For a long time aimlessly he watched the fire, absorbed into the misery of the homeless groups, and afterwards he wandered listlessly in the ruins. But deep inside he was badly hurt, first opened by the suffering of the people, then poisoned by the strange woman's scorn. He couldn't understand her viciousness; her rejection cut him to the heart. It was early morning when he crawled back into bed. William was asleep. For a long time Charles lay there crying until the sobbing waked his brother.

"What's the matter, Chuck?" William asked alarmed.

"Nothing," Charles choked.

"What you crying about?"

"Nothing, I tell you."

"There is something too, you're crying."

"I'm not."

"You are too, and I'm going to tell Mother."

"I'm not, I'm not! I tell you I'm not!"

"Don't cry, Chuck," William consoled.

"I was just crying a little bit," he confessed. "I'm all right, really I am. I was just crying a little because it's all so sad."

"Go to sleep, Chuck," William said. "Everything's going to be all right."

"All right, Will. Don't tell Mama I was gone."

"I won't tell."

As Charles grew older there were many more exciting happenings that he forgot. It was always very hard for him to recall the inside of all the many houses he lived in. But he never forgot the utter loneliness of the woman standing in the darkened doorway, watching the misery of her people, nor the utter viciousness of her rejection.

That year William was very kind to his younger brother. He lied to the teachers when Charles played hooky and never once told on him for slipping out at night. After the first strangeness had worn off and they'd become accustomed to the difference in their mother's attitude, they liked it there. They liked their newly discovered cousins and the thrilling sound of laughter in the streets in the early evening; and they liked the long walks they took through the city with their mother on Sunday afternoons.

The thing they liked best was an old minstrel who came around the school and fiddled for the students. He was a very old man with a deeply seamed face, the color of saddle leather, and a thatch of dirty, yellowish-white hair. His old brown eyes had the bluish tint of age, and but two brown snags hung loose from bare shrunken gums. His clothes were tattered and he stank like a goat, but his fiddle was wrapped with loving care in a square of fine old velvet. The students loved him and whenever he appeared a crowd collected.

"Play 'Hole in de ground,'" they begged.

He played a jig tune and cut a step, then he played a spiritual and mumbled out the words.

"Oh, Mistah Minstrel, please play 'Hole in de ground.'"

His old lined face beamed with pleasure and his eyes sparkled youthfully. He began chanting the endless ballad, sawing the accompanying sounds:

> *Oh once 'pon uh time dare wuz uh hole in de ground*
> *An' de green grass growin' all 'round an' 'round*
> *De green grass growin' all 'round . . .*
> *In de li'l hole dare wuz uh li'l tree*
> *Tree in de hole*
> *Hole in de ground*
> *An' de green grass growin' all 'round an' 'round*
> *De green grass growin' all 'round. . . .*

"Oh, what was on the tree, Mistah Minstrel? What was on the tree?"

> *On de li'l tree dare wuz uh li'l limb*
> *Limb on de tree*
> *Tree in de hole*
> *Hole in de ground*
> *An' de green grass growin' all 'round an' 'round*
> *De green grass growin' all 'round . . .*

"Oh, what was on the lim', Mistah Minstrel? What was on the lim'?"

His old bluish eyes twinkled with delight. And on and on it would go:

> *An' on dat li'l bee dare wuz a li'l tail*
> *Tail on de bee*
> *Bee on de leaf*
> *Leaf on de branch*
> *Branch on de limb*

121

Limb on de tree
Tree in de hole
Hole in de ground
An' de green grass growin' all 'round an' 'round
An' de green grass growin' all 'round. . . .

The children squealed with glee. What would be on the tail?

Sting on de tail . . .

And what would be on the sting?

Pisen on de sting . . .

They loved the old minstrel. But then, the Taylor children loved most things the other children loved. They loved the same games and pastimes; sucking dill pickles stuffed with wine balls, munching peeled pomegranates, lingering over the unfamiliar delicious taste. They enjoyed the holiday celebrations, the outdoor barbecues, running with the football players in the fall, baseball in the spring, the Maypole dance, the Easter Ramble. Quite often they laughed at the same things. The time Pomp came screaming into Miss Rainy's office, "O' Mi Rainy! Mi Rainy! De goat done dead!" It became a classic example of the ungrammatical form. Nor did Miss Rainy show them any favoritism. William escaped; she thought he was a nice, obedient boy. But she paddled Charles several times for fighting, playing hooky, and the hardest of all for calling another boy a "monkey-devil."

The difference was deeper; the difference of upbringing, of perspective. Taking their napkins to the mess-hall in the old worn wooden napkin rings. Saying, "Thank you." The absence of dialect in their speech. The feeling that their teachers didn't know everything. Their unacceptance of the common childish conviction that Negroes were the strongest people in the world. The shocked incredulity both always felt at a collection of Negro heads—in class or in chapel when the students were assembled, the black-burred craniums with bald tetter patches and the short straightened hair of the girls with grease running down behind their ears. And on Saturday night the smell of burning hair permeating the very air over the school and the Patch and the entire Negro community, as if there were a witch-burning of incredible numbers. It always gave Charles a queasy stomach, sick enough to vomit. Yet his own hair was kinky; he couldn't imagine himself without kinky hair; he never thought of it as ugly. It was the atrocities they committed on themselves to be what they were never intended, which he couldn't reconcile. Thin, black girls with white ribbons tied to their crop of short braids always reminded him of Topsy; and the burred white thatch of the Old Minstrel was Uncle Tom again. But Topsy and Uncle Tom were real people like his mother and himself, and why all the shame?

However, they learned to be with other children, and the names and rules of games. And they learned of their family on their mother's side. There was little in the classes they hadn't already learned. But they became accustomed to classroom procedure. And they'd gotten out of Mississippi. If for no more than that, their mother was grateful for that year.

12

THE FOLLOWING YEAR THE CHILDREN ATTENDED school with students twice their age. Their father had missed them the year before. He kept them home that fall and enrolled them in the College. They'd completed the sixth grade at Crayne. Now they were enrolled in the freshman year in college, which was the equivalent of the eighth grade.

Mrs. Taylor fumed and threatened. But she couldn't leave the children. She was trapped.

All that summer she'd talked incessantly as if she'd been

wound up and couldn't stop. Tom was home briefly before going on to Cleveland. He thought his mother queer. Then it was the little children who felt her insecurity.

"Don't ever forget that you are Mannings," she constantly reminded them. Her eyes were vacant, staring off into the past. She frightened them with her ceaseless prattle.

Now, with the frustrating of her hope to take them off again, she was assailed by prolonged despair. It was as if she'd returned to the scene of a long and bitter defeat. The old scars and humiliations of battle opened sharply with new hurt. Before she'd been determined to depart. Now she was obsessed with escape. At times her frustration was so heightened she felt that she'd go crazy. Her eyes were often red from crying, and deep lines of discontent began settling in her face.

"You've done everything in your power to destroy me," she charged her husband. "Now you're trying to destroy me by making monsters of my children. But I shan't let you." Her eyes were wild, her hair disordered. She was becoming a little hysterical.

"By God, they're my children too. And I want 'em here with me."

The course of battle ran the same. Only their ages were different; they had grown older. Professor Taylor had developed chronic constipation.

"You'll regret this, Mr. Taylor. You'll suffer in hell for what you're doing to your children."

The house was sick with fear and hate that morning they entered college. The children spilled their cereal and bolted their eggs. Their mother's face was grim. Finally their father rose to go.

"Now be good boys and don't give your professors any trouble," he admonished.

"Professors at their age," their mother said. "I tell you, Mr. Taylor, it's criminal."

He went off without replying.

"Children," she began without preamble, "I want to tell you how babies are born."

They looked at her from large, startled eyes, squirming uncomfortably. She became embarrassed but went on grimly as if forcing the words from her lips:

"The seed of the male impregnates the womb of the female and the mother becomes pregnant. The baby lies in the womb of its mother for nine months, growing and growing until it is formed, then the mother gives birth. You recall when Mrs. Sherwood was pregnant last year. She was carrying the baby in her womb; her little baby Alice.

"The birth of a baby," she continued, swallowing painfully, "is very sacred and should never be discussed. Only persons who are married are permitted to conceive babies. But there is nothing secretive about it. It is a very natural function—it is as natural as a bowel movement, although we don't talk about that either. I want you children to understand this, and when the older men try to tell you about it you tell them that your mother has already told you and that will shut them up."

She looked away from their huge staring eyes. "Do you want to ask any questions?"

They shook their heads. "No, Mother," William said.

"Do you understand it?"

"Yes, Mother," they nodded dumbly.

Charles thought of Mrs. Sherwood carrying the baby in her womb. He'd never seen a newborn baby. The first time he saw the baby it weighed twenty pounds. He wanted to know how it got out. But he was too ashamed to ask.

Their mother's raw embarrassment had affected them with a strange sense of guilt. They knew less than before, when they'd assumed that babies were born like other animals. Now they were confused. They'd formed no clear association between sexual intercourse and the conceiving of a baby. To them sexual intercourse was still something sly and dirty the grownups did.

The school bell rang. Finally they set off to college in their knee breeches and black cotton stockings, burdened with a vague picture of giant babies in their mothers' stomachs. But they distrusted even this knowledge and felt flooded with shame whenever they saw men and women embrace.

The sight of them was a shock to their classmates.

"You chillun lost, ain'tcha?"

"Them ain' chillun, them's dwarfs."

The men students resented their presence. The women thought it funny. The professors had a problem also. The students thumped the children's heads with their knuckles.

"Naw, he ain' ripe." They guffawed.

"Bastard nigger!" Charles cursed, charging his tormentors.

The students held him off. "Where you learn to cuss, li'l niggah?"

"He bad, ain' he. He tough."

"We take that out 'im."

They trudged behind their elders from one dim basement to another.

"Po' li'l tadpoles, doan you cry
You'll be bullfrogs by 'n by"—the students teased.

The men prodded each other in the rear. The one prodded would jump and strike out, often embrace a girl.

"Uh goosy good time was had by all," some wit would whisper.

"You ain' all that goosy," the woman would protest.

"Ah'd lak to goose you, sugar pie."

The children hovered in wide-eyed attention. The woman noticed.

"Y'all shouldn' be talkin' so nasty fo' these li'l boys. Li'l pitchers got big ears."

The children felt ashamed. The air seemed thick with inuendo. Grown-up speech had double meaning. Only during recitations did they fully understand it. The older students soon discovered their naïveté.

"Hey, Charlie, Ah found uh li'l pussy las' night," the man at the next desk whispered.

"Where?" asked Charles innocently.

"It war hid way down 'tween two fine brown legs." The man winked at his cronies and laughed. Charles blushed.

"I know what you mean," he said defensively.

Jerry Ramsey walked along with the boys when they were going home one evening. "When Fess Williams calls my name one of you boys tell 'im Ah'm gone chasing whores."

The children understood the word to be "hoers." Jerry's parents had a farm not far from the college. It didn't seem strange to the children that he should be going after hoers.

"Where you going, Jerry?"

"You going to Port Gibson?"

"Naw, Ah'm goin' to a whorehouse in N'Orlins."

Professor Williams was a thin, dark, solemn man with a stern visage. He was always afraid his students might try to take advantage of him, and as a consequence was very strict. When he came to Jerry's name during the roll call next morning, William punched Charles. Dutifully Charles stood and said,

"He's gone chasing hoers."

"To a hoerhouse in New Orleans," William whispered.

"To a hoerhouse in New Orleans," Charles repeated.

For an instant the room was gripped in a dead silence. Then the students roared with laughter.

"Shut up!" Professor Williams bellowed.

The boys were frightened. They looked at each other and looked about to see what they'd done.

"Come up here, boy," Professor Williams ordered. His black face was gray with fury.

Charles went forward and faced him beside the desk.

"Now where did you say Ramsey was?" the professor asked through clenched teeth. He was a slow-witted man and hadn't grasped that the boy was the victim of a prank.

"I said he was gone after hoers in a New Orleans hoerhouse," Charles replied straightforwardly.

Professor Williams slapped him. Charles had no awe of the professors. He was a strong boy and now caught up in a violent rage he grabbed the professor about the legs and threw him to the floor. The professor struck wildly with his fists. They struggled and rolled over. The professor beat Charles in the face. Then William ran forward and jumped on the professor's back, pulling him over. Charles came up, turning over, and began beating the professor in the face. Then the students separated them.

Professor Williams sent the children home. Shortly their father arrived out of breath; he'd run all the way.

"It's what you get for putting them in school with uncouth grown-up savages," Mrs. Taylor greeted him.

He ignored her and got the story from the boys.

"Whores are bad women," their father told them. "It's a word you shouldn't ever use."

That afternoon one of the young women asked Charles curiously, "Didn' you really know what it meant?"

"Aw, sure I knew," he muttered, blushing with shame. "I was just teasing Mr. Williams."

Still neither of them were quite certain just what a whore was. Bad how? If it meant what the men were always whispering about, why go all the way to New Orleans? There were plenty bad women on the campus; they'd seen them in the weeds.

Some of the women students often kissed them. Once one pushed her tongue between Charles's lips. He felt like hitting her. But the children began playing with themselves. At night they'd sit in the outhouse and play with each other. William now experienced a definite sex sensation, but it left them both with a sense of shame and guilt. Afterwards they couldn't face their mother. It was more fun to urinate in a long, thin arc.

Often when the children encountered students in the outhouse, the men would shake their penises at them.

"W'en you git sompn' lak that you can call yo'self a man."

The children had such tiny organs that they felt inferior. Once Charles drank a glass of his urine to show how brave he was.

But for the most part that year was very vague to both the boys. The days were filled with grown-up strangers whose names they knew but whose habits they never understood. Nor did they ever learn the subtle connotations of grown-up speech, as other children, less self-sufficient, might easily have done. Their almost primitive, incurious innocence was kept intact.

The deepest impressions came from their mother's incessant nagging. Her voice, like a stream of bile, flowed endlessly through the house. "Mr. Taylor, I'll never forgive you for bringing me to this Godforsaken place. God will punish you as surely as you're sitting there . . . " Bitterness colored the very atmosphere.

Their only escape was into the cold, lamp-lit attic. But even there the voice would search them out. "You children will catch your death of pneumonia up there, and I'll be the one who'll have to look after you. Your father'll run to his shop and chase around what manner of people nobody knows all night long. Come right down out of that cold. If you can't find anything to do but ruin your eyes reading, blame it on your father. He brought us down here to this Godforsaken place among these heathen savages . . . "

However, there were times when Charles escaped and read alone and she seemed to have completely forgotten his existence. In the cold, dimly lit attic he fought a thousand duels and saved as many damsels in distress. He was Ivanhoe and Richard the Lionhearted, Alexander the Great and the Count of Monte Cristo, Genghis Khan and the Scarlet Pimpernel. It was often his face in the iron mask, and his strong back, instead of Jean Valjean's, lifting the carriage from the mud. Most often he was Achilles chasing Hector around the walls of Troy. When all else failed—when he ached with loneliness and Caesar's legions failed to conquer; when Ivanhoe had bad dreams and Horatio couldn't hold the bridge and mud was clinging to his mother's feet—then he was Achilles. There was something poignantly apt about being Achilles in Mississippi.

In the end, Mrs. Taylor got them out. She went to Vicksburg and registered in a white hotel. When she came down next morning the manager confronted her.

"You gave a college for your address. What college is this, Madam?"

"The state college."

"The state college? But that's in—"

"The state college for Negroes."

Again the governor had to intervene. He telephoned Professor Taylor at the college.

"Willie, Ah'll give you forty-eight hours to get that woman out of Mississippi."

Packing was a nightmare. So many of Mrs. Taylor's lovely furnishings and beautiful dishes were lost and broken. The wagons came all day, carting away their furniture. They left at twilight and went down the long dark road, as they had come seven years before, to catch a train at nine o'clock. They were going to St. Louis.

Charles cried. It was the first of a long, unending series of good-byes. It was the end of something; the beginning of change. Charles never liked change; he was more sensitive to it than most. He was affected by its imminence and again by its actuality. It required the readjustment of his two worlds; sometimes he made the one without the other, never both, often none. For all its unpleasantness, his life in Mississippi had been simply wonderful. It was the end. He hated the end of anything. He cried for Mississippi.

Professor Taylor bought a huge old house beside a Catholic school in a changing neighborhood. It was a cold, austere house, once pretentious, with dark oak-paneled halls and cracked marble mantelpieces. When it rained or a north wind blew, the dead smell of old coal smoke seeped from its ancient flues. The dim gas jets filled the gloomy rooms with trembling shades.

The children hated the house. They hated its smell of death. They spent most of their time in the backyard and the shed. They could hear the subdued voices of the phantom children behind the high stone wall next door.

In the twilight after supper they sat on the high stone steps. Below on the pavement people passed. The colored people spoke.

"Good evening."

"Good evening."

From behind came the strained hushed voices of their parents.

"I'm doing what I can, Lillian, honey, Until something better comes I'll just have to take it."

"You'll not talk me into leaving here again, Mr. Taylor."

Other parents were sitting on their porches in the cool dim light. The tip of a cigar glowed. Away on Taylor Avenue a street car passed, its trolley striking blue lightning in the dusk. The lighted windows were filled with people. There were so many people in the city. They lived so close together.

The arc light at the corner sputtered and hissed. Down the street under the distant light, children played wildly. The Taylor children listened tensely to their strange excited voices.

Five . . . ten . . . fifteen . . . twenty . . .
Are you ready? . . .
I'm not ready
Twenty-five . . . thirty . . . thirty-five . . . forty . . .
You're peeping . . .
No I'm not
Count again . . .
Forty-five . . . fifty . . . I'm coming, ready or not . . .

Then the sound of running feet as they peered toward the wild motion; the squeals as one was caught . . .

You're it . . . you're it . . .
Five . . . ten . . . fifteen . . . twenty . . .

They were assailed with loneliness.

"Can we go play, Mother?"

"When you get to meet the children, Mother will let you go

and visit them," she replied absently, her mind on other things. "Mother will take you to meet them as soon as we meet the parents."

"Let the children go, honey, they can't hurt anything."

"I'll not have my children running like wild animals through the streets."

Charles stood up. "I'm going to get a drink of water."

He rushed from the kitchen, flying down the alley. Then he stood in the darkness near the wildly playing children. The white children were playing with the colored. He was taken for one of them in the dark; a hand touched his arm.

"You're it!" a voice cried. *"You're it!"*

He turned and ran like light up the dark alley and disappeared into his own backyard. He was out of breath when he returned to the porch. His parents didn't notice.

The summer passed in a strange lonely tension. And suddenly they were gone. The house was closed and they were on the train. Professor Taylor had accepted another post, in Pine Bluff, Arkansas. Teaching was his way of life. Mrs. Taylor had to face up to it.

13

Out at the end of town, on the flats where the Iron Mountain and Southern Railroads crossed, a group of wooden buildings had been thrown up to house the Negro college.

The Taylors took a house two miles away, along the tracks. Nearby was the Negro business section; out where the pavement ended was the "Patch." The white world was sealed off. By comparison the colored world seemed shrunken and distorted, as if a specimen had been placed beneath an inverted microscope and had become strangely infinitesimal.

In the morning long lines of colored children filed down the railroad tracks, going to the city school. They stood to one side, their ragged clothing flying in the rush of air like the banners of their section, their black faces lifted curiously, eyes intent, as a train went by.

The Taylor children went to college. They loved to walk the rails.

"See, I'm not looking," Charles would say. "You're looking but I'm not."

"I am not looking."

"You are too."

They tried to walk the two miles without once stepping off. Often the other children challenged their right of way. One would push the other off. Then there'd be a fight. Excited childish faces would ring the fighters in. The brothers always fought together. They had become savage again.

A train would pass and they'd race the engine, flying recklessly along the shoulder of the bed. All the way to school they threw rocks at the telegraph poles. They stuck close together and delighted in goading the ragged city children. Hardly a week went by without their getting into a rock fight.

Once Charles tried to hop a fast freight. He ran mightily along the gravel bed and leaped for the low iron rung. His hands got hold, but he was flung about, his back striking the side of the box car, and then hurled to the gravel bed. He landed turning from his own momentum, his outstretched legs across the rail. The onrushing heavy steel wheel struck them as they turned, knocked them away from the rail as it sped on. He kept rolling down the steep embankment, came up skinned and breathless in the gulley.

"Whew!" he whistled, laughing. "Whew!"

"You almost got run over!" William screamed in agitation.

Charles laughed at his older brother. "It threw me all right. But I got the trick. You gotta jump on the journal box."

The next morning he waited for the train and hopped it. A neighbor told their mother.

"I don't know what's getting into you children; you're becoming so ugly," she scolded.

Their father whipped them, and afterwards made them walk to school with him. To show his defiance, Charles hopped a freight and rode all the way to Little Rock and was gone all day. He took another whipping.

They didn't like the college. It was bleak and ugly and everything was strange. It made them wild and restless. They were always running away from it; running away from something. They cut classes to go wandering about the town. They loved to pick a street and see where it would end. Carnivals delighted them, opening up a strange new world.

In the twilight after supper they'd ask:

"Can we go down to the corner, mother?"

"To the corner? What for? What's happening at the corner?"

"Nothing. We just want to take a walk. It gets so tiresome staying in the house all the time."

"You have your homework to do."

"We won't be gone but a minute. We don't have to do any homework anyway. We're way ahead of the class."

Finally their father would say, "Let them go, honey. There's nothing they can get into."

"Well—don't be gone long," she'd call as they took off like a flash.

They'd run the two miles to the fairgrounds out on Cherry Street and stand for a minute, out of breath, watching the fascinating spectacle, the crowds of white people, the ferris wheel and the carrousel and glittering midway—and then run home again.

"Where did you children go?" their mother would ask anxiously.

"Just down to the railroad tracks."

"You've been running; you're out of breath."

"We ran back."

"I've told you time and again to stay away from the railroad tracks."

"We weren't on the tracks. We were standing off to one side watching the signal lights."

"It's getting so I can't believe a word you say," she complained.

It was that way all that fall. Now they'd stay out roaming the streets until nine and ten o'clock. They were always running. Their father whipped them now, but they didn't care.

Their mother was assailed by her old anxiety. They acted so ugly, she thought. More than just naughty; there was a defiance in their attitude that made their acts seem actually wicked, as if knowing right from wrong only bedeviled them. Charles worried her most. There was a vein of violence in his nature that kept her constantly on edge. She lived in constant dread of his killing some other boy, or getting himself killed or maimed for life. She became obsessed with the fear that God was going to punish her for the strange passion she had for him. She brooded for weeks, worrying and fretting between moments of intense anguish. She doubted if he'd live to see his twenty-first birthday. Life would never take his reckless challenge; it would kill him. But what brought her such deep torture was the fear that it would hurt him first. Out of all her sons she dreaded most to see him hurt. He would buck and strain against it and die in abject misery.

And then, it was as if God sent the smallpox to save them from destruction. The day before Christmas both had sore throats and were running temperatures. Their mother thought they had caught common colds. But when her treatment failed to get results she called the doctor. He was familiar with the dread disease and clamped a quarantine. Within the hour the house was posted.

Their father rushed home, but wasn't allowed inside the picket fence. Mrs. Taylor talked to him from the porch. The children had been put to bed.

For three days they were critically ill, drifting in and out of delirium as their fever rose and fell. Their mother waited on them hand and foot. When the pustules came she anointed them constantly with carbolic salve. They lay naked on the slimy bed, the touch of cloth unbearable. Their bodies were covered with eruptions from head to foot, the palms of their hands, beneath their fingernails, the soles of their feet; their faces and lips and ears were a mass of greasy pus. During the long hours when little else could be done, their mother prayed.

"God take my life . . . give me the disease . . . please, Dear God, spare them . . . I'll do anything . . . I'll be a good wife . . . I'll follow Your teaching . . . "

The bodies of her sons seemed rotting away before her very eyes.

"God in Heaven, what have they done?" she cried in anguish. "What have my children done that You should punish them like this?"

Professor Taylor came and stood outside the fence. He brought food which he tossed into the yard. Nights he slept in the men's dormitory. Mrs. Taylor stood in the door and talked to him when she was not too weary. For hours in the settling dusk and on into the night he kept a lonely vigil. Walking back and forth before the picket fence he also prayed. In their extremity there was only God for both. Both had been reared in a God-fearing tradition; both knew no other light.

"Lord, have mercy, have mercy on my boys," he would mutter to himself as he walked back and forth, a little, black, bowlegged pigeon-toed man in a dark gray suit, high celluloid collar and a worn derby hat, fading into the gathering darkness.

"God, have mercy on my sons."

Fear didn't touch the children; they were too sick to know. There was only a cottony haze of unending misery, trancelike in its persistence, almost remote; thirst and the strange sliding into blackness. Charles found it soothing to drift into delirium. When the crisis passed, their mother's heart sang like a mockingbird. Professor Taylor stood crying in the street, joined by friends and curious neighbors.

But the children were assailed by an unendurable itch; their hours were filled with longing to scratch. Their hands were tied in pillows at their backs as the scabs began to form; but in their

136

itching frenzy they tore the mattress with their teeth. They screamed and raged in misery and frustration.

"If you pick the scabs they'll leave pockmarks," their mother said. "You don't want your faces filled with pockmarks."

They didn't care. For the blessed relief of scratching they were willing to pay the price.

Finally the scabs began to fall; the itching passed. They stood in the window and waved to their father and watched the people pass. Soon they were up and about; the quarantine was lifted. Mother and father knelt beside the children and thanked God. Mrs. Taylor felt that God had given her another chance.

Afterwards, she took her husband's hand and promised solemnly, "I will be a good wife to you, Mr. Taylor."

The furniture in their room was burned; the house was closed and fumigated. They went to a neighbor's house and Mrs. Taylor slept; her deep-set eyes were haggard and she was skin and bones. The children found it good to be out in the open again. Both retained slight pocks, almost unnoticeable, on the bridges of their noses. Now they could boast of having had smallpox.

Professor Taylor moved his family from the haunted house out on a hill called Battleville where Negroes lived along untended, weedy roads. Behind them, on a high bluff overlooking a muddy stream, was a skeet trap, and all Sunday long the booming shotgun blasts of white men shooting skeet lay heavily on the singing in the little frame church. Sometimes the children slipped away from home and joined others standing at a distance watching. They loved to climb the bluff, but the shooters made it dangerous.

Although their mother restrained them as she always had, they knew that she was changed. She was thinner and more nervous, but she was kinder, too, and she rarely nagged them anymore. She was more pleasant toward their father, and their home was happier than ever before.

"You are big boys now and must stay for church after Sunday school," she bade them. "You must express your love and thanksgiving toward God for bringing you through alive."

They didn't mind. There was always something fascinating

happening in church. Once a baptism was held way across town in the Arkansas River and there was a fish fry afterwards. The fires were burning smokily in the soft warm dusk and the gaily clad black people, filled with their joy of God, frolicked happily among the shanties and broken-down jetties along the river bank. The liquid laughter and caressing voices, smell of frying cat-fish, dimly moving people melting into the gloom, made magic of the strange night scene, and Charles was lost in fantasy, wanting to hold the moment and never let it end. Soft strange happenings touched him; the dark, whispering river, a young girl's smooth black face silhouetted against the deepening dusk. He liked the mystery of the half-seen, the poetry of the dark. Sharp, hard-angled perspective always kept him tense. And he hated dirtiness and vulgarity in anyone.

Once, at a Sunday afternoon picnic in the far-off woods, a brash young thirteen-year-old girl named Susie kept urging him, "Come on 'n do it to me, baby. Come on, doan be so skeered."

She wore white shorts and her long black legs were goose-pimpled; there were scars on her knees. He couldn't meet her bold, slant gaze. He wasn't scared; inside he was sick with shame. Afterwards, in Sunday school, he avoided her; he wouldn't look at her. Then suddenly a tug, he'd turn; her slant brown eyes were daring him. Finally he told William.

"What do you mean?" William asked.

"She wants me to do it to her."

"You let her alone," William said. "You shouldn't think of anything like that. Besides, you don't know how."

"I do, too, know how."

But shortly afterwards, study began claiming their attention. Their studies had become interesting at last. They plodded eagerly from class to class, along the cinder paths between the crowded buildings, their footsteps ringing hollowly on the worn wooden stairs.

Both loved chemistry. Their happiest hours were spent in the laboratory in the basement of the chapel, arranging complicated apparatus, melting crystals over the Bunsen burners, heating strange mixtures in the test tubes, or grinding solids in the mortars with the complacent patience of a squaw grinding corn. The formation of water by burning hydrogen held them in breathless anticipation. They were intrigued by all experimentation, and were always doing something on their own—silverplating pennies, dropping a tiny ball of sodium to dance crazily on the surface of a beaker of water, dunking copper wire into sulphuric acid. The mystery of the commonplace was especially alluring.

At dinner they'd say, "Please pass the sodium chloride."

"I'll have a glass of H_2O."

"Mother, you didn't put enough $C_{12}H_{22}O_{11}$ in this pudding."

Their mother indulged them laughingly. "Pretty soon there'll be no living with you two."

They were startled to learn that gunpowder was made from common ordinary sulphur, saltpeter and charcoal. And if you mixed it with potassium chlorate and powdered glass it would detonate itself, like the torpedoes used in the great world war. They made little torpedoes to put on the streetcar tracks and stood nearby until the car ran over them. Then they'd run when the motorman got out to see what had caused the explosion.

Explosives held for them a special fascination. They blew up buckets and washtubs and barrels. Their mother became a nervous wreck. Once Charles exploded a dynamite cap on the front porch. Luckily the charge went down instead of up and blew a hole through the floor. The only injuries to himself were tiny cuts all over his face and hands, as if his skin had burst in a hundred different places. After that their mother forbade them to make any kind of explosive.

But in the lab, without her knowledge, they worked industriously at making guncotton and improving their torpedo charges. They often stumped their professor by forming some unfamiliar compound. Once they filled the lab with bromine gas, bringing out the school fire department. The volunteers came galloping across the yard, lugging the carts of hose. Classes had to be let out for the remainder of the day to allow the gas to clear. The children were unharmed.

"God takes care of fools and children," their mother said relievedly. "And fortunately, you are both."

"It's just that we know our stuff," William replied boastfully.

"We can make anything," Charles echoed.

Their mother was struck by their complacency and felt a sudden fear. "Do be careful, children. Chemicals are so dangerous."

"We won't get hurt," William assured her.

"We're careful," Charles echoed.

14

EACH YEAR, DURING THE WEEK OF COMMENCEment, a program was held in the auditorium so the undergraduates could demonstrate their skills. Selected students from every department performed rare feats of learning. A portable forge and anvil was rolled upon the stage and mules were shod, cows were milked, dresses stitched, pies baked, poetry recited; and there were weighty discussions in the fields of science and history. It had a circus aspect and there were always thrills and laughter. Though dedicated to the parents, everyone attended.

The Taylor children were chosen to make explosives. Their mother was torn between pride and anxiety.

"Explosives!" she exclaimed. "And right up on the stage. Why can't they do something less dangerous?"

"They're not going to throw a bomb into the audience, honey," Professor Taylor reassured her. "My students'll have a live forge going and that'll be more dangerous than anything."

"But explosives? What will the parents think you're teaching them at the college?"

Professor Taylor chuckled. "You have a point. But they're very good at it, honey. And since the war everybody's talking about explosives. Professor Tanner thought it'd be effective."

"Effective indeed! I'm sure it'll be effective," she said disparagingly.

The children were thrilled and excited by the prospect. For days before the exercises it was all they talked about. They had made a number of torpedoes in the lab which they exploded in their backyard the morning of the big shindig.

It made their mother nervous. "Do stop playing with those explosives," she called. "I've told you time and again and I'm not going to tell you anymore."

"We're practising," Charles replied.

"You're doing no such thing," she contradicted crossly. "You're just taking this opportunity to disobey your mother."

"What do you know about what we're doing?" Charles said defiantly.

"Don't you dare talk back to me," she said.

In a fit of resentment, when she'd withdrawn, Charles threw a torpedo against the house. It exploded with a terrible bang. She rushed into the backyard.

"Which one of you did that?" she demanded, her face flaming with fury.

Charles looked at her challengingly. "I did."

Her mouth closed grimly with anxiety and rage. "Just for that you shan't take part in tonight's program."

"I don't care," he replied sullenly. "You don't want us to anyway."

His insolence and defiance wrung her heart. "I don't know what's gotten into you."

"Nothing's gotten into me. You're always fussing. Fuss-fuss-fuss all the time."

She never permitted the children to talk back. But now her anger was torn with worry. She didn't know what was coming over him. "God doesn't like ugly," she finally said.

The remark infuriated him; he'd heard it all his life. "Who cares?" he muttered recklessly.

She was profoundly shocked by what she considered blasphemy. He, too, was frightened by his own remark, as if he'd gone beyond the realm of safety. He'd always considered God as omnipresent, able to reach out and touch you at His will. It would not have surprised him had God struck him dead, or burnt him to a cinder.

"God is going to punish you," she said grimly. "God is going to punish you as surely as you're standing there."

And he believed it. But from some compulsion deep inside of him he had to show defiance to the end. "I don't care," he said. "Let Him punish me."

Mrs. Taylor looked at him silently, her face settling into lines of agony. She went into the house, trembling with fear for him. God was going to hurt him in some awful way, and there was nothing she could do to stop it. She closed herself within her room and prayed God to forgive him.

Charles was silent all through dinner. His mother wouldn't look at him. William looked at his brother covertly.

Professor Taylor wondered at the strain. "What's the trouble, son?"

"Charles has been ugly," his mother replied. "And he shan't take part in the program."

"Ugly! Ugly! Ugly!" Charles shouted, jumping from the table. "That's all I hear—ugly-ugly-ugly! I s'pose if I was a sissy like Andy Baldwin you'd be satisfied," he said, dashing from the room.

Suddenly his mother burst into tears, cupping her face in her hands. "God is going to punish him," she sobbed.

"There, there, honey," her husband consoled. "He'll be all right. He's just high-strung, and he's excited. After tonight he'll settle down."

She looked up, her face hardening beneath the tears. "He shan't take part in the program, and that's that! He'll have to learn to control himself."

"But, honey, Professor Tanner's depending on the boys."

"I don't care," she said. "He's not going to get away with his insolence."

"I can do it by myself," William said, looking at his father.

Charles was bitterly disappointed. It was a sad, silent family that set out for the chapel. Charles was put to ushering. When he passed his mother's seat she looked away. He thought she'd put a curse on him. God was going to strike him dead before the night was out. A strange unearthly fear filled the corners of his mind and he began trembling in the dark. The exercises he scarcely noticed. He stood by a window looking out into the night. Orion winked indifferently from the distance and the Milky Way settled on his melancholy. He'd never see the stars again, or his mother or father or brother or anything. His mother didn't matter, he didn't care if he never saw her again; but his brother he'd miss most. He'd be lost without his brother. And he'd never again see him throughout all eternity because he was going to Hell and Will would go to Heaven.

His brother's voice captured his attention. He looked back toward the stage. William stood before a small wooden table, grinding solids in a mortar. He talked as he worked.

"Now I'll add point seven-five cubic centimeters of potassium nitrate, KNO_3," he looked up and grinned, "which is known to you as old common ordinary saltpeter."

A laugh ran through the audience. Charles watched him make the familiar moves, thinking of all the fun they'd had at it. And now they'd never do that again—or anything. He saw William add the potassium chlorate, explaining that it was the oxidizer; and then the powdered glass—the detonator.

Now the pestle moved so delicately in the mortar as William said, "Don't be alarmed, I won't hurt you," getting another little laugh. William moved around the table and stood before the lights.

Not the pestle! Charles was thinking. *Not the pestle, Will . . .*

The explosion came in a sudden white puff, the size of a pillowcase. William stood there for an instant in the center of the stage, the silence deafening about him, holding his face in his hands. There was something of the crucifixion in his posture, a stone of rigid tragedy in a field of barren loneliness. Some instinctive memory, working even then, warned him that to run was dangerous.

Charles leaped forward without thought. Before him was the stairwell down to the landing, and he went off into space. When e regained the chapel floor William was surrounded by their parents, Dr. Lukas and others of the faculty. Men were pushing forward, crying, "Clear the way!" Downstairs he got behind the vanguard. They pressed through the confusion. William was mute. His mother held tightly to his arm, guiding him. He allowed himself to be led; his feet stumbled on the uneven ground. On the other side his father held him up.

"Here! Over here!" Dr. Lukas called in the darkness.

They groped forward toward the car. Doors opened and there was fumbling. Professor and Mrs. Taylor got into the back seat with William between them.

"Where's Charles?" his mother asked anxiously.

"I'm here," he sobbed from the shadows. Suddenly he discovered he was crying; salt taste was in his mouth.

"Get up here with me," Dr. Lukas said.

It was a touring car and there was a hand pump on the dashboard which rendered high compression. Dr. Lukas told him to work the pump. Shortly the motor roared. The car backed and turned and sped through streets of unreality, the bright lights carving strangely distorted scenes out of the dark horror in their minds. Charles wanted to turn and reach over the back seat and touch William. But he was afraid to leave off pumping. All he could do for him was this. He sat tensely, pumping for his brother's life.

No words were spoken. The race was against despair. Prayer fused them within the doubtful hope. Charles was afraid to breathe lest God discover him. The car wheeled into a courtyard, a lighted doorway looming. A sign to one side read: EMERGENCY ENTRANCE. Dr. Lukas sounded the horn and jumped from the car. Two white-clad men came from within the hospital. Mrs. Taylor had gotten out and was helping William down. Professor Taylor ran around the car to help her. Two more cars roared into the courtyard and men leaped out. Suddenly there was confusion. A brief violent conference was taking place before the lighted entrance, the two white men surrounded by a mob of panicky Negroes. Two more white men hastened from within, and Charles saw his father move forward in an attitude of prayer. One of the white men slowly shook his head, regretfully it seemed. And Charles saw his father break down and start sobbing like a baby. He'd not moved from his seat, and now he saw his mother and William at one side, remote from the contestants, forgotten in the contest.

Then another car came swiftly into the scene and a big hatless white man pushed forward through the crowd. After a rapid exchange of sharp, harsh voices, the big white man came forward and took William by the arm and gently guided him across the courtyard and through the lighted entrance. Professor and Mrs. Taylor and Dr. Lukas followed in single file.

The others gathered in clusters, talking tensely. Charles recognized a number of the teachers, his chemistry professor and the college president. He sat lonely in the dark. He wanted to pray. But there seemed something funny about God. At the time he didn't know what. His thoughts were unjelled. Every now and then he'd work the pump on the dashboard. It felt that he was helping.

An eternity went by. Then Dr. Lukas opened the door. Mrs. Taylor guided her son outside. His face was bandaged so that only his mouth and nose were visible. In the light from the open door Charles caught sight of his mother's face. It was gone-gone-GONE! She was an old woman. And then a little stoopshouldered old man came out last, stumbling on the stones. Everything broke loose inside of Charles and he doubled down in his seat crying.

He felt his mother's hand tugging him. "Charles. Charles." Her voice had altered. It was so high and light and tremulous, as if the slightest breath would blow it all away—the voice of an old, old woman.

"Yes, Mama," and he got down from the car and took William's hand. "Will . . . Will . . ." But it was too late.

"Don't worry, Chuck," William whispered through the bandages. "Don't cry."

Emotion came up and cut his breath. They took their places in the car again. Now there was no race. The race was lost. They went now through the dark winding void of tragedy to the colored hospital. Once more Charles touched William's hand. But now William was mute again. Mrs. Taylor went with him into the hospital and the others followed. They waited until he was put to bed. His mother said that she would stay. Professor Taylor took his youngest son and they went out to find a street-car. The car came and they sat huddled in the Jim-Crow section at the rear. Not until then did the nightmare grow complete.

The next day his parents tried to build up hope. As soon as the tissue healed specialists would have to operate. Miraculous things had been done during the war. They were already planning to take William to a famous hospital in St. Louis. They bolstered their courage with talk of its fine surgeons. But they all knew that William was blind. And Charles knew that God, who had taken his sight, would never give it back.

It left him with a sense of shock that never wore off. He might have been able to adjust to his brother's loss of sight. But he never learned to rationalize the error of God's judgment —the profound and startling knowledge that virtue didn't pay.

Before, life had held a reasoned pattern. There was good on the one side and bad on the other. And anyone could tell the difference. One knew what to expect. Good had its reward, and bad its punishment. It had been that simple.

Now it was complex. Who was to say what was good, if you were punished for it? Or that a way was bad when all it ever brought was good? God didn't like ugly, his mother always said: God would punish him. God didn't even know the difference, he thought bitterly. Because he himself was the one who'd acted ugly. It made being good a farce, and took the meaning out of right and wrong.

It was then that time began its nightmare race; incidents crowded together without continuity, days lacked their accustomed familiarity, his actions had no meaning, commotion piled on commotion. And always there was something missing. He'd turn in a sudden catch of excitement and say, "Will—" and it would break off. Hurt would cascade down until he couldn't bear it. He'd have to do something to ease it off. Whatever came to mind. A vague memory of someone saying he had stolen a drink from the bottle of grain alcohol in the lab—and he broke in and drank the whole bottle and lay sick to death, vomiting on the floor, until midnight. When he got home his parents didn't even ask where he had been. His mother looked at him queerly. They'd just returned from the hospital. Now she was faced with a terrible choice. Both sons needed her desperately. Whichever one she tried to save, the other would be surely lost. Should it be the seeing or the blind? But he thought in some vague way she blamed him for it. Her white old face was ravaged with despair, but the grim thin mouth was undefeated. And the curious gray-green eyes, with strange glints, seemed to follow him accusingly:

Why wasn't it you?
Why wasn't it you?

She was so tired. She sat before the dresser with her long silky hair let down, the brush held limply in her lap. He stole timidly into the room.

"Mama, I'll brush your hair."

"All right, my son. Your mother's very tired."

The long brown strands flowed beneath the brush. "Mama."

She waited. And then asked, "What is it, Charles?"

"I wish it'd been me, too, Mama."

The deep strange eyes were sudden pools of tears. She turned and clasped him to her breast.

"My little boy . . . my baby . . . you must be a good boy for Mother's sake."

At that moment she made her choice. He was so close to her, always so much a part of her, instantly he knew.

"It's all right, Mama," he said. "It's all right."

Now both of them were gone. He dried his tears and went back to brushing her hair, prolonging the moment. But finally she was weary. He kissed her tenderly and said goodnight.

The next week Mrs. Taylor took William to St. Louis. He'd come home for the day. Charles took him to the barbershop. Their affection had always been strangely inarticulate, expressed largely in their swift assistance to each other, blind headlong loyalty in a fight, the completion of a sentence should one falter in class, consoling each other at night, the almost mystical sharing of joy and pain, the oneness against the world. They'd talked in a language almost as sparse as signals, cryptic as a code, made up of the said and the known.

"Chuck."

"Huh?"

Walking down the railroad track.

"Something's wrong."

"Old Six knew that."

"Six doesn't know 'bout Joe and Maybelle."

"Ha, but he will. Look, old Billy's loose."

"Pomp oughta be here."

"Mi Rainy! Mi Rainy! De goat done dead."

And they'd stop to laugh.

They'd seldom been out of each other's sight since Charles was born. And though often it seemed the opposite, Charles always thought of William as the leader, even when it was he who took the lead. Now it felt so strange and wrong to be guiding his brother down the cinder lane. He felt a deep sense of shame and embarrassment, as if all the older people whom they passed were hiding something. It was like coming into a church to find all the congregation naked and not even knowing it. As if all of them together had conspired with God to do this, and in some way he knew that they were guilty.

The conversation wouldn't jell.

"Will."

"Huh?"

"That old yellow car with the bay window."

"Car?"

"Boxcar."

"Oh!"

"It came back. 'Member we marked it to see. And it came back yesterday. I saw it on a manifest on the Iron Mountain."

"Yare." But William wasn't interested.

Charles couldn't say *look*. And now he couldn't say *remember*.

They were lost. Charles had the feeling that William was waiting only for the time when he would see again. And he knew that time was never. All that was left was the emotion that flowed between them, like the blood of joined twins. But when William left that night that was severed too.

"Good-bye, Chuck."

"Good-bye, Will."

"Don't let old Percy get you."

"Ha! Not if I can s—er—*hear* him first." He couldn't say *see* but it was worse to stumble.

"Good-bye, Mother."

"Good-bye, son. Please try to be a good boy. Mother worries so when you are ugly."

Ugly! He turned and went off to one side; and he was crying like a baby.

Soon afterwards Professor Taylor took his son away from that house—now it also was haunted with so many hurting memories—and they went to room with a woman across from the campus entrance. They fixed their own meals, sharing the cooking between them, and made the bed in which they slept together. The food was either burnt or raw, and always tasted queer. Once Professor Taylor left a pot of beans to cook and hours later the neighbors broke in to quench the fire. Nothing seemed to go right.

Their home in St. Louis had been leased until September, and Mrs. Taylor and William were rooming too. The treatment on William's eyes was slow; the doctors were picking glass and scar tissue from the cornea. There were many complications; and there was very little hope. Her letters were sad and bewailing; she spoke of taking him to Germany if the operation failed. The gap seemed widening every day.

Professor Taylor had to stay for the summer sessions and Charles worked for the school. He drove the school sedan and cleaned the president's office. The driving took him all about the town; twice a day he picked up mail at the main post office; often he met the trains, took money to the bank. Someone was always after him to transport them some place. He had lunch with teachers in the restaurants off the grounds and was always taking ladies to Wednesday night church. He lived a strange, grown-up life.

On Friday evenings motion pictures were shown on the president's lawn. Once, standing in the shadows, watching a picture the name of which he never knew, sweat started pouring from his body. It was a warm night, but not sultry, not hot enough to sweat. But the sweat came out of his hair and ran down his face and he could feel it streaming down his body in a deluge. He went searching for his father, frightened.

"You're all wet, son," his father observed. "What've you been doing?"

"Nothing. I was standing watching the picture and all of a sudden I started to sweat."

"You'd better go home and lie down," his father advised. "You've been too active lately."

"But it won't stop," Charles complained. "I can feel it coming out my skin."

"You go home and I'll get Dr. Lukas."

He went home and undressed and lay in the dark. But the sweat still streamed from his body as if he was being subjected to some insane process of dehydration. The doctor came and examined him but could find nothing wrong.

"You take these and drink a lot of water," he directed, giving Charles some pills.

But the pills had no effect. A pool formed about him on the sheet and sunk into the mattress. After a time it stopped as suddenly as it had begun.

Most of the summer school students were teachers from the district schools. Charles had a habit of playing tennis with them during the afternoons. But after the seizure his father bade him stop. The next day he went out anyway. His father saw him from the blacksmith shop and came running across the campus.

"Confound it, I'm not going to tell you again," he said, and picked up a rotten stick to whip Charles.

Charles was sick with shame and fury at being whipped before all the grown-ups he'd been playing with. He grappled with his father and they tussled about the court, digging deep holes in the packed clay surface. Finally Charles got the stick and threw it over the fence. His father looked astonished. Without another word he turned and went back to his shop. Charles went off by himself until time for bed. His father never referred to the incident in all his life. He never tried again to whip Charles. But the next day he took his son downtown and bought him new long pants. They made a difference. Now the older women looked at him.

That day he was out on the tennis courts waiting for a game. Classes kept the others later and he was always first. A young woman in a short white skirt sauntered up and sat beside him. She was pretty in a slow, sensous way and he'd never seen a woman wearing so short a skirt. Dark hair grew like tendrils from her strong smooth neck and her full-blown lips were glistening red. She had the ripeness of the South, slumbrous eyes with dark heat circles underneath and that strange look of dissipation found in sultry climates. Her breasts shook like molds of jello beneath the cotton blouse and her heavy thighs were smoothly tan as velvet. The men thought her an exciting piece, but to Charles she was beautiful and inaccessible. He adored her instantly.

"Waitin' for someone?" she asked, the slurred, languid voice habitually affected.

"Oh, no one in particular," he stammered self-consciously.

She glanced at him appraisingly. "Ah haven't seen you 'round before."

"Oh, I'm out almost every day. I work for the president."

"Ah must've seen you 'round. You his nephew or somethin', ain't you?" ;

"You're thinking of Harry. My name is Charles—Charles Taylor. My father teaches blacksmithing."

"Oh, you're Professor Taylor's son." She seemed impressed. "Want to play?"

Her skill was entirely dependent upon her opponent's generosity. He let her win as often as he could, he didn't know why.

151

Usually he played all games with a reckless will to win. But she seemed to expect all the concessions. She'd serve and wait complacently for the return to come to her. After a couple of sets she was winded; they quit to let some others play.

He found some strange emotion at work inside of him. Her proximity sent tingling waves of cold fire coursing down his spine, yet he felt strangely heavy, weak, almost lethargic. To have her enfold him in her full, tanned arms and hold him closely to her heaving, sweating body came scalding through his mind like sinful ecstasy. And yet it had no definition; it stopped just short of sexual desire.

"I'll take you to a show," he blurted.

She looked at him, doubt mingled with expectancy. "How old are you?"

"I'm seventeen," he lied.

Even that would be robbing the cradle, she thought. But the heat and exercise had flamed her blood with passion.

"Ah don' know," she hesitated. "Ah've got to take a bath."

"I'll wait," he panted excitedly. "I'll meet you by the side gate over by the men's dormitory."

"Well—all right."

He ran all the way home and quickly bathed; then dressed himself in his newest blue long pants with a new white shirt and tie. He waited by the gate for two hours before finally she came. She wore a white dress with pleated skirt and patent leather pumps. Now she was commonplace in a way that seemed accessible. His heart pumped flame. But she was nervous and unsure and held herself aloof.

"How old did you say you were?" she greeted him.

"I'm seventeen," he lied again, but uncertainty cut into his ardor.

Two men passed nearby and looked at them curiously. She turned away in shame. "Ah'm too old for you," she said harshly. "Ah'm twenty-two."

His face mirrored his hurt and humiliation. The woman came up in her and she felt sorry for him. Tenderly she held his hands.

"You find a girl your own age. Ah like you, honey, but you're jes' too young."

"All right."

He turned away to hide the sudden tears and walked rapidly around the building. Then suddenly he was running in headlong flight. He ran until he was out of breath. But the shame wouldn't leave him. Finally he went home. He tried to play at making out that he was great and famous and that she would come seeking his attention. But he couldn't find the handle to the dream. There was no defense against his age. Afterwards he shunned the tennis courts for fear of seeing her. There was little else to do. The afternoons became empty. He took to walking out of town and wandering through the woods again. The countryside had always been his friend.

On the last day of the summer session he met a girl his age. He saw her standing on the cinder walk beside the chapel. She looked lost and on the verge of tears. He'd just alighted from the school sedan. He looked at her curiously and would have gone past. But she touched him lightly on the arm and stopped him.

"Could you please tell me how to get to the domestic science building?" she asked timidly, painfully embarrassed.

He felt mature and condescending. "Sure, it's over by the diamond. Hop in, I'll drive you over," he offered grandiloquently.

"Oh, thank you, but I can walk."

Her huge brown eyes shone shyly from a thin, fragile face. She was as tall as he but very thin, her body like a reed in the faded calico dress, but her face blossomed from the long neck like an exquisite flower. Something in the slight droop of her narrow shoulders made him think of dogtooth violets in bloom.

"Why walk when you can ride," he said arrogantly.

Mutely she permitted him to bully her. He drove around the chapel and across the diamond.

"You're new," he remarked.

"Oh, we just came for sister," she blurted out. She was rigid with self-consciousness. "Sister studied here this summer."

He pulled up before the domestic science building. "What's your name?"

She glanced at him and her gaze fled off in panic. "Jessie."

"Mine's Charles," he said. "My brother calls me Chuck."

She saw her parents and jumped guiltily from the car. She ran off, then ran back and cried, "Thank you," and then ran off again. He watched her go with the older people into the building. After waiting for a time he turned the car and drove away. But all that day he thought of her. She seemed so wild and fresh and yet so fragile that should she fall she'd break.

That evening during the exercises in the chapel he saw her on the steps. He took her arm. "Want to go for a ride, Jessie."

Her huge eyes widened in fright. "Oh, I couldn't."

"Let's walk then."

Her eyes sought his and lingered for a moment; her thin taut body seemed caught in flight. "Just for a li'l ways."

They walked along the cinder path toward the campus gate. "I work here in the summer. My father teaches."

"I know," she said. "It must be wonderful."

"You know?"

"I showed you to my sister."

"Oh." And then suddenly it struck him. "Wonderful? How?"

"Everything going on all the time."

"I don't know," he said thoughtfully. "I never thought about it. When Will was here we never—" he broke off.

They left the campus and sauntered slowly up Pullen Street. Neither knew where they were going.

"I guess you miss him lots."

He turned and stared at her. Her face was blurred and softly dreamlike in the dark.

"My sister told me he lost his sight."

They went along in silence.

After a time he said, "He's in St. Louis now." Later he said, "I guess I do."

He felt her slender cool hand groping for his fingers and took it gratefully.

"I always wanted a brother," she confessed.

"I guess we wanted a sister too, although I don't remember ever thinking of it."

Then for a long time they just walked through the cool, dim night, matching strides. Their arms swung a little with their fingers locked together as they walked along without talking, caught in the entrancement of the moment.

Finally she said, "We're going back to Brinkley in the mornin'."

"We're going to St. Louis tomorrow too." It frightened him.

"Don't be scared," she said intuitively. He choked to keep from crying. "You can do a lot of things all by yourself."

"I know," he said. His voice sounded strange and thick. He tried to make it clear. "I'm always doing something."

"Not what you used to do together."

"No, I couldn't do that by myself."

Now they were in the bright lights that extended down past Main. Instinctively they turned into the darkness of Cherry Street.

"But I used to never tell my dreams," he said. "I mean—you know—while you're awake. Just sort of making up things you'd like to do if everything was different."

"Like what?"

"Oh, like I'd say you were Penelope and I was Ulysses returning home from twenty years of wandering. Then I'd make out you'd been waiting for me all those years." He didn't feel embarrassed; he was excited telling it. "But you couldn't really be there; I mean, if you were there I couldn't make it up." The back of the icehouse loomed up, loading docks vague in the darkness.

"Why can't you do it with me here?" she whispered timidly. "You've never tried."

He stopped to look at her and she turned from one step ahead and shyly searched his face.

"I don't know," he mumbled.

Then awkwardly they groped together, clumsy from inexperience. But there was a young sweet poetry in their clumsy hands and awkward motions. His mouth kept searching for her lips as they tried to adjust their faces and his arms about her slender body. Finally their lips were meeting, softly pressing in a clear,

155

cool kiss. The queerest sort of feeling surged from deep inside him; an overwhelming· sense of love and purity gathered in his heart. He was flooded with the impulse to defend her. Wordlessly they broke apart and looked straight into each other's eyes. There was no shame; only the bright, luminous quality of their love. Her long dark hair, worn in loose curls down on her shoulders, made a soft, delicate cameo of her thin, fragile face.

"You're very pretty," he said chokingly. "You look something like my mother used to look. Only her hair was lighter."

"Would you like me better if my hair was lighter?"

"No."

"You're a funny boy," she said tremulously, catchy-like, as if she thought he might vanish or fly away.

He laughed from happiness. "I'm just natural nuts."

Now she laughed along with him. "You are not; you're nice."

"Come on." He took her hand. "There's a carnival at the fairgrounds." He must show her what he knew.

Time and parents were forgotten. The night was filled with magic as they swung along. Clouds drifted in disorder across the moon. He drew her to a stop and pointed.

"See, it's Pegasus. See how the wings spread out and the hoof is raised." He was all excited.

"That's a horse, isn't it?"

He laughed uproariously. "What a question! Didn't you ever do that? Play at finding things in the clouds? Will and I used to all the time."

"Oh, with my sister, yes. But we just found people mostly; just folks whom we both knew."

"You ought've been with us. We used to find all sort of things."

"You and I could too," she said stoutly.

"Race you!" he said suddenly. They leaped and ran with joy. The darkness sang with happiness as they sped along. Then, there in the distance was the carnival, a noisy, crowded, ecstatic wonderland. They wandered down the midway and breathed in the excitement. White people eyed them curiously, but none bothered. They swung along, hand in hand, enveloped in a dream.

But time, that old iconoclast, kept tugging at their elbows. They made the journey home in silence, walking rapidly to keep ahead of tears. But at the end they cried anyway. She wouldn't let him come to where her parents waited with the whipping they held in store for her. He had to say good-bye at a distance and watch her walk away alone. Briefly they embraced, clumsily as at first, clinging for dear life. And as at first, their cool, young lips searched before meeting, and the taste of each other's tears was in their kiss.

The next night he was on the train going to St. Louis. He couldn't stop the crying. It just kept on coming up and flooding out. These good-byes were coming too rapidly for him. He was getting so he cried easily as a baby.

He thought continuously of her. In the outside night that raced along the window he saw her face in all its exquisite moods. And her voice kept time with the thumping of the wheels over the section joints . . . *You're a funny boy . . . a funny boy . . . a funny boy . . . a funny boy . . . a funny boy . . . a funny boy . . . a funny boy* . . . It felt as if his heart would burst with aching. He loved her so . . . *loved her so . . . loved her so . . . loved her so . . . a funny boy . . . a funny girl . . . a funny life . . . loved her so* . . . It seemed as if the turmoil in his head would flame explosively.

"Don't cry, son," his father gestured with vague helplessness. "It's going to work out all right. You boys'll be together before another year."

Charles looked up at his father, choking back his tears. Deep, sinking lines like mutilations pulled down the full, strong features of his father's face. And his skin had lightened, taken on a grayish pallor beneath the black. The settled look of age shocked Charles to reality.

"I'll be all right," he mumbled, knuckling at his eyes. "I'll be all right, Dad, I'll be all right." Then later on he asked, "Can I get you a drink of water, Dad?"

"No, son, thanks . . . I'm not thirsty." The wheels clacked endlessly . . . "I'm just tired . . ."

Gone! It was gone . . . gone-gone-gone-gone-gone-gone . . . Mississippi . . . Then Will . . . Then his mother . . . His love had gone . . . And now his father . . . *Gone-gone-gone-gone,* the wheels clacked. *Came arapping and atapping and atapping and atapping . . . A funny boy . . . gone-gone-gone-gone-gone . . .*

15

St. Louis BECAME A CITY OF FRUSTRATION FOR THE Taylor family. Though they'd gotten back their house, it never became a home. Within it they became prisoners of their despair.

William was being treated by famous specialists at the great hospital. He went five times a week. But no miracle had happened. One eye could distinguish light from dark; the other could make out type print held an inch or two away, and distinguish outlines at a distance of four or five feet. Grafting corneas to both eyes was considered, but only a few such operations had been attempted, and the ratio of success was low. There was the added difficulty of obtaining corneas; they had to be taken from the eyes of living persons or from corpses shortly dead. His mother offered hers, but the doctors didn't think it worth the risk. Charles was never told for fear he might do something rash.

The major hope was to remove sufficient scar tissue so light could penetrate. It was a slow, nerve-racking process that went on all that summer. But William never seemed discouraged, never complained. Charles was awed by his brother's courage. In William's presence he became inarticulate, but worshiped him across the gap.

Tom was there that summer. He did all the things for William that Charles would have liked to do—little things like walking him to the store, taking him to the barbershop, buying him something special. Their mother did the special things, like taking him to the hospital and cutting up his food. Charles felt left out. It seemed as if he was too young to be of any good at all.

Tom was working as a bus boy in a downtown restaurant. He'd

come home with an armache that made him miserable. Then Charles would massage his arm and feel that he was helping.

Professor Taylor had no ability at all for city life. At heart he was a missionary. He'd lived his life in southern Negro colleges. There, a professor was somebody. He counted in the neighborhood. His family counted too. But in St. Louis he didn't count.

He'd gotten a job waiting on tables in a roadhouse out near Carondulet.

"It's a goddamned crying shame about that son of yours, Willie," his boss, Joe Terry, would say, shaking his head in real lament. "You oughta be back teaching your people instead of here waiting on roughnecks like these."

Professor Taylor would smile courageously. "Mr. Terry, the world's not coming to an end because I'm away from teaching for a year or two."

It was in his home that he'd been defeated. He was a pathetic figure coming home from work; a small black man hunched over and frowning, shambling in a tired-footed walk, crushed old cap pulled down over his tired, glazed eyes, a cigarette dangling from loose lips.

His occupation was never mentioned before the children. But they'd overheard their parents discussing it, and were ashamed for him. Usually they were long in bed when he returned from work. But once, going to the bathroom, Charles saw his father slowly trudging up the stairs. He looked so old and stooped and beaten. It frightened him. Suppose his father died. What would become of them?

For a short time at summer's end, after Tom had returned to school, Charles had William to himself. The bandages had been removed from William's eyes but the burnt lids and bluish-tinted irises were more shocking than before. Both tried desperately to recapture the old feeling. They fell into their old-time habit of playing rough, tusseling with each other and doing feats of strength and agility. But suddenly William would turn to shout excitedly and Charles would catch sight of the blueish pebbles in the burnt dark flesh. Agony could cut him to the bone. He just couldn't get over it. Or William would bump head-on into something, and the hurt would course through Charles like brackish, bitter venom. He was always keyed up, too anxious to make his playing seem natural.

They'd rob a huckster's wagon in the early dusk and race wildly down the alley with the apples and bananas. William's foot would catch on some obvious obstruction, an overturned garbage can, a kid's tricycle, and he'd pitch headlong, sprawling on the bricks. Quick, violent protest would shake Charles loose from reason; with a savage insane gesture he'd throw his own stolen fruit in a blind arc, breaking windows, he didn't care.

Once they were out in the alley throwing rocks at a garbage can placed against the schoolyard wall. William had got the range and was doing fine. Their mother called Charles and he was gone for a moment. William went forward to grope beside the can for rocks. Charles dashed back, throwing on the run, and didn't see his brother until the rock was on its way.

"Will!" he screamed in terror.

William looked quickly up, seeing nothing, and the rock struck him in the center of the forehead right between the eyes. Caught in rigidity, hurt surged through Charles like acid in his veins. Then he ran forward. But William had gotten up and was dabbing at the cut with a handkerchief. He heard his younger brother's gasping breath and laughed it off.

"It wasn't your fault, Chuck. I wasn't looking."

Charles couldn't take it. After that he quit playing with his brother. And the gap widened.

Charles hated the city high school. He was given entrance examinations and assigned to the second year. The teachers found it hard to comprehend that he'd attended college.

"Now what's the name of that school you attended in Arkansas?" his home room teacher, Mr. Sawyer, asked.

"Well, they called it a college."

"Oh."

He couldn't say he was Professor Taylor's son because they didn't know Professor Taylor either.

And there was something about the students he never liked.

They were all so preoccupied with themselves, so quick to ostracize and condescend. They seemed to him so cheap-smart and city-dirty. At first they were distant and unfriendly. He was alone now; alone against them all.

William had entered the state school for the blind and Charles went with him on Saturdays. Unlike the city schools, here Negroes weren't segregated. Charles wondered if it was because the students couldn't see.

William enjoyed it. But for Charles, Saturdays became a time of death. There was something unearthly about the blind students moving so cheerfully among the grim, forlorn buildings. He couldn't meet the teachers' eyes. A sense of guilt shattered him. He felt so awfully ashamed for having sight. He'd leave his brother at the door and run until he couldn't breathe.

William studied braille and took lessons on the clarinet and soon was playing in the band. A deep camaraderie existed among the students. Most of them had a wonderful sense of humor. Their errors due to blindness were a constant source of merriment. William was always recounting something funny he'd done, such as entering the girls' toilet by mistake. In the darkness he couldn't see at all. He felt around and his hand had encountered hair.

"I said, 'Excuse me, I'm looking for the urinal.' Then someone said in a shrill voice, 'Wrong department.'" He laughed uproariously.

It made the goose flesh crawl on Charles. Finally he asked in a small, strangled voice, "What'd you do?"

"Heck, I just laughed and went across the hall."

Nights when the band rehearsed, all of them were accompanied by relatives. It was something like a party; they laughed and talked between rehearsals and ate ice cream and cake. Everyone but Charles had fun; he sat apart, self-conscious, fuming with impotent rage, cauterized with guilt . . . *How could they laugh, goddamn 'em! How could they? How could they?* his mind protested. Sometimes his brother turned and spoke to him, thinking him nearby, and he'd have to hurry over.

"What'd you say, Will?"

"Oh—nothing much. Where were you?"

"I—I wasn't listening, is all."

The other relatives looked at him curiously. Frequently they smiled in his direction. But he held himself rigidly aloof and unapproachable. In all his actions he was braced against the world.

Athletics gave some relief. Across from the high school was a public playground where gangs of city hoodlums collected after school and played a dirty, vicious brutal game which they called football. That became Charles's outlet. He played out of a deep subconscious compulsion to kill himself. Bareheaded and wearing only a sweater over his shirt, he'd dive headfirst to make a tackle, flying through the air to meet with full impact a pair of pumping feet.

"Nine—nineteen—twenty-nine—shift!" he'd sing, calling the signals, unconsciously calling the death row in lottery, and he'd receive the ball and start heading, high-kneeing and swivel-hipping, toward the violent men, spinning away from one, jumping over another, until they pulled him down. They'd pile on top of him, dig their elbows into his back, slam his face into the rocky ground. He'd get up grinning, teeth chipped, slightly dazed. And for a moment he'd be free of all the hurt and guilt inside of him.

A curious phenomenon took place within his mind that winter. Whole periods of his past became lost to recollection. There was no pattern, no continuity, no rational deletions, as the editing of a text. Fragments of days, whole months, a chain of afternoons were drawn at random, a word would be missing from a sentence which he recalled with startling clarity, the intended meaning now gone. He didn't remember a single recitation period from all the years of his mother's teaching in Mississippi. The evening of William's accident, the afternoon leading up and the nightmare afterwards, were branded on his brain. But from the time he and his father left the hospital to return home, until William, with their mother, boarded the train for St. Louis, was a complete blank. He didn't remember the girl, Jessie, how she looked, what she said, nor their walk out to the carnival on Cherry Street that night at all. But he remembered the discovery of their love like the lingering poignance of a moving dream, the dream itself having vanished on awakening. And the feeling of the emotion was still so strong within him at nights it made him cry. It was as if a madman had snatched pages from a treasured book, the story stopping eerily in the middle of a sentence, a gaping hole left in the lives of all the characters, the senses groping futilely to fill the missing parts, gone now, senselessly gone, now the meaning all distorted as if coming suddenly and unexpectedly into a street of funny mirrors. In after years it was as if they'd never lived within their house at all; never eaten a meal in the dining room, never sat together in the living room.

But outwardly he was helpful and obedient. He was wonderfully considerate toward his brother. When it became cold enough to freeze the lakes they went sledding in Forest Park. Directly in front of the Art Museum was a long, steep slope adjoining the lake and when the snow was packed the sleds went down at a furious pace and coasted far across the lake.

William loved to sled. Charles sat at the front to steer, William clung behind, and when it came their turn the policeman on duty gave them a mighty push. It seemed as if they soared through the air. William whooped and yelled like an Indian putting out his face to catch the hard cold push of air. Charles set his teeth and braced his body against disaster. He always felt a sense of trepidation, a fragile, fluttery feeling inside, such as he experienced when looking down from heights. He knew if he saw William hurt just one more time he'd come apart inside.

But Forest Park held their fondest times together. On Sunday afternoons their father came with them. The zoo enthralled them both. William, his head cocked, listened to the scolding of the monkeys.

"You can almost understand them, Check."

Charles was fascinated by the lion's silent prowling, back and forth, back and forth, his gaze caught in the lambent, hypnotic eyes coming forward toward the bars, the fluid body turning like running water, his gaze released, caught, released, caught, released, endlessly.

They always tried to reach the birdhouse at feeding time.

"Listen to the babble of the birds," William said. It was his great delight.

In the spring they liked to walk across the ordered acres, down the long stone walks between the sentinel trees, coming suddenly upon the wildness of a rocky hill. It was away, care was momentarily gone, the people here were all trespassers like themselves. And, too, their father seemed a little happy on Sunday afternoons.

Spring in St. Louis was a haunting time. The barbecue pits in the backyards were fired and the soft warm evenings were pungent with the scent of sizzling pork. Excited childish voices floated through the dusk.

Five ... fifteen ... twenty-five ...
Are you ready? ...

Children fled and screamed.

And the morning air smelled of dew and growing things. For that brief period a little bit of country came to the city's cluttered streets.

Once Charles awakened in the night and felt his brother crying. Sharply he recalled a night a long time before when he'd run off to a fire and had seen a strange lonely lady and was crying for her in the dark; and his brother's voice, consoling, "Don't cry, Chuck. Go to sleep, Chuck. Everything's going to be all right."

Now he wanted to console his brother as he had been consoled. But he couldn't find the words. He clenched his teeth and held himself rigid in the dark.

That summer he got a job cleaning and delivering for an old German druggist, and his father bought him a secondhand bicycle. The first morning he swept and mopped the floor and wiped the candy counters. He'd hung his sweater alongside his employer's, and when the old man wasn't looking, stole a package of cigarettes, two packages of chewing gum and a chocolate bar and slipped them into its pocket.

At last the druggist sent him on a delivery. On his return the old man thrust his hand into the sweater pocket and dramatically displayed the loot. "You are a thief!" he shouted, his blue eyes dancing beneath the bushy brows. "I should call the police and have you arrested!"

Charles quaked with fright.

"The minute I turn my back you steal this trash." Furiously the old man shook the loot before his face. "Go! Get out of my sight! Here, take your sweater," he called as Charles ran off without it. "If I knew how to get in touch with your mother I'd tell her you're a thief."

He snatched his sweater and fled. For hours he cycled up and down unfamiliar streets. He was in a daze. He didn't know why he'd stolen. He didn't want the things he'd stolen. And he knew the old man would have given him the chewing gum and candy.

It was late that night when he went home. The house was quiet. A single light burned in the living room. His mother was waiting up for him.

"You must be tired, son," she said. "Why must you work so late?"

"I had to clean up after the store was closed," he lied.

"But why couldn't you do it tomorrow morning?"

"I quit, mother. I told the druggist I wasn't coming back. He asked me to stay and clean up for him."

She looked at him searchingly. He couldn't meet her eyes.

"Did you get into any trouble, son?"

"No, mother, I just didn't like the job."

"Don't get into any trouble, son. Mother couldn't bear it."

She arose and led him toward the kitchen. "I saved your dinner."

He watched her as she busied about the stove. She looked so frail and tiny and so old. Gray streaks fell like stripes of sorrow in the long brown tresses he'd loved so passionately to brush. She was like some strange little white woman he'd never seen before. What had she to do with him? He felt trapped in another person's house, sitting at another's table, looking at a stranger's mother. And then she turned with his plate. He met the greenish glint of her deep-set eyes, and saw the tender worry they held for him. Suddenly she was his own beloved mother in an overwhelming flood.

"Mama, Mama." He groped blindly forward and clasped her about the waist.

She put down the plate and drew him to her breast. "My baby, my baby," she sang tenderly, the crying note of worry cutting through his heart. "My little baby. What have you done now?"

"Nothing, Mama," he sobbed. "Nothing. I haven't done anything, honest. I just love you, Mama. And I hate to see you worry so."

"Mother loves you also, son. That's why Mother worries so."

After a moment he wiped his face and ate his food. He made a vow to himself that he would never steal again.

And three weeks later he was fired from another job for stealing. All that day he'd stolen things to carry home—a camera, a nickel-plated watch, a carton of cigarettes and two quarts of ice cream—and had stored them in an empty barrel in the basement. His employer, Mr. Greenbaum, had been watching him all day. At quitting time he called Charles down and confronted him.

"I didn't put it there," Charles denied, frightened sick inside as if he had to vomit. "I didn't put it there."

"You seemed like such an honest boy," Mr. Greenbaum said. "Maybe if you're stopped now you can make something out of yourself."

"I didn't put it there. I don't know who stole it. It wasn't me."

The ice cream had melted and ruined everything. Mr. Greenbaum sadly shook his head. "The loss. It's nothing to me, boy. I can afford it. It won't break me. But the loss to you, son, you can't afford."

Charles felt the urge to yield, to confess and beg this kind man's forgiveness. But to confess would have made him the defeated one. He felt that if he once confessed he'd be forever lost.

"I didn't take it," he denied again. "I swear it wasn't me."

Mr. Greenbaum looked suddenly old and tired. "Come with me, I'll pay you off," he said.

He pedaled slowly up the hill of Delmar Boulevard. He'd always liked the name of that street; it had such a pleasant sound. People were entering the theatres along the way. They looked so happy. Everyone was with someone else.

At Vandeventer he saw a hot dog man, the shiny, steaming kettle slung across his back. He stopped and ordered one. The man put the kettle on the pavement, spread sauerkraut between a bun and nestled down the long, black, steaming weiner. Charles sat on his bike and ate it slowly. The man lifted his kettle and went along. The night closed in. Suddenly tears scalded down his cheeks. "Goddammit! Goddammit!" he cried. He'd failed his mother after all. Why couldn't she take him as he was, he thought. Why was she always forcing him into making some kind of vow he couldn't keep? Why didn't she let him alone?

He threw the remainder of the hot dog to the street and hurried off. Finally he went home.

The next morning he told her he had quit.

She said sadly, "You worry mother so."

For a time Tom was home that summer and she pinned her hopes on him. He'd graduate from the university.

All that week she'd worked in preparation for his coming; she'd cleaned the house and polished the silver and laundered the curtains. And on the day of his arrival she'd cooked all the things he liked, and had decorated the living room as if for Christmas. Finally the taxi came and brought him home.

She rushed down the steps to greet him. "How handsome you are my son," she sang, embracing him. Her eyes were filled with tears.

Tom was startled by her greeting. "Why, Mother, you're crying!" he exclaimed.

"Why, so I am," she said.

He was a tall, dandyish man with pretentious manners and an affected laugh.

"Hello, Dad," he said, and when the two shook hands it was as if he was greeting a subordinate.

The children resented him.

After dinner he put on his gown and mortarboard. "Now, how does your son look, Mother?"

"You are a man now," she said. Her voice rang with pride.

"Let me see it," William asked, putting forth his hands.

"Here, put it on," Tom said.

"Now I have two titled sons," their mother laughed.

"Mine's no title, Mother," Tom corrected. "It's just a plain B.A."

"Yes, my son, but you must wear it as a title and be proud."

Later she had him to herself. Professor Taylor and the children had gone to bed. They sat in the living room and talked. She asked him what he planned to do. He'd majored in business administration and accounting and wanted to go into the real estate business.

"My son, my son," she said. "You're going to make your mother famous."

He was embarrassed by the intensity of her emotion. "Now, mother, don't expect too much from me," he protested. But he was flattered too.

He got a job working on a commission basis with a Negro real estate firm. And for a time the house was filled with activity. The young women gave him a rush. His mother was so afraid he'd get himself engaged or have to marry before he'd had a chance to settle down she disliked all the girls.

"If you ask me I think Maud is the best one of the lot," she volunteered.

He gave her a startled look. "Maud? Why, Mother, you know you don't think anything of the sort. She's dark and her hair isn't four inches long and you know you wouldn't want her for a daughter-in-law."

"It's not what's on the surface, it's what's beneath," she said sententiously. "Many a golden crust hides a sour pie."

He laughed uproariously. "Where'd you get that one? That's new. I bet you just made it up." Then suddenly he got her drift and added, "You know good and well Maud's not only black but she's evil too. She's not in love with me; she just wants a man. And you're just sticking up for her because you think I'm stuck on Sally."

"Well, son, you're grown," she said, "and if you want to marry Sally I can't stop you. But I'll tell you this much, you'll live to regret it. Sally is a lovely girl and very smart. But she's hard and ambitious and she'll just use you for a steppingstone."

"I'm not going to marry anyone," Tom said sharply, "so you can just relax." He was angry with her for interfering.

But soon the rush slowed up of its own volition. Tom wasn't getting anywhere. The girls turned their attention to young men with better prospects. He began to feel the frustration entombing all of them. More than any of the others, he sensed his father's humiliation and defeat. The house became a prison.

"I'm going to Detroit, Mother," he announced. "A lot of colored people are emigrating there and it's a good field for my line."

"But this is your home, son," she protested, shocked and at a loss for words. "Mother needs you here."

"I'm sorry, Mother, but I can't stay here and live off dad."

"But we want you with us," she insisted.

"I've got my own life to live, Mother," he stubbornly maintained.

She was bitterly disappointed. "You can do as you wish, my son. You're grown and if you want to go I can't stop you. But you listen to your mother. A rolling stone gathers no moss. Your mother knows. I allowed your father to drag us all over creation. And what has he to show for it?"

"I've made up my mind, Mother."

Her mouth closed in a grim, unforgiving line. "If you leave me now, you needn't ever come back."

But she couldn't stop him.

After he'd gone she became assailed by a sense of persecution. She came to the conclusion that all of them were trying to hurt her, Professor Taylor and the children too. At first it revealed itself in their lack of appreciation for all her sacrifices. She'd worked herself to the bone for them, forsaken her own family, given up her friends. And at the first opportunity Tom ran off and deserted her. Nor were the others any better. Now that William could get about a little by himself, he'd forgotten how she'd slaved for him, nursing him night and day, reading to him by the hour. He was all taken up with his work at the school for the blind. His teachers were closer to him now than his mother. And sometimes she felt that Charles actually hated her.

Later she discovered they were doing little things to hurt her physically, to drive her insane. One would put too much salt in the stew pot, or turn the fire up on the roast. Charles—she was certain it was him—sprinkled water in her bedroom slippers so that she would catch a cold. But she was afraid to accuse him of it; he looked at her so strangely now. And she was positive her husband sprinkled red pepper in her bed, although she couldn't catch him at it. But she knew; she'd wake up in the morning with her skin all red and blistered. They'd been sleeping in twin beds in the same room. Now she moved into the room that Tom had occupied and locked the door at night.

At times she became so frightened of them she'd dress and slip out of the house. She'd go downtown and mingle with white people who didn't know her. Their years in Mississippi had darkened her complexion slightly. That was another thing she held against her husband. Mr. Taylor had deliberately planned it to embarrass her; that had been his main reason for keeping her so long in Mississippi, so she'd cease being white. Now she took to coating her face thickly with white powder and rouging her cheeks. She looked white as a corpse. On those days she ate in the white restaurants. Her desire to talk was overpowering. She got into long, involved conversations with strangers. Most times it ended in unpleasantness.

She'd say at some point in the conversation, "I destroyed my life by marrying a Negro."

The shocked, indignant people would rise and stalk away.

But she couldn't restrain herself.

"I think my husband is trying to kill me," she'd say after opening a conversation with some strange woman.

"Why don't you go to the police?" would come the shocked reply.

"My husband is a Negro," she'd reply, as if that were sufficient answer.

The children were affected by her strangeness. Quite often it was left to Charles to cook and serve the meals. William was afraid to ask where his mother was. Their father sat alone and brooded. Charles went off at night and cycled through the lonely streets, sometimes sitting on a bench in some remote section of the city, afraid to think. William visited his blind friends, or went to band rehearsal every night.

Two things happened then to save their mother. Professor Taylor lost his job. Prohibition had come into effect and finally the roadhouse closed. Then William was rehospitalized for a serious operation. A cataract had begun to form across one eye. Suddenly their mother realized that she was needed. They sold the house and bought a rental property in a poorer neighborhood. They moved into one of the flats, taking only the barest necessities.

Professor Taylor found employment doing odd jobs of carpentry work. Sometimes on weekends Charles helped him. At lunch, munching the cold bologna sandwiches, they'd talk.

"Dad, are you ever going south to teach again?"

"I don't know, son. It depends a great deal on you boys. Did you like it as well there as you do here?"

"Oh, I liked it better. We had some good times in Mississippi."

Reminiscence lit up his father's face. "I don't suppose you were old enough to remember the governor."

"No, but I remember hearing you and Mother talk of him."

"We might go there again if Will regains his sight."

"Dad, do you really think he'll ever see again?"

"I don't know, son. We can only pray."

After a long time Charles lied, "I do."

"It depends on God now."

Charles looked at his father queerly. "I suppose so."

Around the first of December the doctors said there was no more they could do.

They were shocked. None of them had been prepared to give up hope.

Professor Taylor lost his will. He lost his grip on ordinary things. Caught out in the backyard, halfway to the shed, with a hammer in his hand, he'd forget where he was going, what he'd intended to do.

Only the mother's indomitable will saved them. Now that she had overcome the attack of paranoia, she was stronger than before. She wouldn't admit defeat.

"We'll go to Cleveland," she told her husband. "They have a

famous clinic there. And we can live with your relatives until we get settled."

16

WILLIAM AND CHARLES WENT TO LIVE WITH THEIR Aunt Beatrice and Uncle George in a two-story house situated on one of those strange back streets inhabited mostly by Negroes in the heart of an all-white community. Their parents rented a room nearby and took their meals with the Coopers. The Coopers had a son, Freddie, a spoiled, fat, mama's boy.

Beatrice had never forgiven Mrs. Taylor for the manner in which she'd been treated when she came, as a girl, to live with the Taylors back at the college in Georgia.

The little house was always crowded and the air was charged with flaring tempers and the clash of personalities.

"You don't like black people but soon's you get down and out you come running to us."

"I married a black man who happens to be your brother."

"Yes, you just married him 'cause you thought he was gonna make you a great lady."

"I'll not discuss it."

"You're in no position to say what you'll discuss, sister. This is my house. I pay taxes on it."

"If Mr. Taylor hadn't spent all of his money sending you and your sister here from the South he'd have something of his own now."

"You dragged him down yourself, don't go blaming it on us. If you'd made him a good wife instead of always nagging at him, he'd be president of a college today."

"Mr. Taylor would never have been president of my foot. He hasn't got it in him."

"Then why did you marry him?"

"Only God knows. I certainly don't."

Mr. Cooper seemed unmoved by the seething dissension. He came in from work, a big man, six feet four, in dirty overalls, blue kerchief tied around his neck, old black hat down over his huge bald head, and sat before the gas grate in the living room waiting for his dinner.

"William, how are you today?" he called in his loud, husky voice that sounded as if his throat was clogged with phlegm.

"I'm fine, Uncle George."

"That's good, that's good."

"How are you, Uncle George?"

"I'm fine, William." He chuckled. "Jes' soon as I get a little food I'm gonna feel better." Then he looked about for Charles. "Charles, how are you today?"

"I'm fine, Uncle George. How are you, Uncle George?"

"I'm fine, Charles, I'm fine. Jes' a mite hungry."

Mrs. Cooper couldn't afford to feed him expensive foods. She cooked great quantities of rice and beef lungs. For dessert she made a deep sweet potato cobbler. The rice was gummy, the pie doughy and the lungs gristly. But it was all the same to Mr. Cooper. His wife served him on a turkey platter. He took a quart of rice and covered it with a half-gallon of lungs and juice, and then looked about the table, smiling at everyone, and from then on ate with silent concentration. The talk went on around him.

Each evening Charles reported dutifully to William how much their Uncle George had eaten, and they'd laugh uproariously in their small back room. Mrs. Cooper resented their laughing, and the close way they stuck together, excluding Freddie. She was always calling them to come downstairs. At every opportunity she set Charles to doing something.

"You haven't got any servants working for you."

"No, ma'm."

"An' you're big enough to help with some of this housework."

"Yes, ma'm."

She couldn't bear Charles. She felt that he was always laughing at her!

During the days William was away with his mother, visiting

the various doctors, Charles bore the brunt of his Aunt Bee's animosity.

"And don't you try to get Freddie to help you, either. He's just a little boy."

"Yes ma'm. He's a year younger than I am."

When Charles entered the neighborhood high school in January, the face of the outside world turned white. He walked down street after street of white residents, the icy blasts from Lake Erie biting into his bones, and was lost in a stream of white faces, rushing up the old stone steps. All of the faculty and all but seven of the pupils were white. He felt strange and out of place, as if he'd gone into another world, a world he'd scarcely ever thought of; and he reacted from emotions he'd never known he had. He felt an unconscious drawing back, a tightening up.

There, among the white pupils, the seven colored pupils noticed him immediately. Only one of them, a lovely girl with olive skin and long black curls, was in his class. But all of them had white friends and ran with white groups instead of with each other. They seemed antagonistic toward him, as if in some fashion he was intruding. Several times, as he passed one or the other in the corridors, he opened his mouth to speak. It was the custom of his upbringing to speak to other Negroes; it was taken for granted that all Negroes were neighbors. But they would look off as if they didn't see him, as if they were ashamed to be caught speaking to him. After that he never spoke to anyone unless spoken to first.

Unlike the other schools he'd attended, here there were many pupils as brilliant as himself, and who applied themselves more diligently. He couldn't coast along and count on being the smartest in the class. There was a freckled, redheaded girl, Martha, who took great pleasure in correcting his mistakes. He did his best to outdo her. But she'd just laugh at him and wait until he faltered.

"That's wrong, Miss Battles. Charles is wrong."

It infuriated him. He hated her. "What's wrong?" he'd challenge, glaring at her.

And laughingly she'd tell him. He wanted to slap her.

When the pupils were paired off in the chemistry laboratory she chose him as her teammate. He was so surprised and outraged he refused to work with her. After class she cried. He didn't know it. But he noticed she was different. She ignored him after that. He was hurt by her lack of interest. It worried him. He felt he'd done something wrong. But he didn't know exactly what.

He built up barriers against the pupils and when one crossed the barriers he was strangely outraged and disturbed. He wanted to reject them before they rejected him. But there was a shy, submerged part of him that wanted them as friends. And when they refused to recognize his rejection, and didn't make friends with him either, he was at a loss, he didn't know how to act. He went into a shell. There were too many of them and only one of him. He was glad when Sunday came and he could go to church.

Their father attended the Baptist church far downtown on Scovill Avenue. On Sundays the church folks had this street, but on weekdays it was inhabited mostly by prostitutes and thieves.

It was very cold in Cleveland that winter. Snow was banked high along the curbs where the plows had been along. Soot rained down from the huge steel mills in the nearby Cuyahoga River valley, turning everything black, the houses and the windows and the curtains and the snow.

Most of the congregation were southern migrants. There was something tragic about the black faces, ashy cold, crowded in the grim slum street fenced by the high banks of black snow, dressed in their dark Sunday best. They seemed so incongruous, so out of place, so lost, the pearl-gray hats and white cotton gloves spotted by the lumps of soot that floated in the air, crowding about the entrance of the black stone church that had been handed down by white people when they'd moved farther east. Charles always thought of the hot, rocking church of Mississippi, when he saw them standing there. Yet during the service they were warmed by the preacher's fiery words; their black faces became greasy with sweat, their white teeth gleamed and their eyes flashed with animation. The old, tired, lined faces lit up and glowed with ecstasy.

Mrs. Taylor attended the Presbyterian church, and sometimes

she visited the Episcopalian church where all the fair-skinned Negroes went. That was another thing her husband's people hated.

Both of Professor Taylor's sisters were short and dark and pressed their hair with straightening irons. Mrs. Hart was one of those women who, from lack of choice, take pride in being virtuous. But Mrs. Cooper yearned to be a fashionable lady. They knew that Mrs. Taylor could pass for white, and very often did. They bitterly resented her white complexion and were envious of her long, straight hair.

Had she been a weaker woman and acknowledged the humiliation of her position they would have liked her better. But she treated them as inferiors even though they had the upper hand. There was no getting along between them. After a time she began taking her meals where she roomed and seldom visited either of her sisters-in-law. Most of her time was spent in taking William to the doctors and looking for a house. The doctors offered little hope of William ever seeing. The corneas of both eyes had sustained permanent scar tissue that could never be removed. They advised her to wait and see what nature did. So William read his books in braille and spent hours writing exercises. All of his father's relatives liked him far the best.

The Harts had moved north, out in the Glenville district, and for quite some time had been the only colored family in that section. William went frequently to visit them. His Uncle Casper had been so long in the postal service he was thinking of retiring. Phillip William, their oldest boy, had been away from home for many years. Now Casper Junior had graduated from college and was teaching in a southern school. Only the daughter, Lucinda, was at home. After graduation she'd taught for several years, but had suffered a nervous breakdown. Mrs. Taylor said it had been brought on by her father's philandering. She hated her father, and hadn't spoken to him for years. But she and William were great pals. Charles seldom went to visit them. They felt that he was more on the Mannings' side than theirs. Lucinda never spoke to him. Charles thought that all of them were crazy.

Professor Taylor took his sister's part. The children were drawn into the feud against their wishes. Charles came to hate all his father's relatives and found it difficult to treat them civilly. Their Aunt Bee picked on him, venting on him her hatred for his mother. William always took his younger brother's part.

The Coopers owned an old enormous car, but they had never driven it. They had bought it and brought it home and it had sat there, in the back yard, rusting and rotting ever since. It was the third secondhand car they'd owned. They felt it necessary to their prestige to own a car. They'd never driven any of them. No one in the family could drive. The driveway was extraordinarily narrow, and where the porch extended, angled sharply. Charles wondered how they'd gotten the big car where it was without having taken down the porch. At times when his mother and aunt were fighting and making the house unbearable, he and William went out and sat on its cold, moldy seat.

Early that summer the Coopers sold this car for junk and bought a secondhand Willys-Knight.

"What, another!" Charles commented at dinner, thinking they would share the joke.

"Just for that you don't get any supper," Mrs. Cooper flared.

He gave her a startled look. "I didn't— Well, all right. I'll get something at the corner."

"Wait a minute," William said, rising from the table. "I'll go with you."

"Now, William, you don't have to go," their Uncle George put in. "Bee, let the boys eat their dinner."

"If your father was here I'd make him punish you," she said to Charles.

"For what?"

"Let's go," William said. "I don't want any dinner."

"You're just like your mother," Mrs. Cooper continued to rail at Charles. "Taking your blind brother away from his food."

"Now what brought that on?" William muttered.

The boys had sandwiches and sodas and went for a long walk. After a time they were able to laugh about it.

"Uncle George is just a fool," William said. "The way he lets Aunt Bee drive him. It was she who wanted the car."

"I don't see how they can buy all that junk. All those funny dresses she wears, and all those feathers in her hats. She must think God's going to call her someday and she's gotta be ready to fly."

William laughed. "Uncle George is all right. He's just dumb."

" 'William, how are you today?' " he mocked.

" 'I'm fine, Uncle George.' "

" 'Dass good. Dass good.' " They laughed.

One day while rummaging through the bureau drawers, William had found one of those gilt-lettered axioms that people hung on walls. By holding it close to his good eye he'd been able to read: A FOOL AND HIS MONEY ARE SOON PARTED.

When they were preparing for bed that night he got it out and said, "I'm going to put this on the mantle."

"Better not let Aunt Bee see it," Charles cautioned.

"I want her to see it. It'll do her good."

The next morning their mother called early for William. Charles was spreading the bed when his aunt came into the room. She saw the slogan on the mantel. Her face went ashy.

"You ought to be ashamed of yourself," she cried in the high, whining tone her voice took in the height of passion. "You ought to be ashamed of yourself! Calling me a fool! The way I've put up with you and fed you and given you a place to live."

Charles looked at her blankly as if he didn't understand. "What are you talking about?"

She stabbed her finger at the mantel. "That dirty, sneaking little thing you stuck up there." Rage had made her quite ugly.

"Oh, that's just something we found and thought—"

"Don't you dare try to put it on your brother," she screamed.

He became coldly defiant. "I put it there. I found it in the bureau drawer and put it there. It belongs to you. I didn't write it; I just found it. If you hadn't wanted it you—"

"Don't you dast give me none of your sass," she shouted. "I'll slap your face."

"What am I supposed to do, just stand here and let you say—"

"If you were my son I'd beat you within an inch of your life. Taking that sneaky way of insulting me. After all I've done for

178

you. You're just like your mother. You ought to be ashamed of yourself."

Watching the contortions of her face, he thought she resembled a black witch singing incantations. He suppressed an impulse to laugh. "I'll take it down, if that'll make you any happier," he said sarcastically.

"You get your things together and get out of my house," she raged. "The idea. I've put up with enough from you. I don't want to ever see you again."

"Yes, ma'm," he said.

Slowly he bundled his clothes and carried them up the street to the house where his parents lived. It required two trips. She watched him like a hawk as if afraid he might steal something. He wouldn't let himself think about it. He moved woodenly, his face blank. It was bad enough without thinking about it. Now there'd be an awful fuss.

His father came home at noon. Charles told him that Mrs. Cooper had put him out of her house.

A deep frown bit into his father's old, lined face. "Now what have you done, son?"

"It wasn't nothing—not much. I found an old saying on a piece of cardboard—it was in the drawer—and I just put it on the mantel."

"What was the saying, son?"

"It just said, 'A fool and his money are soon parted'."

Professor Taylor looked suddenly exhausted, as if he couldn't bear any more. For a moment, he floundered about, gesturing aimlessly. Then he put on his hat and went down to see his sister.

He was still there when Mrs. Taylor and William returned to the rooming house. Charles told her what had happened.

"Why, I put that there myself," William said. "Chuck didn't have anything to do with it."

"It doesn't make any difference," their mother said. "The idea, a grown woman taking insult from a little thing like that."

She went down the street and called to Mrs. Cooper from the sidewalk, "I want to talk to you, Mrs. Cooper, but I won't step foot in your filthy house."

Faces appeared in the curtains all down the street.

Mrs. Cooper charged onto the porch, brandishing a broom. "I'll fix you!" she screamed incoherently. "I'll fix you!"

Professor Taylor came running out behind and struggled to restrain her. They wrestled down the steps and to the sidewalk. His sister fought in a blinding rage to get at his wife. A neighbor called the police. Mrs. Taylor retreated across the street and continued to berate them both.

"The idea, a grown woman behaving like a maniac. And you're no better than she is, Mr. Taylor, I'll tell you that. Letting her persecute your own children."

The police squad car came while they were struggling. Mrs. Taylor turned and walked away and left them to explain. Later she returned and demanded that Mrs. Cooper bring William's belongings down to the street.

"I'll get even with you—you dirty, half-white bitch!" Mrs. Cooper screamed.

Another row was in the making. Professor Taylor quickly intervened and packed William's things himself. Mrs. Taylor waited on the sidewalk. He followed her like a whipped dog, his arms bulging with clothing. The neighbors snickered at the spectacle of the little dejected man trailing behind the grim, determined woman. It was more than just the humiliation. He felt hurt and betrayed by his sister's vengeful act. He could find no excuses for her.

That evening both of his sisters called on them and tried to draw his wife into another fuss. But Mrs. Taylor wouldn't see them. She locked herself in her room. They stood out in the hallway and called through the closed door.

"You may as well come on out and talk, sister," Mrs. Hart said, assuming the role of peacemaker.

"Let's get this settled once an' for all," Mrs. Cooper whined. "You ain't paid me yet for those boys' board."

Mrs. Taylor refused to answer. Now her husband had to take her part. She felt triumphant and vindicated.

The boys were given temporary lodging with their parents. Through the walls they could hear their parents' bitter bickering.

"I should have known better than to let my children ever live with that woman," Mrs. Taylor said.

"It's as much your fault as hers," Professor Taylor charged. "You've always been hostile toward my sisters. The boys wouldn't be so disrespectful if you hadn't encouraged them."

"Disrespectful indeed! How could anyone respect that woman?"

"Maybe she was wrong this time—but you can't excuse Charles either?"

"Charles has always been very courteous to her—more courteous than she deserved," his mother defended.

But inside she was deeply concerned for him. She knew he'd been lonely and unhappy since William's accident. He needed other companions, but it was so hard for him to make friends. She had hoped he would take up with the white children in his high school, but for some reason he didn't seem to like them. It was a bitter disappointment. She had been so pleased when he'd been assigned to a white school. Perhaps next term he would feel more at home. But that would have to work out by itself, she reflected. The problem was what to do now.

Before going to sleep she decided to separate her sons. School would be opening soon, and until they had a home of their own again she would board them out. It would be hard on both of them for a time. But they were old enough now to be apart. Charles had celebrated his sixteenth birthday the past month. It was time he was on his own. In the end it would be the best thing for both of them. Charles would never learn how to live with other people as long as William was about. He felt too protective toward his brother. Of the two, William was far the better off in this respect, she had long since realized. Perhaps his being blind had something to do with it. He could mix with people and make friends, whereas Charles was always self-conscious and aloof.

Through her minister she found a home for Charles on Cedar Avenue. Mrs. Robinson was a colored woman married to a white man and they had a cultured, well-mannered son who was going to college. She thought Gregory would have a wonderful influence on Charles.

William was placed with the Douglas family by the Foundation for the Blind. The Douglas's lived on a quiet residential street and had a son William's age. Both parents went with William when he moved. Charles carried his brother's valise. It gave him a funny sensation to see William in a strange separate room. He had an empty feeling at the pit of his stomach as when he was suddenly frightened. It was something like he felt when Will and his mother boarded the train that took them to St. Louis. Only this time there was no reason to be afraid. He couldn't understand it.

"So long, Chuck," William said cheerfully. "Don't take any wooden nickels."

"Not if I can s— help it." He still couldn't say *see* around his brother.

"Be a good boy and don't give Mrs. Douglas any trouble," he heard his mother say. It was as if he were reliving a forgotten dream, the hurt of the dream coming back in strange cadence. He ran down the steps and out of the house and walked down the street bordered by trees. Overhead the dusty leaves of summer's end whispered in the slight hot breeze. A housewife sweeping her front porch stopped to watch him pass. A dog ran out from another house and barked at him. He felt himself crying quietly inside.

17

CEDAR AVENUE WAS THE MAIN THOROUGHFARE OF the East Side colored section. Streetcar tracks ran down the brick pavement toward the Public Square and Negro businesses fronted on the broken sidewalks. All day long people passed up and down, shouting and laughing, and the noisy streetcars rumbled by, rattling the window panes in the weather-beaten houses.

Mrs. Robinson lived in a pleasant frame house in a residential block. Her husband had been a dining car waiter. Through him she'd met Mr. Sutton, the white steward of his car. For years before her husband's death she'd carried on a love affair with Mr. Sutton. Now she was his mistress and he supported her. Three nights each week his run put him in Cleveland, and he lived openly in her house. Everyone assumed that he was her husband and he was known as Mr. Robinson.

Mrs. Taylor was secretly impressed by Mrs. Robinson's white husband. She wanted Mrs. Robinson to realize that she was almost white, herself. The day she took Charles there to live she stopped on her way out and told Mrs. Robinson all about the white members of the Manning family—the grandfather who was a senator and the one who was the son of a president and the grandmother who was the daughter of an English nobleman.

Mrs. Robinson was a big-boned handsome woman in her early forties. She had a light tan complexion with a scattering of freckles, and wore her hair in a boyish bob with a bang across her forehead. As with many Negroes of her complexion, she was awed by the tiny lady with her superior manners and famous white forebears, and she became very attentive to Mrs. Taylor's son.

When Charles came down from putting away his clothes, she said in her soft, caressing voice, "Just make yourself at home, honey. Ask for anything you want. Greg will be home soon and you two can get acquainted."

Her warm nature and heavily scented femininity affected Charles like a subtle aphrodisiac. He felt a sickness in his stomach and the warmth grow in his groins as he forced a shamefaced smile. He couldn't stay in her presence without having an erection. It shamed him and he was afraid she might discover it.

"I'm going to take a walk. I'll be back in time for dinner," he mumbled, going out.

Mr. Sutton was home for dinner that night. Gregory referred to him as his stepfather and called him "Dad." Although he knew that Mr. Sutton had a family in Chicago, he never admitted it. He was inordinately proud of having a white stepfather. Mr. Sutton treated him as a son; they had a wonderful relationship. The fine-looking, elderly white man took the Negro youth to the best

183

stores and dressed him in excellent taste. At first the clerks were shocked to hear the boy address the man as Dad. But they soon got used to it.

With young men his own age, Greg was insufferable. He was a husky young man with an enormous head which he considered leonine, and he wore his kinky red hair in a sort of lion's mane. Although his complexion was tan, he had the thick, flat features of his father, a squat, black man who'd been fifty when Greg was born. Greg had a strange look of age. His huge, heavy features sagged like those of a man of forty who had dissipated greatly in his youth. Secretly he was proud of his appearance. He thought he looked blasé and sophisticated.

When he discovered his mother had taken a boarder, he was instantly resentful. "Why do you have to go and take a stranger in the house?" he said angrily at dinner.

"Son, I'm surprised at you," Mr. Sutton chided. "Now apologize to Charles."

"Oh, that's all right," Charles muttered, so choked he could scarcely speak.

But Mrs. Robinson made her son apologize. Afterwards everyone was uncomfortable.

For the first few days Charles was tight and lonely and missed his brother more than ever. Mr. Sutton was very kind to the lad. But Greg treated him with studied condescension.

Greg was taking courses in Cleveland College and working lunches as a bus boy at the Union Club. He played the piano and had a fair talent for pencil sketching. They had a very cozy parlor and his friends were always calling. Girls found him interesting, although his charm was lessened by his affectations. He seemed to delight in making Charles miserable.

Mrs. Robinson noticed the lad's painful self-consciousness and tried to put him at ease. What he needed was a girl, she thought.

"Chuck, why don't you bring your girl here to the house," she suggested one day at dinner. "You can entertain her in the parlor; play the phonograph, I don't mind. Does she play the piano?"

"I don't have a girl," he stammered, blushing painfully.

"Don't have a girl? With eyes like those. Shame on you! You shouldn't be so mean to all the little girls."

"He's just a kid, Mother," Greg said irritably. He was intensely jealous of his mother. Whenever she showed Charles the least affection he squirmed with anxiety. "He's not even dry behind the ears. He doesn't even know what it's all about."

"Now tell the truth, honey," Mrs. Robinson persisted. "Don't be so shamefaced. Haven't you ever had a girl?"

Charles writhed in an agony of shame. "No, I—I just never thought about it."

"Never thought about it! What's happening to these little girls in Cleveland. When I was your age I would have thought about it for you."

Greg was furious with his mother. "Let him alone!" he shouted. "Can't you see he's scared of girls?"

"We'll have to do something about that," she said tenderly, ignoring her son's outburst. "You need a girl. Imagine a lovely boy your age who's never had a girl." She turned to her son. "Darling, can't you find Chuck a nice little girl to go with?"

"I don't know any girls who'd even look at him," Greg said hurtingly.

"I don't want a girl," Charles cried. He wished they'd let him alone.

"Sure you want a girl," Mrs. Robinson declared. "Maybe you don't know it but you do." She turned to her son again. "Susie Dean would be just the girl for him."

"Susie Dean!" he sneered. "Why don't you just give him two dollars and let him get his ashes hauled."

"Now, darling, don't be jealous," she chided, unperturbed. "You introduce him to some of your girls then. I'm sure they won't agree with you."

Despite his mother's insistence, Greg refused to introduce Charles to any of the girls who called. But after school began he introduced him to some of the young men who dropped around. For the first time in his life Charles had the opportunity to enjoy normal friendships. But he thought the fellows so poised and

185

sophisticated, he became shy and inarticulate. Whenever forced to speak, he blurted out the first thing that came to mind. The fellows thought him quite witty.

"Chuck's a sly boy," Curly Wright observed. "Tell us about your girls back in St. Louis, Chuck."

"Aw, I didn't have any girls," he replied, trying to keep from blushing. "I just played the field."

Greg gave him a contemptuous look. "Played the field all right," he said sarcastically. "You don't even know what pussy's like."

"Hell, you don't have to have a girl to get that," Charles protested weakly.

It was a signal for the boys to brag of their sexual prowess. There was one tall, handsome lad less extravagant than the others. They called him "The Great Profile" and accused him of holding out on them. But Harvard smiled deprecatingly and said, "It's not that. I just don't find them easy as you guys."

"They're tryna marry you, son," Roy Williams pointed out.

Charles admired Harvard Eaton tremendously. He thought him best looking and most gracious of the bunch. Harvard was always saying something nice to him.

Although most of the young men were high school seniors as himself, he felt so much younger and immature. They attended high schools in the colored neighborhoods and had enjoyed greater social activity. And Greg always kept referring to his youth.

"Shhh, the tadpole's listening," he said once when the talk turned to a girl. "Little pitchers have big ears. You'll be wondering how it got around."

"I won't tell," Charles promised stoutly.

The others took up for him. "Lay off Chuck, Greg. What's he done to you. You scared Marie might fall for him."

"Pshaw, Marie rob the cradle," he said contemptuously.

"She hasn't stooped to that yet, eh?" Bert said slyly.

The others laughed. Marie King was the old date-horse. She was older than most of these young men. Although Greg thought she liked him best, she'd dated all of them at various times.

186

Many evenings the boys and girls got together in the Robinson's parlor. Greg played the catchy tunes popular with their set. The couples whirled gaily about the floor, their feet flying through the intricate patterns of the *Charleston*.

Charleston . . . Charleston . . .

They chanted and panted, their eyes flashing, bodies bouncing . . .

Charleston . . . Charleston . . .

It was an age of daring and sophistication. The young men sought to be blasé, the young women bold and forward. Monkeyback coats and bell-bottom trousers had gone into oblivion; sloppy coats and baggy pants were all the rage. And the girls wore skirts above their knees and stockings rolled below; they clipped their hair in page-boy bobs and wore bangs down to their eyes.

A great motion picture lover of the time, possessed of slumbrous eyes and sleek black hair, had set the pattern for manly beauty in a melodrama of love and passion called *The Shiek*. The young men slicked their hair with greasy pomades and wore tightly knotted skull caps day and night to keep it pressed in place. About the ears and the base of the skull where the hair was left exposed it remained kinky and thick with grease, but the top glistened with gleaming waves. This was called the "pomp," short for pompadour, because of its similarity to the coiffure worn by the Marquise de Pompadour. And when their pomps were mussed, they became unreasonably furious and quite often fought the one who mussed it.

They discussed clothes with a passion, and preened themselves for hours before the mirrors, practising sultry looks from lowered lids. They walked about with burning eyes, seeming half-asleep, and approached their girls with slow, sinuous steps, as if to steal upon them.

Occasionally the boys brought a flask of bathtub gin to animate the party. From his room above, Charles could hear them laughing and screaming in frenzied glee.

Unless the fellows asked for him, Greg never called him down when girls were present. And then all through the evening he made disparaging remarks.

"Little Charley can't dance; he's got two left feet," he jeered as Charles sat mute and sweating between two willing girls.

They looked at him askance. "Come on, baby, let mother show you how," Susie cooed.

Mutely he stood and put his arm about her waist and tried to follow through the intricate steps. But he was wooden with self-consciousness; his legs like rusty rigid joints.

Susie stopped. "Relax, baby. You'll never learn."

"I—I—let's try it later on," he stammered, flaming painfully.

"Oh—" But she was relieved to let him go, and found an older man.

He tried to get the girls alone. Away from the others he could talk to one girl at a time. He sang a rapid monologue to keep his courage up, and the girls thought he had a sly, sweet line.

"Your eyes are like rare wine," he told Marie as they sat swinging on the porch. "Your lips burn like eternal fire; I'd like to quench them with my kisses. Your throat is a pillar of gold, brushed by the lips of men who worship at your feet. Your breasts are softly distant mountain peaks at dusk; between them flows the dark disturbing river down to the mysterious sea."

She was entranced. "You're sweet," she said, her arm stealing about his neck as she leaned forward in the dark and kissed him wetly. Then she heard Greg call and jumped from the swing and ran inside. That was as far as he ever got. With one girl in the dark he was exciting as long as he could think up words and fire them breathlessly, no matter what they meant. Quite often he was shocking.

"I could kiss you like the sea lapping at a virgin cave," he said to Susie Dean once, finding her alone in the kitchen.

"You could?" she whispered throatily. She had no idea what he meant; it was her own interpretation that set her panting.

188

"I'll make you tremble in delirium and cry sweet ecstatic sounds." He was blushing furiously, his voice breathless from the effort of trying to make a hit.

"You lover," she panted. "Feel here."

He felt her breasts.

"Oh shit!" she cried. "Let's go down and put some coal on the fire."

"But there isn't any fire in the furnace," he said uncomprehendingly.

Furiously she jerked away. "You're just a teaser."

There was always this point beyond which he couldn't go. He didn't recognize the moment when it came and didn't know the words to get him over. So many times only a gentle push was needed. But he didn't dream this thing was ever quite that easy. He always got bogged down in a ritual he thought surely was demanded. In his dreams, virtue sat so high on pristine pedestals; gallant swordsmen dueled to the death to kiss a woman's hand. He envied the poised attitudes and glib flattery of the older fellows. He never knew his breathless, incoherent rhapsody brought him closer to actual conquest than most of them had ever got.

Greg made him think the girls just tolerated him. He didn't dare ask one to be his girl, or even for a date to see a picture show. He only saw them at some impromptu party or gathering where the fellows took him. And then his time was occupied by the younger sisters and the unattractive ones. At first they thought him bashful. But once alone with him they changed their minds. He was after the real thing, they thought. He didn't like to play, but Oh Boy, he was really frantic for it.

Often Charles went down to the tennis courts at the neighborhood YMCA hoping to meet a girl. But the players were always paired, the games dated in advance. He wound up on the other field playing rough and tumble football with a gang of ruffians commanded by a young hoodlum called Wop who smoked marijuana and played a remarkable game at quarterback. Charles always played opposite him. They made a great attraction and crowds gathered along the fence. But Wop was too much even for Charles. He tried to get Charles to smoke marijuana and drink whiskey and once suggested that they cut school and steal a car.

"When we get through riding we can sell it," Wop said. "I know a fence that'll give us fifty bucks for anything we bring in. All they do is strip it."

"Suppose we're caught?"

"How you gonna be caught? You gonna be with Wop."

Charles shook his head.

"If you skeered, go home," Wop sneered. He was no older than Charles but was already notorious throughout the city. "*If you skeered, go home.*" He had everybody saying it, even good little boys and girls who'd only heard of him.

Charles didn't envy Wop. He wanted to cut a figure among a different group. If he could just dance like the boy who was winning all the Charleston contests.

On the top floor of the Y was a basketball court that doubled for dances on weekends. Charles went to several of the dances but it was no fun drinking lemonade and eating cake alone. Everywhere he turned was the gimlet eye of some chaperone. He couldn't even smoke and pretend to be indifferent. He sat in the window and watched the couples cavort about the floor.

Charleston . . . Charleston . . .

Envy cut him to the quick. He wondered how they did it; how they came by such natural sense of rhythm. He didn't have it, couldn't learn it, although he was blessed with remarkable co-ordination.

He left the Y and walked out Cedar Avenue past houses with drawn shades and loud laughter from within, where he was certain women could be bought. He stopped at one and went up to the door.

"Er, does Miss er-er Robinson live here?" he asked the red-eyed black man who cracked the door in response to his timid knocking , giving the first name that come to mind.

"Who? Who dat?" The voice was thick with rotgut and suspicion.

"Er, Miss Robinson. She's a nice-looking, light lady with a gold tooth."

"Ah'll see." The red eyes disappeared and the door closed in his face. From behind it he could hear the whiskey-thickened voice. "Mama D! Yay, Mama D! You got an' who' 'round heah call Roberson?"

"Ah'll see," came a high, soft, whining bedroom voice.

The door cracked and the heavily made-up face of a light tan woman popped suddenly in the opening. Glazed muddy eyes looked Charles up and down. "Who you wanna see, baby?"

"Er-er, a Miss Robinson."

"Ah's Miz Roberson, baby. Cum on in."

"Oh!" His nerve deserted him. He didn't want this painted, staring mass of sinister, effluvious flesh. "Another Miss Robinson."

"Git de hell 'way frum heah you li'l bastard!" the voice said harshly; the door slammed in his face.

Frightened and chagrined, he fled down the street and crept to bed. But he couldn't sleep for thinking about girls. He didn't know why he was so unpopular. It disturbed him. He felt that he was growing unattractive. And he wanted so desperately to fit himself into this fascinating life. He wanted girls to admire him and desire his company. He couldn't bear to go unnoticed.

He asked Harvard Eaton what he used to make his pomp so much more attractive than the others. Harvard said he used a combination of cosmetic and vaseline. Charles bought a stick of black cosmetic and applied it to his hair. The result was a fine patent leather shine.

That Sunday afternoon he went visiting with the fellows. It was a warm fall day, very pleasant. It affected him with a poignant melancholy he didn't understand. The small cosy parlor was crowded. Tea was served and young men moped about with narrowed eyes like a strange assortment of sinister sheiks. Their heads glistened like lacquered gourds. The girls sat with their skirts above their knees and their legs tightly pressed together. Their bangs were like pretty painted fans above their flashing eyes and animated faces.

"Where have you been all my life?" the male talk ran.

"What'll I do when you are far from me and I am blue?" the girls countered coyly.

Conversation was marked by self-conscious pauses. Sudden silences caught the entire group. Then chatter burst out to cover their embarrassment. The young men bantered with each other when they could think of nothing else to say. The girls gossiped among themselves. For the moment the gathering was divided into two camps, male on one side, female on the other, each seemingly striving to ignore the other. Then with a concerted shifting about they rushed together again.

"Remember the night, the night you said 'I love you,'" the young man said to his new companion.

"Remember you promised that you'd forget me not, then you forgot to remember," she replied.

Their conversation was made up from quotations from the lyrics of popular songs; without these they couldn't converse. Cleo sat at the piano. Together they sang:

> *Though my dreams are in vain*
> *My love will remain*
> *Strolling again, Memory Lane,*
> *With you.*

From that they went to the rhythmic chant:

> *C'llegiate . . . c'llegiate*
> *Yes! We are collegiate . . .*

The mood passed quickly from frenzied jazz to syrupy sentiment. A famous ballad singer with his guitar and sweet, caressing voice had set the nation crying in its cups. It went with bathtub gin and adolescence.

> *Through the smoke and flame*
> *I gotta go where you are . . .*

Charles kept choked up, on the brim of tears. He didn't know what was wrong with him. The exigencies of social life filled him with apprehensions.

It was a lovely party. But the room grew hot and sticky. The cosmetic with which he'd plastered down his hair melted and began to run. Black streaks coursed down his neck and left black blobs on his fresh white collar.

"Turn around," Harvard said. "What's that on your neck."

"On my neck?" He dabbed at it with a white handkerchief. It came off black.

"Little Charley's hair is running," Greg said heartlessly.

The girls giggled. Charles felt the flame burning in his face. He could have gone through the floor.

"What'd you use, shoe polish?" Greg teased mercilessly.

Harvard took him to the bathroom and cleaned off some of the mess.

"I don't know what happened," Charles said. "I mixed the cosmetic with vaseline just like you said."

"Oh!" A light dawned. "You used black cosmetic. That isn't the kind. I use white cosmetic. It doesn't run."

Charles couldn't meet the others' eyes when he came downstairs.

"Don't let it get you down, baby," Thelma consoled. "These other sheiks have accidents with their pomps too."

But the pleasure and excitement had been destroyed for him. At such times he felt peculiarly cursed with misfortune. A twist of circumstance and suddenly he became the ugly duckling. More than all others he yearned to cut a dashing figure. But when the occasion called for pretty speeches he was inarticulate. While others danced he stood apart on two left feet. His bow ties came askew, his hair grease ran; he couldn't understand just why he exasperated all the pretty girls. He felt a lack of something within himself.

18

THAT FALL, ONCE AGAIN, CHARLES OCCUPIED HIS
mother's thoughts. She reflected how strange it was that he took
precedence in her emotions over her other sons. It was as if the
umbilical cord still held them joined together. Even at the height
of William's need, and during that poignant time when all her
soul had gone to holding Tom, it had never been really severed.
And now again it throbbed with blood and worry as she pon-
dered on the problems of his adolescence. He was so impression-
able, so easily hurt, she knew. And he found it so hard to adjust
to any change.

She knew that he wasn't getting along too well in school, that
he hadn't made any friends among the pupils. She wondered if
their being white exercised some vague restraint, but she could
never bring herself to ask. She visited him often and was pleased
to note that he showed interest in the colored youths. She'd been
so afraid he'd grow moody and introspective away from William.
He seldom talked about the things he did, but Mrs. Robinson
kept her informed. From the beginning, Mrs. Robinson had been
exceedingly impressed by Mrs. Taylor's white blood. It was as if,
by having such illustrious white forebears, Mrs. Taylor had
accomplished so much more than herself. Mrs. Taylor realized
this and acted quite superior. Mrs. Robinson wasn't resentful in
the least; she would have been disappointed had Mrs. Taylor
acted otherwise. She was obsequious in Mrs. Taylor's presence
and very attentive toward her son. Mrs. Taylor was appreciative
and quite relieved that Charles had gotten away from the influence of the Coopers. But yet she knew he needed most of all
a home.

For a time she tried to get him to take piano lessons. Failing in
this, she bought tickets to the symphony concerts and made him
accompany her. With all her heart she wanted him to become

cultured and learn to love the fine things in life. But he didn't like the concerts. The next time she bought tickets he wouldn't go.

"But why, son?" she asked.

"I just don't like them."

"You don't have to like them," she said. "It's like eating olives —you must cultivate a taste for them."

His dislike for the refined and aesthetic offerings of city life was a source of constant disappointment. She attributed it to his father's blood.

It was curious, she thought, how, of the two, William, with his handicap, was so much better able to adjust to circumstances and so much more receptive to good influences. He seemed to be getting along splendidly and scarcely ever gave her cause for worry. The young man, Ramsey Douglas, with whom he lived, had become his most devoted friend. Although no academic schools were provided for the blind, the state paid for readers, thus enabling blind children to enroll in the public schools. Ramsey spent hours reading to William from all his textbooks in preparation for his entering school.

Practically overnight he'd grown into a charming young man, quite different from his younger brother. He was poised in social contacts and talked with ease. No furtive compulsions harassed him in his associations with young women. He was gay and witty and quite frankly liked them all. They found him a wonderful companion, and he'd learned to dance excellently in the short time he'd been away from home. There was always a girl eager to go with him to dancing parties.

The brothers ran in different circles and seldom met. But whenever William mentioned some happy occasion he'd experienced, Charles felt compelled to boast of his own great successes. Secretly he was awed by his brother's adjustment to the grown-up world. It was so hard for him to fit with ease at any level. It seemed as if there just was no place for him, like the day he went out for football practice.

He'd donned a castoff uniform with the others in the locker room. Along with the more intrepid ones, he'd run the three miles to the field where drills were held, only to learn that the varsity lineup was already drawn. He lit a cigaret to prove he didn't care and the coach put him off the field. He didn't go to any of the games.

There was a great deal of extracurricular activity among his classmates that fall. They had undergone a subtle change. They were seniors now, and dignity had been added. Class officers were elected, committees appointed; plans were being drawn for the senior prom. Fierce competition had developed among the honor students. Charles kept aloof, he took no part in anything. He'd never caught the spirit of the school.

His teachers were nice but uninterested. He could have been an A student with but a little effort, but he wasn't particular. His teachers gave him B in everything but Latin. He'd never cared for Latin—only for the stories translated into English—and had just managed to pass in Caesar the year before. Now in Cicero he was failing. Several times his teacher kept him after school.

"I'd hate to see you fail to graduate, Charles," she said. "If you will just make a little effort. I know you don't like Latin and I hope that some day the school system will make it an elective course. But now it is required. And you must pass to graduate."

"I'll give it more time, Miss Parker," he promised. "I'll concentrate on it." He didn't, but she became lenient because she thought he tried.

Again the sense of futility took hold of him. Nothing seemed worthwhile. He wanted so desperately to be important, to stand out; if not that, at least to belong to something. It was mainly because of that, because he had to be different, to be seen, that he accepted his Aunt Bee's offer to drive their car, although he knew his mother wouldn't like it.

His aunt had asked him to drive for them in a funeral procession. She'd gotten his father's consent. And she seemed trying to atone for putting him out of her house. He didn't like her any better. But he loved to drive. Sitting behind the wheel of the big old secondhand car, following the somber procession through the gray afternoon, the black-clad Coopers sitting silently in the back seat, under his control, dependent on him, he felt big and important again. His aur t was so pleased she invited him to dinner and asked him all sorts of questions about his mother. It was pleasant to be the center of attention.

He drove them often after that, without his mother's knowledge. One day he took the car for servicing and stopped in front of the Robinsons' to rush importantly through the house. Greg appeared not to notice but Mrs. Robinson was curious.

"Is that your folks' car, Chuck?"

"No, it's my aunt's. But I can drive it whenever I want," he added proudly.

"Greg, did you see Chuck's car?"

"It's just a struggle-buggy, mother," he replied indifferently, and then to Charles, "Tadpole, how about sitting for me now." He was doing a sketch of Charles sitting at the piano. It was quite unflattering and Charles knew he made it so deliberately.

"I haven't time now," he called, dashing out.

He drove off fast, passing other cars along the way, and waved to a girl he saw across the street. For an instant she couldn't place him, then waved excitedly after he had passed. He was laughing exultantly when, looking ahead, he saw a boy on a bicycle cut across his path. The boy licked an ice cream cone and looked off in the opposite direction.

Charles stabbed for the brake. His foot slipped off the narrow strip of shiny metal. He stabbed again, experiencing the sinking sensation of slipping on a banana peeling. In front the boy and bicycle seemed suspended in mid-motion, the picture rushing forward in growing horror. He wrenched the steering wheel to his right, hoping to pass behind the boy. But even as he did so he knew he'd never make it. With the quick reflexes of a healthy youth, he gave a mighty wrench to his left. The car struck the front wheel of the bicycle, unseating the boy who'd never stopped licking his ice cream cone, never looked, now sprawled spread-eagle on the pavement, the car rushing on as if by some evil momentum, Charles's glance striking on ahead; and then into his vision came the sight of jam-packed men and women, waiting for an approaching streetcar, directly in front of him. Somewhere the horror stopped and never came alive.

197

The car struck them frontally, knocking them down in a mass of kicking legs and flailing arms, crashed broadside into the connecting wall between the corner drugstore and adjoining meat market, shattering the plate glass windows of both, caromed back across the sidewalk. Down the hood Charles saw a short squat man, who'd been hit before, struggling to his knees as the car struck him again, passed over him, crashed into another car parked at the curb. And out of all the incipient tragedy, this single grotesquerie became implanted in his mind, and laughter ripped from him. He couldn't stop it. Funniest thing he ever saw. He didn't hear the screaming.

The door of the car was flung abruptly open. A butcher jerked him to the street, brandishing a bloody cleaver. He looked up into the hard white face, saw the brutal mouth, merciless gray eyes, and felt his consciousness leaving. He tried to hang on to himself, vaguely aware of a violent scuffle taking place as if he had no part in it. When the picture came again he was closed in by a group of colored men. Now he heard the sobbing of the wounded, strident voices raised in anger, the distant crying of the sirens. As far as he could see in all directions was a mass of jabbering people.

The police cars came, pushing through the mob, lining up beside the accident end to end, seven in a row. Charles was taken by two officers in gold braid and placed in a long, black limousine. He sat there with the police driver and watched remotely all that was taking place. There was no order in his mind, the pictures wouldn't register; the persons lying sobbing on the pavement had no relationship to tragedy. Only the eyes were felt, the countless staring eyes, shifting to the victims, to the policemen, back to himself. He looked at his hands. The eyes disappeared. His hands were steady.

The two officials came and sat flanking him, and they drove away.

"Damnedest thing I ever saw," one remarked. "Your car hardly got a scratch. Not even a window cracked."

"All four tires went flat," Charles said. The sound of his own voice startled him. He was astonished by the observation. Both of them glanced curiously at him.

He was questioned at great length at the police station and officers were sent to bring down his parents and the Coopers. At first he thought he couldn't tell them anything. But as he talked the entire picture came alive with startling clarity. He was amazed by his ability to recount in detail sidelights of the accident he had no recollection of having seen.

Over and over he heard himself saying, "The brake pedal was just like grease. Every time I hit it my foot slipped off. The car just wouldn't stop."

Afterwards he was placed in a waiting room. He felt as if it was all a dream. The actual tragedy hadn't gotten him. His mind contained the photographic pictures of the accumulated grotesquerie, but no connection had been made with the resulting pain and awful hurt and terrible consequences. The victims were recalled as adagio dancers executing comic pantomime. Much of it still affected him as funny. The sheer ludicrousness of the poor guy getting knocked down twice. Little sniffs of laughter kept blowing through his nose. There was something monstrous, inhuman, in his mental rejection of the horror. It was as if the dream was known to be a dream, the horror but the artificiality of the dream.

The Coopers were the first to come, he in his work clothes and she with rings of dried soap suds about her wrists, their faces gray with terror. They were taken for interrogation before being permitted to speak to him. Then his mother and father arrived. Her bloodless face was etched with apprehension, her body braced rigidly against the surge of panic. His father was a study in alarm. When he told them what had happened, his mother turned against his father with incontrollable fury.

"You contemptible sneak. God curse the day you ever became the father of my children. After all that woman has done to him you let her make a lackey out of him."

His father wilted. The Coopers came out gray and shaken. Mrs. Taylor didn't speak to them. Mr. Cooper wandered about in a daze. Professor and Mrs. Taylor were questioned briefly. Mrs. Taylor demanded that they prosecute her husband for permitting his son, a minor, to drive. The police officials were confused. Then the Harts arrived. The room seemed overly crowded.

"What have you done to us?" Mrs. Cooper lashed at Charles condemningly. "What have you done to us?"

His mother turned on her in a white rage. "Don't you speak to him. You black evil woman. Don't you dare speak to him. The way you've treated him. You're the one who should be prosecuted."

"He should have gone where I sent him," Mrs. Cooper screamed. "If he wasn't so hardheaded we wouldn't be in this trouble."

"Now, Bee. Now, sister," Mr. Cooper muttered. "We're all in this together."

"My son is not in it," Mrs. Taylor raved. "My son is just a victim."

"Now, honey, I've called a lawyer," Professor Taylor interjected. "Let's just wait until he comes."

"We don't know who's dead," Mrs. Cooper wailed. "We don't know who's dead."

"You black devil," Mrs. Taylor screamed. Clutching Charles's arm she fled into the corridor.

She sensed that as yet the horror had not affected him. She wanted to keep him in that state of mind. She was afraid for him to experience the full impact of the tragedy. Not then, not all at once. She feared a shock; perhaps his mind would become unbalanced. There was no telling how it might affect him. He was inclined toward morbid introspection anyway. And his capacities for good and evil were so delicately balanced. She feared that this might be the very thing to send him off unless she shielded him from all the terrible consequences. They had no right to do this thing to him, she thought. She wanted to protect him at any cost.

Professor Taylor followed them. He realized her purpose and thought that it was wrong. He felt that Charles should realize the consequences of his actions, and suffer in whatever way God saw to punish him. No matter who was right and who was wrong, his son had been the one who drove the car, and he should be the one to face it, he thought.

"Honey, you can't do this," he argued. "The boy must know what he's done."

But she stood between them, shielding Charles with her body as well as with her soul. "Don't you dare come out here and accuse my son of any wrong," she cried. "You're the one to blame. You had no right to let him drive that woman's car. God is going to punish you as surely as I'm standing here for the way you've let your relatives abuse and mistreat your son."

He couldn't stand up to her.

Finally the attorney arrived and Charles was released in the custody of his parents. The hearing was set for the following day. His mother ordered a taxicab to take them home. They passed the scene of the accident. Charles noticed that the car was gone and the shattered glass removed. He looked curiously at the spot where the injured had fallen. And still it didn't register; his mind would not accept the pain and horror.

His mother shielded him from all discussion of the accident. She took him out to dinner and remained with him until bedtime. He dreamed as he'd always done, but only of the usual fantasies that made sleeping such a pleasure. It didn't touch him even in his sleep.

He sat between his parents at the hearing. He felt like a spectator. He'd been charged with reckless driving. When it came his turn to testify, he spoke in a clear, untroubled voice. His father was shocked by his detachment. The court was puzzled. Afterwards policemen testified in his behalf—the boy on the bicycle had ridden thoughtlessly across his path; he had turned to avoid running over him, and the faulty brake mechanism had failed to stop the car. Two of the persons were severely injured, two others were temporarily hospitalized, and the remainder had received superficial bruises. Charles listened to the proceedings in a state of mild amazement, as if they were discussing someone other than himself.

The court reprimanded him for driving without a license and prohibited him from driving again. He was released. There was an action against the Coopers, but he didn't know of it.

His mother took him away immediately. They went to see a motion picture. Afterwards they lunched in a pleasant cafe. They talked of happy things and once he made her laugh. The accident had drawn them closer than they'd been in years. He talked bravely of all the great things he hoped to do. She felt again the intense love she'd always held for him. He was her baby, her beautiful, brilliant baby. And now they'd been through one more crisis and she prayed it was the last. Soon they'd have a house, she promised. And then things would be better again. She promised herself to give him more attention. She'd neglected him dreadfully, but she'd make it up to him.

It hadn't touched him. Secretly he was glad it had happened. After all, no one had died. And it freed him from the curse of anonymity. Already it had acquired the quality of adventure. People he'd never seen before spoke to him by name.

"How'd you make out, Chuck?"

"Oh, I beat it," he answered proudly.

They looked at him curiously, wondering whom he knew, what sort of importance his folks had. "You're lucky, kid."

Now girls seemed thrilled to meet him. Their eyes widened coyly and they ruffled their tails like pullets. "Oh, you're the man who was in that accident."

"Aw, it wasn't serious. Just a great to-do about nothing."

"You should have seen all the people standing 'round. Must have been thousands of them. I don't know where they all came from."

"I saw 'em. You know, people can smell an accident."

"Weren't you scared?"

"Scared? What for? I was just sorry for the people I ran over."

"When that man had that meat cleaver? Mr. Johnson took it away from him. Weren't you scared he was gonna chop you in the head?"

"Naw, he was only bluffing."

"No, he wasn't bluffing, either. The white people were going to lynch you if the colored people hadn't stopped them."

"Lynch me!" He was shocked. But it was a pleasant kind of shock since the danger had passed. It added to the mystery that surrounded him.

Afterwards he'd say. "You know, for a moment, I thought those white guys were going to lynch me. They might have tried at that if there hadn't been so many colored people there."

Mrs. Robinson was very tender with him after that, and even Greg and the gang seemed awed by his experience.

He never knew that the Coopers had been fined, that they'd lost their home and all their life's savings to settle the damages of the injured. His mother kept it from him. Even William knew, but she wouldn't let him tell. Why should he have to know and suffer guilt all his life for what was done to him, she reasoned. His father felt differently. The boy should know; it would teach him to be more careful in the future. But he hadn't the courage to defy his wife. He was doing no better in Cleveland than he had in St. Louis, still working at odd jobs of carpentry to make ends meet. She'd gotten the upper hand. She dominated him by nagging and disparagement. He couldn't stand up to it any longer. To fight back had become depletive. It was easier to let her have her way.

Although they had no legal claim, the Coopers held them morally responsible for half the damages. Professor Taylor felt obligated to pay his share. But the money they'd received from the sale of their property in St. Louis was deposited in Mrs. Taylor's name. She refused to share one cent. Instead she bought a house. Professor Taylor's people never forgave her.

But she felt that she had saved her son from some dreadful kind of horror.

19

IT WAS A SEVEN-ROOM FRAME HOUSE OUT IN THE northeast residential section, across from the high school, and they were the only colored family. Its location in a white neighborhood gave them the prestige of suburbanites. Their colored friends were proud to know someone who lived so far away.

Mrs. Taylor loved the hard, waxed floors and gleaming banisters and flower plots out back. She sent to St. Louis for her furniture and everything was polished to a turn. Their first Sunday they celebrated as a family reunion. For his contribution to the dinner, Charles made a wilted lettuce salad they thought delicious. He was proud and delighted by his success, although he never could recall the ingredients he'd used. He never made another salad although they often begged him. He stood on his laurels to the end.

The house did something wonderful for Charles. He was home again. He'd never realized how much he'd missed a home. First he had Harvard Eaton for dinner one evening after school. Then he invited all the gang of boys and girls for tea one Sunday afternoon. They were impressed by the house and loved his mother. She could be charmingly gracious when she chose. It made all the difference with his friends. Now they took him seriously. Even Greg began to call him Chuck and treat him as an equal.

The brothers were happy to be together again. Charles built a crystal radio set with headphones for them both. The sweet lilting music coming from the swank restaurants about the city stirred Charles with a poignancy he couldn't bear. He'd take off the headphones and walk out in the back garden and cry it out. *Home! It was home!* It was the only house in which he'd ever lived that he could actually see. He loved it with a deep wonderful passion.

William's friend, Ramsey, was often there, and the Douglas

family came to dinner several times. Then there would be a great chattering and laughing as the young men vied to be the wittiest. Afterwards Mrs. Douglas helped their mother with the dishes and the warm, affectionate voices of the women sang above the clatter. The fathers sat in the living room and smoked cigars. Professor Taylor told of his experiences as a teacher and expanded in the pleasant memories. The young men gathered upstairs about the radio. Charles was relaxed, everything seemed to fit. He felt that he belonged.

"What's got into you, Chuck?" Ramsey asked. "I never heard you talk so much."

"It's the spinach," his brother teased. "He's drunk off spinach juice."

Charles laughed. "'Speech is the window of great thought,'" he quoted from some forgotten source. "If I never said anything you wouldn't know how wise I was."

"What Chuck means is he wished he'd kept his big mouth shut," William said.

"Du sublime au ridicule il n'y a qu'un pas," quoted Ramsey, who was studying French.

"In that case you'd better watch your step," said William.

Their father contracted a great deal of carpentry work in the neighborhood and employed two helpers. He had an ingratiating manner with white employers. They liked and respected him. He wasn't servile or submissive, but possessed a profound tolerance for human foibles. Whenever someone said to him, "Well, I don't know, I've never had a colored man do this sort of work," he assumed his most indulgent attitude and quizzically replied, "Now I doubt very seriously if the work will know the difference."

Charles did his mother's nails and often at night she let him brush her hair again. When she decided to wear it short she let him cut it for her. He was careful of each strand and worked hard to get it just the way she wanted it. She let him keep a lock. Quite often he helped about the house. She said that he was as fastidious as a girl. He had a great skill for mending broken china, repairing locks, replacing knife handles and other delicate chores which no one else could do. "If Charles can't do it, no one can," his mother was wont to boast.

His friends organized themselves as the Gnothi Seauton fraternity, and felt quite sophisticated when someone asked the meaning of the name.

"Know thyself," was the proud reply. "It's the inscription on the Temple of Apollo at Delphi."

"Greg will never know himself," Marie teased. "He's his own worst enigma." Bright sayings were the rage and the remark clung to Greg to his annoyance.

Charles was elected sergeant-at-arms, and when they gave their first dance took his duties seriously and marched about the Y gymnasium ordering fellows to douse their cigarettes. They charged admission, made enough to hire an orchestra for their first formal dance, which they hoped would be a social event of great importance, comparable to the annual formals given by the college fraternities. They had a crest embossed on the invitations and the programs printed in Gothic script. Everything was elaborately planned.

As the date approached, Charles was filled with trepidation. He ordered a correspondence course in dancing and got Harvard to coach him after school. They danced together after Charles had memorized the various steps. But he was stiff and awkward.

"Relax, Chuck, relax," Harvard cried exasperatedly. "If you move with the rhythm you can't go wrong."

"I'm trying," Charles said stubbornly.

"I believe you're tone-deaf."

"No, I can hear the rhythms all right. But they just don't go to my feet. There isn't any connection. I hear them with my mind."

"You're just self-conscious. Relax. No girl's gonna bite you."

"I'm not scared of girls," he snapped.

His mother bought him a tuxedo and patent leather pumps. He'd need them later, anyway, for the senior prom, she reasoned. It gave him quite an important feeling in the big department store instructing the clerk that he wished midnight-blue instead of black. When the big night arrived the house was turned upside down getting him prepared. His mother tied his bow and William stood by and gave him sage advice.

"Now when the dance starts, hold the girls at a distance. They'll be worried about their clothes. But at the end—that's when you hold them close."

Their mother laughed. "How do you know so much?"

"I've been around."

"Now, Charles, be a good boy," she cautioned smilingly. She looked at him with eyes of pride.

"If he's too good he won't get any dances," William said.

"Anyway, if I can't be good I'll be careful," he quipped.

While in the presence of his family he felt grown-up and assured. But on the street car, dressed in his new tuxedo and carefully handling the corsage of sweet peas and yellow rose buds which his mother had selected, he felt foolish and conspicuous. Outside the house where Della lived, stage fright suddenly overwhelmed him and his legs began to tremble. It was his first date. She was a new girl he'd met at Sunday school. He felt such a sense of dread he was tempted to throw away the flowers and go home.

But her parents had already seen him.

"How nice you look, Charles," Mrs. Lane greeted, opening the door.

Mr. Lane offered him a glass of wine. "Drink it, son, you'll need it."

Then Della entered the living room. She was an exquisite girl with a rose-brown complexion, dark liquid eyes and long, luxuriant hair. She was wearing a beautiful long gown of pale blue organdy. He glowed with pride.

Silently he presented the flowers.

She took them solemnly with downcast eyes, whispering, "Thank you."

"Oh, you must pin them on her," the mother said.

He fumbled with the pin, his fingers turned to thumbs.

"Oh, dear, let me," the mother offered. Her eyes were bright with tears.

It was Della's first dress affair also. She wouldn't sit for fear of wrinkling her gown. They stood apart from each other, mute and wooden, waiting for the taxicab. The parents chattered nervously.

When the horn blew, everyone started as if caught in the commission of a crime. Charles fumbled awkwardly with her cape and she placed her hand shyly on his arm. She wore the cape loosely so as not to crush her flowers and they went down to the taxi and rode in complete silence to the Y. Upstairs she went immediately to the powder room.

Charles noticed that the young men and women stood apart. Everyone seemed solemn and constrained. He joined the group of club members who stood conspicuously aloof. Although everything seemed to be going as they'd planned, they suffered all manner of apprehensions. Greg suggested that Charles, as sergeant-at-arms, go down to the entrance and direct the guests upstairs. Harvard accompanied him and they stood in the cold on the sidewalk and greeted the couples as they arrived. A group of rowdies had collected about the entrance and picked at the pretty girls. Charles wanted to call a policeman. But Harvard said they always hung around a formal dance. The best thing was to ignore them.

One of the girls who lived across the street ran down for a trinket she had left. Charles felt it his duty to escort her. He tried to wear the mantle of Sir Galahad lightly and be secure and poised in his behavior. But he couldn't take part in any social rite in a normal manner. Inside he was tense lest he make an ass of himself. But he felt impelled to act gallantly, attract attention and be indifferent all at once. His emotions attained a high, explosive quality.

When on their return, some rowdy touched her arm, he wheeled and struck blindly, releasing all his tension in the act of violence. He hit the man solidly on the bridge of his nose and stretched him his length on the pavement. Sharp bone hurt ran up his arm. He recoiled in violent shock; he'd no idea he'd struck so hard. Then terror overcame him. There was the man lying unconscious at his feet. The girl had fled upstairs. Harvard had run for a policeman. He stood alone, facing the crowd, without the slightest notion of what to do. But no one took the rowdy's part.

"That's Dick Hanson," he heard someone say.

The younger men looked at him in awe. Shortly Harvard returned with the officer who dispersed the crowd. The man regained consciousness and the officer helped him to his feet. Charles and Harvard went upstairs. Everyone was talking about his feat. The girls made a great fuss over him. Soon all semblance of his terror left and he expanded with emotion. The driving excitement returned. He felt as if his head would burst. For a time he felt himself vested with supernatural powers, dipped in the river of invincibility. He danced and talked as he never had before. All of his dances were taken with the most popular girls. He soared in delirious ecstasy and found himself saying the most extravagant things.

"Where have you been all my life," he whispered in their ears. "You dance so heavenly in my blue heaven." He chanted in a low caressing voice, looking deep into their eyes:

> *Where'd you get those eyes*
> *Where'd you get those ears*
> *Where'd you get that hair so curly*
> *Where'd you get those teeth so pearly . . .*

They danced the Charleston and the one-step and the waltz; and they fox-trotted and cakewalked and did the old collegiate crawl. And he excelled in all of these.

Everything turned out perfectly. Della was a great hit with the men because he'd brought her. When he took her home she let him kiss her in the taxi. Their eyes sparkled with excitement as their sweet hot breath glowed on each other's mouths. In the dim light he noticed a film of perspiration on her upper lip. Her body felt hot and damp in his arms. They touched the tips of their tongues. Hers was like a small hot rapier. Then the taxi drew up before her house. She ran up the steps. He caught up with her and held her hand. And suddenly he was inarticulate.

He could scarcely mutter, "Good night."

"Good night," she whispered softly.

He turned abruptly away. At his back he heard the door click shut. He felt the urge to run, but the taxi waited. He paid it off and walked toward Harvard's house where he'd planned to spend the night. Young swains couldn't afford to taxi home after delivering their girls. Following every formal dance the nearby streets were filled with tuxedoed dandies wending their way home, many walking in their stocking feet, carrying the too-tight pumps.

Suddenly he was assailed with the feeling of having funked out in the end. After all the high excitement, the passionate responses and his own overwhelming sense of invincibility, he'd walked off right at the very climax. Always it was the same, he fumed inwardly. No matter how intense the build-up, what ardent heights he'd reached, always at the climax he failed to carry through. He should have taken her, he told himself. If not that, made her promise to give herself at some other time. Now he knew she'd expected him to ask; now—after it was over. He wondered what she thought of him, if she considered him too young to know. She must have been keenly disappointed, sick with letdown from her hot passion, he thought. Unbearable chagrin tormented his very soul. He cursed himself bitterly and without mercy.

Soon the moment passed and he was filled with exquisite sadness. It was the emotion of one who has lost in love and carries on in heartbreak. Strangely, the sorrow stimulated him. He reveled in an ecstasy of self-torture, assuming the pain of one who's been deserted. His emotions were vividly alive and hurting. Rivers of heartbreak ran through his soul as he experienced this poignant moment of adolescence. Shortly he began to sing:

> *Me and my sha-had-dow*
> *Not a soul to tell our troubles to . . .*

Farther on he ran into Bert and Clift.

"Where'd you find such a pretty chick?" Bert greeted.

The sorrow vanished instantly and he was happy and excited again. "Never you mind. You just keep your hands off. She's private property."

"I'd like to make her my property," Clift said.

Pride flamed in him and all the chagrin of failure was forgotten. He felt only a sense of conquest.

"Confidentially, Chuck, you ever get any of it?" Bert asked.

"That'd be telling," he replied, slyly insinuating that of course he had.

'Harvard was waiting down the street. The four walked abreast in noisy exuberance and began to harmonize:

> *Now how in the hell*
> *Can the old folks tell*
> *It ain't gonna rain no more . . .*

Harvard lived with an uncle and aunt who were childless. They were asleep. The young men talked in whispers as they prepared for bed.

"Yvonne lets me kiss her and play with her bubbies 'till she gets so hot she cries. But she won't let me go any further. I don't see how she stands it."

"How do you stand it?" Charles asked curiously.

"I don't. When I leave her house I go straight down on Hawthorne and spend two dollars."

Charles laughed self-consciously.

"How do you make out?" Harvard asked; then teasingly, "Visit with the widow?"

"Old widow five fingers," Charles supplemented knowingly, but a hot blush covered his face. "Me? I've been lucky."

"Don't kid old doctor Harvard, son. I know Della won't go. I can tell from just looking at her. She's just like Yvonne. You can get right up to it and no further."

"Not with me," Charles lied. "I don't go for that. There's too many girls that will."

"You mean you've scored with Della?"

"Sure, what do you think? I'd take her to our dance if I hadn't?"

Harvard didn't press it. For a time they talked about the rowdy Charles had struck.

"There was another guy there I just wished had said something. I was going to let him have it too," Charles boasted.

"Come off," Harvard said. "You were just as scared as me."

"Hell, scared of what?"

"All right, Tiger Flowers." That was the name of a great colored prize fighter.

Charles sniggered. But inwardly he felt ashamed and cheapened by his boastful lying. There was one part of himself that wanted to share confidences with his friend, and another part that shrank from revealing any of his inner emotions. It was as if he felt his inner life would in some way be defiled. As a consequence his talk was shallow ,and boastful, his accounts juvenile and false.

If he could have confessed how terrified he'd been after he'd hit the rowdy; and how afterwards he'd become so excited he could scarcely breathe; and how, strangely, this taut excitement had titillated, making him feel strong and powerful as a person and invincible as a lover; or spoken truthfully of kissing Della in the taxi—"We swapped tongues and she was so hot I could have made her promise if I'd insisted. She would have then. But I was scared to ask. I've never asked a girl for that. I've never had a girl. Do you think she would have?"—he would have been vastly relieved of all his torturing frustrations. But he couldn't relate the things he felt. He kept it all bottled up inside himself. He'd never confessed to any of his friends that he'd never experienced sexual intercourse. He felt it was a stigma. To cover up he boasted of the girls he'd had, often giving them bad reputations by the lies he told about them. Afterwards he was ashamed and remorseful. But he couldn't help it.

Early that morning, after the friends had gone to sleep, the Hanson family, father and mother and two sons, called at the house and demanded that Charles be sent out to them. Dick's nose had been broken and he'd claimed that Charles had struck him with a piece of iron. The Hansons ran a trucking business; the older son, Heavy, had been a prizefighter, and the father was a powerfully built man known as a bully throughout the neighborhood. They felt intolerably mortified that anyone would dare attack a member of their family. Their prestige was at stake. For hours they'd been hunting Charles like vigilantes, going from house to house of all the club members. The father had a shotgun.

Mr. Shoemaker, Harvard's uncle, denied that Charles was there. The Hansons demanded to search the house. The father threatened to shoot off the lock. The Shoemakers had no telephone and there was no way they could summon aid. Mrs. Shoemaker peered from the darkened curtains, faint with fright. The sinister clan milled about on the porch. But Mr. Shoemaker refused to let them enter.

"I tell you, neither of the boys is here. Harvard had to go out of town to see his mother. She's sick. He caught the midnight bus. And Charles went on home."

"Where does that fellow live?" Heavy demanded.

"I don't know. Way out somewhere. Harvard knows but I've never asked him. Now I wish you folks would leave. My wife is sick and you'll make her hysterical."

Finally the Hansons became convinced and reluctantly went away. The boys hadn't awakened. For a long time the elders sat debating whether they should rouse Charles and send him home. But they were afraid the Hansons might still be lurking outside.

At breakfast they told the boys what had happened. They sat huddled in the kitchen behind drawn shades, held in the grip of terror. By the light of day the experience became all the more frightening.

"They're maniacs," Mrs. Shoemaker said. "George, you should go out and notify the police this instant."

But he was loath to antagonize the Hansons. "The first thing to do is get Charles home," he said. "I'll walk down the street and see if the coast is clear."

When he returned Harvard accompanied Charles to the streetcar stop. The friends walked in tense silence, searching every nook and cranny with frightened eyes. Charles hunched his shoulders deep into his coat as if to hide. Both of them sighed with relief when the streetcar came into sight. They shook hands solemnly as if parting for the last time.

It was the outlaw quality of the Hansons' act which terrified Charles most. He was afraid should he meet them on the street by accident they'd begin beating and shooting him without a word. And there was no one to protect him. He couldn't tell his parents. His mother would have gone straight to the Hansons and demanded an explanation. He was afraid they might actually injure her. And his father was such a puny man to stand up against such bruisers. Since they'd left the southern colleges he'd never thought of his father as such a mighty man. He never dreamed of asking his father's protection from anything.

For a time he kept off Cedar Avenue. And then one day as he was coming from the Y a strong hand gripped his arm.

"Now I got you, you little son of a bitch!" Heavy Hanson exulted.

He was taken to the Hansons' house as if under arrest and held a prisoner in the parlor until the clan assembled. They tried him as if they were a court. Charles stood before them, pleading for his life, it seemed.

"You know I didn't hit him with any piece of iron. You think I'd carry a piece of iron in my tuxedo pocket?"

Dick wouldn't meet his eyes. "I thought it was a piece of iron. It must have been."

His mother looked at him scornfully. She was a sagging, heavy woman with hair like the Medusa and an ugly mouth marred from dipping snuff. "If you don't beat this bastard I'm gonna make your brother beat you," she threatened.

"I'll beat him," Dick muttered. He was the weakling of the lot.

Heavy turned on Charles. "You gotta fight Dick."

"I'll fight him," Charles muttered.

"I can't fight until my nose gets well," Dick said.

"Then you gotta fight me," Heavy said to Charles.

"You?" Charles's heart sank.

"Let Dick fight 'im," the father said. "He's the one claims the boy hit 'im with a pipe."

"He oughta be flogged first anyway," the mother said.

Charles felt in the grip of a nightmare.

It was finally decided the boys would fight one afternoon on the playground as soon as Dick's nose was healed. Heavy took Charles to the door and cuffed him on the head. He ran down the stairs, limp as a rag. For several weeks he could still see the old lady's sadistic eyes. He was in a state of terror, jumping at the slightest touch. But worst of all was the dark, ugly blot on the memory of his first formal dance. The two were bound together, the triumphant ectasy of the dance and the ugly aftermath of being hunted like a beast, and he could never think of one without the other. Afterwards a cloud of apprehension shadowed every social event. He remained wary of the Hansons for a long time. But nothing ever happened. He never learned how Dick got out of fighting him.

Della became his girl. They were invited to several formal dances. He enjoyed taking her. But there was always this shadow of apprehension, distorting their relationship. He tried desperately to act protective and suffered agony when older men were too pointedly attentive. He wanted her to think of him as a great man of the world, but always underneath was this fear she would discover he was cowardly and weak. He was certain that he loved her deeply and developed a possessiveness that stifled her.

"You shouldn't dance so much with John Webb," he'd say angrily. "He's too old."

"I do just because he's good, Chuck. He's the best dancer here."

He winced with humiliation. "He's just showing off. You know all he wants."

"He isn't. He's nice," she defended. "And he's not so old. He's just a senior at Reserve."

It infuriated him. "That's old enough. And anyway, who brought you?"

"You don't own me," she snapped.

"All right," he said crossly. "Go on and make a fool out of yourself. Everybody's talking already."

"But you want me to have a good time, don't you, Chuck?" she said contritely.

He melted. "All right. But anyway, this one's mine."

Sometimes, after a show, when they sat together in an ice cream parlor, he'd say such sophisticated things as: "Don't you think two people should have sex experiences before they marry? I mean with each other." Sometimes she'd give him a shy, up-from-under look and murmur something incoherently. And he'd feel quite mature and self-assured. But often she'd giggle suddenly and completely disconcert him.

On walking down the street he'd insist, "After all, we both want it."

But when they sat panting in the darkened parlor he couldn't say the words. They'd sit and talk of this and that, listening for the parents in the kitchen. The Lanes were very lenient toward their daughter and trusted her implicitly. Charles didn't know that Della talked quite freely with her mother. And she'd promised solemnly never to give herself away.

"Always keep your legs pressed tight together," had been her mother's sage advice. "And when you can't stand it go take a drink of water."

When finally the parents went to bed he'd say, "Gimme a slobber." Or he'd chant the lyric:

> *Gimme a little kiss, will ya—huh*
> *Oh gee—oh gosh—I'm begging for a kiss . . .*

"Here," she'd say, puckering up her lips.

He'd turn out the light and they'd snuggle closely, groping for each other. They put their tongues in each other's mouths until their lips were wet with saliva. But she wouldn't let him feel her

216

legs. Shortly he'd be frantic, and quite often he became violent, gripping her savagely. The sweet musk scent rising from her body tantalized him and he felt driven crazily through space like a stray leaf in a high gale. But at those moments he could never ask. They struggled silently, he trying to make her yield and she resisting, as desperately as persons fighting for their lives. Yet there were rules constraining both, more felt than realized. Both knew he couldn't take unless she gave. Mutely he tried to make her yield, to have her pant, "Yes! Yes!" because he could never ask. This she knew. It made the game all the more exciting because she kept control. Strangely, both liked it more than they would have the real thing.

They went together until the Christmas holidays. Then she went to a dance with John Webb. Charles never spoke to her after that. He didn't call; didn't write. She wrote and asked to see him. He didn't answer. They met at a dance. She rushed forward and greeted him. Tears brimmed in her eyes. He wouldn't look at her. He turned and walked away. It was always his last resort—*to hell with it!*

He had learned to do this during the first months following his brother's accident. He had developed a credo: *No matter how hurt you are, if you don't think about it, it can't hurt.* It helped him over many a painful situation. Sometimes it worked; sometimes it didn't. The hurt was always there, big and deep. But sometimes the hard quality of his rejection refused it recognition.

20

CHARLES GRADUATED THAT JAUNARY. THE HOUSE was filled with fuss and excitement all during the preceding week. He'd taken the lovely colored girl in his class to the Senior

Prom, held in a fashionable hotel. His mother had been so proud she'd purchased a dozen of the pictures taken there and sent them to all her friends and relatives in the South. His father bought him a new blue suit for graduation. But somehow it didn't touch him. He'd seen commencements all his life. This didn't seem any different. He was just completing high school. Why all the fuss and bother? He attended the exercises with a remote nonchalance, slightly contemptuous of his parents' nervous excitement.

"Relax, mother, all I'm going to do is graduate from high school," he said when it came time to leave them and join his class.

She held him tightly for a moment. Tears brimmed in her eyes.

He sat with the others on the stage of the auditorium, listening to the impassioned speeches with complete indifference. Out in the sea of white faces he located those of his parents and his brother and felt their excitement even from that distance. Inside he was cold as ice.

But when his name was called, and he walked forward, and the principal placed the roll of parchment tied with blue and gold ribbon in his hand, he caught fire. It was as if a miracle had happened. He flamed with one of those rare moments which bring a sense of fulfillment, and felt a confidence beyond all his wildest dreams. In some strange and indefinable manner his earth had steadied. As he walked rigidly to his seat, holding the diploma tightly in his hand, he felt he could do anything he should ever hope to do.

His mother cried. She'd lived so long in tight anxiety for fear of his doing something beyond redemption, now her very bones seemed to melt in vast relief. He'd made it, she thought. At last he'd made it. There had been so many times she'd doubted if he ever would.

William beat him on the back. His father kept saying over and over, "Now, son. Now, son," shaking his head as when greatly moved.

"There's nothing to stop you now," his mother said. "You mustn't let mother down, son."

"I won't," he promised, deeply touched by the flow of their emotion. "I won't. I couldn't." He was always touched by extravagant emotion.

His confidence was contagious. It affected all of them. His parents renewed their hope in it. As long as he progressed, their own future could never die. In the past, while he was growing up, his future had been held within their lives. Now theirs was caught in his. Each night his mother prayed fervently to God to keep his ambition burning, to hold him steadily on the path.

Neither would acknowledge to themselves how greatly they depended on him. Now, after nearly a quarter-century of marriage, he was all they had. They couldn't admit it even to themselves. But his position in the household changed. They catered to him in a number of minor ways.

He realized it and came to feel a great responsibility toward them. He had reached that delicate stage of first maturity where every son feels honor-bound to make his parents proud of him. It was a new emotion, affecting him strangely. He saw sharply the gray in his father's hair, his old, seamed face, now fading to a saddle color; he saw the deep lines about his mother's eyes, how the flesh had sagged down from her high cheekbones, making her jaws more pronounced, squarer. Her lips had thinned and her eyes had become sunken, the lids age-lowered, so that their steady glint was almost baleful. With advancing age her face had taken such a great sternness as to appear mean. He was stricken with pity for them. Once as he tenderly brushed her hair he felt an impulse to cry, "Don't grow old, Mama. Please don't grow old." He yearned to make some great sacrifice to bring back youth to her face.

William entered the high school across the street that month. He remembered his mother as he'd last seen her and missed the poignancy of her gradual aging which so affected Charles. He was a brilliant student and very popular with the teachers and pupils alike. Soon the house was filled with boys and girls who flocked about him. Except for Ramsey Douglas all his new friends were white. William could not see that they were white and never thought of it. They never thought of him as colored. They achieved an intimacy that was wonderful. But whenever Charles came into the group they lost it.

Charles seldom took part in his brother's activities. Their interests had grown apart. He was away from home a great deal of the time, and most of his evenings were spent with Harvard and his friends of the Gnothi Seautons. For a time he had a new girl, whom he took to the St. Valentine's Day dance. They were late getting out and the streetcars had stopped running. He set out for home walking, singing softly to himself:

> *It's three o'clock in the morning*
> *We've danced the whole night through ...*

Two inches of fresh snow had fallen. The old houses flanking the car-lined street were dark and asleep and the park was blanketed with the new white snow. Slanting his hat at a jaunty angle, he became Hermes on winged sandals, bearing a message to Zeus. He could be anything he wanted to at night. It was pleasant to be Hermes through the deserted night.

The days sped swiftly in dreams and it was March before he found a job. His father sent him to a large eastside hotel to interview his old friend, Dick Small, who worked there as the head-waiter.

Charles arrived while breakfast was being served. Across from the elevators two pretty young white women sat in a glass-enclosed booth checking the room service orders. Brisk young waiters with shiny pomps and dark smooth faces, swinging their trays as dancers balanced urns, paraded swiftly past their sharp smiling eyes, hurrying into the elevators. They looked up at Charles as he hovered indecisively, and smiled. He asked for Mr. Small. One of them told him to be seated on the bench beside their booth.

He sat, fiddling nervously with his hat, and looked across the kitchen. Great ranges caught in stark white light loomed in the center of confusion. About them milled the waiters, pushing and quarrelsome, voices cutting across voices, panting with a senseless fury, their bright white smiles and unctuous manners saved for the guests in the dining room. Charles was frightened by what seemed to him a meaningless pandemonium. His first impulse was to slip silently away and forget that he'd ever been there. He'd come up on the elevator but he looked for the door to the stairs.

Before he could escape, a slight, balding man with bird-like movements and bright, dark eyes, impeccably attired, came into the kitchen and beckoned to him. He hurried across the room.

"You're Charles Taylor."

"Yes sir."

The bright dark eyes searched him with a glance, scanned his fingernails, dug into his ears, observed the neatness of his hair, the cleanness of his collar, the polish of his shoes, but so briefly that Charles saw only the warm, cordial smile.

"Son, I've known your father for forty years. We went to school together. Professor Taylor is one of the finest men I know. Come into my office."

He turned away so quickly Charles had to leap to follow. They entered a dressing room off from the kitchen which contained a desk and couch. A row of spotless tuxedoes hung neatly down one wall. Mr. Small sat behind the desk and waved Charles to a chair. A moment later a waiter entered with breakfast and silently served them.

"Son, waiting is an old and honorable profession," Mr. Small said. "I wouldn't hire a man who condescended toward it."

"Oh, I don't feel that way about it," Charles replied, thinking of the hard, hurried confusion he'd just seen. "I just don't know if I would fit. Everything seems so hurried."

"In waiting tables time is the essence, son. Your guests must be served with rapidity. The leisure belongs to the guests, never to the waiter."

"But they sound so—well, violent. You'd think they were going to fight."

Mr. Small laughed. "When my waiters stop fighting at the ranges it is time for me to worry. But don't let that worry you, son. A good waiter and a good chef always get along. I'm going to put you on as a bus boy at sixty dollars a month. The waiters will share their tips. Can you carry a tray?"

"I think so."

"I'll put you on room service until you learn. If you want to learn, I'll teach you. No matter what your aim is in life, waiting tables is a good profession to know. Many of our most prominent men got their start waiting table."

"I want to learn."

"Good. You'll never regret it."

He sent Charles to the housekeeper, a doughy-faced woman with cold, suspicious eyes, for his white jackets, after which Charles found his way below to the locker room. The men sat about in their undershirts, smoking, talking desultorily. A few gambled with greasy cards on the dirty benches. They eyed him critically, without warmth. He felt like an intruder, a tourist who has wandered upon the ceremonial rites of a primitive tribe. He didn't know it was his manner that set him apart. At one glance they knew he was not of them. He had none of the extroversion the occupation requires. Inside he was taut with timidity. Outwardly he strove to show a hard indifference. Silently the waiters resolved to break him in; none offered any assistance. He blundered about helplessly, looking for an empty locker. He was inarticulate; he didn't have the humility to confess ignorance, ask questions. He'd never been able to meet new people, be congenial in strange circumstances. He knew he'd never like it here. Again he had the impulse to throw down his jacket and leave. Just quitting was always the easiest out. But his new feeling of responsibility to his parents held him; he couldn't quit.

Silently he hung his coat and overcoat in a locker that was occupied, and donned his jacket. He didn't have a black tie. There was one in the locker across from him. He took it without asking and left the room. It was like walking through a gauntlet to reach the door. Upstairs he found the women checkers relaxing in their booth, drinking tea. He asked for Captain Jackson.

They smiled at him. "He's in the locker room."

"Oh." He started to move away.

"He'll be up shortly," one of them said. "Are you going to work room service?"

"Yes, I suppose so."

"My name is Theresa and this is Marguerite—they call her Margy. What's yours?"

"Charles." He resented their kindness.

"Where you from, Charles?" Margy asked.

"From?" He didn't understand her.

"Where did you work before?"

"Oh. I just went to school," he admitted reluctantly. "I just graduated."

"Didn't you ever do this kind of work before?" Theresa asked.

"No."

"It's really easy. You'll catch on quick." He looked skeptical. "You'll like it," she said.

"I doubt it," he said, but he had to smile. Their warm, out-going friendliness had encouraged him despite himself. He liked them. "I suppose the first hundred years are the hardest," he grinned suddenly.

"Look, he's got dimples!" Theresa exclaimed, her eyes dancing with delight.

"Don't corrupt my new boy with all your charm," a soft, mellow voice said at Charles's side. "He'll be walking about in a daze soon enough."

Charles started guiltily, turning toward the tall, brown, ascetic-looking man in rimless spectacles. "Oh! Captain Jackson, Mr. Small told me to report to you."

"He didn't tell you to report to these young ladies," Mr. Jackson said with a dead-pan expression.

"No, sir, I was looking for you. I just stopped to ask—"

"Don't be so mean to the boy, Jack," Theresa said.

Mr. Jackson smiled. Charles relaxed.

"These young ladies cause more havoc on my station than a four-alarm fire," Mr. Jackson warned. "You must inure yourself against their charms, son. You won't be able to find the elevators."

The young women laughed. "You know that isn't so, Jack. You couldn't get along without us."

"Come along, son," Mr. Jackson said.

As Charles followed he turned to smile at the two young women who smiled in return. Mr. Jackson took him into the small south dining room reserved for parties and assigned him to sorting silver, folding napkins and filling salt cellars. It was dim and quiet. He worked alone. All of his nature rebelled against the job. He was the servant of servants, required to take orders from everyone. He felt helpless and trapped, knowing all the while it was too much emotion to expend on such a simple job. But he couldn't help it. He was too ingrown to control the emotional impact of the place.

Lunch was served. He went up on the elevators, entered the rooms of strangers, rolled out the wheel trays of dirty dishes. He stacked the dirty dishes in the big tin trays, the silver and the cups and saucers, the plates and coffeepots, rode the elevator down and carried the trays through the mad confusion of the kitchen to the dishwashers. The waiters shouted at him, "Watch out, boy!" . . . "Step lively, son!" . . . "One side, punk, one side!" . . . They pushed him aside. He clung to his tray with his left hand, balanced it on his right. Once in the elevator a coffeepot fell off. Reaching for it, he upset his tray. Soiled china shattered on the elevator floor, silver rang. At the kitchen level he had to get broom and mop and clean up the mess. The two young women, a few feet off, smiled sympathetically. The waiters stopped to look at the debris. Some were angry at being held up, others kidded him cruelly. The bus boys jeered. His face flamed fiery red. He felt sick to the bone with infinite shame. Captain Jackson looked at him curiously. The dishwashers screamed at him when he brought the tray of silver and broken china.

"Take it away! Take it away! Take it away!"

"Where?"

"Dump it in Lake Erie."

He picked up the tray and started off. A waiter pushed him aside. Finally one of the older waiters said, "Take out the silver and throw away the broken dishes, son."

After that he went about his duties with a mute antagonism. Ignorant bastards, they didn't like him, he thought. To hell with them! He'd finish out the day and never come back. To hell with that kind of job! When it came time for him to eat he had no appetite. He dreaded going to the range and asking for his food. He picked at his plate in silence.

"Kind of got you up a tree, eh, kid?" one of the fellows said with a peculiar smile.

He didn't answer. Then finally the day was over. He hurried to get away.

"Good night, Charles," Theresa called.

He turned and found the two young women smiling at him.

"Good night," he said, smiling in return.

"See you tomorrow," Margy said.

"I doubt it," he replied.

His mother asked him how he liked the job.

"I don't like it. I don't think I'll stay."

"It's just until September," she reminded him. "If you stay on until then it will be a great help toward your expenses in college this fall."

"I'll get something else. I don't like that kind of work."

"You'll get used to it, son," his father said. "It's strange at first. But when you get to know the fellows it'll be different."

"I don't want to know the fellows," he maintained stubbornly.

"You must learn, son, you can't have everything just as you would like it," his mother said sadly.

"No, mother," he replied with a tightening of the lips that made them look so much alike. "No, I can't. But there's nothing that says I have to take it if I don't like it."

She winced from the hardness of his manner. All of the old worry and trepidation stirred in her again. "You just watch," she warned. "You're going to make your bed hard."

He looked at her with glinting eyes. "Sometimes it's hard either way."

She let the subject drop. But that night, finding him alone in the kitchen, she tried again.

"You mustn't give up so easily, son. I know it isn't always

pleasant, but you must learn to stick it out. Your grandparents—
my parents—started in life without a cent. When they were—"

"I know, mother, I know all about it," he interrupted rudely.
"You've told me about it a thousand times."

She lit the fire beneath the kettle to make a cup of tea, and sat
watching him finish his sandwich and glass of milk. Except for
his hair, he looked a great deal like her oldest sister, Maggie,
she mused. But he didn't have Maggie's push.

"Has mother ever told you about your great-grandfather, Dr.
Jessie Manning? He was in the United States Senate before the
Civil War." There was the queer note of pride in her voice which
he despised.

"Yes, you've told me all about all of 'em," he said harshly.

She was suddenly saddened by his attitude. Why couldn't he
realize his great potentialities? Why couldn't he be proud of
himself?

"You must never forget it, my son," she said in a tear-filled
voice. "You children have the blood of conquerors flowing in
your veins."

Looking up, he saw the age and disappointment in her face,
and was instantly contrite. "I know, mother; I'm sorry I talked
like I did."

"You must learn to surmount the petty obstacles that arise in
your path, my son."

"All right, I'll go back tomorrow," he consented. But afterwards
he was angry with her for forcing him to do something he didn't
want to do.

Everything was different the next morning. His initiation was
over. He'd come back. In the locker room, while he was changing,
the fellows were friendly and helpful. They joshed him about
dropping the tray.

"You know what to do when you got a bear by the tail?"

"What?"

"Let it go, boy, let it go!"

He laughed. Now he felt more assured, less timid. When he
went upstairs to report for work he didn't feel as if he were
going to his execution.

A good-looking, brown-skinned boy approached him and said, "My name's Roy. You're gonna work with me this morning."

"Okay, Roy. Mine's Charles."

Roy stopped to chat with the checkers. He was a favorite with them.

"How's God's gift to the teen-agers?" Theresa greeted him, smiling.

"You know me better than that," Roy said. "I like my women tall, twenty and terrific."

"You like your women, period," Margy corrected.

They turned dazzling smiles on Charles.

"We didn't look for you back this morning," Margy said.

He grinned. "Well, here I am."

"My, such dashing wit. I bet you slay the girls with your clever repartee."

Charles had to laugh. "Hardly."

"You do it with your dimples, don't you, Charles?" Theresa said.

"With his eyes, dear," Margy amended. "With his long gorgeous lashes. Why don't you give some girl those lashes, Charles? It's unfair."

"I wish I could," he said, feeling the blood rise in his face.

"Look, you're making him blush," Theresa observed.

"Don't pay any attention to us," Margy said. "We're just jealous. We're just two girls trying to find a boy."

"I'll bet," he said. "I'll bet you got so many guys lined up they have to draw straws to see who gets a date."

"Listen to Charles!" Theresa exclaimed. "Who said he couldn't talk?"

Roy didn't like the attention Charles was getting. The waiters, dribbling past to their various stations, kidded him.

"Roy's getting some competition."

"He doesn't like it, either—eh, Roy?"

"He'll have the new boy treed 'fore lunch."

"Better watch it, Roy. You'll lose your pretty home, boy."

The young women were delighted. They enjoyed their popularity with the colored waiters. Their influence on Charles was magic. It changed the face of the day. Now everything was pleasant.

He made several trips with Roy and brought down trays of dirty dishes. The dishwashers shouted to him as they'd done the day before. But he just smiled. The last time up Roy told him that a famous dog that was used in motion pictures had occupied that suite. He was smiling to himself when he brought down the tray. The young women noticed it. When he returned from the dishwashers, Theresa called,

"What's so amusing, Charles?"

"Share it with us, Charles," Margy said. "Don't be stingy. What happened up there. Some dame slip her peignoir?" she asked jokingly out of the side of her mouth.

"I was just wondering how a dog would look in a dinner jacket," he said enigmatically.

The young women exchanged glances, looked at him with raised brows. His laugh was infectious; they laughed with him. The elevator door was ajar; the light was out. He reached inside, feeling for the light switch, looking back at the young women with a secret grin, and they were smiling in return, feeling happy that he liked them, and he was already loving both of them without even knowing it.

He stepped into the elevator. Out and away from where he stepped was nothing. He clutched spasmodically with both hands, finding nothing. For a brief tight instant he was filled with the sense of falling. He was fully conscious of falling. He felt the sensation of his body going swiftly down through the darkness with nothing to stop it. He was aware that he didn't scream. There was no time for fright or panic or the explosion of emotions in his mind. His senses were filled with the knowledge of his falling and he was rational. As quickly it was over. He felt the jarring impact of striking bottom. No instant pain engulfed him. It was an over-all crushing sensation, not localized, but absolute, which should have made a crushing sound. But he didn't hear anything. He was conscious.

Immediately he tried to stand. It was a reflex action accompanied by the self-conscious humiliation of an able-bodied man who slips on ice. He put down his left hand to brace himself. There was a queer, funny sensation as if his hand were some distance away from where he'd placed it. Then fire lanced up his arm and shattered in his brain.

A moment later he heard a tremulous voice as if from a great distance crying, "Help! Help! Help!" His mind was like a spotless vacuum from which all thought has been dynamited by one clean, clear blast. His first rational thought was of the darkness. He couldn't see himself and felt at a great disadvantage. The voice was sharply annoying and he wished violently that it would stop. "Help! Help! Help!" As yet he hadn't realized it was his own. He gritted his teeth in annoyance. Again the white brilliant blast exploded in his head.

Then there was light above him. The basement door to the elevator had been opened. Figures moved against the light like tribal dancers. Voices began penetrating his thoughts but the words had no meaning, as if they were all in a foreign tongue. He thought, "Now they'll help me," and relaxed. He felt queer inside and broken in a number of places. But it was not frightening now that help had come.

A light was flashed into the pit. His body was huddled in a grotesque position against the heavy steel guard supported by a mammoth steel spring rising two feet from the center of the pit to catch the elevator should it plunge out of control. The front of his white jacket was splattered with blood. He was looking upward, faintly smiling.

Someone called above, *"HOLD THAT ELEVATOR!"*

A waiter and one of the garage attendants jumped down into the pit to lift him out.

"Oh!" he exclaimed when the garageman sought to shift him. "I think my arm is broken," he said weakly.

"Watch his arm!" the waiter said roughly. The garageman was sweating.

They straightened him out with infinite care.

"We need some help," the waiter called.

Two others jumped into the pit. The four of them, two on each side with arms beneath his body, the garageman at his head, his greasy hands beneath his armpits, the waiter at his foot, lifted him above where a number of others, lying flat on their stomachs, reached out and took him from the shaft.

"Oh!" he cried faintly as they handled him. "Oh!" The blinding flashes were striking in his brain like April lightning.

Some one had thought of blankets and they laid him gently on the basement floor. He looked up and saw the face of Mr. Small bending toward him. "We've sent for the ambulance, son, and I've sent for your parents." His smile was gone; the head-waiter's face was furrowed with anguish and concern.

"I'm all right," he whispered faintly.

About him were the faces of many others, waiters and bus boys, chefs and many of the hotel's guests, all marked with that morbid recognition of human helplessness. The two young women stood close, their bright, tear-filled eyes, enlarged with shock, against dead-white skin.

"I'm all right," he said again, the sound barely carrying beyond his lips. He felt as if he were crying inside, the tableau held breathless by some powerful emotion, but there was no pain. Way underneath he was remotely pleased, and couldn't help it, to be the center of this absolute attention.

The hotel doctor and nurse arrived and briskly took command. "Clear away these men," he ordered. "Give me the shears, Miss Tate."

While two of the remaining waiters turned his body, the doctor cut away his clothes. He moved his head to look down at his body, which felt so queer. His left arm, he noticed, was broken off completely just above the wrist, blood spotting the white jagged ends of the bones as if the blood were being squeezed from them, and his hand projected away at a right angle, held only by flesh and skin. He studied the fracture carefully without thinking. His eyes were dark with shock, of a velvet, liquid mindlessness, immense in his pale tan face, reflecting no intelligence whatever. The pain had not come. Blood was seeping slowly from his chin, running down his throat. It felt as if he munched a mouthful of gravel. Only the upper part of his body felt covered but he could see his legs were covered also. He tried to move his foot but it didn't respond.

"Now," the doctor said, lifting his right arm. He felt the sharp sting of the hypodermic needle. But he didn't feel it when it went into his hip.

He didn't worry. He'd given himself into the hands of someone and felt content. Almost immediately a drowsiness affected him.

"Is he in much pain?"

"No, he's still in shock. I've given him sufficient morphine for an hour or so of relief."

He heard the voices as from a distance.

The ambulance came down the ramp almost silently.

"Carefully, boys," the doctor said.

The blunt-faced driver looked at him. They were professionals. Charles barely felt it when they slid the stretcher beneath him. The doctor instructed them to take Charles to a large new hospital nearby.

"And what's your name, doctor?"

"He's not my patient. He's an Industrial Commission case. Instruct the hospital to notify the Industrial Commission."

The attendant looked disgusted. "We were called by the hotel."

"Bill the hotel then. But get on with the boy for God's sake."

"As you say, chief," the driver said, shifting into gear.

Charles heard the conversation clearly as he lay drowsily on the stretcher. Just before the siren sounded he heard one of the attendants say, "What kind of goddamn crap is this—no doctor!" He didn't worry. He was confident of being cared for. Underneath all else, consciousness that he possessed a father and mother supported his indefinable faith in the outcome. Now he felt the ambulance slow and turn and stop before the emergency entrance to the hospital.

The attendants opened the door and lifted him out into the bright cold sunshine. He turned his head and saw a dark-haired young doctor step from the doorway and hold up his hand to stop them.

"Ho! What have you got there?" He had dark, well-cut features and his hair was slicked like patent leather in the sun.

"Accident!" the driver said. He was a big, red-faced man with pug features and sandy hair. "Fell down an elevator shaft."

The doctor sobered. He wore heavy, dark-rimmed glasses. He came over and looked down at Charles with sudden interest. His expression went entirely blank. He turned back to the driver. "Where did this happen?"

"Park End."

"Who's the doctor?"

"Commission case."

"Hold him," the doctor said impassively, turning back inside. "I'll see."

"Hold him!" the driver exploded. "What the hell you mean *hold him?* What the hell you got to see? You can see! It's an accident! You can see that! What the hell else you got to see?"

"I said hold him here," the doctor instructed in a cold, controlled voice. Sunlight glinted on his glasses.

"*You* said!" the driver shouted. "So *you* said! Who the hell are *you?*" The doctor closed the door behind him. "What the hell's the matter with that son of a bitch?" the driver raved.

A moment later the young doctor returned with the resident doctor, an older man with graying hair, also of dark aquiline features. As he came, wearing a peculiar expression, he slowly shook his head, looking at the driver with confidential eyes. He carried a hypodermic syringe.

"What do you mean?" the driver challenged.

The resident doctor spread his hands with eloquent appeal. "We can't take him."

Charles watched the red climb up the back of the driver's neck. "What the hell you mean you can't take him?"

"We have no room," the doctor said, emphasizing the statement with spreading hands.

"What the hell you mean no room? In all this goddamn hospital you ain't got no room for an accident case?"

"We have no beds," the doctor said, closing his hands abruptly to end the discussion. "I'll give the patient an injection."

"You'll give this patient not a goddamned thing. He's had an injection. That's all you goddamn bastards want to do, give the man an injection."

The eyes of the resident doctor glinted with anger. "Don't call me a bastard."

"Yes, I'll call you a bastard you bastard. You're not only a bastard but you're both bastards. What's this, a goddamned private exclusive hospital, you bastard?"

The lips of the two doctors folded tightly in anger as they turned, without replying, and re-entered the hospital. For a moment the two ambulance attendants stood outside holding Charles in the stretcher and raved. "Jesus Christ, sweet Holy Mary, these bastards'll leave a man croak right outside their door."

The other one looked at Charles. "Let's go," he urged.

Charles felt the sense of motion. He'd been unaffected by the harsh exchange. It seemed vaguely as if years were passing. He wished they'd stop somewhere so he could go to bed.

He was taken to a hospital on Euclid where Negroes were admitted. The firm of doctors who treated accident cases for the Industrial Commission were notified. He was sponged and prepared for X-rays and given additional injections of morphine. Everyone was cheerful and efficient. He felt safer. But until his mother came he could only wait.

She was out of the house that morning, shopping. His father was at work, and William was in school. So he went through it alone. They were there, anyway, as much as they would ever be. He had never gone to them in his deepest hurts, or shared with them any of his fullest triumphs or his bitterest defeats. They were his parents who had given him birth, and because of this more than for any other reason he loved them with his life and would have died for them. And the fact that he was tied to them by being born of them prevented him from ever being physically alone. There had been many times in his young life when this had been important. It was important now. He needed the nearness and comfort of their physical presence more than he had ever needed it. But inside his spiritual being, where it was still empty of the emotions that would come—fear and panic and despair—they had never touched. His mother had come closest, but always she'd drawn back from the intensity of his longing when it reached that point where he needed someone most. In that respect he'd always been alone.

Shortly, three doctors arrived and he was wheeled into the X-ray room.

"How'd this happen, lad?" one asked.

Charles avoided the bright blue, inquisitive eyes. "I wasn't looking," he answered faintly.

The doctor chuckled. "That epitaph should adorn half the tombstones in this civilized world."

The findings showed that he had three fractured vertebrae at the base of his spine, a compound fracture of the left arm above the wrist, a fractured jaw and twenty-two chipped and broken teeth. The extent of the internal injuries was indeterminable, but there was no indication of internal hemorrhage. He'd landed partly on the elevator guard and partly on the concrete floor of the shaft. His chin, back, and left arm had struck simultaneously.

He was given a local anesthetic and his arm set. They didn't think it was necessary to wire his jaw. His torso was wrapped in a cast. The vertebrae could not be set without endangering the spinal column. As far as they could determine, the spinal column had not been injured, although the bone pressing against it caused paralysis of the lower limbs. The purpose of the cast was to hold the vertebrae in place and give the fracture a chance to heal. They hoped that the spinal column would eventually adjust to the curvature and the pressure be relieved, restoring movement to the lower limbs. His chin was dressed, his mouth washed, and he was wheeled into a private room. The rest was up to God.

Lying quietly on the wheel stretcher, his huge, incandescent eyes drug-widened and remote, he seemed a disembodied spirit floating in a world of unreality. He heard the voices distinctly and watched with mindless fascination. As yet he'd felt no pain.

His mother was the first to come. She was carrying a shopping bag of groceries and her face, devastated as it had been when

234

William lost his sight, older now and haggard to the bone, was held stiffly from within by tremendous will power.

"It's mother, Charles. It's mother, son." Only her voice gave her away, so high and light and dead.

Out of his drugged remoteness he saw the grief there again as it had been the night she came from the hospital with William and walked into the light. Now as the seamed and powdered flesh, the tortured mouth, bent forward to kiss him, he braced himself as if against the kiss of death. All the kinds of mothers he'd wanted her to be bloomed in his mind; the tenderness of doing her nails, the soft delight of fingering her hair, the passion of her whippings—his beautiful mother disfigured with grief. It was not physical hurt but spiritual anguish that came up in him in waves. He closed his eyes as if shutting out the sight of her would dam the flood. But when her cold dry lips touched his forehead, tears made a sudden fringe beneath his tightly pressed lids. He began crying all down inside himself.

"I'm all right, mama. I'm all right," he said in his faint, indistinct voice. "Don't worry, I'm all right."

She sat down beside the bed, holding herself from within, and tightly clasped her hands. She was struck by the immobility of his posture; his body was held so straight and rigid in the cast, laid out almost for burial, his soft, tan face pale as death. He looked final, permanent, as if he might never rise again. The one who'd been so active, so physically assured, whose body had been more expressive of himself than all else, now broken. It seemed a sacrilege against nature. Her baby, she thought, the last of all her sons, the one—. She didn't dare think it. And yet the loss to her, then, as she first suffered it, him lying there in such total disability, was everything, the final, bitter end of all her high and eager dreams. But desperately she tried to hold it, to keep it from her thoughts. If she once thought it she couldn't hold herself. She tried not to think beyond the room.

"Go to sleep, son," she said. "Mother's here. Mother will look after you." Now there was this other thought that she was being punished for having forced him back to work against his will. "You mustn't worry, son." She stroked his forehead. "God always has a purpose and we must trust in Him." But it wouldn't come that God had any other purpose but to punish her for her own incontinent vanity.

"Don't worry, mama," she heard him saying in that faint, pebbly voice. "I don't feel anything at all."

It was his saying that that broke her. All of her body began to cry, shaking. "Forgive me, son," she cried in agony. "Forgive your mother."

He couldn't bear it either, and turned his face away, crying toward the wall. A nurse entered.

"You shouldn't disturb him. The shock should wear off gradually."

The spell of exquisite agony was shattered. Mrs. Taylor exerted a semblance of control.

"I know." She tried to hold herself in, turning to her son. "You must try to sleep, Charles. Mother will sit here quietly."

Her presence, the nearness of her, became uppermost now, and he gave in to her, ceased struggling against her grief, and the anguish slowly ebbed from him, and he became her baby, drowsily in her arms. He went to sleep. When he awakened it was evening. She sat as if she hadn't moved. His father and William were there now, dressed for work and school. In his father's face, also, were the ravages of grief; these two elderly people at this time in their lives having to carry the burden of his hurt because he was born to them.

With William it was different. He sat silently, his face furrowed with an intensity of emotion, his head cocked in an attitude of listening. Over his shocked sorrow he felt a rage of protest. First himself and now Charles. It was unfair—unfair to all of them. It was as if he was hurt again; and poor Charles, so dependent on his physical prowess in all the things he did. He was the first to sense that Charles was back with them.

'Chuck?"

"Will."

"What happened, Chuck?"

"I fell down the elevator shaft."

236

"What's the matter with your voice? Does it hurt you to talk?"

"Naw, not much. I broke my jaw a little and broke some teeth."

"Then you can't eat anything?"

"Just liquids." He looked about the room. There was a great bouquet of flowers from the hotel and the waiters had chipped in and sent an enormous basket of fruit. Professor Taylor had stopped on the way and bought a bag of oranges which looked so pathetic beside the others. He noticed that his father was crying, tears slipping unobtrusively down his black, seamed face.

"Don't cry, dad," he said impulsively.

"Son!"

All were silent for a time. The sons were ashamed and embarrassed for their father, as if he didn't have a right to cry.

"Wasn't there a door or guard or something?" William asked.

"It had a door but it was open."

"Oh!"

"It's a shame," his mother said. "It's criminal negligence. I should think Mr. Small would be more careful."

"It wasn't his fault," his father said. "They have an engineer who attends to that."

"I don't care who attends to it. It was someone's fault and they're not going to get away with it."

William cut it off. "Is there anything you want before we go?"

"No, I don't want anything."

They rose. His father leaned down and patted his shoulder. "We'll go now, son, and let you rest."

"Mother will pray for you, son."

William became tense again. "Let's go! Let's go! Let's go!" he said.

It was dismal in the Taylor house that night. The grief was settling down into the soul, widening into worry, fear, horror. Self-blame attaches inconsistently, and the soul accepts full guilt even when no sin has been committed. If she just hadn't forced him to go back, Mrs. Taylor grieved. She couldn't rid herself of the conclusion that she'd gone against God's will. She'd always tried to force him into doing things he didn't like, and now she knew it had been to feed her own ambition. On the other hand, his father mercilessly condemned himself for having sent his son to Mr. Small in the first place. He'd known, even then, it wasn't the kind of work the boy would like. But because he had had to do it, he'd wanted his son to do it too, telling himself at the time it was for the sake of discipline. Mr. Small blamed himself for not having prohibited the elevator being used when it was first discovered that the door was faulty. He'd simply reported it to the engineer. That had been a week before. The engineer blamed himself for not having fixed it immediately when it was called to his attention. The two young women blamed themselves for having distracted Charles's attention. Both had gone home directly following the accident, prostrated with grief. They had seen him fall.

Later that night, when Charles awakened in the dark, he felt abandoned and alone. But he was not alone; no one can ever be hurt alone. Others are always hurt by the hurt of anyone. Had he known this, it would have made a difference.

21

THE NEXT DAY REACTION SET IN. THOUGHT PATterns returned and the discomfort of lying in one stiff position was now clearly felt. Doubt and fear began to gnaw at his mind, and pain, more imagined than experienced, came throbbingly into his consciousness. As he began to realize the extent of his injury, self-pity settled slowly over his emotions. He tried not to think of himself being a cripple, of all the things he might never do again. But he couldn't restrain himself.

The nurse noticed it. "Our patient is blue," she smiled.

"Just thinking."

"Don't think about yourself. Think of all your pretty girls and what good times you're going to have this summer."

He tried to smile. But that was thinking about himself in the worst possible way.

For a time the visitors helped divert his thoughts. The doctor called early, glancing at his chart.

"How is it today, Charles?"

"All right."

And then his mother came. "Is there anything mother can get for you?"

"Some cigarettes."

She tried not to appear shocked, but her silence revealed it. "Do you smoke, son?"

"Not often."

"Did you ask the doctor?"

"I don't think it matters."

She sighed. "I'll ask him and if he says it won't hurt you I'll bring them to you. Is there any particular kind?"

"Any kind."

Mr. Small and the hotel manager, Mr. Cochran, called before noon. They'd brought along a waiter loaded down with lunch, but he was not permitted in the room and the lunch was given to the nurses. The grip of tragedy still had its hold on Mr. Small. He smiled, but it was different. His poise was gone.

"There's no need for me trying to tell you how I feel about this, son. I couldn't feel any worse if it had happened to my own son."

"I know." He wished they wouldn't talk about it.

"The hotel is at your disposal," Mr. Cochran said. The tragedy hadn't touched him as it had the others.

"Thank you." After a moment he added, "Thank you for the flowers." And then to Mr. Small, "Thank the fellows for the fruit."

"We just learned you can only have liquids," Mr. Small observed. "Is there anything you prefer?"

"Not particularly."

Mr. Small placed a check on the bedstand. "This is a collection the boys took up for you."

"There'll be something coming from the hotel too," Mr. Cochran added. "I think you'd like to know we're going to continue your salary, and we'll see to it that you receive the highest rate of compensation."

The reference to money was meaningless to him. "Thank you," he said again. "I'd like to have some cigarettes."

"Right!" Mr. Cochran beamed. This was something tangible, something he could do immediately. "What's your brand, Chuck?"

"Any brand, sir."

"Right! I'll send them right away."

They stood, smiling, the smiles different, and Mr. Small made one last effort, "I'll send one of the boys over with a thermos of clear turtle soup; and perhaps you'd like some eggnog and juices on hand."

"Yes, sir, that'll be fine."

During lunch hour yellow roses came from the two young women at the hotel and all afternoon the bouquets of flowers and baskets of fruit came from his parents' churches, his Sunday school, the members of his club, and from people he couldn't remember. News of his accident had been reported in the daily papers and all the people who had known him only vaguely felt obligated to send condolences.

The members of his club came during the late afternoon and then his father's relatives and afterwards his own family came and sat with him until the time for visiting was over. The small room overflowed with tokens and flowers were banked about the walls as if it was a florist's shop. He'd had no time to think.

It was late that night, while the hospital slept, that the first blind panic shattered him. He was going to be a cripple, confined to a wheel chair, with a wizened, useless arm. He lit a cigarette, fighting a losing battle. He couldn't bear it. Everything he'd ever dreamed of doing depended on his body. How could one be brave, noble, gallant, without physical perfection? He might never be in love, because it was of the flesh also; might never know what it was like to be with a woman. That was the bitterest thought of all. He pulled the covers over his head to muffle his sobbing.

The next day he was moved into a ward. His doctors thought the activity might distract his morbid self-obsession. There were twenty-three other patients. Something was always happening.

Bitter quarrels ensued between the patients and the orderlies over bedpans. Internes flirted with the nurses, strutted importantly when alone, fawned in the presence of the doctors, and condescended toward the patients with sage demeanors. The doctors came each day, bringing their tidings of good and evil. Food, baths and dressings helped while away the time.

The patient to Charles's right was convalescing from pneumonia; the one to his left slowly dying from a gangrenous arm. Charles watched with morbid fascination the slow decomposition of the horribly bloated arm as it lay floating in a tank of warm solution, the slimy fins of drainage tapes hanging from the rotten flesh like eels feeding on a piece of floating carrion. He shook with fear. Suppose blood poison should set into his arm. Extending from the bandaged splints were the fingers of his hand, waxen and atrophied as were a paralytic's. He thought of the twisted, deformed limbs of beggars he'd seen down on the Square. Tears squeezed through his eyes.

Outside, the gray, dismal days of March's end passed so slowly by the windows time seemed to be standing still. He kept his sight indrawn. From seven until eight each evening was the visiting hour. His parents always came. Sometimes they brought relief, more often not.

His mother had struck up an acquaintance with the wife of the patient who was convalescing from pneumonia. Her conversation consisted for the most part in denouncing the hotel. Charles was tired of hearing it. But the woman was a patient listener.

One night she said, "My man is going home tomorrow."

"Oh, how nice. Then I won't be seeing you again."

"I'm afraid not."

"I know your husband will be glad to get away from here."

The patient looked up. "You can say that again." Afterward he was restless, anxious for the night to pass.

Charles loaned him one of his western story magazines. The cover held a lurid picture of gunfighting, and the stories were equally gory.

Later Charles heard a weird, inhuman gasp and turned his

head. The patient, sitting half upright, sucked desperately for breath. His neck was stretched, elongated, the thin neck muscles taut as cables; his hands clawed at his throat.

"Nurse!" Charles screamed. "Doctor!"

The other patients yelled. For a moment there was bedlam. The nurses came running and drew a screen about the patient. Then the resident doctor and his assistants arrived. Charles heard the low urgency of their voices, the rustle of swift movement. An oxygen tent was ordered. But before it arrived, the doctor came slowly from behind the screen.

"Sometimes it happens like that," he said to his assistants. "Undue excitement. The heart can't take it."

The nurses retired. A few minutes later two orderlies removed the screen and wheeled the cot, on which the covered body rested, from the ward. Now in the empty space beside Charles's bed, where a few short minutes before there'd been a man going home next day, was death. A frightened silence fell upon the ward. After a time the patients talked intermittently in whispers. Shortly the lights were turned off for the night. Charles lay in the darkness contemplating death. It seemed to him then, in the wake of shock, as if death negated all life. All the splendid glory that life offered and people dreamed came to nothing in death. All the talk of good and bad he'd endured throughout his life, everything that he'd been taught, chemistry, Latin, religion, good manners, were senseless, he concluded. There was nothing in the end but nothing anyway.

Finally he slept and dreamed that he was falling. Three nights in a row he dreamed that he was falling. The death had softened his emotions, left them in a state of flux torn between fear and protest. He didn't want to die himself; he didn't want to see anyone die; he didn't want to think about it.

But the patient with the gangrenous arm died, and death came again into his thoughts. During the day a blood clot had become dislodged and moved slowly up a vein toward his heart. The doctors gathered about his bed and worked desperately to dissolve it.

Early in the evening, when the patient became aware that he

was dying, he began reciting the Lord's Prayer, over and over and over, and after the lights were turned off, only the night lamp left above his bed, the voice went on and on in the strained, rigid darkness. Doctors and nurses tiptoed through the ward, sibilant whispers came from behind the screen, but the praying voice continued, indifferent to the fuss and bother, growing weaker as the night wore on. A shroud of horror descended on the ward. No one slept. When one dies prayerfully it is always infinitely more despairing to those who have to listen.

Slowly, inexorably, Charles's mind hardened toward the voice; some defense had been erected; his anger and resentment crystalized. After that he thought only of getting well, getting out, getting what he could and enjoying it while he still lived. He fought bitterly, desperately, against acceptance of infirmity. Inside he cried continuously.

But outwardly he was cheerful. He learned to smile to hide his inner feelings. When the panic came and fear rose like bile from a ruptured bladder, he spread his lips so the dimples showed and widened his senseless eyes. He smoked incessantly to combat the driving irritation of his confinement. He laughed in quick, staccato bursts. He was so brave, they said.

"And how's our cheerful young patient this morning?" the nurses greeted him, bringing the monotonous trays of juices and milk toast.

"As ever," he smiled.

Only his mother could kill the smile. Slowly his heart turned against her. Now when she called he hated the sight of the grief that lived in her face; he was repulsed by her bickering and denouncements.

"Mother, will you please-please-please shut up," he'd say whenever she launched into a tirade against the hotel. "You're as much to blame as anyone."

These outbursts cut to her heart. "Mother's doing the best she can, son," she'd plead, tears brimming in her reddened eyes.

She had tried to sue the hotel, but the day after the accident the hotel had filed for bankruptcy and declared itself insolvent. She meddled with the hotel employees, seeking those who might testify to the hotel's solvency. The tiny woman with rouged and powdered face, strange deep-set gray-green eyes glinting behind nose glasses, dressed in the old brown fur coat, the brown felt hat pulled low across her forehead, became a familiar sight, incongruous and pathetic, somehow frightening too, at the back entrance where the colored waiters came and went. They knew her as Charles's mother and greeted her courteously with furtive sidewise glances as they passed. She'd become such a nuisance that Mr. Small had requested Professor Taylor to keep her away.

"You're just making a fool of yourself," he charged.

She flew into a rage. "You're just as bad as they are. You'd see your own son a cripple, broken and penniless for life."

"What you're doing isn't helping any. Do you think you're helping him to walk?"

"At least I'm not just sitting down and letting everyone run over me."

"No, you're just antagonizing everyone who might help us."

They began shouting at each other. The neighbors came to the windows to listen. One stepped out on the porch, debating whether to interfere. William sat in his room, engulfed in shame. Finally he went down to the kitchen.

"Dad! Mother! Please. That isn't doing any good."

The sight of him standing there, blind and helpless, his face shadowed in humiliation, quieted them for the time.

But she couldn't rest. She had to do something. She couldn't bear the waiting, the praying, the hoping. She felt compelled to exculpate herself of blame. It was as if she believed that by some self-sacrificial act she could at once, restore her son, free herself of guilt and win him back to her.

She called upon the district attorney to prosecute the hotel for negligence.

"Do you wish to swear out a warrant, Mrs. Taylor?"

"They're so full of tricks I don't know who to charge. It's your duty, anyway; it's not mine. You're required to prosecute lawbreakers."

"Our office has no evidence to act on, Mrs. Taylor."

She was enraged. All evening she fumed. "They're not going to get away with it," she informed her husband.

"They're not trying to get away with anything," he defended them. "The Industrial Commission takes care of these cases. That's the law. The hotel is paying the boy his salary." But even as he said it he felt himself a traitor.

Both suffered in their own individual manner. It robbed their efforts of all purpose, turned all the long years of struggle into bitter waste. They had no direction for their anger, no outlet for their hurt; their emotions turned against themselves.

Mrs. Taylor's long and bitter fight was to save herself as much as anything. She didn't realize this. She thought of herself as doing what a mother should. And yet, in the end, she lost herself. Both lost themselves. She became mean and petty. And although Professor Taylor had been without a teaching post for four long years, he had still felt he belonged. Deep down he had still considered himself a teacher. Now he didn't. It broke him inside where it counted. He gave up. He lost his will to try. In many ways, the effect on this little black man born in a Georgia cabin, who'd tried so hard to be someone of consequence in this world, to live a respectable life, rear his children to be good, and teach his backward people, was the greatest tragedy of all. Mrs. Taylor never gave up as he did. But she had to feel the world was turned against her to justify herself.

In turn Charles was affected by the change in them. The essence of their defeat was insidiously transmitted to his consciousness. His confidence was shaken. The fact of having parents was no longer reassuring. He became frightened of the world. He dreaded their visits and wished they'd never come.

His mother's eyes were always red-rimmed and something had happened to her face; something was missing, some quality that had given it distinction. Two red spots of rouge stood out on her high cheekbones in startling fashion.

"They ought to be made to pay for what they've done to you," she'd say piteously.

"Let it alone!" he'd shout. "For God's sake let it alone!"

22

AFTER SIX WEEKS SLIGHT ARTICULATION HAD returned to his fingers.

"Keep kneading them," his doctor instructed. "Pretty soon we'll have those splints off and see how it looks." '

One morning he discovered he could move his feet. He was afraid to mention it. For two days he kept his secret, wiggling his toes and finally moving his legs.

"Look," he showed the doctor.

The doctor was amazed. "Wonderful!" he exclaimed. He tapped the knees for reflexes. "Wonderful! Wonderful!"

From then on Charles knew that he would walk again.

Several weeks following, the splints were removed. His arm was slightly bent, terribly emaciated; it was attached to a brown, atrophied hand. On the inside of the forearm, where a bruise had festered, was a large dark area of rotted flesh, and below the red serrated ridge of the scar where the bones had protruded. At first sight he was frightened, but the doctors seemed well pleased. They gave him cocoa butter for massaging and a ball of putty to knead. He followed their instructions zealously. For long hours while reading, holding the book with his right hand, he kneaded the putty with his left, unthinkingly. The strength came back without his realizing it.

One day he looked outside and noticed it was summer. Three months had passed. He decided he would walk. Waiting until the ward was unattended, he threw aside the covers, inched his body to the edge and stood. He was exceedingly weak, his knees buckled and his legs felt numb, half-asleep. The cast cut into his flesh. But his back did not hurt at all.

The nurse returned and caught him standing. Her face whitened. "What are you doing out of bed?"

He grinned at her. "I'm just trying out my legs."

Several of the other patients laughed. She flushed with anger.

"Help him, Clyde. Don't let him fall," she called to one of the convalescents while she ran for help.

Clyde came over and grasped him about the cast. "Steady, boy, steady."

"I wasn't going to fall," he protested, but by then he could barely stand.

The nurse returned with the resident doctor, several internes and the orderly.

"The army," Clyde murmured.

They lifted him back to bed. He felt a high, lightheaded exhilaration. Laughter bubbled from his lips.

"How does the back feel?" the doctor asked.

"It doesn't hurt a bit." Excitement slurred his voice; his face was flushed and his eyes were bright as fire.

His own doctors were incredulous. They ordered X-rays and warned him not to move. But several mornings later they came in grinning.

"We're going to let you walk a bit, Charles. See how you like it."

With their help he walked across the ward and back. They looked at one another.

"I fooled you, didn't I?" Charles laughed.

On the third of July, four months to a day, he was discharged. The cast had been removed. He now wore a strong back-brace with two steel bars flanking the spinal column and straps about his shoulders and thighs.

His perceptions had sharpened. He felt things more strongly. Situations that had been commonplace were now stark and ugly. He was more easily irritated. His reactions had become hard, abrupt and violent. His world had filled with blacks and whites, harsh purples, vivid greens, blinding yellows. There were no shades, no tints, no grays, no in-betweens. His emotions were either intense or non-existent.

He'd thought how wonderful it would be back in the world of healthy people. But everything seemed strangely different, as if the world had gone out of focus while he'd been away.

He was struck by the atmosphere of animosity that existed in the house. His parents' incessant quarreling became insufferable. Before his accident those bitter family scenes had filled him with anguish. He'd shared their suffering, longed for their happiness. But now he felt only a harsh rejection, devoid of any tenderness or concern. He didn't care whether they were happy or not. They were alive, and that was enough. Everybody was hurt. William was hurt—terribly, irrevocably hurt. He, himself, was hurt. Goddammit, one didn't have to cry and fight about it all the time, he thought. One didn't have to make a goddamned spectacle out of every emotion. It seemed as if he floated in emotion. He wanted to get away from them, so he wouldn't have to hear them, share in their bitterness and defeat, or even think about it.

He still had only partial use of his hand and required his mother's help in dressing. And the doctors had instructed him to sit for an hour each morning in a tub of hot water. But once these chores were done he left the house only to return for dinner.

He was self-conscious about the brace and wore a jacket even on the hottest days. It held him abnormally erect. His face was tight from the discomfort and frustration. His posture was mistaken for a sign of arrogance, his expression for disdain and condescension. He shrank from the antipathy in people's eyes. He avoided going places where he was known. He never went to visit any of his former friends.

When he began visiting the dentist he found temporary escape. He was a garrulous old man with a great curiosity concerning Charles's background. He was fascinated by the stories of the southern Negro colleges. Sometimes they talked for hours.

Most afternoons Charles went to the movies, sitting alone in the obscurity of the loges, smoking an endless chain of cigarettes, absorbing the organ music, watching the fantasies unfold on the screen. And for a time he felt safe from the prying eyes. Nothing mattered then but the emotion which engulfed him. He could dream away his infirmity for an hour or two.

For a time the members of his club came to visit. He and Harvard took short walks in the park. Occasionally they went together to a show. But the old intimacy was lost. He found himself strangely intolerant of the fellows' social life. He couldn't bear to hear about the parties or the girls. There was little for them to talk about.

Finally he realized he didn't like the people he had known. They stopped coming. He was relieved. He liked it best alone. He sat alone for hours in the park, half-relaxed, unthinking, just sitting there hidden from the world. There was a high, grassy knoll where no one ever came. He lay there, stretched on the grass, and watched the lake. He never tired of watching the constant ripple of the waves. It soothed him. In the big expanse of water, like the world almost, nothing was permanent but change. Strangely, he liked the thought of that. A wave rose on the surface, took a million different contours as it rolled its six-foot span of life, and was gone; another took its place. Like all the countless people of the world, assuming the various shapes of life and then death.

He had always liked the night from the time he'd first discovered it. He had liked it then because of the difference in himself and in others too. Now he liked it because it hid him. At night no one could tell that he was infirm; no one could see the back-brace bulging from his jacket. And he could revel in the various wonders of the night—the lighted marquees of the theatres, spilling magic on the flower-gardened people; the long, amber necklace of the High Level Bridge across the inky Cuyahoga; railroad trains with their thousand yellow eyes gliding down the dark lakeshore; moonlight on the great expanse of water like ever-crumbling dreams. He was imbued by that moving, inarticulate awe of beauty given only to the very young.

And from it all he had to come back and listen to his parents quarreling bitterly. At such times he hated them.

He began walking until late at night, going far from the neighborhoods he had known. He liked to walk among the dwellings of the rich, past the old mansions hidden deep behind the night-black landscapes. Shaded lamps glowed cheerfully behind wide windows; here and there someone sat in a cone of light placidly reading, guarded by the shrubs and evergreens—sentinels in the outside darkness. From afar they seemed so peaceful, enveloped in serenity, impregnable to all the irritations and distractions that were his lot. He imagined the residents as happy and contented, filled with the joy of living. He felt it was wonderful to be rich, have all the things one wanted, nothing to worry about, and so many marvelous things to do to fill the lonely hours. He came to feel that by a tiny twist of circumstance he might have lived there too. Deep down it was the life he yearned for.

It made him discontent. He lost all liking for his own home. He became restless, slowly desperate in his loneliness.

His thoughts returned to girls, but to none he'd ever known. The summer's heat and sexual urges boiled within him. His hot, naked stare bore into women, sought their lips and breasts and hips, undressing them. Walking down a quiet, sexless street, he'd pass a woman with firm breasts, and catch afire, unable to control the throbbing in his groins. He had to walk with his hands in his pockets to hide his agitation. And all the hippy, full-breasted girls about the neighborhood drove him frantic.

Finally, in desperation, he turned to Scovill Avenue. He'd been there often in the daytime. By day there were the aged and smoke-blackened churches, grubby stores, barbecue joints, pool halls, dismal tenements, funeral parlors, flanking on the filthy gutters, no different from another slum street. Deserted for the most part, it was pitiably forlorn. But at night it teemed with a sinister life as the wretched inhabitants crawled from their dark vermin-ridden holes to traffic in prostitution, mugging and murder.

He moved warily as one picking his way through hostile territory. His breath was short from tension, congested in his chest, his muscles taut. A vein throbbed in his temple.

"Wunna see uh girl, baby?" a hoarse, whiskey-thickened voice spoke indifferently in his ear.

He jumped, startled, wheeled about. Beside him loomed a hideous hag, her scarred, painted face twisted in a lewd grimace. The vile reek of her breath poured into his face, polluting his nostrils. He drew back, shaking his head, and hastened his stride.

"Go tuh hell den, you sissy li'l bastard!" the whore reviled, waking up the darkness. The shadows crawled with unseen life.

He heard a snicker slither through the gloom, a laugh, another whiskey voice, "You tell 'im, Mayme."

He shuddered beneath the scorn that flowed over him like filth. His impulse was to flee. But he couldn't give up so easily. An ungovernable urge held him to his purpose. There must be some that he could bear. The fellows in his club who'd said they'd gone by way of Scovill couldn't possibly have lain with these wretched hags.

Suddenly a beam of light struck across the street, catching a horde of cruising women and stealthy men in stark tableau. The next instant the street was deserted, as if the figures had dissolved instantaneously into the night. He found himself alone. A police squad car creeped up beside him at the curb, its red light blinking, the spotlight searching down the street.

"Where you going boy?" an officer addressed him.

His heart stuck in his throat. "Just walking."

"You don't belong down here. You'll get hurt."

"Go over on Cedar," another said. "Get some clean ass. This here's filth."

"You know Billie on Thackeray? She's got some nice girls. Treat yourself big. Tell her I sent you—Monahan."

"I'm not looking for a girl," he denied. "I'm going to my father's church."

There was a moment of silence. "He's going to church," the second officer said.

"Don't let me catch you on this street again," said the first officer as the car moved off.

"No, sir."

He hastened over to Thackeray, knocking at doors indiscriminately, asking for Billie. Some of the occupants invited him in, others chased him away. Finally he found the right house. Billie let him enter a pitch-dark foyer.

"Mr. Monahan sent me."

"Mister?" She had a heavy masculine voice.

"Officer."

"What you want?"

"I—well—I want to see a girl."

251

"We don't have no girls here."

"Oh! Well, I—"

For a fleeting instant the light came on. He was blinded in the glare. Then it was darker than before.

"All right, baby."

She ushered him into the living room. Soft light spilled on luxurious furnishings. It resembled his idea of an opium den.

"Set down, baby. You wanna buy a pint?"

She was a big, dark, thickset woman with a heavy mustache. Her blouse was open and he noticed hairs growing from between her breasts.

"Yes, I want—I want a pint."

"It's five dollars."

He fished for the money. "I want a pretty girl—a *nice* girl," he stammered.

She looked at him curiously. "All my girls are nice and pretty."

After she'd gone there was no sound from the house or from the street. He felt entombed in a sense of unreality. He wondered what would happen when he went to bed. For a moment he was frightened. Then a young woman clad in a transparent negligee entered silently, bearing a tray with the whiskey and setup.

"My name is Margaret," she said affectedly, giving him an artificial smile. "What might be yours?"

"Oh! Charles is mine," he replied.

Placing the tray on the coffee table with an air of formality, she appeared astonishingly shy. "And how would you like yours?"

Dark curly hair fell about her shoulders. Her complexion was like coffee and cream; her eyes ringed with mascara. He could see the outline of her legs through the chiffon negligee. He thought her the most beautiful woman he'd ever seen.

"I—" he choked. "Just like yours."

She mixed the drinks and came over and sat beside him, holding her glass with the little finger extended in what she thought was a gesture of refinement. Billie had instructed her to act like a nice girl. "You're cute," she said.

Her soft, perfumed contact heightened his excitement unbearably. He gulped his drink, coughed and strangled.

252

"Don't rush, baby, we got all night." Her voice seemed to caress him.

He stole another look at her and swallowed hard. "I'm ready now," he blurted.

She laughed. "All right, baby."

Upstairs in the perfumed blue room a soft pink light bathed her naked body. She screened herself with her hands. He throbbed with exquisite tension, his blood on fire. His fingers turned to thumbs; he couldn't undo his buttons. She helped remove his shirt.

When she came to the brace she exclaimed, "Oh, your back's hurt!"

"Not much," he gasped, panting, throbbing as if he'd burst.

Before turning toward the bed, she said, "That'll be five dollars, baby."

He gave her ten dollars in his excitement. She smiled, then took him in her arms, embracing him with warmth. His body sealed against her velvet skin. At the instant of contact it was over. He was done, spent, finished. His face burned like frostbite; his blood congealed. What must she think of him? He felt miserably ashamed, mortified, unutterably chagrined. He wished he could die on the spot.

Though devoid of sensitivity, her sexual appetites were flagrant, intense, consuming. Frantic and trembling, she held him tight and forced her tongue into his mouth. He struggled to free himself. Locking her legs about him, she made a strange moaning sound and bit him on the lip. He thought she was trying to hurt him. "Don't!" he screamed in terror, striking her blindly.

She threw him aside and sprang to her feet, blazing with an idiot's rage at this greatest indignity to a whore. "Goddammit, you son of a bitch, I'll kill you!" she mouthed, clawing at his face.

He turned to escape and wrenched his back. Pain and terror gripped him in blind panic. "Oh!" he sobbed. "Oh! Please!"

She hung over him, her long, polished fingernails gleaming in the dim light like bloody talons. "You dirty freak! I oughta have you shot for hitting me. I'm not the kind you can hit you son of a bitch!"

He raised his hands to ward her off. "I didn't—I'm not—I couldn't—" His mind groped dazedly for the words. "I mean I didn't mean to hit you. I just—it just happened. I thought you—"

She was partly mollified. "If you wasn't a cripple bastard I'd kill you. Get your clothes on and get out. If I told Billie you'd hit me she'd have you beat to death."

He fumbled with his clothes, trembling with shame and terror. In his haste he couldn't fasten anything. "I'm—I'm trying to hurry," he pleaded.

She lit a cigarette and sat on the bed and watched him, smoldering with rage. Her mouth was brutal and in her eyes was a look of animal stupidity. He was afraid to look at her. His broken arm was useless.

Finally he got up courage to say, 'If you—if you help me dress I'll give you five dollars."

She relented and took the money. She helped him strap on his brace and tied his laces. He shuddered at her touch, looking away.

"You're a strange one," she said curiously. "What kind of kick is that?"

He didn't know what she meant. "Is what?"

"Is that all you ever do? Just—" she snapped her fingers "—and it's over."

He was ashamed to tell her but was afraid to keep silent. "I—I never did it before."

She stopped helping him. "Oh!" Then she sat down and laughed until tears came into her eyes.

He worked with his buttons frantically.

"Look, baby, you don't have to go. Mama'll show you what it's like."

"I got to go," he muttered desperately. "I got to go."

"You can spend the night, baby. You got a lot to learn. And I'll be nice."

"No, I got to go. I can't stay."

"But you'll come back?"

"Yes, yes, I'll come back. But I got to go now."

"Don't go with any other girl now. Promise me."

"Yes, yes, I promise. But, please, I got to go."

He was crying inside from shame and desperation. She buttoned his clothes and went with him to the door. She kissed him in the dark. He was trembling all over. "Come back and see me, baby," she urged in a sensuous voice.

He ran down the stairs without looking back, and walked at a dizzy pace. His back ached unendurably. He shrank from the people he passed on the street. His chagrin became unbearable. He boarded a street car but couldn't sit still. At the next corner he alighted, walked over to Euclid and slunk into a movie.

An all girl orchestra was playing:

> *When day is done*
> *And shadows fall*
> *I dream of you ...*

His emotional turbulence quieted to a steady pulsation; his trembling slowly ceased. The picture came on and in the quiet darkness he devoured the youth and beauty of the heroine's face. His stare never left the soft, mobile mouth, the tender smile, the expressive eyes, and the thousand exquisite movements of the facial planes. For a time he was lost in his spell of adoration. Then the picture ended.

He returned to the street, forced to face living people in this living world. He shrank from them as if he had leprosy. At last his thoughts caught up with him. Finally he admitted to himself that his accident had incapacitated him sexually. He felt that women could see it stamped on him. And the shame of having spent himself, his first experience, on such an ill-tempered prostitute made him, by the time he reached home, morbidly depressed.

His mother was waiting up for him. "Why must you stay out so late, son?"

For the first time, although vaguely realized, her color separated them as Cedar from Euclid, as himself from the heroine on the screen. But her scolding was brackish and cutting, and her worrying about him, picking at him for every little thing, always nagging, when it was herself, he thought, who'd done this monstrous thing to him, so enraged him that for a moment he couldn't breathe. He hated her—God, if she knew how he hated her, he thought.

"You're not well yet and mother worries so when you stay out so late."

"Goddammit, let me alone!" he exploded.

She was shocked speechless, her old flaccid face falling into ruins.

He ran clumsily up the stairs and sat in the bathroom, sobbing bitterly. Finally he undressed and examined himself long and thoroughly. His back ached. Shame and fear combined in excruciating agony. He'd never be a man, he thought. And the shame of having revealed it to a senseless whore. How could he have done this to himself, gone to that den and bared his naked soul to a brutal prostitute? How could he have so debased himself?

For days he wouldn't leave the house. He felt his shame and inadequacy as visible as a torch. He kept everyone on edge. His mother went about with a tight, grim look, sick with anxiety, but still she refused to speak to him. He wouldn't apologize. She wouldn't forgive him. But finally the shame quieted to passive resignation. He rationalized by telling himself that all the fellows visited prostitutes. And when the sexual urge returned he became frantic again. Now his incapacity took precedence over his shame. He poured through all the textbooks on physiology in the house, seeking information about the sexual act. He didn't care what Marge was, he wanted her. But he could find no information to help in his dilemma.

Finally he consulted his doctor.

"I want to know if I can get married?"

The doctor was alarmed lest he'd made an oversight in his diagnosis. "I'm sure your accident didn't affect your spermatic cord. We found no evidence in our examination."

"It isn't that. I can't hold it." He felt his face burn.

The doctor laughed with relief, but sight of the desperation in the youth's face sobered him. He explained that it was not uncommon. "There's nothing to worry about. If it happens again just wait for a resurgence. At your age it should come back within a half hour."

Charles felt juvenile and foolish but immensely relieved. Next day he drew fifty dollars from his account and visited Billie's early. He slept with Marge until midnight. They had whiskey and food brought to the room. He was ravenous but didn't drink because the whiskey made him sleepy. He paid her recklessly and she enjoyed lying lazily in bed, drinking, and being paid for it too, and she made him feel competent. She had the body of a debauchee who seemed bursting with love, and her smooth, flawless skin against the pale blue sheets in the pink light had a warm, glowing tint. She was coarse and vulgar and much older than himself, and called him "Daddy" in the immemorial manner, but each time he gave himself he closed his eyes and imagined she was young and virginal and a beautiful princess from the land of dreams. He remained excited the whole time and there were moments when he felt almost completely recovered.

After that he spent much of his leisure time at Billie's. With Marge he was hidden and reassured at the same time. He confessed to her how frightened he'd been the first time when he'd believed he'd lost his sexual capacity. He told her many things about himself he'd never told anyone before. Sealed in the strange room, safe from the hard, critical world, secure in her love, he could confess all his hurts and dreams, his fears and disappointments. She sipped her whiskey and pretended to listen, her thought on other things. And then he'd take her furiously.

"Daddy," she'd say with professional excitement. "My frantic little daddy. You just had to warm up."

And he thought she loved him. Afterwards he could walk down the dismal slum streets and look the critical, staring people in the face, feeling daring and manly because he'd slept with a whore. And if he could think of her as young and virginal, he could wink boldly at the young girls his own age, feeling gallant and experienced.

257

His mother would be waiting up for him. She'd look at him accusingly, her mouth hard and grim. He would go up to his room without speaking to her.

Although he knew he would miss Marge and the sanctuary of her bed, he was relieved when it came time for him to go away to college.

23

So MUCH HAD HAPPENED TO HIM DURING THE PAST year that college, inescapably, was anti-climax. The flame of confidence that had caught fire the night of his graduation from high school had been extinguished by his accident. To still his fears of lost manhood he'd poured too much of his will into Marge's receptive body. The hot flow of his ambition had cooled to stumbling blocks, and during his seizures of depression his earth had begun to quake again.

As a consequence college never got him, never got down inside him; he never became a part of it. He matriculated and went to classes, but he never became a student. He missed entirely the purpose of college, the idea, the realization that it was a place of higher learning. He was always just outside.

Much of it appealed to him: the artificial sense of freedom that college gives, the beautifully landscaped grounds, the great stone stadium, the impressive buildings surrounding the huge, green oval. And there was a feeling of exclusiveness, like being a member of a superior club.

Temporarily he had escaped the constraining authority of his parents, his mother's constant nagging and fear of his father's defeat. It was as if he'd shed a great burden he'd borne for many years, or got rid of an irritating sore. He could do as he chose, go where he pleased. He felt that he'd grown wings.

But, paradoxically, many of its appealing aspects also repulsed him. Greater freedom incurred greater self-reliance. The impressive architecture was overawing. It was too big, too impersonal. There were too many students, six thousand of them, of which only five hundred were colored. He felt outnumbered again. And the exclusiveness which at first he'd found so appealing carried its own bitter sting of exclusion.

So much that he liked was negated by its pattern of segregation. The city itself was segregated in much the same manner as St. Louis had been. But in St. Louis he'd attended a segregated school; he'd been a part, he'd belonged. While in the university he had no part in any life outside the cold and formal classes. Negro students were barred from all the fraternities and sororities whose houses bordered the university grounds, nor were they invited to join any of the student clubs and honorary societies of the university itself. Nor could they patronize any of the privately owned restaurants, cafés and theatres of the neighborhood, which seemed so essential to a sense of ease. From the very first he knew he didn't really belong, and that he never would.

The colored students had a social life of their own, but it was not the same. They gathered in the garden of the library, flirted and became acquainted and made dates, their sugarcoated laughter floating through the open windows to distract many a serious student bent on research.

"Oh, introduce us to the pretty mens."

"Lucy, Chuck Taylor, Steve Adams—and this little flapper with the gleam in her eyes, boys, is Anne."

"It's not gleaming for you, big boy."

"Steve is taken, Little Sister: Edith's got her brand on him."

"Aw, Ben—"

"And who's nursing you, pretty mans?"

Charles blushed. "I—I'm in the field."

"Don't let her rope you, kid; she does it to all the guys. That's just a wriggle in her jiggle."

"Rhymes with pants," Lucy said.

"Don't tell me, honey, let me guess," Big Ben whispered stagily. "Could it be, by any chance, you mean ants?"

Their soft orgiastic nuances flowed along the edges of Charles's mind. He came out of himself at such times; he loved it.

That bit of the campus, by common consent, had been conceded to the colored students.

They had their own fraternities and sororities which met in private residences. Charles was tapped for one of these. One night the pledges were blindfolded and taken in a truck to a city park where they were paddled and thrown into a lake. After which they became Pharaohs. They had made the grade and were invited to all the popular parties. They gave dances in the Crystal Slipper on Long Street and wore their black ties as handsomely as any in the university section. Crowds collected from the nearby pool rooms, gambling clubs, barbershops, whiskey joints and greasy restaurants to meddle and admire.

"Ain't that purty—the purple one, honey; ain't that uh purty thing?"

Or some young pomaded petty pimp leering, "How 'bout some of you, baby?"

That section of Long Street was called "The Block." Soda parlors abutted filthy dives, doctors and hoodlums drove the flashiest cars, and prostitutes and school girls walked side by side.

They had their own restaurants and theatres. On weekend nights they crowded into the Empress, along with the people of the neighborhood, to listen to a prissy young man play provocatively on the piano, while a tall brown handsome man with marcelled hair sang *Moonlight On The Ganges* in a voice that made the coeds scream. For days following the showing of a romantic picture the coeds went about the campus distorting their faces and wrinkling their noses with all the sex appeal of the heroine on the screen.

Or they patronized the whiskey joints on the side streets, drank cheap home-brew with salt, and debated points of higher and lower learning, as the brothers in the fraternity houses did.

And on Sunday they ate in groups at Brassfield's popular restaurant and afterwards walked their girls along the pebbled paths of Lincoln Park and lay on the dusty grass.

But all of this took place four miles away from the university, on the other side of town, in another world.

Charles was in conflict with the university from the day of his arrival. He was at once inspired by the thought of being a student, and dispirited by the knowledge this thought inspired. On the one hand he began to run, not outwardly, but in his emotions, like a dog freed from its leash; while on the other he was fettered by every circumstance of the university life which relegated him to insignificance. He dreaded the classes where no one spoke to him, he hated the clubs he couldn't join, he scorned the restaurants in which he couldn't eat.

He found it irritating and humiliating to discuss his courses with his advisor, to reveal his infirmity and tell about his jigsaw academic background. Although his advisor was a pleasant young professor who kept smiling encouragingly, he was glad when the ordeal was over and he could escape to the Student Union, a four-storied brick building overlooking Mirror Lake. There in the large, cool, dark-paneled lounge, he could sit in a leather chair, puff his pipe and imagine he looked upper-class and relaxed.

Some of the white students drove old battered roadsters with rumble seats, painted in bright colors and bearing crude legends of college wit, and wore yellow slickers adorned with names and dates. They seemed to him the true collegians, the only ones who counted, and he emulated them. Beneath his yellow slicker, inscribed with the names of girls taken from the appendix of his college dictionary, he wore a red-and-gray striped blazer, tweed knickers, Argyll hose and yellow brogues. With his black slouch hat pulled low over his eyes, chin jutting forward, jaw muscles knotting as he gripped the long pipe stem between his teeth, he roared about the campus, screeching to a stop, frightening upperclassmen and stepping defiantly on the grass forbidden to freshmen. For the moment he'd feel less lost.

He'd taken a room in a minister's home near the campus, and had arranged for his meals at Mrs. Johnson's, a colored rooming house nearby. Most of the students who lived there waited on tables for the white fraternity and sorority houses in the vicinity. They bunked four and five to a room and twelve in the attic. Only a select few, most of whom roomed elsewhere—Randy Parker, a Chicago politician's son, Steve Adams, son of a St. Louis undertaker, Jesse Sherwood, whose father was principal of a colored high school in Kentucky—could afford to pay for their meals. The others ate where they worked. But together they formed a strangely loyal and closely knit unit, like members of a rather shabby but furiously animated and happy fraternity.

Living in such close proximity they had no secrets, no privacy. Their possessions, clothing, financial status, intellectual capacities, social diseases, personal habits, state of cleanliness, size of each other's genitals; their girls' reactions—who liked them big and who didn't—were topics of general discussion. Without provocation they would reveal their most intimate emotions, their most sacred associations, with startling candor. Charles was always shocked and repelled by such raw confessions.

But strangely enough, he liked them. He enjoyed their bantering and badgering until it turned on him; then he couldn't bear it. He dreaded their discovering he wore a back-brace, but it was inevitable.

For the most part they liked him too and, realizing his sensitiveness, seldom teased him as they did one another. He had money to spend and a red roadster, and they found him useful to drive them the four miles to the colored section. They'd pile on, eight or ten at once, and he'd drive them to their favorite whiskey joint.

He was a reckless driver, turning corners at full speed, and every now and then he'd throw one off.

"Hey, hold it, Chuck, stop, man, you lost Josh!"

He'd tramp down on the reverse pedal, killing the motor, the car lurching crazily to one side, throwing others off. John would limp forward, hands and knees bruised, trousers torn, a big swelling on his head.

"Goddamn, Chuck, take it easy, man," he'd say, having great

difficulty controlling his anger but knowing he must since all of them would also be depending on Charles to pay for their drinks. "Damn, son, you Barney Oldfield or somebody?"

He'd grin and roar off again. He always drove with the hood up and a floor board removed to provide a current of air to cool the motor, and from his seat behind the wheel he'd watch the exhaust manifold turn white hot.

Mrs. Johnson allowed them to entertain their girls in the living room. On Saturday nights when they could play the phonograph late the girls came over and they drank bathtub gin and did the slow, belly-rubbing dances in the dim light.

But the best times for Charles were the hot bright Indian Summer Sunday afternoons when he'd load his red chariot with other lonesome boys and drive up and down The Block, waving at all the pretty girls out in their many-colored glory. He'd park before the soda parlor and the girls would be magnetized. For an instant out of time the scene would catch fire, emotions would burn with the extravagance of youth, wit would spill like blood, as boys and girls engaged momentarily in the immemorial tussle of the sexes. Charles would be caught up in an incontinent excitement. His face would glow with an inner life. He'd feel carefree and wanted and included.

But he never got started in the academic life. He was like an airplane that crashes before it gets off the ground. He could have, but he wouldn't try. He contrived all sorts of excuses to keep from trying: the studies were too difficult, the classes too strange and formal; he didn't have the academic background for the pre-medical courses he'd elected; his see-saw schooling from Georgia to Mississippi, from Arkansas to Missouri, had left him pitifully unprepared for university study.

Deep down, where he wouldn't look at it, he was rebelling. If he couldn't take part in everything, he wouldn't take part in anything. He'd always been like that; if he couldn't have it all there was nothing in it for him.

Had his mother been there she would have pushed him. Subconsciously he had come to depend on her pushing. He was not complete away from her, not a whole person. He was still joined to her by an artery of emotion. Independently he could only exercise his will against her, never against others. Against others he needed the joining of her will.

He might have overcome all his aversion to the university, his lack of confidence, his feeling of exclusion, everything, had she made him know how much she depended on his succeeding there. He might have caught fire again. That part of his heart which meant most to himself was dedicated to her. He lived for his mother.

But by himself he wouldn't make the effort. He began to feel inferior and became resentful and withdrawn. It was as if the artery of emotion joining them began bleeding at one end.

His professors were lenient because of his injury and made unconscious allowances because of his race. They considered him a good boy from a nice background and didn't want to flunk him out. On several occasions his advisor requested his professors to give him another chance and he was often permitted to take tests over in which he had first failed.

But he never got his academic wings. His studies left him morbidly depressed; his social life excited him unnaturally. He had come out of his shell but it was not healthy. His excitement was sick; he couldn't control it. There were too many things to do, too many pretty girls, too many wonderful fellows; he had too much money to spend, too much leisure. He became slightly hysterical from so much excitement. As he bogged down more and more in his studies, his resentment toward the university increased. He felt imposed on. He had an awful row with his laboratory instructor. He began cutting lectures. And finally, slowly he withdrew completely to the frenetic escapes of the city.

He began haunting a house where the students often went to drink home-brew with salt and patronize the girls. Instead of studying he spent his nights at the Pythian Theatre where the colored musicals played, sitting in the front row, watching the sensual shimmying of the half-nude bodies with lust-filled eyes, the dark columnar limbs rising above his tortured gaze like gates to infinite ecstasy. Afterwards he'd go backstage and try to date the girls, but always the ones he wanted were already dated. He ended up by finding some prostitute or other.

On Hamilton Avenue in a house run by the Williams brothers he found a prostitute named Rose who reminded him of Marge. He slept with her so often that she became possessive. She called him her "lover" and said that he was full of steam.

He contracted gonorrhea from her and for a time was terrified. One of his friends suggested that he go to the university infirmary where he could receive treatment free of charge, but he was too ashamed and went to a private clinic in The Block.

The students at Mrs. Johnson's teased him mildly.

"Chuck's got his credentials."

"He's a man now. You're not a man until you've had the clap one time."

"Hell, I've had the clap for seven years," Clefus said. "It ain't no more than a runny nose."

The fellows laughed. No one seemed to take it seriously. But Charles found it dirty and disgusting and had to use a syringe and wear a supporter and quit drinking.

He was sick and morbidly depressed when the quarterly finals came, and was incapable of coping with any intellectual exertions. In German he turned in a blank paper. It didn't seem to him that he did much better in any of the other courses. But miraculously he was passed by all his professors. It was a question of whether he should feel glad or sorry. Now he'd have to continue; he owed it to his parents. If they had flunked him out he could have gone home in peace. By then he knew he couldn't make it, he'd never make it. All that had happened was a postponement of the inevitable end.

He went home for Christmas. He was thin and extremely nervous, always on the go, haunting the cheap cabarets on 55th Street, coming home late, drunk and exhausted. He couldn't even have the satisfaction of visiting Marge. He knew he shouldn't drink, but he couldn't bear his thoughts. Once he was caught in a heavy snowfall and there was no way of getting home. He had to spend the night in the downtown hotel. It was crowded with other stranded people. Some strange men tried to come into his room. He had a fight before the management came to his assistance. Afterwards he propped a chair against his door and sobbed bitterly. His life had become revolting.

It was obvious to his parents that he wasn't getting along well in his studies. They tried to draw him out but he wouldn't talk about himself. William was preparing for graduation from high school the following month. The house was always filled with his many friends, and he gave a gay New Year's Eve party. But Charles was uninterested.

The only reason he returned to the university was because his things were there. By then almost all the students knew he was a goner. Two of the fellows offered to coach him but he resisted all their efforts to help. Toward the end of January he wrecked his car. He'd been to a private party down the street from where he lived. One of the fraternity brothers called him aside.

"Are you well, Chuck?"

"Not quite."

"Then what the hell you doing here?"

"It's not catching," he protested.

"No, but dammit, it's dirty."

Anne came up in time to hear the last remark. "What's dirty?"

"I am," Charles said bitterly, and went to get his hat and coat.

He put the top down so the snow would blow in on him and sped toward the booze joints in The Block. The snow was in his eyes and he drove blindly into the abutment at the end of the viaduct. He was jarred slightly and his ankle sprained. For a long time he sat there in the wrecked car, letting the snow fall on him. His back began to ache. A car drove up and stopped.

"You hurt, buddy?"

"No, I'm all right," he heard himself reply.

The car didn't move so he climbed slowly from the wreck. A colored man was driving and offered him a lift. He got in and rode over to the house on Hamilton and drank himself blind. The next day his back ached so badly he couldn't move. The proprietors put him in their car and drove him home. His gonorrhea took a turn for the worse. For two weeks he was in bed. But he wouldn't let them notify his parents.

266

"It'd kill my mother if she knew I had gonorrhea," he told Mrs. Miller, the minister's wife with whom he lived.

"Poor boy," she grieved for him. Later she told her husband, "He's trying so hard to be brave."

His professors permitted him to make up for the time he'd lost. For a while he made a valiant effort. He felt as if he were drowning and made this one last desperate attempt to save himself. And for the first time in his life his mind would not respond. He couldn't concentrate; his memory failed him.

It was in a state of utter frustration that he attended the Pharaohs' grand ball, by which they metamorphosed into full-fledged fraternity brothers. Due to the number of guests they gave it in a larger, less fashionable ballroom than the Crystal Slipper, located near the red light district where Charles had become a patron. As he stood on the gallery, watching the couples whirl gaily below, everyone seeming so happy and excited, he felt debased beyond redemption, lost, cut off from all those fresh, clean, pretty people.

"Cheer up, Chuck. Have a drink," someone said.

He took the flask without looking at the donor, emptied it down his throat.

"Hey! Hey!"

"I'll get you some more," he promised.

"You know a place?"

"Right around the corner."

"Wait a minute. Maybe some of the fellows want to go."

He had drunk a pint of bathtub gin and it built a forest fire in him. Suddenly he was dancing, his despondency burnt away in the alcoholic flame.

Someone tugged at his sleeve. "You ready now, Chuck."

"Sure, anytime." He looked at the girl with whom he'd been dancing and was surprised to discover that she was Anne. "You want to go with us? We're going around the corner to buy some grog."

She hesitated. "Who all's going?"

"A bunch of us," Jesse said. "Steve and Edith, Randy and Jay, Johnny and his girl too." The last was a fraternity brother.

"All right. Wait until I get my coat."

The gay little party clad in formal finery tripped lightly through the dirty snow, faces flushed, eyes glowing with excitement. It was a lark.

"Won't they object to so many of us?"

"No, it's a pad—I mean a place where they sell home-brew too and people sit about and talk. There's a victrola too."

"How does Chuck know about these places?" Edith asked.

"Don't ask the mans that," Anne murmured.

"My knowledge is wide and varied; I was educated like Gargantua," Charles said with drunken flippancy.

As they clustered on the porch of the house of ill fame, whispering excitedly in the dark, startled eyes peered from darkened windows across the street. Finally a man cracked the door and peered from the darkened vestibule.

"It's me, George. I got some friends."

"Okay, come on in; there's nobody here."

He opened the door and they groped forward in the dark, striking against each other. Someone gasped. Then the door was opened into the dimly lit parlor. They surged forward in a body, sighing with relief.

"What'll it be?" Charles asked grandiloquently.

"Gin," Jesse said.

"A quart of gin and setup, George. You don't mind if we play some records."

"Don't play it too loud. Rose is sleeping."

The couples found seats and snuggled down in the semi-darkness, whispering, here and there a nervous giggle. George brought the drinks and served them. Charles put in a soft needle and played a blues recording. Slowly the girls relaxed, succumbing to that delicious sense of naughtiness as the gin took effect. They began to dance, rubbing their bodies together, giving themselves to the ritual of the sex act. Steve whispered in Edith's ear and she began to laugh hysterically. The other girls tried to quiet her; the young men's voices were raised excitedly.

George came into the room. "Shhh, don't make so much noise," he cautioned.

When Edith's hysterics subsided she began hiccuping. Everyone suggested a cure.

"We better go," Randy said.

Anne laughed nervously. "I bet Ben's looking all over for me."

Charles put on another record. "You're in good hands. Just one more dance."

They stood locked together, their bodies fused, scarcely moving.

Rose came into the room. She was dressed in a soiled green kimono and her coarse, straightened hair stood on end. She looked at Charles through narrowed lids. Her eyes glowed like live coals in the dim light. She hadn't seen him since he became ill. Now seeing him in the arms of a sweet young girl she was scalded with jealousy.

"What kind of dryfucking shit is this?" she screamed.

The girls gasped. A shocked silence fell. Slowly Rose looked about the room, her sleep-swollen face puffing with rage. Everything about the scene infuriated her—the air of innocence worn by the girls, the young men's concern for them, their horror at sight of her. She went berserk, lunged forward and dragged Anne from Charles's embrace.

Charles was outraged by her violence and vulgarity. He'd never known her to be like that. The times they'd been together she had been sweet and gentle. He clutched her about the waist and threw her roughly to one side. "Shut up, goddammit, and get out of here!" he shouted.

She clawed at him. "I guess mine ain't good enough for you." He pushed her away. She ran to the victrola, snatched off the record and smashed it.

The students began a headlong rush toward the exit, carrying their wraps in their hands. They stumbled through the pitch-dark vestibule, surged out on the porch and down the walk and through the dirty snow in panic-stricken flight, ruining their shoes and gowns. They didn't stop until they'd rounded the corner.

George came from the kitchen in time to see them leave. He closed the door after them and returned to the parlor. Charles and Rose stood looking at each other with bleak hostility. There was something deadly and debased in the battle of their wills.

"You quit me, didn't you?" she accused.

He didn't understand her. "Quit you?" He had never gone with her. "I was sick," he said.

"I fixed your little red wagon, pretty boy," she said vindictively.

A dazed look came into his face. All the sickness of despondency he had momentarily thrown off returned to castrate him. His shoulders sagged; his eyes had the look of death. "Yes," he admitted wearily, "if that makes you happy."

George felt sorry for the lad. "Go up and go to bed," he ordered Rose.

She looked at him defiantly. "I'm gonna take baby with me."

Charles covered his face in his hands. He couldn't look at her. His soul felt naked and defenseless. He knew if he looked at her he'd be lost; her brazen stare would conquer him and she could bend him to her will.

"Go on! Go on!" George said roughly, pushing her from the room.

Dazedly, Charles put on his coat and hat. Suddenly it struck him that he'd done a terrible thing. Now I'm in for it, he thought.

George walked with him to the door. "I'll see you, kid."

He turned around and looked at George, and was shocked by the sympathy he saw in the panderer's face. "Jesus Christ!" he said, thinking: Even this son of a bitch is sorry for me.

All the next day he kept to his bed. The following morning the postman brought a notice for him to report to the dean's office. The dean was a shy, crippled man with a thatch of graying hair. His clear blue eyes, always so warm with sympathy, were immeasurably saddened.

"Mr. Taylor, I have here a report on your misbehavior sent in by one of the students."

He read aloud the letter, recounting the episode with Rose, which Edith Rand had sent to him. "I have not had this investigated."

"You don't need to, sir. It's true."

"I had assumed so." He folded his hands, studying Charles's expression. "You have given me the necessity of making a very difficult decision."

"I'm sorry, sir."

"Do you feel that your failure in adjusting to the academic and disciplinary requirements of this university is due, in part, to your ill health?"

"I—" He groped for the words to explain it. "I suppose I don't fit."

"Because of your injury?"

"I guess that has something to do with it."

"If I permit you to withdraw for the remainder of the term, do you believe your health will be sufficiently improved by fall to enable you to make good?"

"Yes, sir, I do." What else could he say, he thought.

For a time the dean fiddled with the letter opener on his desk, then came to his decision. "I shall permit you to withdraw because of ill health and failing grades." It was an unprecedented clemency.

Charles stood up and when the dean extended his hand and said, "Good-bye and good luck, Mr. Taylor," the warm tone of sympathy and the dry, firm, encouraging clasp tore him apart.

"Good-bye, sir," he choked. "Thank you. Thank you."

For a long time he stood on the stone steps of University Hall, looking across the snow-covered oval. He was saying good-bye again, this time to many things, to all of his mother's hopes and prayers, to so many of his own golden dreams, to the kind of future he'd been brought up to expect, and to a kind of life, which, on the whole, had been the happiest he'd ever known. But at the time he didn't realize it. He felt trapped again, pushed into something against his will. *Why hadn't the dean let him go? Why did they keep pushing him? His mother had pushed him all his life and now, goddammit, she'd start pushing him again. Why hadn't the dean let him go? Then, goddammit, she couldn't push him. She wouldn't have anything to push him toward and he'd be done once and for all . . .*

Sudden tears blotted out the sight.

He packed early while most of the students were in class and spent the remainder of the day and night in hiding with Rose. He couldn't face the students. And some strange compulsion had sent him back to the source of his initial hurt. He didn't know what he expected to get from her.

The next morning he was on the train going home. He imagined his mother's shocked expression, her face folding into deep, harsh lines of hurt and bitter disappointment. A flash of hatred burnt through his mind, followed by despair.

What's wrong with me, he thought. Why must I always be some kind of disappointment to everyone?

Came arapping and atapping and atapping and atapping . . . The strange words kept time with the clacking of the wheels . . . He looked out the window. A farm sped by, a cow standing disconsolately in the dreary sweep of snow.

"Gone!" he said involuntarily. "It's gone!"

24

CHARLES WAS SICK AND CONFINED TO BED FOR TWO months after his return home. Complications had developed from his gonorrhea and his back ached constantly. He had to engage a private doctor and he was always nervous and on edge for fear the Industrial Commission doctors would discover his disease. He was afraid they might stop his compensation.

It was hard to keep it from his mother. She wondered why he needed so many doctors. Torn between concern for his health and anxiety over his state of mind, she couldn't keep away from him. He lived in torture for fear of her discovering his disease. He hated for her to come into the room. She wanted to nurse him. He had to invent all sorts of reasons to keep her from touching him. They fought each other in bitter silence, the spoken words that passed between them seldom conveying their true emotions. During the day when everyone was out, or at night when they were all asleep, he'd slip into the bathroom and treat himself. Once she almost caught him.

"What's the matter, son? Does your back ache? Why don't you let mother rub it?"

"Let me alone!" he shouted, wishing she was dead.

A black pall hung over him which none of them could pierce. William couldn't gain his confidence. They slept in separate rooms and were almost strangers. Now when they met they treated each other with that delicate diffidence of persons who've been close but have lost contact. William kept away.

No one had told his mother about his episode with the prostitute. But she knew there'd been something more than what was said. She couldn't conceive of him failing in his studies; he was too brilliant, she thought. He'd done something bad, she knew. Ever since his accident she'd lived in constant apprehension that he'd do something to destroy himself completely. She'd been relieved when he finally went to college. Now she was more apprehensive than before.

For a time, following his enrollment in college, his father had taken new ambition too. He'd tried for a civil service job. But the years away from teaching, without reading, unthinking because thought hurt, had taken their toll of him. He'd deliberately dulled his memory. Now he found he couldn't draw upon it anymore. As a consequence he didn't make an eligible grade. It hurt him more than if he hadn't tried. When winter came on, his carpentry work had fallen off. He had taken a job as a laborer. That, too, added to Mrs. Taylor's anxieties.

Now William was his mother's only consolation. He'd graduated from high school that January and had received a gold medal from the school board in honor of his high scholastic record. There had been a glowing tribute in the press. He had many nice friends; everyone loved him. She often wondered at the fate that had taken his sight and yet left him so much more ambitious and nobler than his brother. She couldn't conceive of where Charles would end. He acted so ugly. Disaster seemed to hang above him like a Damoclean sword. At times she felt he'd be better off if he were dead.

Only his father sympathized with him. Professor Taylor sensed his son's problem of adjustment, not only to every new phase of his own life, but to every change in theirs, to the over-all uncertainty in which all of them were caught. He knew that the various facets of metropolitan life combined with the strangeness of nonsegregated institutions had put him under a strain. He felt that Charles would have been better off had they remained in the South, or even if he'd been enrolled in a southern college. "Let the boy alone," he'd say when Mrs. Taylor complained about Charles's attitude. "Let him alone; you're killing him."

"I'd rather see him dead than ending up in the penitentiary or on the gallows," she'd reply.

The sound of their bickering went on night after night, her harsh, nagging voice, his whining rebuttal. Charles would close his door but the voices leaked in. He tried to close his mind, but suddenly he'd hear them shouting at each other, as if it were a dream, a nightmare. He'd struggle to awaken and discover he'd been awake all along.

One night he dreamed that his mother had slipped from a high precipice and was hanging perilously by one hand. He was standing nearby and one part of himself fought furiously to save her, but his body was immobilized. He couldn't will himself to move. He could only stand there, watching in utter horror, while she slowly lost her grip. The sound of her screams rang in his ears, awakening him. He felt a sharp, burning pain in the region of his disease and discovered he'd had a sexual discharge. Immediately, before he had even cleaned himself, he tried desperately to tear the memory from his mind. He felt utterly debased; he wanted to die. In the bathroom he saw his father's razor and thought of slashing his wrists. Then he saw the sleeping potions his mother often took. He swallowed six and went to sleep. It was late the next day when he awakened. But all the devastating details of the dream were still with him. He felt defiled, impure. He couldn't look his mother in the face.

It was then that strange demons began pursuing him. He never saw them, but he always felt them just behind, closing in on him. At the slightest sound he'd wheel about, his face gripped

in the horror of death. He tried to escape in study, suddenly determined to re-enter the university that fall. But he got a queer,
unnatural reaction from his textbooks. Sight of the printed text
made him physically sick; he wanted to vomit. He couldn't force
himself to read.

One night he went into his brother's room. "Will, I think I'm
going crazy," he said.

William was startled. "What's the matter, Chuck? What happened?"

He told of his reaction to his textbooks.

William was puzzled. "You mean you actually feel nauseated?"

"That's it. That's just how I feel—nauseated."

"I wouldn't worry about it," William said. "It's just nerve
tension. I used to feel that way too when I was in the hospital.
Why don't you just relax, let the studies go. Why don't you just
rest, Chuck."

He tried but he couldn't. For days he remained in complete
despair. William tried to comfort him, but after the first con-
fession he could never talk of it again.

One day his doctor said that he was cured. He dressed immediately after the doctor's visit and left the house, intending to
spend the night with Marge. It was a warm May day. The last
of winter's accumulation of soot-laden snow was thawing and the
thick black slime running in the gutters affected him strangely.
He felt a strong desire to wade in it and get his clean white
shoes filthy. He could barely restrain himself.

At the bank, on sudden impulse, he drew out three hundred
dollars. He wanted to impress Marge with being rich and pros-
perous. But Billie's house reminded him of the fiasco at George's,
the living rooms were quite similar, and he was struck by Marge's
resemblance to Rose. All the bitter hurt came back. Suddenly he
felt nauseated again. He left abruptly, walking rapidly along the
cheap slum street, avoiding the eyes of the whores in the windows. In his mind he was running. He went out Cedar Avenue,
but everything he saw reminded him of something he wanted to
forget—couples playing tennis on the courts behind the Y, the
corner where he'd wrecked his Aunt Bee's car. When he ap-

proached the Robinson's house he crossed the street and looked the other way. The three blocks between 97th and 100th Streets, known as "The Avenue," a congested area of vice and destitution, was a city paradox. Even though it was early afternoon of a working day, crowds of black and yellow people drifted up and down the street, shouting and laughing and cursing, threading in and out the whiskey joints, the gambling clubs, the whore-houses, as if it were a summer Saturday. Sleek fat pimps and hustlers sat in their parked cars, talking about their money, while starved, diseased flotsam shuffled past, living on a prayer.

Charles had seldom lingered in the vicinity. But now it intruded on his consciousness. A group of mothers with their babies chatted in the sun. A car roared down the street, screamed to a sudden stop. Several youths his age were pitching quarters on the sidewalk. All the different tones of laughter fingered on his mind. A sudden wave of loneliness swept over him. He turned into a pool hall to seek companionship.

"Give me change for a twenty," he said to the rack boy.

All the hustlers and hangers-on saw his roll of money. Suddenly he found himself hemmed in.

"Play yuh a game of rotation, kid?"

"Don't you play that guy, he's slick."

"The kid don't gamble. You don't gamble, do you, kid?"

He was rescued by a big light-complexioned man with curly hair who had once been his barber. "Let that kid alone; he's a friend of mine. Whatya say, Chuck, long time, no see."

"Hello, Dave."

"Wanna buy a car?"

"I hadn't thought about it."

"Come on." Dave took him outside and showed him a big sporty-looking touring car parked at the curb. The top was down and it had red leather seats. "I'll take you for a ride."

They drove out into the country and Dave increased the speed. "Listen." He kicked a pedal on the floor. Motor roar spilled out behind like thunder from a speeding plane, the sound enveloping them whenever they passed underneath a tree. "It's got a voice, eh?" he shouted over the roar. "A four-by-seven cutout."

Charles felt as if they were hurtling through space. His blood raced down the black road with the speeding car. "Let me drive," he shouted.

They stopped and exchanged seats. He gripped the wheel and pressed down on the accelerator. The big car leapt forward in an open-throated roar, throwing him back against the seat, and the road came up over the hood like a tidal wave. Nothing in all his life had equalled that sensation. He leaned forward into the onrushing road, his mind sealed shut in a feeling of invincible power, the whole past dropping away behind him, cut off; for the moment every thought he'd ever had was blotted out by the bright blue beautiful unknown sensation ahead, all else gone in his consuming sense of might. He knew then that with that car he could outspeed all his fears and trepidations, his shames and humiliations, the gnawing self-consciousness imposed by his injury, the terrible depression that had settled on his thoughts. With that car he could defy everyone. He could take that goddamned car and drive off the edge of the world. And later, after they'd gotten back to town and he was driving slowly down Cedar Avenue, looking at the passing girls, he knew somehow without actually thinking it, he could also rescue damsels in distress.

He bought the car from Dave, paying down two hundred and fifty dollars and having the balance financed for monthly payments. He had to give his age as twenty-one to sign the contract.

Owning a car gave him a feeling of importance. His mother noticed the change in him immediately. But she didn't know he'd bought a car. He never took it home. He knew she'd disapprove and he was afraid she might, in some way, force Dave to take it back. So he always parked it on the street beyond the high school and walked home.

Dave was having an affair with a married woman named Cleo and introduced Charles to her younger sister, Peggy, so the four of them could ride around together. Peggy was a soft, voluptuous

woman with reddish hair and fair skin, and she had that clinging, insistent femininity of women who want only to bear children. She was twenty-two years old and told Charles he was
the second man she'd had. Cleo's husband worked in a hotel
garage and was away on weekends. Peggy lived with them.

During the afternoons while the husband was at work the
four of them drove to nearby towns and rented rooms in various
brothels. But on Sundays Dave drove off alone with Cleo while
Charles and Peggy stayed at home. For Charles these were the
best times. All day long they lay in each other's arms. Peggy
slept on the couch in the living room, but on these days they
used her sister's bed. The shades were drawn and they could
hear the voices of the neighbors as they panted in delirium.
For a time they'd lie lazily apart.

"Why don't you want to marry me, baby?" she'd murmur in
her soft southern accent.

"You know I do," he'd lie.

They could hear the children laughing in the yard. It was
cool and dim and pleasant in the secret room.

"Why do you always put it off then?"

"But we're just getting to know each other."

"What else you want to know? Ain't it good to you?"

"Yes, yes."

And she'd take him, enfold him in her soft hot body so that
he drowned in ecstasy. She seemed to respond the moment he
touched her. Their mouths would be glued together, their tongues
fused, their bodies thrashing in a struggle each to consume the
other.

Once she screamed and bit his shoulder. Instantly he was
flooding, overflowing, all of himself gushing into her.

By afternoon the sheet would be spotted with their love.
They'd jump up guiltily and run about the house, naked and
laughing, while she washed the sheet, and she'd dress quickly
and hang it on the line to catch the last sun. The neighbors
watched her curiously, wondering why anyone would wash a
single sheet on a late Sunday afternoon.

Finally his mother knew, not from any telltale evidence, but from something in his look. His tension had gone, he was relaxed but more implacable than ever. He didn't fly into a rage when she scolded him for staying out so late. He scarcely paid any attention to her at all. She was overcome with a fierce, unreasonable jealousy.

"You just wait," she screamed at him. "You're going to end up in the penitentiary or on the gallows yet."

She wanted to hurt him, to beat him unmercifully. She told herself it was to save him. Several times when he left home she tried to follow him. But when he got over on the next street he seemed to disappear. She didn't know he simply got into his car and drove off. She thought the woman lived nearby. It was a white neighborhood. She was shocked. That he would take up with a white woman was unendurable. She couldn't realize that she wanted to be the only white woman in his life. And she was certain the woman was mature.

Her fury became uncontrollable.

"Charles is living with a woman on the next street," she told her husband, hoping to enrage him to action.

"Living?"

"He's having an affair."

He went over next day and found that only white people lived on that street. He was relieved.

"You're going crazy," he told his wife.

"You may think I'm crazy but I know what I'm talking about." He put down his paper. "Only white people live on that street." She couldn't bring herself to say the woman was white.

"Why don't you quit making up things to nag the boy. Let him alone, he's coming out all right. He just needs some peace."

She left the house; she couldn't control herself. After that she nagged at Charles whenever he was home. She found herself incapable of charging to his face that he was living with a woman. Instead she accused him of spending his time in dives and gambling dens. No matter what hour of night he returned home, she would arise and come into his room and turn on the light and stand in the door, her hair in braids and her face greasy with night cream, and nag until he turned his back and drew the covers over his head.

You're throwing away your chances . . . you're throwing away your chances . . . The words would slither and crawl through the room like figments of insanity.

Then one day Peggy told him he'd have to marry her.

"You've made me pregnant, honey."

They were returning from a drive, just the two of them, and had parked for a moment in front of her house. He had his arm about her and was leaning down to take her kiss. Abruptly he drew back.

"Pregnant?" He was frightened.

"You knew you were doing it, baby. The way you poured it into me."

"It's only been a couple of months."

"How long you think it takes?"

To marry her was beyond his comprehension. It seemed impossible; impossible that she would even think he would. She didn't know. He just couldn't marry a common ordinary colored woman like herself. What would his mother think? She'd feel betrayed after all the things she'd told him about his white forebears. She'd really die, he thought.

It was the first time he'd been faced with such a choice. He knew, at that moment, he could never leave his mother.

"Well, let's go inside and talk it over with your sister," he said.

She got out. He reached over and closed the door and sped off, driving as if the demons were chasing him.

The next day Dave said, "Cleo and her husband been lookin' for you. They asked me where you lived but I told 'em I didn't know."

"Was Peggy with them?"

"Not at the time. What happened?"

"We broke off."

"Is Peggy pregnant?"

"She says she is."

Dave looked at him curiously. "That's rough, kid."

"Goddammit, she ought to have been more careful," Charles flared defensively. "She knew I couldn't marry her."

"Well, you'd better be careful too, and hope they don't find you."

For several days he kept to himself, spending his afternoons at the movies, driving through the parks at night. He told himself he was glad to get out of it. But he couldn't get over the realization that he'd done something horrible, despite how his mother might have felt. It kept coming back how he must have hurt her. She loved him. The strange part was he loved her too. It haunted him. It was the bitterest good-bye of them all.

His mother knew that it was ended. She could almost imagine how he had ended it. She suffered for him, and yet she was elated. She felt triumphant over the woman he must have hurt.

One day he ran into Dave downtown. He couldn't keep from asking, "How's Peggy?"

"You sent her back to Georgia, kid. You sent her home."

After that he tightened up again. The demons were catching up. He began going out on the country roads, trying to lose himself in speed. But the demons ran along beside the car. Sometimes it was all he could do to keep from taking off from some high precipice and roaring toward the sky. He'd look up, and there'd be Peggy's naked body straight across the road; or he'd find himself suddenly back in George's house that night with Rose breaking up the party and the students fleeing out the door. He'd catch himself just in time to keep from running into something. It was as if the current of his life, having passed its crest, was now running downhill. It was swifter, more dangerous, infinitely more destructive as it gained in momentum. It became dangerous for him to drive alone.

Danger and the loneliness drove him back to town. He began picking up women from the street, taking them to liquor joints, waking up in strange rooms with half-remembered details of drunken orgies. Often he was utterly shocked by the memory of a scene.

There was a popular cabaret in the downtown colored district where he often went. It had a bar that sold setups for the drinks sold by the bootleggers hustling at the tables, and a bandstand at the end of a big dance floor. On weekend nights the place was crowded with women on the make. Charles smoked cork-tipped cigarettes and wore his white linen suit and black crepe silk shirt and the floating, seeking women began picking him up. When the trumpet player came forward and began blowing the *Bugle Blues* the women became wild and abandoned, were caught in a hypnotic exhibitionism. Some tried to take off their clothes, screaming, "Let me run naked!" while husbands and lovers struggled to restrain them. Others stood atop the tables with their dresses pulled above their waists and screamed, "Blow it out, daddy, blow it out!" During these moments some predaceous woman or another always captured Charles, throwing her arms about his neck and devouring him with her whore's look, crooning in her whiskey voice, "Give me those eyes." He'd go home with whatever one approached him first; sometimes with women who paid the bills, sometimes with those who thought themselves queens, sometimes with others, atrociously ugly, who made up for it by mothering him. Several times he went home with a prizefighter's wife who'd tremble stagily whenever she saw him. The men never bothered Charles; they called him "Pigmeat" and joshed him about his conquests. Only the older women were infatuated, the young girls were hunting older men. And always, sooner or later, as he lay in bed with them, the expression came up, "With eyes like those you can break any whore's heart."

One night he spoke to the trumpet player who was standing at the bar between two teen-age girls.

"How do you do it, Pat?"

The tall dark man in his ice cream suit with his glossy hair gave him a confidential grin. "Keep 'em barefooted and knocked up."

Charles returned the grin. A woman came and took his arm.

"You the one got the best go and the mojo," Pat called after him.

He became friendly with Pat after that and met the others in the band. Frequently when the place closed he would drive them home, or to some after-hours spot where they met their women.

When their contract was up at the cabaret the band went on the road. Charles began driving them about the state to the steel-mill towns where they played one-night stands in the local dance halls. Those nights were caught in fantasy. A dreamlike quality descended on the violent dances in the strange, distant cities, the wild abandoned rhythms animating the black figures milling about the floor in the dim light until reason seemed to have fled the mad orgiastic weaving of their bodies. Then followed the bloody cuttings, the grotesquely funny shootings in the under-brush, a "brass-lined forty-four on a forty-five frame" blazing in the night, some poor victim dancing an agony of death. And afterwards the mad drive homeward, racing blindly through the early morning fog, riding the sound of the motor roar, like some-thing out of the "Inferno"; the band boys half drunk and dead tired, draped about each other, another car or two following, and himself crouched over the wheel, foot jammed to the floor, feel-ing invincible, as if he could drive his goddamned car right straight down through the solid goddamned earth, daring death. Most times he couldn't see a curve thirty feet ahead.

"Jesus Christ, kid, take it easy," some band boy would say, suddenly awakening as the car lurched from disaster.

"Have we ever had an accident?" he'd challenge.

"No, but goddammit, the way you driving we ain't gonna have but one."

"Do I charge you anything to use my car?"

"What the hell's that got to do with it if we all wake up dead."

"Listen—" shouting over the roar. "All I ask you to do is close your eyes. I'll get you home."

Those times he'd completely escaped all his hurt and loneli-ness.

His mother kept after him constantly to study for his examina-tions that fall. But nights he was always gone, coming home drunk to sleep away the day. She didn't know where he went or what he did. She feared any day they'd bring him home dead, or that she'd be notified he was in jail for some terrible crime. He couldn't tell her that the sight of his textbooks nauseated him, that demons pursued him, that once he'd dreamed horribly of letting her die—that the only way he could escape these things was by his nighttime odysseys. She began to fear that he didn't intend to return to college. She felt his life would be irrevocably destroyed unless he did.

In her desperation she tried to get control of his compensation but was told it required a court order. She tried to engage an attorney to file an action. He told her the concurrence of both parents was necessary. But her husband wouldn't support her.

"For God's sake, let the boy alone," he said. "He's coming out of it. If you keep pushing him and nagging at him you'll run him away from home like you did Tom."

She closed her mouth in a grim, hard line. They hadn't heard from Tom in more than a year. It was a source of hurt. But she could never bring herself to admit she had run him away.

"I'll not sit by and see him throw away his life," she said.

So she went to the hotel and demanded that they give her his monthly pension so she could save it for him.

The manager sent for Charles and told him of his mother's visit. "If you wish we'll be glad to mail your checks to her," he said. "But we won't do it unless you consent."

"No, I don't want her to have them. I'll call for them after this."

When his mother learned of his decision, she threatened to have the courts force them to give her his pension. She and the manager had an awful row.

"You've cheated him out of a settlement," she accused, "and now you're trying to ruin his life."

"Rather than do that," the manager said angrily, "we'll stop it entirely."

Charles never learned exactly what happened. When he called for his check the first of that month the cashier told him that his pension had been discontinued. For a moment he debated whether to see Mr. Small, then decided against it. He didn't know what his mother had done but he dreaded becoming involved; he'd rather not have it than be caught up in a long, bitter quarrel.

Later he overheard her quarreling with his father. "I'd rather he didn't have it," he heard her say, "than throw it away running

284

around with God only knows what kind of people and getting himself into all kind of trouble."

"What kind of trouble has he got into?" his father defended.

"He got into trouble at the university. I don't know what it was, but if he hadn't had too much money he'd have been better off."

After that she nagged his father to make him study; she nagged at him whenever he was at home. The sound of her nagging filled the house. All of them tried to escape it. William spent most of his time at his friend's house. His father began staying out until all hours of the night; none of them knew where he went. She accused him of having a woman. He was more interested in running around with some loose woman than in his own flesh and blood, she said. By then his father had begun to realize that Charles needed some kind of discipline; but he just couldn't bring himself to apply it.

Without his pension from the hotel Charles was pressed for money. He missed a payment on his car. A collector from the finance company called at his house. His mother discovered he owned a car. She became desperate. Without her husband's support there seemed nothing she could do. But Charles had to be restrained at any cost.

So she swore out a warrant for his arrest, charging him with forging her name to a check for twenty-five dollars. The check was among those that had been returned with her bank statement; it was the only check for that large a sum. Two policemen came for him early in the day, before he'd left to pick up the band. At the time both William and his father were away.

He was shocked. "You know I didn't forge your name to any check," he told his mother.

Her mouth was grim and unrelenting, but she couldn't meet his eyes. She looked away. "Someone did, and you're the only one with access to my check book."

He turned without replying and went down the steps with the policemen. That night his father put up bail. When they came home his mother was in a mood to fuss. But no one spoke to her. Later William came to Charles's room.

"Don't worry, Chuck. Mother's just upset. She found out you'd bought a car."

"Hell, it wasn't exactly a secret. I just didn't want to have her fussing all the time."

He was arraigned the following morning. His mother had no evidence that he'd forged the check.

"But he's bought a car," she said. "And run around all night with God only knows what kind of people."

"Is that why you think he forged the check?" asked the judge.

"It's not only the check. He's wasting his life. Sooner or later if he isn't controlled he's going to wind up in the penitentiary or on the gallows."

"Do you want him prosecuted for this charge? Forgery is a felony. He could go to the reformatory if convicted."

She relented; she didn't want it to go that far. "I can't swear he did it," she admitted, "but he ought to be disciplined. He has no right to own a car; he's still a minor. They had no right to sell him a car."

"That's something else. Of course, they can be prosecuted. But this concerns itself with your charge that he forged your name to a check."

"Even if he didn't this time it won't be long before he does, unless something is done to stop him. He spends his compensation as fast as he gets it. There should be some way to make him save it."

"Yes, but that is more or less a problem for his parents. That is outside the jurisdiction of this court."

Professor Taylor came to his son's defense. He told of how Charles had been injured, and of how it had affected his subsequent behavior.

"My son has been sick and upset," he admitted. "But my son is not a thief." There were tears in his eyes. For a moment he was cloaked in the dignified humility he used to assume in years long past when talking to the white trustees of the southern colleges.

The judge was sympathetic. He turned to Mrs. Taylor. "Unless you can present more evidence of forgery I am going to dismiss the charge."

She withdrew the charge herself. She hadn't intended to have him prosecuted, but she'd thought the court would give her some sort of legal authority to control his money. She was bitterly disappointed with the outcome, and went off without looking toward either her husband or her son.

Professor Taylor left the courtroom with his arm about his son. There was something infinitely tender in his attitude. The court attendants looked curiously at the strange couple, the old, short, black man who seemed shrunken in his seedy clothes with a son a half-head taller, lighter complexioned, wearing an expensive white flannel suit with an air of arrogance.

Charles liked his father then; he'd always liked him in a way. What he liked most was the manner in which his father had taken up for him. He hadn't thought his father had it in him.

But at the same time he felt a sense of utter loss. Before, no matter what had happened, he'd always felt he could come back to his mother in the end. He'd always believed, despite everything she'd done, that she loved him most of all. He had never felt she would really hurt him. They had always fought, but he'd thought, deep down, that it was a fight of love. It was a secret between them; their own private conflict. He'd always felt he wouldn't hurt her either; that in the end, at some time, he would have to die for her. This more than anything had kept him home; that some day she would need him to give his life for her. He'd never consciously thought about it, but he had always felt it was his one and only obligation to anyone. And now that she had taken their own sacred fight out into the callous, critical world, to be pawed over by strangers, he felt he could never go back.

"I'm going to see a movie, Dad," he said. "Want to come along?"

"No, son, I've got work to do. But don't stay out too late. We worry about you, son."

He went and sat in the darkness of the theatre, thinking of his mother and himself. I guess she must have been pretty worried, he thought. He wondered what she could do to help if he told her how his textbooks affected him.

The organist began playing *Among My Souvenirs* and the soft, cloying chords seeped down into his emotions, the plaintive melody spelling out the words:

> *There's nothing left for me*
> *Of things that used to be . . .*

He felt the warm flood of tears pouring down his cheeks. "What's wrong with me?" he sobbed aloud, stumbling through the darkened aisles, escaping to the street. It came to him again that he'd never leave his mother. All the way home he felt a poignant overwhelming longing for her love again. He wanted to cry out his heart to her, to say, "I forgive you, Mother," and have her say, "I forgive you too."

But he found her waiting for him with an agent from the finance company. "I've ordered them to take your car," she said.

The agent said, "I'll go with you to get it."

For a long, bleak moment he looked at his mother, ignoring the agent. Then he said, "I'll turn it in myself," and turned and started out.

He became aware that the agent was following him and stopped and faced about, "I'll take it in by myself."

The agent hesitated. "Be sure and get it in by five o'clock or we'll notify the police it is stolen."

He drove around for a time. Once he thought of driving to another state, of just getting on some road and going wherever it took him. But he knew they'd catch him somewhere and he'd be charged with automobile theft. He stopped by the house where the band leader lived and told him he wouldn't be driving them about any longer.

"What's the matter, Pigmeat, tired of us?"

"No, I lost my car."

"Lost your car? That's it outside, ain't it?"

"Yes, but I got to give it up."

"Can't you make the payments?"

"I guess I could, but my mother doesn't want me to have it."

"That's tough titty, kid, but that's your and her business."

He left and drove down Cedar Avenue. Exactly when it came to him he couldn't give it up, he never knew. All he knew was that if he gave it up everything he'd ever dreaded would catch up with him again. It was already settled when he started down the hill underneath the viaduct at Ansel Road. And this seemed as good a place as any. So he stepped on the accelerator and pulled head-on into the concrete abutment beneath the railroad line.

For a short time he was unconscious. When he came to, policemen were holding back the crowd and an ambulance was coming. He felt such a sense of frustration he was sick all down inside. There was a small cut on his forehead from broken glass and his chest hurt from the impact with the steering wheel. His back had been wrenched and it was painful when the ambulance attendants lifted him out. But he derived a perverted pleasure from sight of the smashed front end of the car.

"Now they can have it," he muttered.

"What?" asked a policeman hovering over him.

"Nothing."

They took his name and address and he was driven to an emergency hospital. But his injuries weren't serious; there was no indication of hemorrhage. He could walk well enough although his back ached and his chest hurt inside. The cut was bandaged and he was put in a taxi cab and sent home with instructions to remain in bed for a couple of days.

But he couldn't bear his home; he couldn't bear the sight of his mother. He had to get out. He sought the parks. He came to know the banks of Lake Erie as he knew his hand. He'd lay for hours on the ground, feeling the closeness of the earth. He couldn't bear to be indoors anywhere. At times he wondered how it would feel to be buried alive.

The physical pain lingered for a time. But he didn't mind it.

What he minded most was the loss of his escape. He was left walking in a world of running demons; every way he turned they had him cornered.

When William went off to college, Charles took him down to the station. They tried to talk but it was embarrassing for both; one was going away to college and the other was staying home. What could either of them say? Both felt relieved when the train finally came.

Charles took his brother into the coach. "Good luck, Will." He wanted to say something wittier, but he couldn't find the words.

"I hope you'll get back next quarter," Will said.

"Me, too, if for no more than the ride."

"Don't worry, Chuck."

"What's there to worry about? If we die we go to heaven, the streets are paved in gold, angels playing harps, everybody's happy. Is that a cause for worry?" He tried to make it sound flippant, but it went another way.

William was silent.

"All aboard!" the trainmen called.

"So long, Will."

"So long, Chuck."

For a long and bitter moment Charles stood on the platform, watching the train pull out. When it was out of sight he raised his hand in a wide, slow wave, he didn't know why. Then suddenly it struck him that this was the first fall he'd missed entering school. And he knew the reason he had waved. He himself was on that train, all of himself that had ever meant anything to himself, and all of himself that would ever mean anything to anyone. He was waving goodbye to himself. He was stricken by the thought.

Like a sleepwalker he went down the steps to the tracks and walked out to where they curved over toward the lake and then turned off through a woody, undeveloped park. All about him were the signs of fall. The painted colors cried inside him and he sat down with his back against a tree until the hurt had quieted.

It was such a perfect time of year, he thought musingly. All the disturbing heat of summer had cooled into a sort of peace. His body always felt good in the fall. And yet why was it always such a poignant time? Slowly, as he tried to reconcile the signs about him of nature dying, leaves falling, plants drying and withering, to his first feeling of respite, his thoughts turned inward again and he came face to face with death.

And to himself, death had always been a source of hurt and bewilderment—the death of anything, even of a time. He hated all endings; he couldn't bear finality. The giving up of any life; the senseless cessation of dreams and emotions; all the ecstasy and beauty, all the strange, deep, moving melodies that came from the sight of flowers, the feeling of early morning in the country, the sound of a running brook, all ending in death.

Fall had always touched him thus. The end of summer had always been the death of freedom too. School had assuaged and channeled this sense of death. Now he was caught adrift without an anchor.

After what seemed to be hours he arose to go home. His back was stiff; he could barely walk. Some section hands passing down the tracks on a handcar gave him a lift to the nearest highway crossing. He went home.

"Did your brother get off all right?" his mother asked.

"Yes."

She looked at him accusingly. "If you don't begin studying for your examinations I'm going to put you out of the house. If you're going to throw away your life you'll not live here; you'll have to eat and sleep with those people you spend your money on."

"What money?" he said bitterly.

"I'll not argue with you. If you want to—"

He left the house and slammed the door behind him, cutting off her voice. He went over to Cedar Avenue, wandering aimlessly, stopping first in one pool hall and then in another. In one he ran across Dave.

"How you doing, Chuck?"

"All right." He wanted to ask about Peggy but was too ashamed. "What you doing these days?"

"I got a little crap game going in my pad. Why don't you drop by later on."

"Okay."

For a moment he contemplated going down to Billie's. But he had very little money now. Maybe he could win some in the game, he thought. He'd never gambled seriously, although he'd watched a number of games. Just the thought of risking his money on the roll of the dice gave him stage fright. He began drinking to bolster his courage, drifting from one liquor joint to another.

It was late when he got to Dave's. He was blind drunk. He lost his thirty dollars before the dice were passed around the table. He borrowed twenty from Dave and lost that. At the thought of having to go home, broke and defenseless, and face his mother's tirade, he was assailed by a sense of desperation. He felt his legs begin to tremble. His gaze slid across the stacks of money, then went off in a blind trance. When he came out of it the dice were back to him.

"What you shoot, kid?" someone asked.

"Not this time," he said. His throat had contracted until his voice was barely above a whisper.

He backed from the crowded table and left the smoke-filled room. A voice was crooning, "Shooter for the game." A sense of unreality settled in his mind; the night turned weird. He was overwhelmed by a kind of fear he'd never known. It was the first time since his injury he'd been completely broke. He felt naked and without friends.

As he went down the stairs a big, loutish-looking youth wearing a grass-green suit overtook him.

"You can't beat them chiselers, man, they use crooked dice."

"I didn't lose much," he muttered defensively and kept on walking.

The youth fell in beside him. "I seen you down at the cabaret. They call you Pigmeat, don't they?"

"Sometimes." He could scarcely remember it; something seemed to have happened to his memory.

"They call me Poker; I used to run a poker game in the Alley.

My real handle's John—John Parker. I know where there's a game downtown that's jumping. Ain't nobody but squares. You stake me to a half a C and we can win ourselves a grand."

It took a moment before Charles comprehended; he couldn't think. "I got broke," he finally said. "I haven't got any money."

"Hell, get some from them whores. I tell you, man, we can win a grand." When Charles didn't reply he said, "You collecting from them whores, ain't you?"

"Collecting?" The persistent intimacy was picking at his nerves, but he didn't have the will to send the fellow off.

"All them whores I see you with? You mean you ain't getting nothing from 'em?"

He walked a little faster as if to get away. They came into The Avenue of shabby store fronts and dingy buildings crowding on the broken pavement. Dim light spilled grotesqueness over the squalid scene. Drunken men and women, milling about the doorways, argued profanely about inconsequentials. The pungent scent of marijuana drifted in the air. Revulsion knotted in his stomach. He turned suddenly and crossed the street. But Poker stuck with him; he couldn't get away.

"Not anymore," he finally lied. "I don't see them anymore."

"Hell, man—" Two light-complexioned prostitutes, cruising by, caught his attention. "Hellooo, babes," he drawled.

The whores slowed, raked him with their appraising scrutiny. From them came a scent, both putrid and perfumed. "Did you order coal?" one asked the other superciliously.

"This year, dear, I'm burning nothing but chalk in my fine box," the other said with a spitting sound.

"You burning it all right," Poker countered, argumentively.

Charles walked away. But Poker caught up with him. "Where you got your car?"

"I haven't got it anymore." He stopped suddenly; he couldn't stand it any longer. "Look, fellow, I'm broke, I don't have a car; there's nothing you can get out of me."

"Hell, man, don't be like that," Poker said obsequiously. "You an' me, man, if we run together we'd always have some money."

The desperation and revulsion had clotted in his mind. He

just had to have some money, he told himself. He just couldn't get along without it; he couldn't go home; he couldn't do anything. He didn't want to become involved with Poker, but he couldn't break himself away.

"Well, how?" he finally asked.

"Come on," Poker said.

After a moment's hesitation, he went along. What did he have to lose? he asked himself. They went down a quiet side street and stopped before a cleaning and pressing shop in a delapidated frame building. The windows in the apartment above were dark.

"Wait here," Poker said. "If you see a light come on upstairs start whistling the *Bugle Blues*. You don't have to worry 'bout the cops; they don't never come 'round here."

"What are you going to do?"

"I'm going to get some layers, man."

Poker went around toward the back of the building and vanished in the dark. Charles crossed the street and stood in the darkness beneath a tree. Once he started to leave, but no one came in sight, and the pull of desperation held him to the outcome. Finally Poker came into sight, looking furtively up and down, then hurried over and took Charles' arm.

"Come on, let's beat it."

He had thirty-two dollars. They divided it evenly. Suddenly Charles was conscience-stricken. "I'm going home," he said.

"Okay, I'll see you tomorrow night at Dave's."

It was a long ride home, and he couldn't keep from thinking. He hadn't stolen anything for years, he realized. He wondered if he was going to end up being a thief. The thought frightened him. All of a sudden he wanted to see his mother; he didn't care what she said to him. He just wanted to see her, be near her, be reassured by her presence.

She was waiting up for him. "I'll not tell you again," she said. "The next time you come in at this hour you just pack your clothes and get out of this house."

Now that he'd seen her he lost the desire. Her presence didn't

294

give him anything. He felt the same as when he had left the house earlier in the day.

After that he went out every night with Poker, and stood watch while Poker broke into small, isolated stores and robbed the tills. His mother tried to force him to leave the house. But his father said he didn't have to go. William was away in college. Again Mrs. Taylor became assailed with the conviction that Charles and his father were plotting to harm her in some way. She became frightened and moved into William's room and locked the door. They were trying to run her away, she thought. But she refused to go. She couldn't go and leave Charles there to destroy himself, she thought contradictorily. Once she dreamed of seeing him sink slowly into quicksand while she stood by, powerless to help.

One morning Charles awakened to hear his parents struggling in the bedroom. He heard his mother's choked scream.

"You bitch, I'll kill you!" he heard his father shout.

A chill ran down his spine. He leaped from his bed and ran into their room. His father was choking his mother. Blood streamed from a gash on his father's forehead and a shattered hand mirror lay on the floor. His mother's face was turning purple. When he pulled away his father's hands she sunk to the floor.

"Jesus Christ!" he cried in utter agony. "You've killed her."

Then everything went blank. He didn't know he'd hit his father until the words seeped slowly into his mind, "Son, don't! . . . Son, don't! . . . " His father was trying to struggle from the floor, one arm raised protectively, while he stood above him, gripping the stool of the dressing table as if to strike him with it.

"Jesus Christ!" he said again.

His mother had regained consciousness and was screaming in a strained voice, "You murderer! You beast!" Her face was livid and the tendons stood out in her neck.

He had to hold her to keep her from attacking his father again. He picked her up and carried her from the room. "I'm not afraid of either of you," she screamed. "You can kill me if you want but you'll go to the electric chair."

"I don't want to hurt you, Mama," he found himself saying over and over as he took her into William's room and laid her across the bed. "I don't want to hurt you, Mama." He smoothed her hair. "Nobody's going to hurt you, Mama. Nobody's going to hurt you," he crooned.

He heard his father going down the stairs; heard the front door close. "He's gone now," he said.

"I'm going to have him arrested for murder," she said, trying to get up.

"Please don't, Mama," he begged, gently pushing her shoulders down. "Please don't, Mama. Please just lie down until you feel better. Please don't do anything now."

She made her body passive but her eyes condemned him bitterly. "You may think you're helping him escape," she said in a harsh, unrelenting voice. "But he'll not escape; he'll pay for this."

"Jesus Christ!" he said.

He left her and went to his room and dressed quickly and left the house. He went over on The Avenue and began drinking. But the whiskey filled him with despair. He was crossing the street toward the pool hall when he was struck by a terrible fear. Suppose his father returned while he was away and killed her. He began running and ran until he flagged a taxi and urged the driver to hurry.

"This may be a matter of life and death."

He found his father packing a suitcase. His father's sister, Mrs. Hart, sat in the bedroom while he gathered up his clothes. It was the first time either of his sisters had ever stepped foot in the house. Mrs. Taylor stood in the door berating them both.

"If it wasn't for my children I'd have you arrested and sent to the penitentiary," she was saying.

"Now, Lillian, you brought it all on yourself," Mrs. Hart came to her brother's defense.

"This is my house," his mother began to scream. "Don't you dare—"

He rushed up and pulled her away to her room. "Now, Mama, don't start another fight."

"You just wait and see," she said harshly, more to herself than to him. "He'll not get away with it."

Charles walked down to the door with his father and his Aunt Lou.

"Take care of your mother, son," his father said.

"I'm sorry, dad, I didn't mean to—" He couldn't bring himself to say the words.

"I know you didn't, son. I lost my head too. Your mother aggravates us both. But you must take care of her."

"I will."

That evening his mother telegraphed her brothers for some money. When it came she engaged a white attorney and sued for a divorce. At the time she didn't intend to carry through on it. She wanted to punish her husband, and at the same time frighten him into doing his duty as a father. She knew how deeply he opposed divorce, that he regarded it as a mortal sin. She thought she could make him face up to Charles, take a firm stand, commit him to an institution if need be.

Professor Taylor pleaded with her for a reconciliation. "Don't break up our home, honey. We've been married twenty-six years."

She acceded on the condition that they send Charles to a boarding school the city maintained for recalcitrant youths.

He was trapped. As much as he wanted to save their marriage, he couldn't do this. He was convinced it would kill his son to be locked up. The boy was hurt somewhere deep inside, he thought. He needed time for it to heal. If there were some way to get him among good boys his own age. Maybe he'd decide to return to college if they let him alone for a time, he argued.

"It would kill him, honey; it would kill him," he said.

"It would do no such thing," she contradicted. "He must be disciplined—he must! You won't do it, so you must let others do it for you."

"I won't do that," he said.

She couldn't change him. So in the end she carried through

her suit for a divorce. She charged him with cruelty and desertion and deliberately shirking his responsibility as a father; and requested that Charles be placed in her custody. She would rather get rid of her husband than lose her son. For in the final analysis, even though she no longer admitted it to herself, he was still her own lovely baby, and deep down she loved him in the same intense, passionate manner she always had.

Charles had remained at home ever since his father left. He'd become fearfully concerned for his mother. He'd noticed her absentmindedness and her habit of locking herself in her room at night. He was afraid she might do something to herself, or hurt herself accidentally. She didn't seem able any longer to perform the common chores about the house. He did most of the housework and cooking.

One night at dinner she said, "If your father had been any account at all you children could have had a decent home all your lives and wouldn't have been running around all over creation getting yourselves maimed and crippled and into God only knows what kind of trouble."

He was frightened by the consummate bitterness in her voice, and tried to pacify her. "Try not to think about it, Mama. It's going to be all right."

Suddenly she began to cry. She rose, crying, and fled upstairs to her room. He followed in alarm. She had flung herself across the bed and was crying disconsolately. He stroked her hair.

"Don't cry, Mama. Don't cry."

But she couldn't be consoled. Although she'd told herself, ever since their wedding night, how much she hated and despised her husband, in the end it hurt to give him up. He was the only mate she'd ever had, the father of her three sons, and there was still a part of her that wanted him for herself. It was as if he was bound to this part of her in some unbroken way. And there was the memory of all the years they had spent together. Even now she didn't want another woman to have him.

Charles became so immersed in her suffering that all the world blacked out. The urge to sacrifice himself for her became his only thought, and for that instant she was his beautiful young mother again and he wanted to take her in his arms and go out beyond the edge of life, where it was dark and peaceful and they could be together and free from all the troubles they'd ever known.

"I'll look after you, Mama," he choked. "I'll take care of you. Don't cry."

Down in the old deep-sunken eyes, red-veined from crying, the bitterness flickered. "If you had just tried to be a good boy," she sobbed.

It was as if she had suddenly slapped him. He felt a sharp, brackish shock such as he had experienced as a child when attending Crayne's Institute in Augusta, Georgia, the night he had run off to a fire and had offered his services to a strange, lost whore standing in the doorway of the one remaining shack. The memory returned vividly in the wake of his sensation. He could see the bitter forlornness in the young woman's posture and recalled his tremendous urge toward self-sacrifice as he went forward to help. And he could hear her harsh cursing voice, "Git der hell away frum heah an' mind yo' own bizness," and feel again the cold shocking hurt of being utterly rejected.

He stood up and groped blindly from the room. He went down to the dining room and tried to finish his dinner. He took a mouthful of food and chewed and chewed, but he couldn't swallow. Suddenly he felt the deluge coming up from down inside of him. It was as if his blood had begun to cry.

25

CHARLES WAS SUMMONED BY HIS FATHER'S ATTORney to give a deposition for the divorce proceedings. He was handed the summons on the eve of Thanksgiving as he was leaving the house to buy a turkey for his mother's Thanksgiving dinner.

A small gray man came up the steps. "Are you Charles Manning Taylor?"

"Yes."

He placed the summons in Charles's hand and grinned. "A present for you."

Across the street the high school was letting out and the sound of laughter drifted in the air. Charles read the summons without moving. It directed him to appear in the office of his father's attorney the following Monday morning. The cold legal phraseology conjured up the thought of courts and jails and policemen and stern-faced merciless men sitting in judgment over a defenseless world. He could see his parents standing before the bar, caught in utter helplessness, hanging on his words that would betray one or the other. He would have to tell of how they'd fought and suffered; he would have to reveal all the mean, secret things about them which he'd tried so hard throughout his life to keep hidden from himself. They would ask him terrible questions: "Did you ever see your father strike your mother? . . . Did you ever hear your mother curse your father? . . . What did they quarrel about? . . . Was it you? . . . " For a moment his mind was gripped in terror.

"What is it, Son?" he heard his mother ask from behind him. She'd noticed him standing there and had opened the door.

He slipped the summons into his inside overcoat pocket. "Nothing," he said. "It's nothing. I was just thinking."

"If you're going to get a turkey you'd better hurry," she said.

He went down the stairs and started toward the store . . . *Did your father's color have anything to do with it—because he's black and your mother's white?* he heard them ask. *Do you know whether he was ever unfaithful? . . .*

"Jesus Christ!" he said aloud.

Two high school girls passing by gave him startled looks. Suppose someone asked them was their mother a little off, he thought. Suddenly he was panic-stricken. He began running. A streetcar came and he climbed aboard. But it didn't go fast enough. He got off and began running again. An empty taxi passed and he hailed it.

300

"I got to get over on Cedar Avenue in a hurry," he panted.
The money for the turkey went for whiskey. But he couldn't
get drunk. His body got drunk, his legs wobbled, but the sharp
bitter panic kept flaring in his mind. He started looking for
Poker. It was night before he found him coming from the pool
hall.

"I got to get out of town," he said desperately.

Poker drew back instinctively, frightened by the raw terror
blazing from his eyes. "The cops after you?" he asked tensely.

"My parents are getting a divorce—"

"Hell—" Poker breathed in relief.

"You don't understand. I got to testify."

"Hell, what about it?"

He looked at Poker for a moment as if trying to focus him.
"I got a summons." Now the paper seemed to come alive within
his pocket; he could feel it burning against his chest, like some
sinister invitation to his own execution. "They're going to make
me."

"Hell—" Poker thought it over. "We could steal a car and go
somewhere."

"All right."

Poker borrowed a car from the pool hall proprietor and they
drove over past Euclid. When they found the car they wanted
Charles got in to steer and Poker drove up behind and pushed
it back to Cedar. Poker knew how to short-circuit the ignition
switch and when they got it started Charles drove swiftly out
of town. He drove as if the demons were after him again, the
long lights lancing down the road as it came up over the hood,
dropped away and turned, and came up again. The high sullen
whine of the speeding motor rent the quiet night. Houses loomed
eerily in the moonlight, like the abodes of ghosts, and the motor
whine echoed back like the wail of banshees. Charles crouched
down over the wheel, caught in the unreality of the night,
almost but not quite free, not quite escaped, his foot jamming
the accelerator to the floorboard as if to push still greater speed
out of the laboring motor. *Faster! Faster! Faster!* it kept saying.
Just a little goddamned faster! And he would be completely

gone from all of them. *If he could just get this goddamned car to go a little faster . . .*

He was on the inside of a turn without slackening speed when the headlights of a truck loomed up ahead.

"Hey, goddammit!" he heard Poker yell and through the corner of his vision saw his hands fly up to his face.

But it didn't penetrate his concentration. He was sealed within the single determination to hold to the wide arc of his curve. Given the exact relation of time to speed he'd make a perfect tangent, which for once, goddammit, even his physics professor at the university could appreciate, and come out safely on the right side of the road. He crossed in front of the big truck lights without once veering, the whole goddamned putrid sickening world coming up inside him like vomit at the instant of infinite danger, and then he was past, his left rear fender pinging faintly against the heavy steel bumper of the truck. Letdown spread through his mouth and down into his stomach like the acid flow of bile. Now only the brooding sense of safety lay in the long, empty road, filling with all the hurt and panic, and for a moment he closed his eyes.

He opened them to the sound of retching. Poker had vomited.

"Sonafabitch, goddammit, you tryna kill us," he heard him gasp.

He pulled over to the side of the highway and stopped. He felt totally depressed.

"Here, you can drive."

Poker had a pint bottle of gin. They drank in the dark beside the car. Afterwards they cleaned up the vomit. Poker got behind the wheel. Charles sat silently, watching the night go by. It was almost as if some complete certainty had failed, like the night God erred when his brother was blinded.

"Where we going?" Poker asked.

They hadn't thought of it until then.

"Let's go down to the university," Charles said. He didn't know why he thought of the university, but thinking about it, as they drove along, it seemed as if something were waiting for him there, something he had left, forgotten.

They drove up to Mrs. Johnson's boarding house. It was late and most of the students had gone to a Thanksgiving dance. He went in and spoke to Mrs. Johnson and she said she could put them up for the weekend. Two freshmen whom he didn't know were on their way to the dance. Charles offered to take them. One of the freshmen gave him directions. He drove around the university campus and came into a colored shanty town beyond the railroad. He felt a strange sensation when he drove past the university. It was as if he were revisiting a city in which he had lived during a former life and there were something peculiar about it which had affected him. But at the moment it had slipped his mind and he couldn't recall whether it was good or bad.

The dance was being held in a big, dilapidated barn that had been converted into a dance hall. He parked and let the freshmen out and he and Poker lingered for a time about the entrance, watching the dancing couples inside. They didn't have the price of admission. No one came out that he knew.

"Come on," he said. "I know a place I can get a drink on credit."

He drove across town to the house where Rose had lived. Rose was gone. "Left right after you did," George said.

George didn't seem happy to see him, but he gave him a pint of gin on credit and loaned him five dollars. They drove back to Mrs. Johnson's and she fixed two cots in the third floor dormitory. They were asleep when the others returned from the dance.

Next morning Charles asked for some of the students he'd known. Most of them had gone home for the weekend. Only those who couldn't afford to go had remained. Charles knew several of them by sight, but none very well. They asked him what he had been doing, whether he was coming back. He felt so depressed he found it difficult to talk. Poker was nervous and ill at ease. Charles used whatever toilet articles he found about, brushed his teeth with someone else's toothbrush, found a clean pair of sox. Poker had already dressed. They went down to breakfast and Mrs. Johnson sat and talked to him.

"Aren't you coming back, Charles?"

"Oh, I suppose so."

"Don't you want to?" She seemed as concerned as if he were her own son.

If she asked him another question he felt he would scream. "I'm coming back next quarter," he said. "I've been doing a lot of studying."

"I'm so glad," she said.

He was shocked by the sight of tears brimming in her eyes. I got to get out of here, he thought as the panic began building up again.

They were interrupted by the sound of a crash out front. One of her daughters rushed in and said someone had run into Charles's car. He and Poker ran outside. He was glad of the respite.

A well-dressed, middle-aged white man had driven an expensive car into the rear end of theirs. The man was so drunk he could barely stand.

"There's no need to call the police, boys," he said. "I'll pay for everything."

Charles examined their car. The gas tank was punctured and the luggage compartment smashed in. Gasoline ran down the gutter.

"Don't nobody strike a match," Poker said.

The man was fumbling for his wallet. "We'll fix this up between us, boys. Here's my card." Charles noted that he was an insurance company executive with offices downtown. "Here's twenty dollars. Now—now, that's not all," he added quickly, seeing Charles about to protest. "That's just for your trouble. Come down to my office tomorrow morning and I'll give you a check for the garage bill."

Charles took command. "Okay."

"If the police come tell them everything's been fixed up."

"Okay."

"I've had a few drinks. You know how it is."

Several of the students who had gathered extricated the

304

stranger's car and pushed it down the street beyond the flow of gasoline. The front end had been smashed but the motor started.

"I'll see you boys tomorrow morning," the man promised as he drove away.

"We'll call a tow truck and see how much it's going to cost," Charles said. He had already begun to feel he owned the car.

Poker called him to one side. "Hell, man, we can't take this car to no garage. It's hot. We better get out of town and leave it where it is."

But something about collecting for damage to a stolen car appealed to Charles. It was a strange sensation, as might be experienced by standing on a ledge fourteen stories high and looking down. At the time he had no intention of jumping. But it gave him a wonderful feeling of power to know he had a choice. So far the only element of risk existed within his mind. It offered a completely absorbing diversion—to jump or not to jump.

"I'll do it myself," he said.

He went inside and telephoned until he found a garage that was open. They promised to send a tow truck. Poker was thoroughly frightened.

"Hell, man, you're crazy," he kept saying. "I'm gonna get out of this." He could break into a deserted store after dark. But handling a hot automobile in broad daylight was too much. "Gimme some money, man. I'm going over where we was last night and get a drink and let you handle this."

Charles derived a perverted pleasure from Poker's fear. He gave him the five dollars he'd borrowed the night before. "I'll meet you at two o'clock in front of the gates to the university."

"If you ain't in jail," Poker said, hurrying off.

Charles laughed for the first time in days. While he was waiting for the tow truck a police car drove past and the policemen got out to investigate the wreck. Charles told them that it was his car.

"I talked to the fellow who ran into me and we've gotten everything fixed up."

"Was anybody injured?"

"No, no one was in my car and the driver was alone in the other car. He didn't get a scratch." He laughed; he was in a gay mood. "Only my feelings were hurt, and he paid for them."

The policemen grinned. They drove off without writing a report. Charles became lightheaded with exhilaration. He was standing up there on his ledge and way down on the street a crowd was forming. People were pointing at him now. It was as if he had drunk the wine of the Gods; he'd never been drunk like this.

When the tow truck came he told the mechanic he'd drop by in the morning and get an estimate of the damages.

"I'm not paying for them so make them high," he said, winking at the man.

"I'll give her all she'll take," the mechanic promised.

Poker was hiding behind an arch when Charles arrived at the university entrance. Charles bent double laughing. A couple of white students grinned in his direction. Finally he choked, "Come on out, Poker, the enemy's gone."

"You crazy, man," Poker muttered angrily. Fear had got down into his body, his spine had tightened; he stood with his shoulders hunched and his hands rammed down into his pockets.

Charles took him to the Union cafeteria for Thanksgiving dinner. They sat at a table with several fellows he remembered and he was in high spirits throughout the meal. Poker was silent and uncommunicative. Someone passing in back of him inadvertently bumped his shoulder. He gave such a start his fork fell from his hand and clattered on the table. Everyone looked at him.

"Don't pay any attention to my friend," Charles said, laughing impishly. "He's just escaped from Alcatraz and he's still a bit jumpy."

The fellows laughed. Poker gave Charles a look of such fury they became silent again. Soon afterwards the fellows left.

"Man, you sho' nuff crazy," Poker said. He believed it now.

After dinner they went back to the Johnsons'. Poker was afraid to go but Charles insisted. Between the time they'd left Cleveland and then, Charles had become the master. It added to his exhilaration. He began contemplating ways to add to Poker's fear. They found the boarding house deserted.

"Let's go back to that place where we were last night and hole up," Poker suggested. "I couldn't find it."

"Let's steal another car," Charles teased. "Why should we walk around on a day like this?"

"Man, gimme some money," Poker demanded. "I'm going home."

"I haven't got any money," Charles lied. "I had to pay Mrs. Johnson. You've got to wait until we collect tomorrow."

"I'm gonna go down and set in the station. I'm cuttin' out, man. You crazy."

Charles watched him go, laughing to himself. He went down to The Block and hung about the pool halls, and from there over to George's where he drank until bedtime. He was beginning to feel depressed, let down again. But sight of Poker asleep on the other cot when he returned to Mrs. Johnson's perked him up again. It was as if everyone had finally gone home except Poker, who was still down there on the street, fourteen stories below, held in morbid fascination. He was laughing to himself when he went to sleep.

Next morning they went to the garage to get the estimate of the damages to the car. Poker waited for him at the corner a block away. It was just as Charles had hoped. The exhilaration began building up again. The estimate was less than he'd expected.

"Only eight-five dollars?" he protested. "I thought it'd be at least a hundred and fifty dollars."

The mechanic grinned. "Eighty-five is tops. I wouldn't charge you but fifty."

He pocketed the itemized statement and rejoined Poker. "See," he said. "No cops."

From there they went to the office building to collect. "You don't have to come up—unless, of course, you want to," Charles said.

"I'll wait for you down here somewhere," Poker muttered.

The man had a hangover. He had discovered, after he'd gotten home, that he'd bitten his tongue in the accident. He was in a vicious mood.

"Eighty-five dollars!" he fumed. "For that amount of damage! This bill is padded."

A feeling of unlimited power swept over Charles. He felt as if he held the man's destiny in the palm of his hand. He laughed. "Maybe it is."

The man reddened with fury. "How do I know it's even your car?" he raved. "You haven't shown me any registration. It might be stolen for all I know."

Charles met the challenge head-on. "Why don't you call the police and ask them?" he dared.

For an instant their eyes locked. Charles felt stifled by the sensation of danger. He leaned forward, his breath catching, as the urge came up to press it to the limit. But the man unlocked his gaze and flung himself into his chair.

"Who shall I make it out to?" he asked, opening a check book.

The flat, sour feeling of letdown flooded ever Charles. He felt his body sag. The man looked up, waiting.

"Taylor Manning," he said finally.

He watched the man write the check. He felt depressed again.

"Here, boy," the man said. "You'd better be glad I gave you my word."

He took the check woodenly. "Thank you."

Poker noticed the change in him immediately. "Didn't the man pay you?" he asked anxiously.

"I got a check," he said indifferently. "I'll go to the bank and cash it."

He didn't have any identification and expected difficulty, but the teller cashed it without comment. On sudden impulse he asked for a book of checks.

"Do you have an account?" the teller asked.

"Yes, I do."

The teller passed him the book of blank checks.

"Thank you," he said, struck momentarily with a sense of unreality. It seemed for the moment as if everything he'd done was lawful.

Poker was waiting for him down the street. They stood on the sidewalk and divided the money.

"I ast the man in the station last night and he said we could get a train at one o'clock," Poker volunteered. Now that the danger was past he'd gotten over his fear.

Charles was finished with him, through; Poker without fear was no good to him. "You go ahead," he said. "I'm going to stay."

"You gonna press yo' luck too far, man," Poker said, and hurried off alone.

Charles looked the other way. The sensation of daring danger that had kept him in such high exhilaration was gone. He had taken every risk and nothing had happened. He felt depleted and at loose ends. People jostled him. He realized that he was standing at a busy intersection. The lunch hour crowd milled past. He began walking along aimlessly. A squirrel scampering up a tree attracted his attention. He noticed that the building in back of the park was the courthouse.

Suddenly he remembered the summons. It was as if he had opened Pandora's box. All his panic and despair surged back like a tidal wave. He thought of his mother waiting for the turkey he'd gone out to buy two days ago. It was all he could do to keep from breaking into a run.

The next thing he noticed was the railroad station. The idea came to him to buy a ticket to some place where he could never be found. Then he realized he didn't have enough money to carry him as far as he had to go. His thoughts, moving in a cycle of association, took him back to the bank where he had cashed the check. Next he recalled the book of checks in his pocket. He suddenly realized that with one of the green identification cards issued by the university, he could fill them out for small amounts and cash them almost anywhere. His mind became aflame with the possibilities.

No one was in the dormitory when he returned. He searched through the various lockers until he found a green card some-one had left over the weekend, and substituted the name Taylor Manning. Before leaving he filled out all the checks for twenty-five dollars each, payable to Taylor Manning, and signed them with the name of the man who'd given him the check earlier.

Next he went down to the shopping center across from the campus and entered a haberdashery. He bought two pairs of woolen sox.

"I wonder if you can cash this check for twenty-five dollars," he asked the proprietor, presenting his green card.

The proprietor looked at the check, turned it over and extended his fountain pen. "Endorse it."

Charles wrote, "Taylor Manning."

The proprietor compared the signature with that on the green card, then counted out the change in bills and currency.

He went from one store to another, making small purchases. He encountered no difficulty anywhere. In a tobacco shop he ordered a carton of cigarettes. Another customer came in as he presented the check. He was a big ruddy man, hatless, and in his shirt-sleeves. He recognized Charles immediately.

"Say, I just cashed a check for you at my bookstore."

Charles looked up, startled, and tightened into a knot. "What about it?" he challenged.

The man reddened. "What about it!" He took the check from the tobacconist's hand and glanced from it to Charles. "By God, you're passing bogus checks," he shouted.

"Give me my check," Charles demanded and tried to take it from the man's hand.

The man held it out of his reach. "Oh no you don't."

Charles turned suddenly and started toward the door. It was more a reflex action than from a conscious desire to escape. His mind had gone completely blank.

The man leapt after him and clutched his arm. "Call the police!" he shouted to the tobacconist. "I'll hold him."

Charles's first impulse was to break loose and run. But two students entered the shop at that moment.

"Help me hold this fellow," the man appealed to them. "He's been passing bogus checks."

The students looked from the man to Charles uncertainly. Charles caught a sudden picture of them chasing him down the

310

street. Revulsion came up in him. To be chased had always impressed him as an intolerable indignity. It was an impression from his childhood, indelibly implanted in his mind when he first read of Achilles chasing Hector around the walls of Troy while all the city looked down, weeping in anguish at the sad spectacle of this once brave and mighty warrior fleeing for his life. Then all of a sudden he was consumed with rage. His body stiffened but he didn't struggle.

"Take your goddamned hands off me," he said in a low intense voice.

His voice had such a tone of deadliness the man drew back in alarm. Charles turned and looked at him. "I'm not going to run."

By the time the police arrived a small crowd had collected. They stood about looking at him with fear and embarrassment. He glared back at them defiantly. They thought he looked desperate; they expected him to make a break at any moment. He resented their staring at him; otherwise they didn't matter. Deep down he felt triumphant. It was as if he'd broken out of prison, escaped.

Over the weekend he was held in a strange, cold jail in a cell with other prisoners waiting for the Monday morning court. At mealtime he was taken with the others into a large barren mess hall where they sat at long wooden tables and ate their potatoes-and-cabbage soup. Across from them sat the city prisoners who were serving jail terms. The prisoners wore overalls and talked across the aisle, trying to frighten them.

"See dat li'l nigger dere." The speaker pointed at Charles.

"Which 'un?"

"Dat li'l nigger dere in de gray suit. Ah'm gonna ast de man tuh gimme dat li'l nigger. Ah'm gonna wo'k his ass off scrubbin' dem flo's down in numbah one. W'en Ah git through wid dat li'l nigger he ain' gonna look so hincty." Raising his voice. "You heah dat, doncha, li'l nigger?"

Charles didn't look up. He dreaded the meals most of all. He was frightened by the viciousness and obscenity of his cellmates and outraged by the callousness of his jailers. But all of it together kept him preoccupied, enclosed in an impenetrable nightmare, shutting out all thoughts of his parents and his home. He drifted in the horror, letting it enfold him.

His parents had been notified of his arrest. But by the time his mother arrived late Monday afternoon, he'd been bound over to the grand jury and transferred to the county jail. There was nothing she could do. His bail had been set at fifteen hundred dollars. She couldn't raise it. She sat across from him at the wooden table in the visiting room along with the other mothers and fathers and relatives of the prisoners and cried as one or two of the other mothers did.

"You'll just have to stay here until your trial comes up."

"That's all right," he said.

He felt sorry for her, but underneath it all he was glad he wouldn't have to testify at her divorce. Now no one could make him.

"I'll engage an attorney for you. There's a friend of my sister Gert who's practising here. I'll ask him to take your case."

"I haven't been indicted yet."

"You'll have to pay him out of your compensation. Your mother doesn't have any money now."

"That's all right."

"You'll have to tell him the truth, son, if he's going to be able to help you."

"There isn't anything to tell. I just forged some checks, that's all. I needed some money and forged some checks."

Her face hardened into the grim, bitter mold. "If you had listened to me and saved your money—" she began in her harsh nagging voice, but he cut her off:

"You had me arrested for forgery once. Only this time I'm guilty."

They tore at each other until it was time for her to go.

His father came down the next day and brought him a package of cigarettes.

"You keep them, Dad," he said. "I have some money and they let me buy what I want."

"I'll see if I can make bail for you, Son."

"Don't bother, Dad, I'm all right."

"If there is anything you need, Son—"

"I don't need anything, Dad."

Neither of his parents visited him again. They were embroiled in their action for divorce. His father contested her plea for alimony on the grounds that she had destroyed his earning capacity by refusing to live in the South where his profession would take him. She contended that he resigned every teaching post he'd held without consulting her and that he hadn't returned South for the simple reason he could no longer get a teaching post.

His father's relatives testified for him, and all the old bitterness of color that had smoldered for years between the families was brought out in their testimony. His wife had ruined his life because she hated black people, they swore. William was called from school to testify for his mother.

It was a bitter, vicious action filled with abuse and recrimination and colored with disorder as the contestants screamed at one another. His mother pictured his father as a debased and spineless scoundrel who had tried to kill her on more than several occasions. She brought out the whole long, sordid story of Charles's behavior in an effort to prove her husband incapable of parental discipline. He countered that she had ruined her son's life by nagging him beyond endurance. She reiterated that he had destroyed Charles's life to hurt her. Although he was absent, Charles became the bone of their contention as his mother fought to have him given in her custody.

The proceedings dragged on and on, bleeding them both. Charles read his mother's letters and was glad he wasn't there. At first it was just the relief of having escaped that torture. But after a time he came to like it in the jail. He'd been assigned to a single cell in a row that faced an identical row across a wide corridor called the "bull pen." Colored prisoners celled on one side, white prisoners on the other. They were let out into the bull pen between meals. They shot dice and played cards. During mealtimes they were locked up and their meals brought around in tin plates and shoved beneath the doors. There were many fights between the white and colored prisoners and something exciting was always happening.

At night a short black prisoner with a barrel chest sang "low-down" blues in a bull-tone voice. Some nights he'd sing:

> *Ah'm blue*
> *But Ah won't be blue always*
> *Cause de sun's gonna shine*
> *In my back do' some day . . . .*

And other nights:

> *Ah feel like layin' mah head*
> *On some railroad line*
> *An' let dat midnight special*
> *Pacify mah mind . . . .*

From over on the other side of the jail came the sound of women screaming, "Sing it, lover!"

It was the first time in Charles's life he'd been completely without responsibility or obligation. He didn't have to worry about what he did or what his mother thought or what he thought himself. He didn't have to think at all. All his thinking was done for him. He didn't care what happened to him. And there was nothing else to worry about. He felt completely safe at last.

Mr. Baker, the attorney his mother had engaged, came over to see him once. He had a tic on one side of his face and Charles thought he couldn't be a very good attorney.

"What did you do with the money?" Mr. Baker wanted to know.

"The police took it. I guess they're keeping it somewhere."

"Is it all there?"

"Yes, and the things I bought too."

"Good, we'll offer to make restoration if they reduce the charges. How many checks were there?"

"I've forgotten. Eleven or twelve."

314

"So many?"

"Something like that."

"Well, I'll get the names and addresses and drive out and talk to the people. You know, I was engaged to your mother's sister once."

"Is that so?"

"That was before you were born." He stood up. "Your mother says this is your first offense. That's in your favor."

His mother came down at Christmas and brought him a box of food. He had never seen her so nervous. She sat across from him tearing her handkerchief into shreds.

"Your father and I are now divorced," she said.

Although he was prepared for it, he felt a sense of shock.

"Your mother is a single woman now." Her attempt to be casual was pathetic.

He was stricken with guilt. "I'm sorry, Mama."

She reached across the table and took his hand. It was against the rules but no one reproached her. The skin on her hands was rough and reddened and laced with tiny cracks and the knuckles of her fingers were swollen. Her hands were burning hot. He could feel them trembling as they clasped his. The trembling went into his own hand and traveled up his arm and he could feel his legs begin to tremble.

"You must come and live with mother, son. The court has awarded me fifteen dollars a week alimony." She was trying desperately to be matter-of-fact. "You are eighteen now and it was left up to you to decide which parent you want to live with."

"I want to live with you, Mama," he choked.

"I talked to Mr. Baker and he said your case will come up sometime next month. He hopes to have you placed on probation."

"Don't worry about it, Mama. Everything'll come out all right."

"Be a good boy and do as Mr. Baker says. Mother will pray for you."

When it came time for her to go he said, "I'll be home soon, Mama. You take care of yourself."

She laughed. "Your mother has been taking care of herself so long now she's used to it. If I had depended on your father I'd have been dead a long time ago."

He winced. She sounded like a stranger. He didn't know her at all.

For a long time he lay across his bunk, trying to adjust his mind to the thought that never again would his parents live together. What would his mother do, who would she have to nag, how would she live? The questions turned over and over in his mind, hypnotically, and he went into a trance. He felt his body swaying from side to side as if he were riding on a train. He heard the wheels clacking over the section joints. The lulling motion of the train and the monotonous clacking of the wheels were ineffably soothing. Then he realized they were going somewhere again. He felt himself crying all down inside. Finally he turned his head to ask his mother where they were going. The chain by which his bunk was suspended from the wall angled down across his vision, breaking his trance. He got up and drank a cup of water.

"Well, I guess that's gone too," he said without realizing he had spoken.

Later on he lay down in his clothes and went to sleep. When he awakened he was stiff and cold and his head ached. By morning he had a severe cold and laryngitis. He didn't report it because it kept his brain fuzzy and he couldn't think. He'd rather feel bad than be able to think.

The first week in January he received a letter from his mother:

Dear Son,

We have sold the house and most of the furniture. Most of the money has gone to pay the cost of court and lawyer's fees. I was able to hang on to my silver and a few of my dishes. I want you and William to have my silver, some of it has been in my family since my childhood. I have moved with a family on Emmett Street, but the lady puts mice in my room at night and I have to find another place. I also want a separate room for you and William. I don't know where your father is living and I don't care. I suppose he has written to you. I have your things with me. Mr. Baker says your case will come up soon. I will try to be there. You must pray and put your trust in God.

Your loving mother.

It made him sad to think of her living alone and feeling persecuted again. But by then he had let his cold get to the point where his eyes were swollen almost shut and his head ached constantly; and nothing mattered very much.

He was still sick when his trial came up the following week. It was quite different from what he had expected. The courtroom was practically deserted save for the court officials, his attorney and himself. He wondered why his mother hadn't come but he wouldn't ask. He hadn't heard from his father since the divorce so he hadn't expected him.

Mr. Baker stood beside him at the bar while the clerk read the indictment.

"How do you plead, guilty or not guilty?" a voice droned.

Mr. Baker pleaded guilty for him and placed him on the mercy of the court. He stated that full restoration of the money had been made. And due to the tragic background of the defendant, his injury and subsequent illness which had contributed so greatly to his delinquency, and now his broken home, the prosecuting witnesses had agreed not to appear against him. He asked that sentence be suspended.

The prosecuting attorney said he would raise no objection.

The judge looked down at Charles. "I am inclined to let you go home," he said, "but I want your promise that you will keep out of trouble."

Home! Charles thought. He tried to meet the judge's eyes but his gaze turned away. From outside came the clear, hard sound of an automobile horn, bringing a sharp, vivid memory of the night ride down from Cleveland, and he wondered momentarily if the car had been found. "Yes, sir, I promise." His throat was still inflamed and he could barely whisper.

He was given a bench parole with directions to send the court

317

written reports monthly. And then he was placed in the custody of his father.

Mr. Baker requested the court to parole him to his mother. "Mrs. Taylor has always exerted stronger discipline over this son than his father," he contended. "And she has already prepared a home for him."

Charles thought suddenly of a line from his mother's last letter: ". . . but the lady puts mice in my room at night . . ." He wanted to tell the judge she needed him.

But the judge wouldn't change his ruling. "No, the boy needs a strong hand to discipline him."

Mr. Baker accompanied him back to the county jail where he got his overcoat and hat. "Your mother will be very disappointed," he said.

Charles didn't reply. While Mr. Baker was driving him to the station he realized that he didn't know his father's address. He thought perhaps Mr. Baker knew, but he wouldn't ask. He didn't want Mr. Baker to know his father hadn't written.

"I'll mail you the money from my compensation," he promised.

"Don't worry about my fee, son. Just be a good boy and make your mother happy."

He bought Charles a ticket and stayed with him until he boarded the train.

Charles dreaded the ride. He wished he could have stayed in jail. The dreary winter landscape passing by his window reminded him of his trip home from college the year before. Only this time he didn't know where he was going.

He had a box of bitter brown quinine tablets he had been given for his cold. He'd been instructed to take one every hour, followed by a glass of water. Instead he chewed them, one after another, letting the dark, bitter taste spread out in his mouth. Somehow it was comforting. He chewed the bitter tablets and tried not to think.

26

It was snowing in Cleveland. A cold, biting wind, coming across the lake, whistled through the smoke-blackened rafters of the old wooden station and slanted the snow into Charles's face. He turned up the collar of his overcoat and climbed the rickety stairs to the gloomy waiting room. He began coughing again. His throat felt raw and inflamed. The unutterable dreariness of the surrounding scene matched his mood. He felt a strong desire to sit there among the shivering, bundled-up foreign-born travelers and never move again. He dreaded having to talk to anyone.

Finally he telephoned his Aunt Lou and asked for his father's address.

"Is that you, Charles?"

"Yes."

"Where are you now?"

"I'm at the station."

She wanted to ask about the outcome of his trial but he didn't give her any opening. She told him that his father lived at an address on 100th Street off Cedar Avenue. He thanked her and went outside through the smoke and sludge and caught a street car. It was already dark. He huddled over the coal-burning stove at the rear of the street car and shook the grate. Someone had placed orange peelings on the lid to kill the smell of garlic. He opened the door and added a shovelful of coal.

Beyond the flats falling away behind the municipal buildings he saw the yellow lights of the bridges across the river. He wondered if William had come home for Christmas. He hadn't asked his mother. He looked out at the ugly city and tried not to think. It took ages to reach the house where his father lived.

A middle-aged, dark-complexioned woman came to the door.

"Oh, you're Charles." She gave him a close scrutiny. "Come on in, your father is expecting you."

He stepped inside.

"Professor Taylor isn't here right now, but you can go right on up to his room. You and him are gonna share the room."

"Well, I'll come back," he whispered. "I got to get some things anyway."

She gave him a suspicious look. "Now don't you come in late waking up eve'ybody. We're all working folks an' got to get up early. An' your father don't sleep well as it is."

"I'll be back shortly."

The house was only a half-block from The Avenue. As he was standing at the corner waiting for a street car he saw Poker come out of the pool hall diagonally across the street. He turned his back to keep Poker from recognizing him. Black faces drifted past, breathing out the smell of rotgut liquor. He felt the need of a drink, but he didn't want his mother to smell it on his breath. Finally the street car came.

She was living in a strange neighborhood off Kinsman Road, out near the city line, more than an hour's ride away. He hadn't eaten since breakfast and as the slow street car plodded through the dismal night he felt himself filling up with tears. A soft droning sound filled his head, and his throat and chest burned as if on fire. He was grateful for the distraction.

His mother was surprised to see him. She was clad in an old kimono and her hair was braided and her face cold-creamed for the night, and he thought of all the times she had come to the door of his room late at night, looking as she did then, to scold him.

"Oh, why didn't you let me know you were coming?" she said crossly, extending her cheek to be kissed. "You're all alike. You never think of me. I haven't made your bed or anything."

He kissed her, tasting the perfumed cream, and felt a sudden wave of nausea. "I didn't know myself until this morning," he whispered, and then added, "I have a cold."

"Are you free?" she asked anxiously. "Were you placed on probation?"

"I was given a bench parole."

He took off his coat and she moved some clothes from the

chair. She sat on the bed facing him, her hands nervous in lap.

"What are you taking for your cold?"

"I got some pills."

They were embarrassed and constrained, as if they were strangers. Both found themselves unable at the moment to discuss what was uppermost in their thoughts. She wanted to know about his trial, why she hadn't been notified, and all about his future plans. She wondered if he'd heard from his father, what his father was doing. He wanted to tell her he was sorry they had to sell the house, that he was sorry now about everything, about all the hurt and heartache he had caused her all his life. But there was a wall between them which neither could break through.

"I've taken the room across the hall for you and William," she said, "but I don't know whether we'll be able to stay. These people, the Morrows—he's a waiter on the railroad—they have a twelve-year-old son who sneaks in here while I'm away and breaks stink bombs in my room."

He felt a chill run down his spine and it was a moment before he could speak. "Why don't you tell his parents?"

"I have, but Mrs. Morrow says he doesn't do it. She's just as bad as he is. Mr. Morrow promised to make him stop, but he's away most of the time and his mother encourages him."

"Why don't you leave?"

"Oh, one place is as bad as another." She laughed. "Your mother is used to people trying to hurt her. Maybe he'll stop now that you're here."

He wondered how long she'd been laughing like that. It was a weird, mirthless sound that seemed bordering on hysteria.

"Mama—"

She looked around at the tone of his voice and he saw the deep oblique lines of sudden fear cut across her face. He looked down at the floor.

"I was paroled to dad. I was paroled to dad for five years."

For a moment she was perfectly still as if her blood had frozen. It was the bitterest disappointment she had ever suffered. All for nothing! All waste! She wouldn't have him after all. Finally she

forced herself to speak. "I suppose you'd rather be with your father. He'll let you do as you like." She didn't mean it. She was trying desperately to stem the hurt, to hold herself together. She knew if she broke then she'd never mend.

"I didn't ask for it, Mama."

"You're old enough to know what you want," she said. Instead of the old, harsh, nagging tone her voice was now light and brittle as if it might break into tiny pieces in the middle of a word. "You'll find your things in the other room."

He went across the hall to the small bedroom and packed the suitcase he had taken to the university. When he returned she was sitting in the chair, painting her nails. A cork-tipped cigarette was burning in an ash tray on the dresser. He was scalded by shock, blinded. His stomach knotted with nausea and he had to fight to keep from vomiting.

"Mama—"

She didn't seem to notice his agitation. "I suppose Mr. Taylor is living with his sister."

"No, we have a room on 100th Street." He felt that she was slipping away into oblivion, down into the deep, dark, sordid world she had so despised. He wanted to save her, to draw her back, to swear on his knees he'd love her and take care of her forever. But she gave no indication that she needed his help.

"Now you can walk to all the dives," she remarked, trying so hard to dam the torrent of tears welling up in her. She was nearer to defeat than she had ever been.

He put on his overcoat and picked up his suitcase. "Yes, they're just around the corner," he whispered bitterly.

His father was in bed reading a pulp magazine when he returned. The magazine cover had a gory picture of gunmen killing each other. His father wore a pair of steel-rimmed spectacles he'd never seen before and was smoking a self-made cigarette. He laid the cigarette in a saucer on the chair beside his head and greeted Charles.

"Hello, Son."

"Hello, Dad."

Smoke curled slowly from a pile of smoldering cigarette butts

322

in the saucer, and hung in a haze at the ceiling. Charles noticed that the ends of the butts which his father had held in his lips were stained brown with spittle. The room reeked with a horrible stink of burning spit and wet tobacco.

"Have you had your supper?"

"Yes."

"You can come with me tomorrow and get your breakfast."

"All right."

He undressed and got a pair of pyjamas from his suitcase. He couldn't breathe. "You mind if I crack a window."

His father looked blank. After a moment he said, "You must make yourself at home, son. It isn't much." He took another cigarette from a paper bag resting on the chair. The one he'd just put down smoldered with the others on the saucer. He seemed to have forgotten it.

Charles crawled into his side of the bed and looked away. The sight of that pile of smoldering butts had filled him with blind anguish. He closed his eyes and tried to go to sleep. After a time he opened them. Ash hung from the end of his father's cigarette. His eyes were open, staring at the print. Charles noticed that he hadn't turned the page.

"Why don't you put out your cigarette and go to sleep, Dad?"

His father closed the magazine and laid the cigarette atop the smoldering pile. "I was thinking of the time I lived in Savannah. I was just a raw young buck right out of college, just begun to teach but everybody called me 'Fess.' They'd stop by when they came up from the docks. 'Want a li'l kittle o' eyesters, Fess?'" He chuckled. "You like oysters, Son?"

"Sometimes."

There was a cord tied to the head of the bed, connected to the drop light in the center of the room. Charles reached up and pulled the cord and turned off the light. Every now and then he could hear his father chuckling in the dark.

Professor Taylor was working as a porter for a night club on Euclid, run by two racketeers named Manny and Benny. They liked Professor Taylor and trusted him alone in the club. Charles helped with the work every morning but left before

Manny and Benny came in around noon. He emptied and washed the ash trays, ran the vacuum sweeper, cleaned the dining room, dance floor and bandstand. His father cleaned the stairway and foyer, behind the tobacco counter, and scrubbed the kitchen. At eleven o'clock they ate breakfast. Charles tried to eat enough to last him for the day. He'd eat a bowl of oatmeal, six eggs, four pieces of toast and a half pound of bacon, or occasionally a steak. He was always gone by noon.

Every afternoon he saw a moving picture show. If he became hungry again he'd eat dinner in a restaurant out on Cedar Avenue. The days were easy. He could get through the days. It was night he couldn't fill. He couldn't cope with his nights. After six o'clock he was always at loose ends.

For a time he tried keeping to his room and reading. But he couldn't bear the sight of his father reading the same page of some blood-and-thunder story hour after hour, endlessly smoking the stinking cigarettes. His father never mentioned the divorce, never mentioned his mother, not once did he ask about the trial or Charles's sentence. He never referred to their former home, never spoke of William, never asked Charles where he went or what he did. But he often spoke reminiscently about some happening in the distant past, before he was married. He'd recount in infinite detail what someone had said to him and what he'd said in reply, as if it had happened yesterday, and often he would chuckle to himself, causing Charles's blood to curdle.

Charles would get up and leave. He tried visiting his mother. But that was worse. She had developed a strange new personality. She'd dyed her hair and wore her nails painted, and although Charles never saw another cigarette in her room, there was an ash tray on the dresser and he was certain that she smoked.

She complained so often of the Morrows' son putting stink bombs in her room that he finally persuaded her to move. But at the next place she complained that her landlady was jealous of her husband.

"Who'd want that man?" she'd say, laughing mirthlessly. "He's as black as your father."

She asked only once what he was doing.

"I'm helping dad in the morning. He's got a porter's job."

"What do you do the rest of your day?"

"I go to the show. Try to read a little. I can't find anything to do."

"You're not trying," she accused. For a moment the old harshness returned to her voice. "If you don't intend to return to college you should at least try to get a job in some business with an opportunity for advancement, instead of wasting your time hanging around your father."

"But what can I do?"

"You know how to get into trouble well enough."

He got up to go. "Yes, I can do that well enough."

Her voice came after him. "Oh, my baby, if you would only try. With your blood you should be able to do anything."

He turned and looked at her. It was your blood first, he thought. And what did it get you? But aloud he said, "Yes, shouldn't I?" After that he found it very hard to visit her.

Quite often he felt the urge to look up Poker. But he was afraid of his parole. He kept away from The Avenue. Occasionally he slipped into a whiskey joint, but he was afraid to get drunk again. He was afraid of what he might do.

Most of the time he didn't have anywhere to go. He began walking again through the lonely parks at night. It was then he became assailed with a sense of drifting. One night he stood on the parapet at Gordon Park and watched a full moon turn the lake into molten silver. Far up the bend of the lake, car lights bobbed on the Drive, turned and were lost in Bratenahl. He recalled how he used to walk out there. Here he was alone.

Down below, the sharp-tongued waves beckoned with a strange fascination. It was as if they offered sleep—cool, deep, caressing sleep. Suddenly he felt tired. He had never been so tired, so utterly exhausted. A smell of snow was in the air. He listened to the faint sighing of the wind in the overhead crags. He felt a strong sweet longing to lay down on the waves and sleep. The thought frightened him. He found himself struggling to break the hypnotic hold of the shimmering waves.

He turned and ran in headlong flight down the vague footpaths, as shadows of the skeletoned trees danced weirdly in the moonlight. At home he found his father lying in the middle of the bed, his blank gaze resting on the pages of an open magazine, a pile of wet brown butts smoldering in the saucer at his side. He crawled in on the edge to keep from touching him. But he hated his father with such a violence he had to get up again. He went into the bathroom and drank the tepid water from the tap. It nauseated him and he vomited into the stool. But when he returned to the room he began sweating profusely. He went back to the bathroom and took a bath.

"Don't you feel well, son?" his father asked.

"I feel fine," he said.

He began dressing to go out. His father didn't ask where he was going. He put on his overcoat, drew on his gloves, and put on a dark felt hat.

"Do you have your keys, son?"

"Yes."

He closed the door behind him, tiptoed down the stairs and let himself out into the night. It was snowing and he turned up the collar of his overcoat. He walked along The Avenue without any idea of where he was going. A drunken man and a drunken woman staggered along in the slush, clinging to each other to keep from falling. At first the snow felt cool and pleasant on his face. He recalled his mother's suggestion about getting a job, turned over the possibilities in his mind. God knows he'd have to do something, he thought; he couldn't keep this up. Then he thought of Mr. Small, at the hotel where he was hurt. Mr. Small would give him a job, he knew. He could become a waiter. That wasn't the worst thing in the world. Many of the waiters earned a good income. He resolved to go and see Mr. Small the very first thing in the morning.

Sometime later he found himself at 82nd Street, not far from where the Douglas family lived, with whom William had stayed that summer. He found himself thinking intently about Will. He wondered how he was getting along in college. It must have been an ordeal for him to testify at their parents' divorce proceedings, he thought. He wondered what William had said. His mother had never discussed William's testimony. She'd said very little about the entire action. And his father had never mentioned William's name. It was very strange how Will had got so far away in so short a time, he thought. He had a sudden impulse to catch a train and go down and visit Will. Then he realized he would arrive there at an ungodly hour of morning. He wasn't certain that Will would be glad to see him. He hadn't heard from his brother since before Christmas, when he was still in jail. Thinking about it, he realized he hadn't written to Will since he went to college.

"I'll see him another time," he said. He spoke aloud without realizing it.

When he came to the Y he turned and started back. Snow had collected on his hat and coat. He suffered a sudden chill. He'd never completely gotten rid of his cold and going out into the snow immediately after taking a bath had been dangerous. He'd better stop somewhere and get a drink, he told himself. Then he thought of Dave; he'd stop by Dave's.

At the house where Dave had lived he was told that Dave had moved to The Alley. He went around to the dark, unpaved alley back of the buildings that fronted on The Avenue and found Dave's shack. There was a coal-burning, pot-bellied stove in the middle room and a group of half-drunken men and women stood around an oilcloth-covered table shooting dice. The air was thick with whiskey fumes and tobacco smoke. It was stifling hot. The mutter of thick voices rose from the intent players like a blasphemous miasma.

"Whass de mattah with you, niggah, Ah bet you a fin."

"Ah put down a fin."

"Where it at?"

"How Ah know?"

"Doan hold up de dice, niggah."

Dave looked around and saw him. "Chuck! Whataya say, boy. Where you been? I been looking for you everywhere."

"I was in jail."

Several of the players turned around and looked at him.

"What for?" Dave asked.

"Nothing much. I'm out now, anyway, so let's have a drink."

Dave put his arm about his shoulder. "Same old Chuck," he laughed. "Take off your coat, man." Then he turned toward the kitchen and called, "Hey, Veeny, bring in a pint and some ginger ale."

"I'll drink it in the kitchen. It's too hot in here," Charles said. "Come on and drink with me."

They went in and sat at the kitchen table and Charles threw his coat across a chair. The woman served them. She was a well-formed woman about thirty-five years old. Her light-tan complexion had a strange indoor pallor as if she'd been in prison. Long black hair hung down her back and her dark brown eyes, fringed with long lashes, had a muddy, beaten look. She wore a black satin dress with a high collar which didn't quite hide the thin embossed scar that circled down across her throat from ear to ear. In her face and body were signs of wanton dissipation, and, looking at her, Charles thought that she must have been ravishingly beautiful in her youth. As she bent over to pour his drink, their gazes locked, and he felt the shock of sickness run through him as if he saw himself mirrored in her beaten, lustful look. He was at once revolted and entranced.

Dave caught their look and laughed. "Veeny, this is Chuck. He's my pal. Take care of him."

"He's a pretty boy," she said.

When she went out of the room for a moment Dave said, "I keep her to run this joint. I got another whore downtown."

Charles felt an intense revulsion toward Dave. "I think I'll gamble," he said abruptly.

He went back into the middle room and squeezed into the group about the table. But he couldn't keep his mind on the game. He kept thinking about Dave's woman. Something about her frightened him; she seemed to smell of death. And yet she incited in him an almost uncontrollable desire. Several times he forgot to pick up the bets he'd won. Soon he was broke. He borrowed some money from Dave and when he'd lost that he went out to the kitchen to get a pint of whiskey on credit.

Veeny was sitting at the table, drinking with another woman. "Where's Dave?" he asked.

She held his gaze. "He's gone already. He goes about this time every night."

"Oh, I wanted to get a pint but I haven't got any money with me." He couldn't unlock his gaze from hers.

"I'll give you a drink, baby."

The other woman got up. "I'm gonna try 'em again, honey."

Charles took the chair she'd vacated. Veeny held his gaze. Her huge muddy eyes were glassy. She slowly licked her lips. He felt the hot sick lust come up into his own eyes like something wet and sticky.

"I'll give you some money if you want to keep on playing."

"I just want to borrow ten." His voice was thick as if something had caught in his throat.

She raised her skirt and took some money from her stocking. He gulped his drink and went back to the game. The heat made him sick and the room began to blur. When he'd lost the ten he started to leave but he felt too sick. He staggered back to the kitchen. Without realizing how it had happened he felt Veeny's body in his arms. Her face was blurred. All he could see were her huge glassy eyes. He felt her tongue move across his lips, search his nostrils, then dart between his teeth down into his mouth like a small, wet flame.

"I want a drink first," he begged.

He remembered vaguely bending over the sink to vomit. She was holding him about the waist. His next conscious thought was on awakening. Sunlight on the tan window shades filled the room with a soft yellow glow. He noticed the short black hairs on Veeny's arm, against the yellow pallor of her skin. Her arm had a dead look, as if it were just beginning to decay, he thought. Then his gaze moved upward and he saw the dark embossed scar about her throat. He felt shock pour over him.

"I got to go," he said, trying frantically to escape.

She pulled him back toward her. "You were too drunk to do anything last night."

He looked down at the dull yellow composition of her breasts, trying to avoid her eyes. "I know, but I got to go," he said hysterically. "I'm late now. I got to go."

"Take me," she said.

He jerked free of her. His head seemed to split open with pain. "Goddammit, I got to go!" he shouted. "Suppose Dave came in and caught me."

She gave him a peculiar look. "He's been here already, baby."

He felt suddenly caught in something he didn't understand. "He was?" He felt defiled, as if he had debased himself, as if he had wallowed in pollution. But the lust surged back into him until his blood pounded. The conflict of lust and revulsion held him, he shivered with a sudden chill. The splitting headache of his hangover blinded him. He let her force him and gave in. The touch of her skin was like death. He spent himself uncontrollably over her legs and the bed.

She said, "Oh, goddammit," in a strange aching wail.

He fled to the other room, found his clothes and dressed, and ran out of the house. It was past noon, too late to go and help his father. He went downtown to a show, but became so ill he had to leave. He went home. His compensation check had come that morning, but he was too sick to go out and cash it. He undressed and went to bed. When his father came in he awakened.

"I'm sorry I didn't get over to help you, dad. I went to see mother and stayed for the night," he lied.

"That's all right, son. Just take care of yourself."

His father undressed and got into bed, opened a magazine and lit a cigarette. Charles got up and dressed.

"I'm going and get something to eat, dad."

"All right, son."

He started to eat in a restaurant on The Avenue, but found that he didn't have but thirty cents besides his check. On sudden impulse he rode out to see his mother. He was almost within sight of her house when he realized he couldn't face her. He rode back to The Avenue and wandered about for a time. It was as if he were struggling against returning to Veeny. But finally he gave in and went back to her.

The dice game was in progress. Dave looked up and grinned. "How'd you make out, Chuck?"

He wasn't certain just what Dave meant. "I got broke again," he said.

"How much you need?"

"I got a check for seventy-five dollars I want to get you to cash."

"Sure thing."

He paid Dave and took the change and went into the kitchen. Veeny was cooking pigs' feet. She came up to him and ran the palms of her hands down over his waist and hips. "Hungry, baby?"

Suddenly he was very hungry. "I want a drink first."

She mixed two drinks and sat down across from him, devouring him with her eyes. "Don't get drunk, baby."

"I won't," he promised.

By midnight he was broke and blind drunk. He vomited in the sink again. She took him into the bedroom and undressed him and put him to bed. An hour later Dave left. She stopped the game and put the people out, then came in and went to bed and held Charles's head against her breasts. It was noon the next day when he awakened. She played her tongue over his lips. He felt too weak to struggle. He gave in. It was like a terrible horror of ecstasy; as if his blood were being sucked by a vampire.

Afterwards she fixed breakfast. While they were eating, Dave came in. He had a pair of large green dice.

"Let's try 'em out," he said.

They began shooting on the kitchen floor. At first they bet a half-dollar on the roll. But as Dave began to lose he raised the bet. He lost twenty-five dollars, then took all the money Veeny had. They gambled for two hours. When Dave got even Charles said, "I quit."

"Goddamn, all that work for nothing," Dave cursed. "If you weren't my pal I'd cut your throat."

"I didn't want to gamble against you," Charles said.

Veeny smiled.

"I'll be back later," Dave said and left.

Charles couldn't understand what was happening. He was sick and frightened.

"Why does Dave let me sleep with you?" he asked Veeny.

She came over and ran her tongue across his eyes. "He's got to, baby. I want you. He's got another whore and I got you."

He wanted to leave and never come back. But he didn't have the strength. He didn't know what was happening to him. Instead of leaving he began drinking again. He was drunk every night for a week, awakening to be loved, fed, and begin drinking again. His thoughts became vague. He seemed floating in a nightmare of sensuality. Heat began growing in his brain in a thin, steady flame. When he couldn't bear it he'd call her to bed. Each time he felt himself pouring out of himself into her as if giving her his life. He began to love the sensation of dying he derived from her.

He went to his room only for a change of clothes. Sometimes he saw his father. He made some vague excuse. His father never questioned him, never scolded him. He wondered if his father were sane.

He hadn't visited his mother since the night he first met Veeny. He couldn't understand why he felt such an intense fear whenever he thought of her. There was a period each night just before he became unconscious, when his mind seemed sharp and clear. Quite often, during this period, which sometimes lasted no longer than a fleeting moment, he thought of his mother. He'd recall an episode from his early childhood in Mississippi . . .

He and William had been to the store with their mother. They were returning down the long, dusty road in the magic twilight, the two tots trotting along beside their mother, vying for her attention.

"Mother, we saw a jackass."

"We saw a guinea."

"We saw something we didn't know what it was."

"Mother, there ought to be something on an animal to tell you what it is."

"Something in its fur."

"Suppose it's got feathers."

"In it's feathers then."

She had to laugh. "I'm a bear," she said. "Be-ware."

They laughed uproariously.

"I'm a fox—I'm sly."

"I'm a weasel—I steal chickens."

"I'm a rabbit—catch me."

"I'm a rabbit—fry me."

She laughed delightedly. "In case you've never cooked a rabbit here is a recipe for rabbit fricassee."

Her gay, tinkling laugh thrilled them . . .

For that instant he felt happy and excited. Then the memory was gone, leaving a bitter aftermath, in which he thought it strange that he couldn't recall ever having heard his mother laugh with his father. Suddenly he remembered her laugh as he had heard it last. The next moment he was blotto.

27

HE HAD SLEPT DRUNKENLY ALL DAY. ON AWAKENING he felt exhausted and helpless. Veeny was kissing his chest and the sensation of her hot sharp tongue sickened him with revulsion.

"I can't this morning—I can't. Please don't make me," he pleaded.

"Pretty-pretty," she moaned in a thickened voice, kissing his eyes and face. Her hair fell down about his head, covering him like a shroud, and he could barely breathe.

"Don't, please don't," he begged, but his voice was muffled by her mouth.

She sucked his breath, forcing her long sharp tongue between his lips. He wrenched his face away, feeling faint. Savagely she bit his neck. He struggled to push her away but she clung to him tenaciously, like a carnivorous animal, devouring his flesh.

"My baby," she moaned, scouring his ear with her tongue. There was a paralyzing evil in her consuming desire.

A strange wanton sensation overwhelmed him. It was as if she was drawing all that was good from him and poisoning his blood with something that was repulsive and weird and abnormal. He tried to hold on to the good but she was the stronger and pulled it loose from himself. Finally he gave up and let his will go. He closed his eyes and felt himself sinking down into her womb.

For an instant he thought he would faint. Then suddenly his blood flooded up in a warm ecstasy of surrender as if he was the whore of the two.

"Oh, give it!" she cried, wailing as if in the throes of death.

He felt the sweet acid shock of utter evil. Then he whimpered like a child as he gave himself to her. Afterwards he lay in a trance of passivity, looking into her eyes, for the first time realizing that she was on top. Now he wanted to give himself to her again in this different way where nothing at all mattered but the strange sweet ecstasy of defeat.

But she arose and said, "I'll fix us some breakfast, baby."

With the sound of her normal voice his revulsion returned. He jumped out of bed and began to dress in a world suddenly gone in filth and depravity. His soul vomited up the strange sensation of surrender and, as he looked at her, death flooded from his eyes.

"Where are you going?" she demanded.

He avoided her gaze. If he looked into her eyes he would kill her. "I'm going home and change clothes," he said.

"You'll come back, baby." He heard the triumph singing in her voice and felt nauseated with shame.

It had been raining earlier but now it had turned to soft wet snow. He stood for a moment outside the door, breathing deeply the damp cold air, trying to orientate himself, to adjust his emotions to the normal world. His mind was enveloped in weird unreality, as if he had awakened in a world he'd never seen.

Two men passed and their soft Negroid voices sounded the tone of reality. Slowly the street took perspective in a row of shabby houses. He saw a dog sniffing a wet pile of garbage beside a broken step. He discovered with a shock he was thinking of his mother. He could hear her saying with a crying note of worry, "My little baby. What have you done now?" He closed his mind to her and began walking toward his room. He wanted to get his clean clothes before his father returned from work.

But his landlady met him in the hallway and said, "Now don't you go disturbing your father. He's sick."

"Oh, I didn't know."

"You ain't home enough to know anything," she accused.

He tiptoed up to his room and found his father in bed. As he entered the room he heard his father mutter, "Don't hurt the boy, Lillian. Don't do it, honey . . . "

He bent down and shook his father. "Dad!" he said softly.

His father opened his eyes and made an effort to focus his gaze. "It's all right, Son, it's all right," he mumbled. His breath reeked with the odor of rotgut whiskey.

Charles drew back. He was surprised to discover that he felt no shock. It was as if he'd passed the point where degradation mattered; as if he now expected only the worst in everything.

"Is there anything I can do for you, Dad?" he heard himself ask.

His father didn't answer. He had already closed his eyes. A moment later he was breathing stentoriously.

Charles put a pitcher of water and a glass beside the bed, and straightened the covers over his father. Then he began to change clothes. After a time he became aware of tears streaming down his face. He didn't know how long he had been crying.

Before leaving he searched the room for whisky. He intended to throw it away. At least he could do that much for his father. But he didn't find any.

It had darkened outside, filling the early night with gloom. He began walking. There seemed something sacrilegious about his father drinking. He tried not to think about it. For a time he didn't think of anything. He felt the tears trickling down his face, and every now and then he sobbed spasmodically. He blew his nose and wiped his face.

Suddenly he realized he was thinking of his mother again. She must have been in his thoughts all along. He wondered if she had begun drinking too. The thought fired him with unbearable horror. He hailed a taxi and rode out to the home where she lived. The window of her room was dark but he knocked anyway. A pleasant middle-aged woman with a kind brown face came to the door and he asked if his mother was at home.

"No, she went out early this afternoon and hasn't returned."

"Did—did she seem ill?" he found himself asking.

The woman looked at him strangely. "Why, no—no more than usual."

"Oh!" He wondered what she meant but couldn't bring himself to ask.

He thanked her and said he would return. Then, for more than two hours he walked about the neighborhood, passing the house on the opposite side of the street every fifteen or twenty minutes to look up at her window, hoping to find a light. He felt such a craving for whiskey he was tempted to return to Cedar Avenue, but the deep dark sense of dread anchored him. A movie theatre loomed up before him. He went in and sat in the dark. But after an hour the urgency returned. He jumped to his feet, rushed outside and ran all the way back to her house. Her room was still dark. He wondered if she had returned while he was in the theatre and had gone to bed. He was afraid the woman might think it was he who was in trouble if he enquired again, so he stationed himself across the street to wait. The soft wet snowflakes blowing against his face were like the touch of cool gentle fingers.

"Please don't let anything happen to her," he prayed.

The cold seeped through his clothes and he began trembling. He needed a drink the worst way. It began to snow heavily. After a time he had to give up his vigil. He rode back to Cedar Avenue on the streetcar, but the moment he alighted the dark terrifying dread returned to haunt him. He went into a whiskey joint and drank a half pint of the strong rotgut, hoping to calm his fears. But instead his emotions were intensified and the dread began roaring through his mind like a chimney afire.

He took a taxi back to her house. The jolting of the car over the bumpy streets made him sick and his mouth ballooned as he strained to keep from vomiting.

Now the whole house was dark. But he staggered up the front steps and knocked anyway. A man clad in a red flannel robe came to the door. In a thick blurred voice Charles asked for his mother.

The man looked at him sympathetically. "You're Charles?"

"Yes sir."

"You were here earlier this evening, weren't you?"

"Yes sir, I was."

"Your mother went down to the college to see your brother and hasn't returned yet."

"Oh!" He swayed drunkenly as the porch rolled crazily beneath him.

"You can wait for her in her room if you wish," the man offered.

He thanked him and followed up the stairway, trying to keep from stumbling. The man opened the door to his mother's room and turned on the light. Charles thanked him again, closed the door and, without removing his overcoat or hat, fell across the bed.

After a moment he turned to make himself more comfortable. His gaze lit on the ash tray on the dressing table. It held the butts of two cork-tipped cigarettes marked with lipstick, and the butt of a homemade cigarette stained brown with spittle. His body went rigid; his neck was caught in the angle of turning, frozen in shock. *His father had been there. . . .*

Abruptly he sprang to his feet. For a moment he stood perfectly still, his head tilted as if listening for a sound. His gaze was unfocused, inturned; he didn't see anything now. He could feel his heart beating in the sealed silence. *That was why he was drunk.* He looked again at the cigarette butts, studying them as if they contained a clue. Suddenly, uncomprehendingly, his senses were stunned in the manner of a lover's by discovery of his loved one's infidelity. Then he was caught up and hurled into a sea of bitter torment. Everything he had tried to forget, to push from his consciousness, to drown in drink and dissolution—the despair over the loss of his home, the breaking up of his family, his parents' divorce, his failure in school; the open sores of sorrow in his father's face, the unread blood-and-thunder stories, the vacant stare, the pile of smoldering cigarette butts; the bitter hurt living in his mother's eyes, the brittle laugh and hennaed hair; and his own remorse for all the things he had done to bring them to such an end—all of it was dug up and brought alive in the picture presented by those three cigarette butts.

"Jesus Christ!" he gasped.

His mind blazed with panic, setting off motion within him as the lighting of a fuse. He was running even before his feet began to move. He ran from the room, hurtled down the stairs. He heard the man shout, "Hey, what's going on!" He fought the front door, trying to get it open. The demons had broken out and were charging down behind him. He got the door open, leaped across the porch. His foot slipped on the fresh snow and he skidded headlong down the stairs. His hat flew off. He got up and ran bareheaded down the street. Behind him he could hear the man calling, "Taylor! Taylor!"

He ran until he was exhausted. But he could not rid his mind of the agonizing picture. He sat on the curb and sobbed, "Goddammit, goddammit," over and over. *Why couldn't his father leave her alone; just leave her alone and let everything rest?* The sour flow of acid, brought on by his torment, mixed with the rotgut whisky, spewed up from his stomach and made a brownish-yellow blot on the white snow. He wiped his mouth on his sleeve, feeling the snow melting in his hair. He looked down the long white street, his thoughts turned inward. "I can't go through that life again," he thought.

Then he rose and walked all the way back to Cedar Avenue. His body was giving out but he was unaware of it. He returned to his room. His father was sleeping drunkenly as he had left him, his wide bold nostrils flaring as he snored. His mouth was open and saliva drooled from one corner of his lips.

For an instant hate blazed in Charles with murderous intensity. But his father looked so completely defeated and helpless in his drunken sleep that compassion welled up in his mind, putting out the hatred. He felt an impulse to wipe his father's mouth, but he didn't want to awaken him. He turned out the light and stood quietly in the darkness, listening to his father snore. Strangely, he felt his heart listening also, straining itself to hear something, he didn't know what. It ached from the effort of listening. He held his breath. Some sense warned him of another presence in the room. Quickly he turned on the light again. But there was no one. He stood for a moment longer, wondering what it was, and his emotions were invaded by a sense of death.

"That would be all right," he heard himself say softly. "That would be fine."

He turned off the light and tiptoed from the room, down the stairs and from the house.

The street was still and silent beneath its mantle of snow. He walked down toward Cedar Avenue, his footsteps muffled by the snow. For a moment he experienced the queer sensation of moving in a dream. *He'd get a taxi and ride out to the lake and just keep on walking out into the water until he'd left the world behind.* But there were no taxis in sight, and when he came to the first whiskey joint he went inside.

Mrs. Taylor returned home shortly after one o'clock that morning.

Early the previous afternoon Professor Taylor had called to plead for a reconciliation. He'd been offered a teaching post in a small southern college, and he proposed that they remarry and begin over.

"They'll give me a house and we can have Charles with us."

The thought of having Charles again almost tempted her to accept. But deep inside herself she could never forgive him for having let her go.

So she refused. "After what you and your family have done to me I wouldn't live with you again if you were the last man on earth. Never! Never!" Her voice was pitched in the old harsh tone she had always assumed when addressing him.

But afterwards she was beset with doubts and uncertainties. Was she denying her son his last chance for a normal life because she couldn't abide his father? She didn't know. She was tired—so tired. And living alone made decisions so difficult to reach, so hard to defend; she was becoming afraid to trust her judgment any longer.

It had been different when she'd had her husband and her sons. Even when they'd opposed her, the fact of them belonging to her and her belonging to them gave her support. And now there was only herself in her lonely room.

She felt an overwhelming need to talk to someone who loved her, someone who needed her, if just for a moment. From that love and need she would draw her strength.

Her heart thought first of Charles. She knew how much he needed her; how much he loved her. But her mind rejected him. She knew that he was afraid to admit his need or any longer confess his love for her, that he was afraid of committing himself again to a way of life which had disappointed him in the past. Sometimes she had the feeling that since his release from jail and parole to his father instead of herself he was deliberately trying to destroy himself. She had nothing to go on, but at moments her heart was so filled with foreboding she could see him lying dead and neglected in some den of iniquity. There were times when she couldn't bear to think of him. It was that which made her decision so hard to bear.

So she went down to the college to see William. She did not mention his father's proposal. She just sat and talked to him about his studies and himself. He took her out to dinner and was very cheerful. He was extremely well liked on the campus, and on every hand the students and professors came forward to meet his mother. She was immensely cheered by her visit.

On the train returning to the city she felt a new growth of hope. She'd try to get Charles into the college. Perhaps William could steady him. Or perhaps she'd get William to talk to him first. The more she thought about it the more feasible it seemed, and by the time she let herself into her house she had convinced herself of its certainty. She felt suddenly happy for the first time in years. An old tune from her childhood came back to mind and she was humming it softly as she mounted the stairs.

Hearing her footsteps, her landlord came from his room and told her of Charles's visit. "I let him into your room. I don't know what happened, but all of a sudden he jumped up and ran out of the house."

Her blood congealed, frozen by a premonition of disaster. "Was he ill?" Her voice was so thin from fear it was barely audible.

"He didn't seem so. But he was very drunk."

Now the whole sea of worry washed back over her and she felt the room tilt. She groped for a chair and sat down. Her landlord brought her a glass of water.

"Do you want Mattie to help you to bed?"

"No, thank you, I'm all right now."

When she had recovered she telephoned for a taxi and went immediately to his father's room.

Professor Taylor awakened, groggy and uncomprehending. "I haven't seen him all day. Where has he gone?"

"But doesn't he work with you in the mornings?"

He was muddled and defensive. "Now don't start hounding the boy again. You don't want to make a home for him, so let him alone. He's getting along all right."

Her face took the old bitter cast. "God is going to punish you, Mr. Taylor, as sure as you're alive," she said harshly. "You just watch what I tell you. You're going to burn in hell for what you're doing to your son."

"The boy's all right," he muttered angrily, feeling for his paper sack of cigarettes.

She left the room and walked down to Cedar Avenue in search of someone who knew where Charles could be found. But at that late hour the stores were closed and the houses dark and the street deserted of humanity. Snow sifted soundlessly on the broken pavement and her foreboding grew in the dead silence. She was assailed by the thought that he could be dead in one of those dark houses and she wouldn't know. Then she saw a drunken couple stagger from a darkened areaway.

She approached them hesitantly. "Pardon me, do you know a young man named Charles Taylor?"

The man eyed her with greed and cunning, thinking she was white. "Now does I know Charles Taylor?" he began, instinctively clowning. "It seems as if I knows a boy named Charles. Is he a big boy or a medium-sized boy or is he a liddle boy?"

The woman snatched his arm, her red-rimmed eyes narrowing with animosity. "Come on an' leave that white trash be. You know you doan know nobody by that name."

"But he's my son," Mrs. Taylor pleaded.

The woman softened and took pity on her. "Then try that whiskey joint back there where we just come from. They's a lot of young men in there an' one of them might be yo' boy. Just go 'round to the back there an' knock at the door."

Mrs. Taylor thanked her and went up the dark walk between two buildings. She screwed up her courage and knocked at the door. A panel opened and two muddy eyes raked her suspiciously.

"Pardon me, I'm looking for my son—" she began.

The panel closed abruptly in her face. She heard a voice behind it saying, "Some white whore say she lookin' for her son."

The brutal inhumanity of the statement terrified her. Suddenly she was afraid for her safety. She felt her body trembling as she hurried back to the street. Now her foreboding grew out of control, sapping her strength. She felt lost, without friends or help, no way to turn, no one to turn to; and every fiber of her being felt exhausted. The dark dismal stretch of Cedar Avenue gave the impression of another world. For an instant she had the impression of reliving some horrible nightmare. She had to have help.

So she returned to the man who'd been her husband and was the father of her children. She found him still awake, smoking his vile-smelling cigarette and staring at the ceiling. A butt smoldered in the saucer on the stand beside the bed. She made him get up and dress. His face was lined and haggard, creased with sleep wrinkles; his chin bristled with dirty gray whiskers;

his eyes were runny and redlaced; his kinky hair matted in a peak. But he was Charles's father and he had to help her find him. He dressed slowly, as if in a daze, his hands fumbling with the buttons.

Her own face was white from fear and fatigue, and in the bright overhead light the rouge stood out like a mask, and her dyed red hair resembed a wig. Her eyes had dulled from the excessive strain and had receded into her head.

They resembled derelicts. But for a brief moment their appearance meant nothing. They looked into one another's eyes, all the regret and pity welling from their tortured souls, their twenty-six years of marriage come to this, knowing in that instant that neither could go it alone. For the first time in more than twelve years she wanted him to take her in his arms. But after her rejection of the previous afternoon, he could not try again. She couldn't make a move to let him know she wanted him. The moment passed. He turned his eyes away. She was blinded by tears.

"We must hurry," she said in the harsh voice she'd always had for him.

He turned and opened the door without speaking. They made an odd couple trudging through the snowdrifts on Cedar Avenue, the haggard white-faced woman with dark-circled eyes and the shabby little black man with his cringing walk. There was a quality of prayer about the woman, etchings of defeat in the man. The few drunks and late prostitutes whom they approached along the street eyed them curiously. Finally a taxi driver told them to try Dave's in the Alley.

Charles was lying across the bed in his shirt sleeves and stocking feet. He had the feeling of having been there for a long time, and of awakening suddenly from a strange dream which he could not remember. Something had drawn his attention. He raised his head and looked into the other room, trying to focus his vision. His mind was in a state of semi-stupor and his sense of perception dulled almost to blankness.

343

As if seen through a dense gray fog he made out the blurred figures of two people in the outside doorway, barred by Dave's bulk from entering.

"You vile hoodlum, I know he's here and I'm going to have you arrested for selling whiskey to a minor," he heard a woman's voice and when he recognized it as his mother's, the first sense of shock penetrated his consciousness.

He heard Dave's bullying voice reply, "Goddammit, don't argue with me, lady," and then Veeny say fearfully, "Just close the door."

He saw his mother push Dave aside and come quickly into the room, calling, "Charles!" He saw Dave clutch her arm and jerk her about.

"You son of a bitch! That's my mother!" he cried thickly, pushing to his feet. His legs buckled and he was trying to get his feet underneath him when he heard his mother say sharply, "Don't you dare touch me," and then he saw her slap Dave.

Fury rent his heart as he saw the sudden pimp rise in Dave's flushed face, the moronic bestiality in the character of men who murder women, and heard Veeny shriek, "Don't hit her, hon!" He knew that Dave was going to strike her, and he groped for a weapon and tensed himself to leap even before Dave actually struck her, knocking her off balance. But the actual sight of his mother being struck by a depraved pimp cut his will loose from his mind, and turned his mind back thirteen years to its first impression of horror. *He saw her hands grope desperately for the spokes of the first wheel, and then fall limply, jerking spasmodically in the dust as the hurt came overwhelmingly into her bulging eyes.* The two scenes fused together and were sealed in transcendent horror. He felt the flood of brackish bile drenching him in shock. He was caught, anchored in paralysis, stripped to his naked soul in a sudden world of no values, no right, no wrong— his mother struck down by a sullen brute and himself helpless in the flood of brackish bile. He was standing half crouched in the doorway between the rooms, gripping the bedspread he had seized for a weapon.

As he tried vainly to move, his will still severed from his mind,

344

he saw his father strike Dave across the forehead with a chair. He saw Dave stagger back, the white cut over his eye not yet beginning to bleed, whip out his knife and loom above his father like an enraged monster, stabbing him in the chest. He saw his father grapple with the brute, struggling desperately to clutch his wrist, the knife rising again through the solid terror of Veeny's screams. All happening in nightmare perspective, too rapidly for his mind to rationalize, too horrible to retain. And then he saw his mother rising from the floor, moving to his father's aid, entering the area of ultimate danger. He tried to leap to her defense, to call out a warning. But he couldn't move or cry or breathe. Then he felt himself going down-down-down into the cool dark valley of oblivion. . . .

They drove through a land that had no roads and parked on the crest of a hill without trees and scores of laughing brown men, seeing the shiny car, scrambled up the steep ascent and beckoned to him, their black eyes glittering and their white teeth flashing in the sun, saying, come on, we'll get you some fine sexy girls, juicy as melons and sweet as honey, there are thousands of them down there just waiting to be had, pointing to the village of huts without doors that lay in the valley below. His mother said no, don't go, my son, there's only destruction and ruin down there, but he could see girls with thighs as firm as river banks and breasts as sharp as mountain peaks dancing on the rooftops, their red mouths smiling up at him like the sun rising from a sea of pearls as huge as cannon balls, and his desire was too great to withstand. He sprang from the car and left his mother sitting there on the pinnacle of the hill, turning away his gaze from the entreaty in her eyes, and followed the brown men down the precipitous slope. Like ravenous wolves they chased the girls through the dusty streets of the village and caught them and threw them down and ravished them in the sight of each other in the bright sunshine in the hot dry dust and their blood blazed with carnal lust and they chased still others and ravished them. Then he felt a burning pain pass down through his body like a bolt of fire from heaven and he looked to the sky to see from whence it came and he found himself in a narrow street of a

345

*city that was ancient before Rome was born where the crooked
houses were seven stories high and men with satyrs' heads were
leaning from the upper windows shooting down at him with
guns that made no sound and laughing insanely as he danced in
agony. He ran headlong in blind panic, the terror eating at his
loins, not knowing which way to turn, and the buildings grew
higher and the streets narrower and darkness descended and
men of all nations with bestial faces fought savagely with gleaming knives, cursing in a thousand tongues, gutting each other
with inhuman ecstasy, while the screams of the women trampled
underneath rose from the dark narrow crevices like anguished
wails from hell. He was fighting desperately with no weapons,
with all his might and soul, swinging his own body like a broad-
ax to cut a path through the bloody slaughter back to the pinnacle of the hill where he'd left his mother defenseless and alone,
his heart caught in the grip of an unearthly fear. But when he
came to the path that ascended to the pinnacle of the hill his
way was blocked by an ancient hearse drawn by four black
horses standing before the entrance of a crude stone temple and
flanked by hundreds of very old women clad in long black gowns
who were showering their heads with dust scooped from the
ground and wailing lamentations to heaven. And twelve short
black men with identical faces graven in grief, six on each side,
bore a plain black coffin from the temple and lifted it into the
hearse. His heart stopped beating, caught in a terrible presenti-
ment. He pushed the old women aside and ran forward and
leaped into the hearse and tore loose the lid of the coffin, but he
knew it held the body of his mother even before he looked down
and saw her face, the mouth opened and twisted in infinite
agony and the marks of the brutality livid on the fair skin of her
neck and body. It was as if by taking part in the carnival of lust
and savagery he had ravished her himself. He was struck down
with a bolt of guilt that burned like the fires of hell.*

"Oh God!" he cried aloud, the anguished cry torn from the
very depths of his soul.

"Easy, lad," he heard a voice say.

He opened his eyes and looked into the face of a policeman

who bent over him, holding a bottle to his nose. He turned his head away. For a moment the dream seemed so real he thought his mother was dead. He felt the deepest, bitterest torment of all his life.

Then he heard the policeman saying, "Better get up and get dressed. Your father's been hurt. They've taken him to the hospital.

He looked about the room. There was only another policeman present. To one side was an overturned chair. Dark patches of blood made a grim arabesque on the floor, dots like macabre footsteps leading toward the door. Suddenly the horror returned.

He heard his own voice, torn from the constriction of his heart, "My mother—"

"She's all right. She's with your father."

Slowly he got to his feet and put on his shoes and coat. With the knowledge of his mother's safety his mind had ceased to work. They drove him to the hospital in a police car. He was permitted into the operating room.

At first he had eyes only for his mother. She stood beside the operating table with her back to the door, holding his father's hand. Her small, worn body was immobile, held in a posture of absolute faith. He knew that whatever the outcome, she had placed her trust in God. Somehow, it was reassuring to see her thus.

Then he looked at his father. His nude black body lay passively on the white stretcher, almost as if resigned. His eyes were closed and the deep lines about his mouth and nose were relaxed. All of the signs of frustration and defeat had gone from his face and it was calm. There was a great dignity in his calm as if he had prepared himself to meet his Maker without excuses or deceit.

Cotton swabs covering the wounds were stained with blood. Two doctors were rapidly tying a suture. Another, assisted by a nurse, was giving him a transfusion. Charles could not tell whether he was under anesthetic or not. He went forward slowly and stood beside his mother. He didn't feel anything at all. His body was drained of all emotion. His head was light and empty and he was fearful he might topple and fall. His mother didn't look about or give any sign that she was aware of him.

But suddenly, as if sensing his presence, his father opened his eyes. He saw his father's lips moving, the struggle to speak mirrored in his eyes. He leaned forward to hear.

"Son, be a good boy," his father whispered.

One of the doctors looked up, frowning. "You mustn't talk, sir," he cautioned.

His father gave no sign that he had heard. "Take care of your mother, Son," he continued to whisper.

Charles nodded and looked at his mother's face. Its set composure was held in a complete and untouchable grief. She was looking at his father's face. She didn't see him.

He felt a strange sense of rejection, as if he didn't belong there, as if he were intruding on an intimate scene between the two of them.

"Mama—" he began, but she didn't hear him.

"We—we all made mistakes," his father was whispering. "Don't —don't let them—"

He knew, even before the doctors exchanged glances, that his father had died. His mother leaned down and kissed his father's lips. She didn't speak or cry. The nurse covered the body with a sheet and wheeled it into another room. His mother walked along beside the stretcher. He reached down and took her hand but it was cold and did not respond and he felt that she was not aware of his touch.

Suddenly he was too exhausted to stand any longer. "I'm going home and go to bed for a while, Mama," he said.

She did not reply. He waited for a moment and then asked, "Are you coming?"

"Mother will just stay here for a while," she said without looking at him.

He knew then, in that instant, that she had gone back to his father; that she would belong to his father now forever. He felt as if he had been cut in two; as if a part of himself had been severed from himself forever. But at that moment it did not hurt; the hurt had not come.

348

He went quietly from the room and left her standing there, her small white hand with its swollen red knuckles resting atop the dark lifeless hand of his father which she had drawn from beneath the sheet. He walked slowly back to Cedar Avenue. When he passed a whiskey joint he felt an impulse to stop and buy a drink. But he knew he didn't need a drink; he'd never need a drink again.

He turned and went to his room. The picture of his mother standing there, holding his father's hand, blotted out everything else. It seemed to fit. But he was out of it now. It was his mother and his father in the end. And he was out of all of it. But somehow it seemed wholly right. It seemed the only wholly right thing he'd ever known.

He was blind from exhaustion. He undressed slowly and sat naked on the side of the bed.

Then he looked up and saw the pile of stained butts in the saucer beside the bed. Sudden tears cascaded down his face in a tidal wave. Now the horror came over him like a shroud. He was inside of the horror and it was all about him. But it was different now. It was not like it had been all the other times, such as when he'd been in the automobile accident. His mother was not there now to shield him. She'd never be there again. He was alone within the horror and he knew he'd never get out. He'd always see the world through his veil of horror.

But even that was all right now, he thought sobbingly. Everything was all right now. Even his father was resting.

He slipped beneath the covers, smelling his father's smell. But that was all right too. It would go, and then there would only be his own smell, for always. He was quiet now, in his complete and sealing horror. He folded his arms behind his head, staring at the ceiling. He wondered if his brother Tom was still alive. His mother would have to tell Will, he thought. He wondered what Will would think of him. He found himself thinking about Will's accident. That was the beginning, he thought; that was where it started. He thought about it for a long time, from the perspective of his horror; about his mother saying God was going to punish him for acting ugly, and how he'd thought about

God afterwards when it had been Will who'd been blinded. Now he knew: *God didn't make a mistake, after all.*

Finally he thought about himself. He wondered what would become of himself now. Maybe he'd look up Mr. Small and become a waiter. He'd look up Peggy too. She had his child somewhere. He'd find out where she was and write to her. He'd tell her everything. Maybe she'd understand. If she would have him after that he would marry her. If she wouldn't, maybe she'd let him help the child.

His thoughts began to drift away. Just before he went to sleep he said aloud, "Good-bye, Mama."

ABOUT THE AUTHOR

CHESTER HIMES was born in Jefferson City, Missouri, in 1909. His childhood was spent in Cleveland, Ohio, in Mississippi, in Pine Bluff, Arkansas, in St. Louis, Missouri, and finally in Cleveland again, where he graduated from East High School in 1926. After two years at Ohio State University he lived in Columbus and Cleveland, working as bartender and bellhop in hotels and country clubs until 1938, when he became associated with the Ohio Writers' Project and wrote a history of Cleveland for the WPA Guide Series. From 1941 to 1944 he worked in several ship-yards and war industries in Los Angeles and San Francisco, California.

Although Chester Himes's stories and articles have appeared in many magazines since he was first published in *Esquire* in 1934, it was not until he received a Rosenwald Fellowship in 1944 that he was enabled to complete his first novel, *If He Hollers Let Him Go.* When published in 1945 the book was extremely well received by the critics and has since sold well over 450,000 copies in all editions, and has also appeared in England, France, Norway, Sweden and Denmark. He has published two other novels—*Lonely Crusade* in 1947 and *Cast the First Stone* in 1953 —and his work is included in a number of anthologies. The French edition of *Lonely Crusade—La Croisade de Lee Gordon—* was chosen by French critics, along with the works of Hemingway, Faulkner, Wouk, and Hersey, as one of the five best novels by Americans published in France in 1952.

For the past year—after having resided in the East since the publication of his first novel—Chester Himes has been in Europe, principally in England, France and on Majorca, an island off the coast of Spain, where he is now completing a new novel with a European locale.